PENGUIN TWENTIETH-CENTURY CLASSICS

AND AGAIN?

Sean O'Faolain was born in 1900 and educated at the National University of Ireland. For a year he was commercial traveller for books but gave it up to fight on the side of De Valera in 1921. He was a member of the Irish Republican Army for six years, taught for a further year and then studied at Harvard University. For four years he taught at Strawberry Hill Training College for Teachers, after which he turned to writing and went back to his native Ireland, where he now lives in Dublin. He has written some twenty books, including travel and literary criticism, novels, biographies, and several books of short stories. He has also contributed to many well-known periodicals in Great Britain and the United States. His other publications include an autobiography, *Vive Moi!*, and a history of Ireland, *The Irish*, which he calls 'a creative history of the growth of a racial mind'. Penguin also publish three volumes of short stories, *Midsummer Night Madness*, *The Heat of the Sun* and *Foreign Affairs*.

Sean O'Faolain is a D.Litt of Trinity College, Dublin.

SEAN O'FAOLAIN

◆

AND AGAIN?

PENGUIN BOOKS

PENGUIN BOOKS

Published by the Penguin Group
27 Wrights Lane, London W8 5TZ, England
Viking Penguin Inc., 40 West 23rd Street, New York, New York 10010, USA
Penguin Books Australia Ltd, Ringwood, Victoria, Australia
Penguin Books Canada Ltd, 2801 John Street, Markham, Ontario, Canada L3R 1B4
Penguin Books (NZ) Ltd, 182–190 Wairau Road, Auckland 10, New Zealand

Penguin Books Ltd, Registered Offices: Harmondsworth, Middlesex, England

First published by Constable and Co. Ltd 1979
Published in Penguin Books 1982
3 5 7 9 10 8 6 4 2

Printed and bound in Great Britain by
Cox & Wyman Ltd, Reading
Typeset in Linotype Pilgrim

A Note from Olympus

I am writing this for myself. I need to remember. Only the immortals can live forgetting. Without cherished memories a man's imagination must fly wild; lose touch with common life; go off its chump. I need to remember precisely what happened to me that March morning in 1965, and thereby come to understand it in terms of its effects on me ever since. But there must be no dramatics, nothing souped up, no sensationalism. Anyway it all started so smoothly that I was not even aware of it at the time. I was half asleep when my eyes lifted slowly to a whispery sound like a mouse outside my bedroom door. Dozily I looked down sidewards and saw a couple of foolscap-size sheets of yellow paper being edged forward under the door along the carpet. Still only half awake, I looked around the room, found it uncomfortably unfamiliar, rolled out of bed, slid back the curtains and was startled to see below me an equally unfamiliar and unshorn lawn some thirty yards by twelve, bordered on both sides by a few nascent colours – half-opened daffodils, flecks of forsythia – suggestive of March rather than May, ending in some tall, blackish-greenish macrocarpas rising raggedly against the backs of other houses and a pallid sky. To my right and left, perspectives of similar gardens and houses. I put my palm to my chest and said aloud, 'Where the devil am I?' – to which my only response was a sense of blankness inside my head that made me look around for a mirror to stave off the more personal question already nibbling at my ear.

In the left-hand corner of the room there was a pink wash-basin with a white splash-back and mirror above it. I looked into the mirror and saw an old man, thin hair, light as dust, mostly white, red-nosed, mouth pursed like a witch without her dentures, pink eyelids, staring at me crossly out of bright blue eyes. He made a hostile face at me. I shot around to see if he was standing behind me, saw again the yellow pages angled under the door, puffed away the notion that I had been drugged and kidnapped, crept cautiously to the door and flung it open. An empty landing. I gathered up the long yellow pages, sat on the side of the bed and began to read the closely typed message:

Department of External Affairs
Olympus
Timeless

ref a/z

To: Mr James J. Younger. Journalist. 17 Rosmeen Park, Dunlaoire, Dublin, Ireland, Europe, Northern Hemisphere, Earth.

Sir, You will be interested to know that for some time past Our Celestial Divinities assembled on Olympus (5,000 years in human time; in celestial time a wink) have been considering how best to make the experiment of permitting some mortal to live again. Our interest is solely to decide, once for all, whether what you humans call Experience teaches you a damned thing.

I have the pleasure of informing you that Our Divinities hereby offer you the privilege of being the object of this experiment. Your decision to accept or refuse Our offer must, of course, be voluntary, but since We are who We are We supernaturally foreknow your decision although We do not foredain it. Congratulations, Mr Younger. Today is your sixty-fifth birthday, and your second birth day.

I must, however, warn you that two restrictions, of necessity, attach to your reincarnation. 'Of necessity' because although Our powers are unlimited they are restrained by a divine regard for consistency. Allow me to explain.

Much that happens in your world surpasses human understanding, but of one thing men have never been in doubt: that everything that happens on earth is implicit in its creation. There *is* a pattern down there, as even your earliest human beings observed on observing certain repetitions in the world about them:

The iteration of day and night,
Of storm and calm,
The lovely cycles of birth, growth,
Disease and decay,
Soothing death,
Blooming happiness, blasting disaster,

Silver planes traversing the stainless blue,
Thousands burned in crashes,
Cities ever spreading out and out,
Workers bombed street by street,
Millions wasted by wars and famines
Human charity always prompt to help a few,
The skies' birds, the earth's beasts,
Morning, day, sunset, the dark, the sun . . .

And every single life since time began linked with every other life. Without Babylon there could be no Ballymacoolaghan, no Bethlehem, no Belsen, no Belfast. Because Tutankhamen sneezed Queen Victoria caught a cold. Because Greek traders sailed past Sardinia a Corsican lost Waterloo. Where would you be now Mr Younger if England had not walked on the face of your country and produced the Duke of Wellington? Cleopatra's nose? Because Adam saw Eve's nakedness allured by a fig's leaf you exist. It all hangs together. Got it? Okay!

All this being so we supernaturally regard with caution any proposal that might seem to contradict it. For example, if after all these consistent aeons we were to tolerate what some amongst you misguidedly call a miracle (a word allied, I may remind you, to the word *smile*), e.g. if we permitted a dead man to rise from the grave, or a new limb to replace a lost limb, mankind's faith in the gods would at once be shattered. Men would say, 'The gods are capricious. They are playing tricks with us.' It is true that we could do those things. We could do anything. Being gods we may not. As you, a journalist, would say we 'miraculously' do not perform miracles. Law and Order.

From all of which come these two small restrictions on your second coming: *Viz.*

One. Whenever men entertain the fantasy called 'living it all over again' they are victims of a terminological contradiction. What they are really thinking of is getting a Second Chance at an Identical Problem. It is out of the question. In life nothing happens twice. The weather would be just a bit different the next time for Columbus. The second time round, Brutus will have forgotten to bring his dagger. Napoleon will have eaten bad fish before his second Waterloo. Exact repetition would eliminate everything that makes life life – challenge, free will, ignorance, chance, choice, the unforeseen. Anyway who would want to relive the same old part in the same old human comedy? He would die of boredom like an actor condemned to play one single character night after night for ever.

Having devoted quite a number of seconds to the inherent problem We have decided that there is only one way in which you may experience a second period of life full of similar, but not identical, challenges; it is by severely limiting your memory of the details of your first sixty-five years while permitting you to retain all the fruits of your experience. Accordingly you may remember of your former fellow actors such odds and ends as the Gravedigger and the Sentry, the Herald, the Ghost, possibly a Rosencrantz, even a Polonius, but not his daughter, or Claudius, or Gertrude or Laertes. No close intimates, no formative personalities, no David, no Jonathan. As in your past life you will make your new intimates as you go along.

Two. You cannot be discovered at the start of your second life gabbling in a cradle like a man of sixty-five. Neither can we have you growing more and more silly until you become one hundred and thirty. Instead, starting from your present age of sixty-five you will live backwards for sixty-five years, growing younger, and younger, until at the ripe age of zero you are whisked back into the womb of Mother Time.

In this way your iteration will trouble nobody. Any late-won wisdom that you may display at the age of forty-bis or thirty-bis will be attributed to oncoming senility. As you enter your teens you will be dismissed as a precocious brat. To avoid any embarrassment that your built-in juvenescence may cause to others you will do well to change your habitat as soon as your phenomenally youthful appearance ceases to be attributable to monkey glands, royal jelly, yogurt, wheat germ, cosmetics, corsets or Guinness.

So much for the restrictions. We anticipate no difficulty in disposing of the old you. People disappear nowadays quite undramatically every day of the week. The requisite documents for your new public identity will be supplied to you when you have formally accepted our offer, but not before you have meditated thereon for one hour.

The reason for this delay is that you are already wondering whether this is really happening at all, and why on earth (Where else?) to you. It is happening to you because we are obliged to select somebody of no consequence. It would be too much of a good thing to revive a Cromwell, a Napoleon or a Hitler and allow them to bother or bore mankind all over again. You are also a convenient choice because you were in any case due to die within the next hour, felled by a blue truck careering past the corner of your avenue at precisely 9.32½ a.m. as you emerge to purchase your morning paper at the neighbouring kiosk. It is now 8.32½ a.m. You will have proof of the reliability of Our offer and ample opportunity to enter or to withdraw your acceptance thereof by stationing yourself at the corner of your avenue at 9.32½ a.m. when the truck will follow its appointed course.

That is all. We shall have no further verbal communication, though you are certain to infer our presence now and again, incorrectly.

Is mise le meas
Secretary to the Department of External Affairs
Olympus.

As I read that last word the yellow pages began to crumple slowly in my hands, dwindle and vanish, leaving an old man sitting on the edge of his bed in his faded blue pyjamas, his white hair all porcupined, his face screwed up like a Michelangelesque cartoon of old age, hollows under cheekbones, eyes pouched, nose approaching chin, his belly churning gall, honey, fear and hope, staring before him in a frenzy of joy at that exquisite inflection known as The Future Tense.

What else would any man of sixty-five do after reading such a message? Huff and piff and sniff? Say, 'Now who is the smartiboots who has been up to this big practical joke? Put me to bed last night, blotto? Shoved this rigmarole under my door to take a rise out of me this morning?' Allow me to sing the quiet joys of age, all of them awaiting us as ye approach the psalmist's three score and ten: debility, impotence, incontinence, diverticulitis, colonic cancer, stones in the gall bladder, sand in the eyes, a tongue like a henhouse, dullness of mind, belching, yawning, farting, constipating, enlarged prostate, obstructed gut, friendless days, empty nights, muscular aches, markets falling, prices rising, pension contracting, no more plans, a slow rusting, coronaries, strokes, at the best a sleepy drive to the airport's departure lounge there to wait for the chirrupy voice, 'Will all passengers on Flight Omega for Hades now kindly proceed to boarding gate number zero-zero-zero?'

I believed in that offer as utterly as a prisoner condemned to death would believe in a warder's consoling whisper that he was about to be reprieved and would merely have to die as a lifer. I wanted that offer to be true. I wanted to take a somewhat later plane.

None the less, I was going to verify that bit about the blue death truck.

I rose, looked into the cool sky beyond the macrocarpa and added my own little test. If, as they had rudely told me, I had already effectively said 'Yes' (which I damned well in fact had not) how much could I now remember of my past life with this new, allegedly docked and bobtailed memory of mine? I could remember from this immediate past only what I could see around me in the room or through the window. From my remoter past, that is from my sixty-five years of lived experience, floods of images, ideas, judgements, attitudes, opinions, facts, places, happenings, a mass of what is vaguely known as general knowledge. I felt dashed. They had been talking nonsense. My memory was just as good as . . . I stopped, both frightened, and relieved. I called up faces, lots and lots of faces, but I could not remember their owners. Total loss of specificity? A forgotten Crusoe forgetting totally? I recalled being at the Curragh Races recently. I saw and heard the crowds, but no familiar faces. At a dance years ago. No embraces. I had been a journalist, I summoned up a great public demonstration in Trafalgar Square, recalled the speakers, something of the speeches, but of small, intimate encounters not the faintest traces. But wait! I remembered one man who smiled at me. He was a ticket checker in a train. I recalled a cheerful woman – was it in Manchester? – with whom I used to exchange a chatty word every day. A waitress in a tea shop.

Well? And a submissive 'Well!' So that was how it was going to be. I resolved that I found the vacancy soothing. Years of responsibility rolling off my back, loads of guilt, innocence scenting the air. It would be pleasant to have no relations, no connections, no genealogies, a seagull volplaning over the wind-tracked sea, and I might have gone on languishing for an hour in this pleasant feeling of a new kind of freedom if a church bell had not recalled me to the urgent moment. I shall just have time to wash, shave and dress and be at the end of the avenue to exercise the first (or last) option of my entire life. I refuse to accept that foreknowledge can imply foreordainment, even when power speaks. I reject the idea that both these f's cannot be toppled head over heels. I insist that I have a free man's power to choose! And it duly transpired that I had – up to a point.

I moved to the pink wash-basin and found myself leaning on either side of it confronted by a pale-green toothbrush, supine on the glass shelf that terminated the mirror. Here was my past, present and future. Had I chosen this disgustingly pallid object? If it was not mine whose was it? I picked it up, observed that it looked worn, and replaced it unsurely and distastefully. Every toothbrush is somebody's toothbrush. A toothbrush is one of man's more intimate possessions. I would lend to or borrow from a friend a piece of soap, even a razor, at a pinch a comb, never a tooothbrush. I apprehended a dilemma. I had no way of knowing whether or not that toothbrush belonged to me because I could not recall the Me who had compassed it: which means, my mind and my electric razor whirling madly in twin circles, that – 9.19 – I have been conned. I could spend half my second life accumulating a Me sufficiently reliable to know a toothbrush or for a toothbrush to know. It would take me years and years to establish Me to Me. 'Which', gurgling furiously through the water, 'means that You bastards up there are offering me not sixty-five years of life but half, or less. What sort of a bargain is that to offer any man – a whole memory for half a life to be lived asswise! Thank You for nothing!' I spat it as I dragged on my tie and pounded down the stairs, grabbed a hat – 'Mine? Thank you! So I *am* somebody? I own a hat!' I kicked the hat-stand and opened the door on a blaze of sun that gleamed on the chromium number 17.

Come on, death truck! It is a far, far better thing I do than I have ever done, a far, far better rest I go to than I have ever known.

I must polish that number. What a balmy, birdsinging sweet scented spring morning. It was going to be a lovely spring. Daffodils coming up. Almonds? Across the avenue a girl and a boy arm in arm, woozing along, gazing at one another, bumping hips, laughing. O lost and by the wind grieved ghost come back again. After all what is a memory? A ghost telling half-lies. I shall have to cut that piece of front lawn – glancing at the early-cut lawn of my neighbour, divided from mine only by a white railing. Down the line, along a brief, smooth, black-asphalted avenue a series of other lawns, flower beds, shrubs and trees before similar semi-detacheds on either side. As I banged my door behind me an elderly lady, portly, hair-cropped, in ample slacks, appeared on the doorstep of the house to my left and addressed me cheerfully. She spoke with an English accent.

'Good morning, Mr Younger. Settling in all right?'

The alien accent informed my gapped memory that I was not English. Could she be a nudge in the ribs? An exceptionally godly push in the back to get me going? See how informative even so small a thing as an alien intonation can be! For I noted that I noted it with a tinge of nostalgia. Why nostalgia? Was I part-English? Could this possibly mean that there could also be tiny leaks in Their Lordships' lordly prescription against over-intimate reminiscences?

'I'm getting along very nicely indeed, Mrs Er. Very kind of you, I am sure. Most kind.'

Again! My accent was English, not Irish. Amiable, not cordial. Which in hell am I?

'Well, do not hesitate to call on us. We are the Windele sisters. Glad to lend a hand. Always hard to be a lone man. Especially after such a sad bereavement!'

I lifted a sadly amiable hand in hail and farewell and went down my miniature car drive through its double iron gate, white and twanging. Had I detected a certain tone in those last five words? Inside knowledge? Sympathy? Dubiety? Antipathy? Or just plain, kindly human interest in a recent arrival? If I had had time to dally with her I would have found out how and when I had been so sadly, it would even seem unpleasantly bereaved. Did she mean widowed? Whom had I lost? I had time only to observe that some, at least, of my history must be known, correctly or incorrectly, to others. A few more such hints must lead me to friends I once knew. And so back to that lost historical Me? To my right the avenue dwindled to a cul-de-sac. The other way I saw a public street at right angles to the park, passing traffic that included at that moment a blue and cream bus. I walked thither as briskly as my sixty-five years and an ingrowing toe-nail would allow.

Smallish houses of, I hazarded, two-three bedrooms; perfect for newly-weds and retired couples. Quiet. Every lawn railed like my own, in green, or white, or china blue, or priestly black or nuns' grey. Do black priests wear white? Do black women look exciting in white panties? The noble thoughts of a man facing the guillotine. Everything well cared for here. Nobody wealthy. The parked cars all popular makes. Fords, Fiats, Renault 4s, Minis. *Petit bourgeois.*

God save Ireland. Still, some taste too. A silver birch, a cherry, a willow, an almond, a mountain ash, a cordyline, sometimes called a club palm such as I had seen in Devon, the Isle of Wight, Glengariff, the Riviera. If only I could remember as many people as trees! This modestly select retreat must mean that I have a small bank account somewhere, current, not deposit, never in the red, occasionally close to it. They had informed me that I am or had been a journalist. Living here I could as appropriately be a salesman, a civil servant, a dentist, a forester, a teacher, a con man, but not a doctor. My cul-de-sac ended with the corner of a wall standing parallel to the public road, bearing a metal plaque giving the name of the cul-de-sac in Irish and English. Páirc Rosmin. Rosemary Park. The corner where, if I so decide, I shall calmly await the careening truck.

Two and a half minutes to go. I heard my heart echoing into my left ear. My gut belched. I looked up and down the road. To my left the man-high railings of a public park carried the perspective towards irresolute traffic lights. To my right, at a little distance, a church, with two zebraed ears sticking up like a donkey's. No steeple. No campanile. Slight traffic. Few pedestrians. Near to hand I became aware of a red-curled child on a bicycle, a girl of five or six, circling the black, smooth tarmacadam of my park. That blue and silvered machine was probably her main gift last Christmas. I was pleasantly distracted by her childish air of power, her show-off vanity, her first skill – until some twenty yards away I saw a structure beside what looked like a bridge over, I presumed, a sunken railway, evidently a surburban commuting line to and from Dublin, and at the same moment I also saw in a sudden terror, between the station and the church, a dusty bluish two-ton truck swaying wildly in the reckless speed of its approach.

'Well?'

Was that *my* voice?

My chest became taut. I had the sensation of a swimmer who has stayed seconds too long underwater. I let my breath go in such gasps that a man passing the mouth of the cul-de-sac stared at me as he went onward. That truck is doing sixty m.p.h. The driver must be mad. Thirty yards away.

'Well?'

Twenty yards.

'WELL?'

At ten yards I see a hirsute face, eyes glaring, mouth shrieking, his klaxon screams, his fists twist the wheel as if his sole intention is to mash me against the corner pillar of the park. He is glaring at the child on the silver and blue bicycle who has incautiously swerved out of the park on to the public street right into his track. In that million-times-less-than-an instant I knew that the child had only two chances of life. One: the trucker could swerve off his legal channel to the other side of the street, a chance immediately made impossible by an outward-bound bus sweeping along that side of the street. Two: As the child curved proudly towards me I might hurl myself at her and fling her across the park like a rugby ball just before I get flattened by the flying tackle of the flying truck.

When I was twenty I was a pretty good centre-forward; then my muscles would have responded to any demand like a finger click. Turn thirty-three and you discover that what you should do, and once upon a time would have done easily, is in your mind but not in your muscles. Did I at that second weigh the chances? Decide that I couldn't do it? Were the gods having the timelessness of their timeless lives staring as intensely as spectators at the last seconds of a bullfight? Or laughing their fatheads off at me? Did I think of the sixty-five years of livingness waiting for me?

It is difficult to report with accuracy what happens in moments such as this. I wish to record that I was in some manner aware of the two aforementioned contingencies and that I am now aware only that I threw myself three yards away from the colliding truck. I cannot testify whether or not there was a connection between the former observation and the latter action. *Post hoc ergo propter hoc?* That second between the challenge and the response is the one arena that constantly challenges the judges, poets, dramatists and novelists of the world. All I can do is to report that, twisting like a lizard, I witnessed the trucker's final effort and defeat. For a moment he triumphantly evaded the child. Then his nose crashed against the sharp column at the corner of the cul-de-sac in an explosion of steam, shattered windscreen, sprays of blood. He sacrificed himself uselessly – his tail swung around, scooped up the child, sent her flying through the air, and lobbed her on her head on the pavement like a squashed tomato. I rose to my knees, got up, saw her, buckled and sank.

I heard dim voices and saw blueness behind overhanging faces. Who's the ould fella? He'll be okay. Just fainted. Arms helped me to my feet. But what really uplifted me was rage. I had been tricked into 'choosing'. I assured my helpers that I was all right. I lived a few yards away. I saw that they were eager to investigate the child, the driver, the truck now pouring steam from its crumpled bonnet above the heads of a crowd of onlookers. As I wavered back to Number 17, as numbed as a knocked-out boxer sinking to the canvas, head humming, heart battering, I heard the siren of an ambulance. It was not until I was halfway through my second cup of black coffee that I grasped that I had begun my second life.

I did so by sedately recognising the flavour of chicory in the coffee, by connecting this flavour for no reason that I could at first define with the smell of incense, which smell recalled the image of a woman who had passed me on my way back from the death of the little girl. Her blue eyes peering shortsightedly over my shoulder at the hullabaloo at the end of the park had been smallish in nature and her peering made them still smaller. She wore no hat. Her hair, light as new wheat, was brushed from its central parting like a man's. She was large of mouth, her ringed hands were large, she had pearls in her ears and wound about her throat, her waist was androgynous, her skin breathing of pale pink sweet-peas, her bosom mild, in all she was an interesting blend of two sexes. What had struck me most forcibly about her was that as she approached, front face, she had looked undistinguished, almost plain, too pink, frosty-faced, and then just as she passed my eyes she presented a profile of the most delicate, dignified, even stately fineness, an outline fit for an empress on a Greek coin.

I have paused to reread that poetical bit about the profile on the Greek coin. It sounds trite. I would not change it, though when I say that her profile was 'stately' I say better: an ideal image, as all profiles on coins and medals are, of what-is-meant-to-be a symbol of Majesty, Power, Liberty, Fecundity as with the Irish salmon, bull or horse, the American eagle, ear of wheat, sower of seed. There had been one reality of her facing me, and at her side another, her shadow, her dream? When this Jana-Juno, who must be half my age, passed me in a waft of sandalwood (that evergreen whose heart-wood makes the aroma of incense) I had looked back at her. Her carriage, her movement, her stately neck, her imperial shoulders, her whole frame lifted up by her desire to see what was this that was happening ahead of her were all such – or so I might have said if I were young and romantic – as to make Vikings fight to possess her.

I am aware that such an interest at such a moment does not

stand to my credit. The desires of the young are regarded with an indulgent smile; of the old with contempt. I record the moment only because my anger exploded again on the head of it. What sort of man, I raged, is this who inside fifteen minutes welcomes life, surrenders memory, takes fright at a toothbrush, despises life, hails death, salutes the spring, is moved by its death in a child, frightened by a truck, faints at blood, relishes chicory, remembers incense and lechers after a woman? What a feeble tangle to be pitted in age against the birth of life? Was I always like this? Whatever I now am what was it that made me like this?

That basic question was to haunt me for twenty-five years.

For the moment there was no point in my pretending that I had not chosen life for Me as against death for a child. So? All life, my lords, is one? Since Adam? This is my pattern? This is your pattern? Then why has she been dragged into it? Liars!

I could hear their unruffled exchanges:

Well, it was his choice, ye know. We did not coerce the poor fellow. It is a simple concept. We had, to be sure, foreseen that the child would be there. That was her choice. We foresaw that she would be killed unless he saved her. Unfair? Over-fair! We offered her bait to his virtue. By not forewarning him we also left the issue open to him. Had we forewarned him about her that would have brought a considerable degree of coercion to bear on him. Odd that he cannot see this! Stupid old fool. He got every chance.

'Chance! Whose chance?'

Our chance, of course. When we created the world we created Chance. We had to or everything would be predetermined. Chance is the ultimate proof of free will. And the most persuasive proof that Heaven is a reality.

'And the child? Was she free? You bastards!'

Now, now, Mr Younger! Watch your language.

'You can do nothing to me. I have sixty-five years of life to go.'

And afterwards? You used to believe in a Hereafter. The child? Alas, yes. Her death was foreordained, as yours is. Things pay for things. Death for Life is one such. The Inexorable has to be there. Otherwise there would be no pattern. But Chance is also the way out. Chance is the brother of Courage. It is what people are always trying to seize. It is what makes life interesting. Anatole France said Chance is the pseudonym of God. Certainly one has to distinguish between the true and the false chance, the good and the bad chance, one has to be careful as well as brave. You were careful. We expected you to be. Our congratulations, Mr Younger.

I fled from the kitchen to the hallway, howling up the empty well of the stairs, 'This is casuistry, I will have nothing to do with it, I was entitled to know beforehand that I am a careful, cowardly, calculating bastard. A man can come to no free decision about anything until he knows the kind of a man he is. I want to know who and what I am! I insist on knowing!'

I started to try to find out by examining my groundfloor quarters foot by foot. It was a pleasant living room, long, divisible by sliding doors, painted wholly in white. Some books but not many. With the natural reaction of a journalist I noted that most of them had a referential value – directories, year books, biographies, travel guides, historical books, dictionaries, a fair amount about the arts, few works of fiction. They did not look unfamiliar; neither did they have the feel of one's own worn doorstep. Indeed, on examining the titles I responded only to one book. *A Sportsman's Sketches*, by Ivan Turgenev. It gave me a familial feeling; if I could only remember it, some intimate connection. (Why make a pother about it now, seeing that it later turned out that the connection was with my dead brother, a sportsman.) The whole place had otherwise the distant feeling of a rented, furnished house emitting faint human vibrations, a transmitter running down as intermittently as a heart with a disorder rhythm. Its reticence about Me so irritated me that I felt like throwing the whole room out through its own window. 'I want an ego' I shouted and looked around me like a baited bull or bear.

The buzzer buzzed at the end of the little hallway. Calming myself I opened the front door.

I saw on the roadway a delivery van in orange, white and black bearing the logomark *pt*, meaning Posts and Telegraphs. At my door its rumpled Mercury handed me a parcel with a gift-bearing grin, asking only 'Mr James Younger?' When I nodded, he rolled himself away into his van and in it rolled away. I took the parcel into my living room and cut the cords with my pocket knife. A complete 'I' slid out of it all over the table in sheaves. Passport, bank book, insurance policies, baptismal and marriage certificates . . . And what were these? A bundle of diaries! A bulging photograph album! Press cuttings. Riches to occupy me for weeks.

I began with my passport. Here I am. On stage. Me for real. *James Joseph Younger.*

Number	H 291010
Profession	Journalist
Place of Birth	County Cork
Date of Birth	17.3.1900
Residence	Ireland
Height	5′ 11″
Colour of eyes	Blue
Colour of hair	Grey
Face	Oval

It puzzlingly bore an American visa, franked on arrival in New York on December 20th, last year, but bore no stamp to show that I had returned. Had I returned? When? How? It had been issued in Dublin. As with all passport photographs the likeness was of the very-like-a-whale sort, meaning that a smart crook could have faked the whole thing inside a couple of days.

The next document informed me that I had been duly born and duly christened, i.e. baptised James Joseph Younger on March 20th, 1900, in the parish of Castletownroche, in the County of Cork. I had, naturally, no memory of this incident, and I found on consulting myself that neither had I any memory of Castletownroche. Before the afternoon was out an Ordnance Survey map showed this place to be a small village on the little Awbeg River which flows into what one tourist guide eloquently describes as 'the salmon-crowded Blackwater', which flows into Youghal Bay and St George's Channel, that is into the Celtic Sea. This put my village about nineteen miles north of Cork city as the crow flies, about twenty-five miles by road, about one hour and a half by motor car or about two and a half hours by bus, allowing for halts, drinks, breakdowns, wayside chats and winding roads. An ancient guide-book further informed me that there had been, at one time, a railway station and a railway line some two miles away from the village. On further inquiry I found that this line is now defunct; which makes the village a very out-of-the-way little place indeed. To establish this much took me several days. Old guide-books and Ordnance Survey maps had to be bought. One digressed down interesting if irrelevant side-roads. Timetables for modern buses and trains had to be purchased. I found it all an interesting piece of research.

The same certificate listed my mother's maiden name as Whitley. This fact I found suggestive since neither Younger nor Whitley are traditional Irish names, by which I mean that I felt reason to wonder whether my parents might not originally have been English, or Anglo-Irish Protestants, even though I observed that I was baptised 'according to the rites of the Roman Catholic Church'. I record this notion of mine solely because it was accompanied by the feeling that I would have been gratified not to be wholly Irish, or if not wholly English at least no more than half-Irish. This was some sort of a clue. But to what? It likewise pleased me that one of the sponsors at the ceremony bore the unIrish name of Lindsay. I likewise regretted that the other sponsor was one Pat Joe MacMahon. But all this referred to some sixty-five years ago. Not much hope of tracing down contemporaries of a childhood so far off in time. The facts were clear, but as for their human associations had one of the scrivener's grey hairs stuck to the page it would have been more eloquent.

I studied the next three documents many times then and for weeks after, each time more sombrely. The first informed me that I had married one Bridget Olden. There was a copy of my marriage certificate to prove it, dated 1925, printed in ecclesiastical maroon and black, its contents compiled from the register of the parish church of SS Peter and Paul in Cork city. I found that I remembered the old place, large, high, in red sandstone and grey limestone. I was moved by its dusky smell and ponderous image. I did not remember Bridget Olden. Nor did I recollect the witnesses, Robert Olden and Hanora Foster, nor the celebrant, the Revd G. Quain. One omission – the addresses of all concerned – defined for me what was fatally missing in everything I had so far read: those simple factual details that alone allow us to visualise forgotten or half-forgotten people – their features, clothes, accents, tics, their preferences in food or drink or politics, their prejudices, whether they had come on foot, by taxi, tram or private car, those trifling minutiae that so often point to personal idiosyncrasies whether or not under the stress of unusual occasions. I suppose I am talking of that plenitude of tiny depth-giving brush strokes that marks off the first-rate portrait from the shallow blur. If I am a reporter I must have lived by these human details. Here there were none. Merely facts.

The next two documents felt like two punches in my diaphragm, bang right, bang left. The first was the birth certificate of my son, Henry Younger, born on June 6th, 1926, at Number 5 Sunset Villas, Lower Glanmire Road, Cork. I had no recollection of him. Then came a brownish card, my entitlement or 'Grant of Right in

Perpetuity' to burial in St Joseph's Cemetery, Cork, Plot number 30, Section One, St Finbarr Row. I had apparently purchased it for the burial of the aforementioned son one week after his birth.

Since those early days of my second life I have come to believe myself a man who respects all long-standing institutions and traditions: accordingly, when I here saw marriage and fatherhood ripped cruelly from me I saw for the first time how many other old, intimate precious, domestic memories I must have surrendered for the satisfaction of a second life. I was not proud of myself. This experiment had already cost me a son. For somebody else a son, father or brother who, up to this morning, used to drive a blue truck. Somebody else had lost a child of six. How many lives can one life cost?

I did no more work that day. I wandered around the precincts of the harbour and the bay until I saw a lightship briefly gleam across the still daylit sea. I was unaware of hunger, or of the wind from the east. Were those the lights of Bray three miles down the coast? More homes, families, close-knit lives? Behind me were the comfortable lighted homes of Killiney, and more and more about the tiny harbours of Dalkey and Sandycove. The dusk of Dunlaoire offered closed boarding houses, boarded-up tea-rooms, locked salt-water baths, the soughing swaying of wintry seaweed clotted on the low-tide rocks. The lighted mail boat emitted its one brief hoot preparatory to steaming out of the harbour for Britain. I was irrationally moved by the memory of George IV's landing here in 1821, moved much more by the distant sight of James Joyce's martello tower on its promontory, a man whose bottomless memory gave him inspiration, torture and a courageous acceptance of life. By the time I had visited my last pub on my blind way I had begun to wonder, thinking of him, whether time can ever assuage pain. It can if it can bury loss under the clay of fresh experiences to be in their turn remembered with tears. I watched a crowd struggling into a bus bound for Dublin. That is Life to the greater part of mankind. Catching the bus. For the thoughtful few? A tragedy that we treat as a comedy to save our sanity, or else an absurdity that we treat seriously to preserve our dignity, and to spare the blushes of the silly gods who begat it.

If I were at this moment a man writing a novel I would probably leave the informations and misinformations of my dossier lie where they have so far alighted, postpone explanations, annotations and elaborations to later on, create a little harmless mystery to tease or amuse the reader. But no man can afford secrets if he is writing to clear his mind. I do not wish to obfuscate myself. I have stood by the grave of the child Henry Younger in the multitudinous cemetery of Cork. The spring birds called. I have stood outside the house where his mother gave birth to him and he died, having earlier assured myself from old Rate Books that a Mr and Mrs J. Younger did indeed reside there in 1925. I have suffered the feelings of loss and loneliness that I have just described. Therefore, no deceiving. I have told no lies except insofar as I have been lied to myself. It took me a long time to discover that that dossier was not my dossier. Within weeks I was to uncover several deceptions in it that should or could have led me sooner to its final exposure: such as that I did not marry Bridget Olden, so that Henry Younger was not my son. Not until I went down to Castletownroche did I find out who I really am. Even after that I had to go through a lot of what meteorologists call turbulence before I fully surrendered to the fact that James Younger was in fact my brother. Long afterwards I was to discover that I missed a third brother, Stephen. Nevertheless my search was not based wholly on deception. I had dug like the sons of the old man in the fable who told them as he died that there was treasure buried underneath his land, but did not say where, so that they dug every inch of it, and the harvest was their treasure. If my search had been pointless I could have said so at the start, spilled out its emptiness like a tip-up truck. I have had to, and still must, riddle, pan and sift the sand to uncover the grains hidden in it. So, back, feverishly, I might say venomously, to that dossier to make it speak.

I melted at once. I even began to laugh with joy. The rest of the new material waiting for me seemed plenitude itself, impossible to fake, every word of it easy to verify; income tax demands and receipts, lists of investments, the registration book of an old Wolseley 1500 in my garage, demands and receipts for rates not only in regard to this house but other houses in various parts of Dublin and around England, a long list of local telephone numbers and useful names – doctor, oculist, dentist, grocer, greengrocer, wine merchant, window cleaner, plumber, gardener, firms that would or would not hasten to correct faults in my central heating or my dish-washer. All I needed to do was to circulate the Borough, have a chat with a few of these good people, and I could already hear them: 'Hello! Is this Jim Younger? Haven't been seeing you for some time!' Then a few leading questions from me.

I lifted the telephone and rang the first name on my list.

'Hello! Dr Cusack? This is J. J. Younger speaking. You remember me? Number 17 Rosmeen Park.'

He was polite, but formal.

'Good morning, Mr Younger. Alas, I don't remember you. Have you been a patient of mine? I did, of course, get your letter from London a couple of weeks ago saying that you were coming here to live. Are you in trouble?'

'Not in the least,' I called out breezily. 'Just checking. I look forward to not seeing you,' and after a few more pleasant words I hung up and stared.

Would they all be like that? To them all would I be merely a name, a digit? With a gulp like the fear you gulp when you first hear bullets spewing over your head – where in hell had I ever heard bullets spewing over my head? – I realised that all I had been promised by the gods had been a *public* identity, and this was it, strewn mockingly in front of me on my desk. My passport? All any passport had ever 'done' in its life is to oblige some immigrant official to accept that its bearer is Citizen A and not Citizen B, whereas all I want to know, I implored my desk, paper-strewn, is what sort of bloody creature *is* Citizen A! How else can I become aware of my own awareness – not just how I struck the Sentry, Gravedigger, First Murderer, or Ghost but my close friends who know me, in whom I confide, who confide in me.

My dossier edged towards me two more memorials: a bulging album leaking photographs at the seams, and a large bundle of pocket diaries tied in hairy string. I found that they ranged back to the year 1912. I tore open the album. There I was, as a boy, a youth, a young man, a mature man, peering at the sun, grinning at a friend, smiling at the photographer, one of a group, in a paper hat, golfing, playing tennis, with a girl there, with two girls here, with a woman and a child. I filled my lungs. Pictures can't lie.

I took three cheerful, whistling days to select twenty-five pictures, and started to play patience with them. This goes with this, that with that, both these around twenty-four or -five, two here at least forty, this blonde could be my wife Bridget, this a brother though much older. Where was my son Henry? One face turns up several times. These kids always turn up with that pair so I can discard them. That pair always appears with me. A close chum? No, that one was not my wife, she keeps turning up with 'him', the man of the pair that keeps turning up with me...

Suddenly I came on my first truthful picklock: a picture of me about twenty-fiveish in a jaunty panama hat and a cream linen jacket, the sun blazing, the background either Italy or Southern France. So far, nothing remarkable. But if this woman, over here, really was my wife, why have I no picture of her in this same blazing sun? People on holidays always take photographs of one another. Fishy? Besides, in the whole album there was no other showing a continental background. Very fishy! Hurrah! On the back of the panama photograph a date: 20/4/1924, and a place name. Can . . . ? Cadam . . . ? Cadenabbia? Cannobio. On Lake Maggiore. I scrambled for my 1924 diary, and sure enough there it was, an entry on April 18th nervously insisting – *Victoria, meet C. on boat-train platform 10.30 for 11 a.m. Repeat, 10.30. Gare de Lyon for Stresa. Steamer for Cannobio.* C? Who was C? (Those diaries, by the way, were really my own diaries.)

I leaped up with that jaunty snapshot in my hand to compare its gaiety with the picture in my mirror, fish mouth, baggy eyes, fish nose, veins on nose, sagging jowls, thin hair, all laughing back at me and saying, 'Haha! You old bastard, you SEXagenarian, I won't have you for long. Roll back time, roll back the Italian lakes, the godly sun, all those girls waiting for me in a line!' I waltzed around the room. Back to my patience game, concentrating solely on the women's faces.

One did hold me, a dark, bold, handsome, self-assured, masterful-looking young woman in her mid-twenties, seated on a harbour bollard, showing a fine leg, a narrow waist, rich hips. On the verso was pencilled the letter B, and the word, Wexford. B? Bee? Beatrice? Beatrix? Trixie? Bridget it could not be. It could not be Bridget Olden. This was not my wife. Not my type. I felt sure of it.

What about this one, a much more alluring, smallish, blonde woman, not young, not at all young, possibly in her late forties, standing against a public statue that bore a white bird on its head? I warmed to her at once. Gulls. Far calls. I looked at her for a long time. I felt that if I were a younger man I would want to order a case of her, and was frustrated when I searched the fat album over and back and found no other picture of her. On the verso of this photograph I found another single letter, A., and in front, at the bottom, the written word *Seagulls*, as if this were the artistic reason for preserving the picture, which I could not believe because it was not at all a good photograph – it was the kind of poor photograph one keeps only because it reminds one of some special place, occasion or person. I took my magnifying glass to examine the woman's face and instantaneously recognised the statue. It was William Harvey, the seventeenth-century discoverer of the circulation of the blood. This I knew because I knew that I had written a piece about him on the three hundredth anniversary of his death in 1957. The recollection at first disappointed me. It offered a less romantic reason for my having taken the picture. On consideration, it gratified me all the more. It meant that if somebody, inquisitively turning over the pages of my album, had said, 'Why are you keeping this picture?' I would have glanced and casually said, 'Oh! William Harvey!'

I next peered at the woman's face through my glass, uttered the word *fountains* and thought *horses*. She was carrying a case for field glasses by a strap over her shoulder. We had probably been to the races at Folkestone? But why *fountains*?

I believe that that was the moment – I was by now trembling like a dog after game in a wood – when I really broke through my enemy's defences into those vast, undefended spaces before even the gods were, where all memory lies sleeping, a harp string in the air, indestructible, speaking in the image of a horse-race, or a lake or a quivering nimbus of spray blown prismatically across a fountain that, whenever I concentrated too much on it, sank into itself on the turn of a tap. For it was futile for me, then or any like occasion, to try to remember deliberately or forcefully; to evoke races in Kent or fountains in Versailles, Holyrood, the Villa d'Este, even in the music of Respighi.

A.? Horses? Fountains? Fifty-seven? I turned in a frenzy for my 1957 diary. There it was, in September, *Folkestone*. A. Arabella? Anthea? Alma? Ann? I did nothing else that day but sieve every page of my diaries in a vain search for that enchanting first letter of the alphabet. However, the next morning I found a picture postcard of the fountains in Trafalgar Square to which I had hitherto paid no attention. It was addressed to me c/o *The Evening Gazette*, Colchester, Essex. It carried one scrawled, comic(?), flirtatious(?) sentence: *Je meure de soif auprès de la fontaine*. It was signed with a big sprawling A. But the date was June 1924. Thirty-three years before Folkestone! Surely the cocked panama hat also harked back to the summer of 1924? I checked back. I was mistaken. That was April, and on double-checking with a perpetual calendar I saw that Easter that year had been on the 20th, two days after my diary's record of that nervous meeting with C. in Victoria Station. No connection with the A of the postcard two months later. Or, rather, no obvious connection.

About C. one thing nostalgia told me, sitting back and staring back at a damp and chilly April morning so long ago in Victoria station's dust, steam, steel, fish, shuffling feet, echoes of generations of dead trains and dead travellers. It was that she was a she and late. No Charlie, or Cyril, or Clive could have recalled as I now did the 'O my God!' of joy and adoration breathed over my shoulder as I in memory looked out, the next morning, above Pallanza, at a blazing sky over snow-tipped mountains and, below us, the greater lake with its cypressed islets and its encircling oleanders, azaleas and camellias that breathed a happy goodbye to London's damp from this early-morning transformation scene beyond the Alps. Nostalgia told me nothing about A. – nothing. Yet she may once have meant everything to me. Now lost autumn leaves meant less.

Younger! Watch it! Mystifying? Romancing? What we are doing is mathematics, adding up, looking coldly for a total. Bad novelists and poor reporters are two of a kind. Remember that your job was journalism. Write down the facts as you ultimately established them, and only the facts. Okay, they are that I had been married to a C. for Christabel Lee. That I met A, for Ana, again, face to face, about three months after I began to go through the gods' lying dossier with a pair of tweezers, and that I fell madly in love with her again, both of us aged sixty-five, she slowly ageing, I swiftly younging. She told me a lot about me which was true when she did not think that she was revealing anything and that was more or less untrue when she did. I was by this tired but not worn out. Research had become an obsession. From photographs and diaries I went to stubs from old cheque-books, press cuttings, inscriptions on pill-boxes, doctors' prescriptions, dog-eared receipts. Most of these turned out to be genuinely my own personal property – smaller objects such as even the most peripatetic bachelor drags from digs to digs – books, discs, even framed pictures. Everything else, all the furniture from the doormat to the dustbin proved to be my brother's property, including the house and gardens, bought and held in his and his wife's name. As I smelled around the house for clues I would be filled with triumph on finding an old label, brown and curled, on the back of a picture (it was of a sailing-boat – mine?) framed in Colchester; be cheered if I discovered in a tuxedo that fitted me a cloak-room check naming a hotel in Stockport; welcome with a happy wink a printed invitation to a National Union of Journalists' Anniversary Dance, i.e. booze up, in Sheffield; half-recognise the lease of a flat in Leeds; laugh at the receipt for three bags of coal delivered to a house in Highgate, London.

Two weeks later, with the help of the diaries and all my bits and pieces of paper, I was able to map my presumptive route through life from the village of Castletownroche to the city of Cork (*The Evening Echo*), to Dublin (*The Evening Mail*, now defunct), to Colchester (*The Evening Gazette*), Leeds (*The Yorkshire Post*), Manchester (the old Manchester *Guardian*), finally London (*The Daily Mail*). There the trail seemed to go underground after the end of the war. However, since my gods still called me 'Journalist' in 1965 I must have continued as a free-lance.

To the road! Or would Olympus, annoyed by my hubristic efforts to circumvent their restrictions on memory, thwart me? At first I feared so, when I rang my bank for the total of the balance in the current account and was told that I was good for £15.11s. Hoping for even a small cheque from some unremembered quarter I scuffled through the scatter of letters, circulars, bills or advertisements that had been hitherto kicked aside on the mat. They were mainly bills for electricity, telephone, gas. I noted that the largest bill was for liquor. (I do not know what I ate while I had been sifting and panning, delving and digging, but my wine merchant informed me that I had drunk a sizeable quantity of brandy.) I became aware of the gods' vengeful smile.

I have occasionally thought since that I misjudged them. Were we all not partners in that dig? For, surely, a dig is what living-it-all-over-again amounts to: a preternatural eagerness to lay bare in layers the composition of one's present by excavating one's past. Before I was reborn I was incomplete because still living. Now, dead and alive I am become an appealing green site of hump and hollow which, like any archaeologist, I may dissect with spade, trowel, spoon, scalpel and dusting toothbrush. I recall the French pedagogue's punning sentence, intended to point the nature of a homonym, which I learned while at school in Cork and now see was not true. *Je suis ce que je suis, je ne suis pas ce que je suis* ... etc. (I am what I am (follow), I am not what I follow (am) . . .) I am because I do follow. A spadesman recording his dig.

But I had no money to finance my dig! As I kicked the letters and circulars from my hall mat the telephone chimed. A bird-frail female voice said gently, 'Mr Younger? This is Gore-Goodbody, solicitors. Would you please hold the line for Mr Harold Gore-Goodbody?' A moment later an assuringly fruity voice took over.

'Mr Younger? This is Harold Gore-Goodbody speaking. Greetings. First of all may I offer you my deepest sympathy in your recent bereavement. I am ringing you on the suggestion of Mr Rubinstein of Sensible, Hicks, Breach and Rubinstein of Bedford Row, London, WC1, who suggest that since you have now taken up residence in Dublin you might find it more convenient to round off your various affairs here in Ireland rather than on what some old-fashioned Irish people still call – Haha! – "the far side". This will be, of course, entirely as you prefer, but there *are* papers to be signed and a certain amount of money to be handed over to you under your late brother's will.'

Money? My brother? How much?

'The will of your brother James Younger, who with his wife Bridget Younger died in that unfortunate air disaster in the U.S.A., has gone through probate. No objections have been raised to it. The insurance company has also paid up. The total estate reverts to you, which, all charges paid, including taxes, legal fees, and the like, amounts to £75,543.3s net. So, if you are agreeable and wish to make an appointment with me you may drop in here any time that suits us both. We can complete the whole matter in a very few minutes, and I can hand you the final cheque. Oh! Mr Rubinstein has also forwarded your passport to me . . .'

'My passport? But I have it here in front of me.'

'Impossible, here it is in front of me. Robert Bernard Younger. Journalist, born County Cork, the 17th of the third, 1900, et cetera. That will be all the indentification you will need when you come. We also have the Indenture, Assignment and Lease of the residence in Rosmeen Park that your brother James Joseph paid for in full previous to his fatal trip to the United States . . .'

The voice went on explaining long after I ceased to listen. 'Your brother . . . Your passport . . . Robert Bernard Younger.' When I became aware of myself again the floor was another draggle of trampled, battered, tattered papers, photographs, diaries, documents and I, panting and blaspheming in the middle of them, was still kicking them. I halted, gasping. I focused on my large scratch pad leaning against the leg of an armchair. It bore a few numerals in my handwriting. I bent to read them.

'£75,543.3s.'*

It was late April, sunny and not cold as I drove south for Castletownroche. Every mile of the road came back to me until I reached the Blackwater and deviated into smaller and unknown side roads. Every field I drove past, through Kildare, Queen's County, Tipperary, North Cork, gleamed as if, washed clean of the sodden winter, it was drying sweetly and freshly in the soft south-west winds of spring. The newborn fields were speckled with wild plum, blackthorn, Easter lambs. Small clouds barely moved against the blue sky. In the ditches were celandines, tiny stars of Bethlehem, primroses. What did it matter to me who I was? I am! Rejuvenated, delighted, exhilarated to be able to recognise so many small things along the way, a casual turn of the road, a well remembered pub, a noble Georgian country home, a line of muscular beech trees, a favourite glimpse of a distant view. I slept soundly at Cahir so as to arrive early enough at the village the next morning, there to define whatever there was finally to define and then push on to Cork, get it all out of my mind, be master of a known Me.

The village was a street. I had decided to make two calls only, to the schoolmaster in order to see his registers, and to the priest to see his. Castletownroche looked so empty that April morning it might have been a film set waiting for me. Or was that whole story shot? At any second would a voice shout 'Strike the set!' and the village collapse? The hour was half past ten in the morning. The schoolhouse was easy to find: new, rough cast, serviceable no doubt, it should have borne, like one of those Italian headstones, a china-ware photograph of the defunct schoolhouse it replaced. The

*Postscript: In 1965 the pound sterling was still perpendicular. When I invested most of that £75,000-odd in house property and land I was able to buy eight new houses with it and some ten and a half acres of what I (correctly) hoped would duly become desirable building land. Ten years later the houses had trebled in value and the land was being purchased by the square foot. Meanwhile I had the income from the rents of those houses, roughly £7,000 gross per annum and as I lived fairly modestly as a bachelor with what is called no 'cares', I was able to reinvest a fair part of my income every year. This tells me as much about the sort of man I am as anything else I have so far observed. Only Ana has told me more; apart from my favourite reading – i.e. books like Dumas and Fenimore Cooper, romantic adventures; especially my Cooper – the American Eden where men were upright, honourable, brave and true of heart. Idealist? Sentimentalist? Or just escapist? With a fairly strong *SOSP* (sense of self-protection). Nothing odd there. I remember as a boy hearing an aunt say of a countryman in her shop in Cork: 'He has a grand flood of ghost stories and fairy stories, but he would skin a flea for the hide of it.'

schoolmaster was (to me) a red-headed boy, and no sooner did I look at him and tell him about my interest in my own pre-youth in Castletownroche than I realised that he would have nothing to tell me. He was bright, quick, alert, on the ball, three pens in his breast pocket. He did not waste my time or his words. He just led me to the porch and silently pointed across a field to the roofless and stone-cropped shell of what had obviously been the National School of Castletownroche when I was a child. The sight of it – melancholy to me, a profound relief I did not doubt to him – informed me that to him I was a similar victim of rust and time. He lifted his empty palms.

'Too bad!' he said briskly. 'And we have no records from before the First World War.'

Bright lad! TV-trained. A grandchild of Yeats's terrible beauty. He had my age stamped and stapled in one click. He smiled and I followed his pointing-down-the-street directions to the parochial house where he indicated I should probably find the parish priest, Father James Carney, reading *The Irish Independent*. So he was. My hopes rose a trifle at the sight of a man not much junior to myself. Here, with the Church I was back in the thirteenth century. Gregory IX. The Holy Office of the Inquisition. He was slim, small, dainty, bald, open-eyed, welcoming and surprisingly, unlike the teacher, he was only too ready to chat. He did not appear to me to be oppressed by work. He offered me a whiskey (at eleven a.m.) in the best nineteenth-century tradition of rural clerical hospitality, and delicately efficiently picked me over for every detail about myself that he assumed (and that I wished) I knew to find out exactly why I was interested in his registers. When I told him that I was pursuing a search into my father's and mother's history for purely filial reasons he professed to understand fully while doubting if his books would tell me very much. He took his hat and umbrella and led me across to the church. His presbytery smelled of candle wick, floor polish, the past of this world and some rather thin hopes of the next. He rubbed his hands as if to defrost them.

'Younger?' he mused, putting on his modern plastic-rimmed glasses and hauling out a couple of large and heavy ledger-like records. 'The name is unfamiliar to me, but I have been here only for the last thirteen years. And that certificate of yours goes back sixty-five years. But let us lift up our hearts and hopes, we have the exact date and there should be no difficulty.' His tiny hand gracefully turned the leaves of fate, murmuring to himself as he did so.

'Eighteen ninety-eight . . . Eighteen ninety-nine. Nineteen O. Here we are. January. February.' He paused tantalisingly to blow his minute nose. 'You know, February and March are often very busy times of the year for christenings. June brides. I had seven baptisms last month. March? Here we are. Up she comes. Born, you said, on March 17th. That is an easy date to remember, St Patrick's Day. Baptised, your piece of paper says, on March 20th. Now, let us see!' His wrinkled finger sidled featly down the page and stopped. 'Here it is,' he cried delightedly, and I leaned across his arm to look at my name. 'Younger!'

He paused, frowned, turned his spectacles to mine – our faces were only inches apart – his eyes enlarged, his brows uplifted, his mouth a puss of comic dismay as he tapped the page with his index finger.

'You were twins. You, James Joseph as your certificate says. And the other, Robert Bernard.' He drew back, looked at me over his glasses, poised on the edge of suspicion. 'You didn't mention your brother Robert to me?'

'Robert is dead,' I said quickly. 'And I am interested only in checking the date, my parents' names, and hoping to see where they lived hereabouts. Your book, I see, does indicate that they resided in the Main Street.'

His lower lip protruded like a horse's. He removed his glasses, breathed thoughtfully over the lenses, polished them, glanced at me like a headmaster who feels that he must not discourage a pupil from whom he had expected better things, and said with a melancholy good cheer as he closed his ledger, 'Never mind, we're not beaten yet. We have an old chap here named Ike Smith who claims to be eighty-two. That means that he was born in 1883. He would have been seventeen when you arrived on this earth. He may be worth a try.'

All this should have persuaded me to give up, but I clung to my scrap of Me-ness that I still felt or hoped I had sifted out of that otherwise lying dossier. After all, a true twin – I knew this somehow or other; journalists know bits about all sorts of things – a true twin is the product of a single fertilised ovum, not just the synchronous development of two eggs, and therefore may well be the mirror of its mate. We had not far to go. From the steps of the church his Reverence pointed his umbrella at a human tortoise, that is to say at an old, hooped man who with the help of two sticks was not so much walking as slowly inching along this empty Main Street, sliding one quarter-step by one quarter-step, patently a cripple from advanced arthritis, never once lifting his tortoise head from the earth that once as a youngster he bestrode.

'He can't walk,' my guide observed. 'He can't hear. He can't see. I doubt if he can smell. I presume he can recognise his sticks by their touch. I gather that he tastes a pint of stout every day. He comes to me to confess his sins once a month. I could not, of course, tell you what sins he confesses to me – presuming that I ever knew what they were! – but there is one thing that he can do very well! He can spit like a cuckoo. We must stand well back from him.'

We advanced and halted him and the P.P. began a shouting conversation with him that, I was sure, every faceless window heard. This humped tortoise was a blade of twenty-two when I was five; he would never again know, as in time I would, what it is to be twenty-two. His voice was so feeble, throaty, toothless and broguey that I could not understand more than a word or two of his croaking responses to the priest's shouting, but his Reverence must have understood because the conversation went on a long time, with many chuckles and many gestures, and at the end the priest shook his paw elatedly, whispered to me, 'Give him a bob,' and when I had passed across the coin, he took complete possession of my arm and my search.

'We have done it, Mr Younger. We have made contact with your childhood. Not very much but perhaps enough.' As we went through the empty main street he chuckled at some private joke which he choked to draw my attention to some recent 'improvements' and 'developments' which were to me indistinguishable from their surroundings. Presently his grip on my arm obliged me to halt on the pavement's edge and face the opposite side of the wide street. Watching me he nodded discreetly across at a pub, surmounted by four storeys of privacy, the whole building painted from ground to roof in a red startling enough to make it as prominent as a skyscraper. 'Ike Smith says it was painted green in your father's time,' and sure enough I could see pale green blotches in its red, like a green petticoat showing through the ragged rifts of a scarlet dress.

'Look at the fascia board,' he whispered with (what I felt was) an unpleasant relish. 'It could do with a lick of paint. The name is DANAGHER. Ike Smith says that we can read traces of another name underneath the Danagher. I can make out a Y. and an O.

Can you? When Ike Smith was a boy this pub was run by two brothers. Bob Younger, our uncle. Gerald Younger, our father. This, Mr Younger, is the rock from which we were hewn.'

I could not understand why he should suddenly have developed a bud of malice towards me, unless it was that I was a nosy, superior Dubliner and he was a nosy, superior Corkman; also he may have thought that I was asking his assistance in my search while concealing some element of it, which indeed I was, and in a priest as in a policeman concealment always arouses suspicion – an awareness on my part which simultaneously told me something further about myself.

'Well?' I pressed, 'Ike said more than that.'

His Reverence refrained, wavered, could not resist it, lunged mock-humourously.

'Ike Smith says that our forebears went off with themselves very suddenly on Sunday night a touch over fifty years or so ago.'

He was enjoying himself hugely. At his next clerical dinner party all this – whatever 'all this' was – would be his great story.

'Go ahead,' I said crossly. 'Let it fly. I can take it.'

And there on the pavement's edge he built up his comical story about the simple, enquiring Dubliner who thought he could cod the Cork people.

My uncle Bob, I gathered, had one weakness long suppressed, as my father had another not long enough suppressed. Being only the brother of the titular proprietor, therefore in the eyes of the customers of *The Green Man* a titular subordinate, and being by nature far less genial than my genial father, and therefore naturally less popular with the customers, Uncle Bob was one of those people who for long periods can conceal their resentments in utter silence and then suddenly let them explode with multiple force. 'They didn't get on' would be how some customer like Ike Smith would have put it, thinking no doubt of their long horrid silences rather than their occasional storms. In between these silences and these explosions Bob had, naturally, to have some safety-valve to let out the gathering head of steam, and it took the innocent form of betting in farthings. Not in half-pennies, pennies, threepenny pieces, six-penny bits, shillings and certainly not in any coin higher than that (he was a man frugal to the point of miserliness), only in farthings, the fourth part of a penny, the most minute temptation possible, which temptations his genial brother, out of his expansive hatred of such despicable coins, put in his way by collecting farthings in a tin box on the shelf near the till into which he contemptuously threw every such lousy farthing that came his way.

'There,' a customer might idly say, looking at the window, 'is the first fly I saw this year.'

'That,' Bob would say, giving the counter a wide sweep with his palm, 'is not a fly. It is a bluebottle.'

'Ah no!' the customer would say. 'I know a fly when I see a fly', and if there were a couple of other customers in *The Green Man*, or more than three if it was a very busy day, one of the others would join in, and yet a third customer, and on the busy day, the fourth, always siding against Bob to get him worked up to the point where he had to say, 'I bet ye a farthing it's a bluebottle.'

These passionate discussions provided a pleasant entertainment for the clientele, released some of Bob's bile, pleased my father insofar as they got rid of a farthing or two and disgusted him because the coin involved was so low and mean, a disgust that also pleased the clients. While Bob was planking down the farthing, exactly the same size as an old-time half-sovereign, my father would be rattlingly rearranging the bottles on the shelves, and was on rare occasions even known to pour himself a half of a half-glass of whiskey to soothe his gut. Finally, one day he intervened. Whatever the subject under discussion was – the name of the second last Pope, or whether it was Goldsmith or Sheridan who wrote *The School for Scandal*, or was Kruger's name John Paul or Stephen Paul, or whether or not the Jews have Lent – my father suddenly said to my uncle Bob, 'I bet you sixpence you're wrong.' And to everybody's astonishment, that is everybody in, and within fifteen miles of Castletownroche when the news spread, Bob put his hand in his pocket, fished out a sixpenny bit, and planked it on the counter.

It was a symbolic gesture, clearly intended to establish once for all that he was co-partner on an equal financial footing with his brother in that pub; if Jerry was ready to risk good money in this feckless way let it be clear that what was at risk was the fortune of the *whole* family. Quietly and fatally, the customer who had started the argument, whether about Kruger, the Pope, the Jews or *The School for Scandal*, raised my father's bet to a shilling. My father at once put down a florin, and helped himself to a whole glass of whiskey. Uncle Bob had no option. Pale as a peppermint he laid his florin on top of his brother's, raced upstairs for his twenty-year-old *Pears' Cyclopaedia* and, beaming, returned to display it on the counter. He had won his bet. Filled with a sense of relief that he had never yet known he gathered his gains, put them in the till and stood drinks all round, including a double whiskey for my father. From that day on Uncle Bob became a slave both to gambling and to drink, outpassed the popularity of his brother, and *The Green Man* became the most frequented of the seventeen pubs of Castletownroche.

'That house,' said his Reverence, looking across at the red sky-scraper with the pale green blotches, 'became the Monte Carlo of the Blackwater, from Mallow down to Cappoquin, until our congenial forebears duly departed from it in the early hours of one wintry morning. It was the horse-betting that ruined them.'

He pressed my arm with a sympathy that I found so revolting that I asked him the coldest question I could think of:

'What happened to the tin box where my father used to throw those despised farthings?'

He looked as wounded as I expected him to look. Yet why should he? Priests have also been known to cut themselves off by coldness (sexual?) from their kin. All the same, I stared for quite a while at that pock-marked house trying to see myself coming out of its hall door, with my school satchel, as a small boy of five or six. It did not work. Nobody came out with me. I left nobody behind. No pals met me. The gods had not lied. Nobody can live the same life all over again unless the same world lives it with him.

I extricated myself from my priestly Virgil's web of malice, curiosity and human sympathy, heeding only of the many voluble vacuities with which we both tried to hide our differing feelings of failure, his final remark (he squeezed my arm again and again as if to make my pulse exude the truth) that my parents might well have left Castletownroche when I and my brother were mere babies. For one mean second I suspected another unkind cut – that the Youngers had not lasted long after that. Then I thought, No! He means well. He is merely suggesting that I should not be hurt by Castletownroche. Any man who wants to know himself needs to go through all the generations. I thanked him for his kindness. Huffily he walked away. I returned to my old green Wolseley and drove out of the village. A mile out from it I halted, sank into my arms on the steering-wheel and became unconscious.

By the time I found myself again my mouth was full of cobwebs. The windows of my car were heat-fogged. About me a field beset by scattered stones like giant sized hail under an occluded sky.

When that lawyer told me that I was not James Younger but Robert I should have surrendered. Now that I had seen those baptismal registers I had even less reason for trying to recover the memories forbidden to me. But could I, a grown man, face life blank and faceless? My jaws clamped. I crouched back into my Wolseley and drove off to do further battle with whatever windmills and wine bags lay in my way.

I cut it short. Why record failure? I saw Bridget Olden's grave. I read the obituaries in the *Examiner*. 'Her sorrowing husband James Younger.' I consulted the Vintners' Association. I consulted Rate Books. I went from church to church. The gods must have yawned at my childish *hubris*. Whether in Cork, Dublin, Leeds, Sheffield, Colchester or London I was to find no rational evidence of any Younger's former existence even when I clearly recognised streets, houses, pubs, railroads, towns, cities, theatres, parks. Every human association that should have been connected with these places raced from me like the foam hissing away behind a liner's propellers at midnight. As for my fellow actors of forty or thirty years ago I did meet and recognise a Gravedigger or a Messenger here and there: such as that old landlady in Leeds, gabbling, 'Yesh, yesh, yesh, I do seem to recall a Mr Younger. Or was his name Young? He had a little white dog. Did you have a white dog? No! Or was his name Oldham? But Younger? My memory is gone to pieces . . .' Or the cheery, cackling, retired old compositor in Colchester who half-thought he half-recognised me. 'Wot year did you sye? That's a mere forty years ago! Let me see. Hold on! Of course, I remember you. The young fellow named Younger we used to pull his leg down in the old *Kat and Kytten* about Younger's ale? See the joke? O Lord! Hayhayhay! How we used to laugh at it. So! After all these years! You still like Younger's Ale?'

I did not like to tell him that I had never in my younger life drunk anything weaker than brandy and soda.

I allotted my last week to London. On the last day of that week an absurd incident, or it may have been just my exhaustion, convinced me. It was probably a minor Olympian cocksnook at my obstinacy. I had ticked off every possible contact and address in my itinerary except one, a pub near the Inner Temple. I went down there and one glance told me the trail was, again, gone cold. The area had been neatly bombed, the pub neatly rebuilt. It was a few minutes after the reopening hour for the evening session and the sole occupant of the pub was a ruddy, grumpy man wearing a coloured flowery waistcoat and no jacket who silently uncapped my bottle of Guinness. I said, more from habit rather than hope, that when I was on the *Daily Mail* during the war I used to occasionally drop in here for a Guinness and a Spam sandwich. He held the bottle, looked out the door, said nothing, then, on due consideration he uttered one mildly companionable word.

'Retired?'

'Five years,' I lied. 'When are *you* going to take to playing bowls and growing dahlias?'

When he grimaced with his nose I presumed that that was the end of our friendly chat. He poured my stout with due and proper care down the side of my glass and then, still holding the glass, he looked straight in front of him, said 'Spam!' and laughed heartily. (The English are, *au fond*, a most warm-hearted people.)

'Not,' he admitted judiciously, yielded eye-squintingly, 'that I minded the war. I didn't even mind the Blitz. Not even the night this place,' one elequent finger rose an inch, 'went up. That night I was on top of the roof of St Paul's. Air-raid warden. You remember when they did the City? Now that I look back, awful. At the time I felt nothing . We just stood there, four of us in a row, up on the gutters looking at it. They came in waves. The whole City of London on fire. I remember three things vividly about the war. Spam, as you say. That night listening and looking. And what I saw when I came in here to open up the following morning.' He nodded and I looked over my shoulder at an irregular shape of brick wall neatly outlined in red, white and blue, with a bowler hat hanging on it. 'Six square feet of wall, that bowler hat, and rubble, and beams all around. When we came to rebuild the place we preserved that bit of wall, and that hat, just to show they did not knock us out completely.'

He had left me to attend to a couple of young chaps who had just come in, fellows in painters' white overalls. I looked at my watch. I would have time to stroll, pack, have a meal, catch the Irish Mail for Holyhead, the mail boat for Dunlaoire, and be home for breakfast. Mission unaccomplished. In pub silence I finished my drink, slid off my stool, said good evening and out of recent habit, 'The name is Younger.' Like a shot, like a young man, he cried commandingly, 'Hold it!' I turned in surprise. Had I not paid?

'Did you say Younger?'

'Yes.'

'Used to drop in here from the *Mail* during the war?'

'Ye-e-es.'

'Would you mind handing me that hat?' pointing to the historic object.

Unwillingly I lifted the thing from its crook and handed it to him. The top half of it was grey with dust. He turned it over and pointed inside it to the two dulled gold gothic letters printed on the leather sweat band. *R.Y.*

'Your initials?'

I shook my head. If that hat was mine it would be the big belly laugh of the gods, my reward for nosing into Bluebeard's Chamber, Aladdin's Cave, clambering after the forbidden apple. I muttered about R for Richard, Roderick, Rupert. Y for Yeoman, Yonge, York, Yardley, and a man I had once interviewed named Yashiro. Anyway I had never worn a bowler hat.

'Try it for size,' he ordered and the two painters watched while I tried the dusty hat. It was not the gods' revenge, though it must have been their last and final warning. The hat was so big that only my ears stopped its descent. One of the painters said, 'Naow! He's not Cinderellar.'

'You see!' I said delightedly. 'Not mine.'

As I walked up Bouverie Street into the boom of Fleet Street and along the Strand to Charing Cross I gave up, and said so, quietly. 'I give up.' As I said the accepting words I thought I felt a door opening and a door closing, as if somebody had come into a room and looked at me and gone out again. Under an impulse I crossed the Strand at Charing Cross station and went into Trafalgar Square and wandered around to stand with my back to the National Gallery. I was in a relaxed mood, unaware of the buses, vans, taxis circling anonymously behind me. A cloud-canopied, summery afternoon light spread behind the statue on its top column. I started wondering again about an element in Nelson's career that had always interested me, the large part that chance had played in his life ever since he happened to join the navy as a child of twelve, which is, perhaps, a good moment for me to say that if anybody, not excluding myself, ever comes to read this record of my life, my second life, in ten or twenty years' time he might easily conclude from everything I have written so far that nothing interested me during my travels but me: this had not been so. Far from it: many recognisable but uninformative things along my way had given me considerable pleasure, and I enjoyed recollecting each of them, impersonal and unassociated though they were: the splendid collection of pre-Raphaelite pictures in Manchester; the boats about the Royal Solent Yacht Club in Yarmouth that I used at one time visit from Colchester; the moors above Sheffield where I often spent a whole Saturday or Sunday tramping alone; even in Leeds I had old haunts to revisit, and, of course, here in London where I had spent so many pleasant years. So, that last afternoon in London I was just on the point of turning into the National Portrait Gallery to have a look again at a few portraits I had always liked, especially the Gainsboroughs, when my eyes sank down from Nelson's silhouette on his lofty column into the water of the fountain beside me and a precious bit of my London past suddenly revisited me.

As I looked into the basin of water it took on a lightsomeness, both disturbing and curious, like the oncoming light of the almost risen sun. The blown spray of the fountain sprinkling it became prismatic like a rainbow presaging the end of a storm. In the freckled water of the basin I saw a familiar face, that A. whom, within a few days, I was to know again as Ana ffrench. I actually turned to my right to see if she stood beside me and knew, then and there, as I had long faintly hoped or suspected, that there is in every man and woman another memory, that I now call a nocturnal memory, existing behind everything we clearly remember by the light of day. This dark memory comes from where all myths are born, primordial, adamite, as animal as the instinct of the garden cat that I am watching at this moment scratching the ground behind her to hide the spoor of her droppings as carefully and daintily as if she were the primal tigress who begat her kind in the silence before Eden lived. No power, human or divine, can completely kill those subliminal echoes, as suggestive as they are unintelligible, whispered from some U.F.O. of the imagination hovering like a dragonfly on the edge of time. I swore by that fountain that I would listen in future only to these soft tappings, never again to the oompah oracles of the gods.

I did see my Gainsboroughs, had a dry martini in the Café Royal for old times' sake, dined well in Soho, caught the Irish Mail. Later that morning when returning to Rosmeen Park, now in full leaf and flower, from some necessary bachelor shopping my ear was dusted by a soft tap-tap that I failed to heed above the pleasant clack of a lawn-mower until I was at my own white gate. There its echo came back to me like the last meeouw of a kitten up a tree. It was the word 'Zanzibar'. I said it many times. It evoked nothing, not even Africa or Madagascar. I must, I guessed, have seen it on some other garden gate among the *Mellifonts, Chattertons, Innisfrees, Magentas, Jilljoes, St Mary's* along my way. But why did just this one word stick?

As I opened my gate I saw a primrose Jaguar parked outside the adjoining house and a familiar figure, blonde, powerful, standing beside it, fingering awkwardly in her hand for the correct car key while clasping a bulky flat package in brown paper to her side with her left elbow. Jana, wife of Janus, the god with two faces, one facing back, one forward, the patron of all beginnings. The first day I saw her she had sent me a waft of sandalwood. I had thought her younger then. Today she looked a richer thirty-five – which proved to be her age – a woman still, at least to me, old man, *à la fleur de sa jeunesse*. She would have looked splendid on horseback, not so good nude, or in a swimsuit, the waist too heavy. Her head was yellow as laburnum, her pallid eyes smoke grey, smoke blue, dark lashed as I remembered them from our first passage. I saluted her.

It is easy for the old to accost the young. To them we are all foreign tourists, unresented unless, future-less ourselves, we try to cadge theirs. Our proper tense is the past habitual. We seem absurd or comical if we claim any of their powers, such as passion; disgusting if suspected of copulating after forty. So much blood in us? Hamlet should be their patron saint, the youth who, to his horror, when his loins were aching for his girl discovered that his mother a venerable old lady of forty or so, much respected in court circles, had loins too. His roar was, 'Frost on fire!', his oath to destroy this world root and branch, her paramour, his girl, her father, his school chums, himself, his entire line. Those areas and prescriptions apart we old fading shadows of men beyond fifty are welcome to say hello to our young.

She responded laughingly to the old gentleman who soapily introduced himself as a newcomer to the park. She said she knew all about me 'already'.

'In this cul-de-sac everybody seems to know everything and everybody "already".'

An intelligent young woman, warm and friendly, she chatted easily until I noticed that while she was talking to me and looking at me her lower eyelids kept lifting and her eyes kept peering at me as if she were focusing myopically at something far away. If I had been a young man I would have seized my chance with. 'Yes, we *must* have met before? Was it at Eden Roc or Brighton?' Things being as they were it was she who said it. I shook my head, knowing that she had not noticed my existence that March morning of my rebirth.

'Unless,' I probed, 'you have always lived here and seen me come and go?'

'We bought our house only last March. The painters, and all the rest of them, have been at it up to a week ago. Still, it is my first very own Irish house so I am quite excited about it. I mean up to this I lived in England, or New York, or Berlin, or Paris. Studying painting. My husband is a sculptor. So, if I ever did meet you it would have to have been a long time ago. No! It is just that I got an odd feeling that when I was a girl I had seen somebody very like you once or twice in my mother's house. In Number 118 Ailesbury Road?'

'I am sure,' who was by this unsure of everything, 'that I have never known anybody who lived in the select elegance of Ailesbury Road. What was your mother's name?'

'Her name is,' stressing the 'is', 'Ana ffrench, with two small f's. We are the Longfields. You must drop in and have a drink with us sometime. Oops!' The cry came as she turned towards her car, having found the right key while chatting, and smacked her flat package against the silvered lamp post on the kerb. She puffed comically, adjusted her package. 'It's my birthday gift to my mother, an old painting of me she had done years ago. She is sixty-five today although she'd kill me for telling anybody. She looks as young as me.' Humouring the old gentleman, she opened the car door and before depositing the picture folded back the brown paper over it for a second. 'He was a black painter.'

She had sat in, the door still open, one hand ready to close it.

'Did you say black? You said a black painter.'

'Oh, that? Yes, he was a doctor studying here. A gynaecologist visiting the Rotunda, my father is a real gynaecologist – Reginald ffrench. He was not a real painter. A Sunday painter. From some place like the Congo, or was it Tanganyika? I'm awful on geography. I must fly. It could have been Zanzibar.'

She closed the door, started the car and with a smile roared off. Earlier there must have been a little shower of rain – I found myself looking at a dusty oblong patch on the road. Longfield. Ana ffrench. Other words began to slide slowly along the wire of memory like beads, close but not touching. *The Regina.* A yacht? Or a hotel? Was it when I was in Colchester and did a bit of sailing out of Harwich that I was told that if you are grand enough to own a yacht you must modestly call it a boat. If you own a boat it is also a boat – *Three Men in a Boat.* The word Nice slid by. I was confused. 'Longfield' was coming back, but as a priest. Ailesbury Road meant nothing, but Ana meant fountains, and seagulls. I went into my house, so empty and fusty, no letter on the mat, not even a bill, plugged in my electric fire and poured myself a whiskey. A week ago I might have pursued the hint. Not now. People in silk-sock places like Ailesbury Road were always giving parties, indiscriminately, Horse Show parties, Diplomatic parties, Dog Show parties, Sunday morning sherry parties. If I had been to any one of those affairs it could only have been for some journalistic reason and I would have been no more than a digit among the crowd. I found the name in the telephone directory. Reginald ffrench with the modest letters M.D. after the name, at 118 Ailesbury Road, Dublin 4. Suppose I did ring the old lady? And suppose she did grant me an interview?

'This is very kind of you, Mrs ffrench. Great intrusion, etc. I will explain at once, etc. Your daughter Mrs Longfield happened to mention . . . The fact is I am suffering from a really grave loss of memory. So when I heard . . . Enormous help . . . A long shot . . . Far-fetched . . . Nevertheless if you by any chance did . . .'

I could imagine the sympathetic smile, eyebrows floating, wrinkled palms holding up nothing, falling helplessly.

Three days later I again encountered Donna Jana on the avenue. She halted to say that her birthday party had been great fun. 'But it's always fun when my mother throws a party.' She had mentioned that her neighbour was a Mr James Younger but, 'Apparently, I was mistaken. She knew no James Younger.' I gestured submissively that I had expected nothing else. She gestured resignedly that that was that. We parted. She turned back to say that Leslie and herself were having a few people in for sherry next Sunday morning about eleven-thirty. I would be most welcome. In fact Leslie said he used to know a man named Younger. I said I would love to come and decided to forget all about it. But that night I recaptured Leslie Longfield. Of course. That young sculptor! I knew him very well indeed. I had written about him. But why had I confounded him with a priest?

That was a Friday. On Sunday morning I was alerted by the cars arriving and turning outside their 18 and my 17. It was an overcast June morning. I had gone through the Sunday newspapers. I was a man without a friend. If only to meet Longfield I went to join the party next door.

PART ONE

Ana

1965–1970

I noticed with interest that there were two or three fairly expensive cars by the kerbs, including the daffodil Jaguar, two Mercedes and an eyebrow-raising Jensen which I took to be the gynaecologist's. The rooms were crowded, the company more or less what I expected, wives spreading conscientious good cheer, business men relaxing clubbily, two doctors, one affable (still some steps to climb), the other giving forth portentously (probably Mr Reginald ffrench), a Belgian diplomat, a British second secretary, two barristers matching the two doctors, one at eleven o'clock, the other high noon, but no parson or priest – a sign of the times? The words 'per cent' were heard. A secular club. Could be anywhere in Europe, except that here the feel was more amiable, less successful, more egalitarian, striving, chummy, amateurish, a touch of Tammany, all very incongruous in the home of a sculptor and a painter.

For a while I quite enjoyed the unwonted sociability. Then gradually I caught myself trying to justify my presence, which made me decide that whatever my swim was I was not part of this swim, though I did not gather what sort of a swim it was until Donna Jana, whom I shall henceforth frankly call Anador, introduced me to a slight, middle aged, red-and-grey-beared man with the alert figure of a light-weight boxer, a Jimmy Cagney figure, once handsome. It took me half a minute to recognise the Les Longfield who had once been more than an acquaintance, almost a friend or, qualifying the sacred word, a wartime friend many – say twenty-three? – years ago. Then I understood. He was, I knew, and knew I knew, not more than fifty-five and not less than fifty-three because I had first met him as one of the crew, a youth, probably a student, on somebody's yacht somewhere before the war. Otherwise I retained only a subliminal awareness that he was not a very good sculptor. For his part he was so over-delighted to meet me again, so eager, laughing, sociable that I was just on the point of thinking him a most friendly fellow when I heard Anador telling me that he was going to have a show of his latest sculpture in Dublin next week. This morning's swim was his swim. A public relations party. I had been to hundreds of them. 'Do meet my husband, son, brother, cousin, dear friend, the famous sculptor who is just about to ...'

'Good Lord!' he said, shaking my hand with fervour. 'So you really are our neighbour! When Anador said our next-door neighbour was one James Joseph Younger I said, Well, I used to know a Bobby Younger, he always gave me good notices in his paper. He used to be one of my best pals. We lost sight of one another after the war. But I always knew you as Bob Younger! And here,' slapping my arm heartily, 'you turn up suddenly next door, and you really *are* Bob Younger! What paper are you attached to now?' He did not wait for the answer. Quick, I thought, on the uptake. 'Let me show you a couple of nice things I've collected.' He led me to corners of the room, and into the front room. 'See that? A piece of sculpture I picked up in Paris when I was studying there before the war. Giacometti. Worth a nice penny today! Actually I think I prefer his drawings. I have, see, three of them! Cost a fortune now! But for me Modigliani is the man. And I include his sculptures. Look! This! And that little beauty! And these little wax models by Degas ...'

I was puzzled. Modigliani died in – was it? – 1918, anyway during the First World War. Long before the second he was famous, and expensive. Les Longfield must be a man of means, and circumspect.

'You are a lucky man,' I enthused, 'to be able to afford gems like Modigliani sculptures.'

He laughed, saluted around the room with his glass of champagne.

'Tea!'

'Tea?'

'Longfield's Lovely Tea. Don't you know it? My people are tea importers. You don't suppose I or any other sculptor could live on sculpture!'

I looked at the Modigliani. Drink, drugs and misery. Persecuted by the police for indecency. No – not made happy on tea.

'Did you ever meet anybody who had known Modigliani?'

He pfoofed, braggingly.

'Lots. I met his widow once.' I held my tongue. What was her name? Herberterne? Habuterne? She threw herself out of the window the day he died. 'Come to my studio in town some day and I'll show you more of my treasures.' He led me back into the babbling room, out through the crowd to a little conservatory behind it – the house had a façade identical with mine but had more rooms – and pointed up the rear garden to a new wooden hut. 'That's Anador's studio. She paints, you know. And very well too. A present from her mother. Well, well, well! And so we have met again, Bob Jim Jo Younger! A drink on that!'

I let the nominal confusion pass. It was easy to fob him off in that shouldering crush, to swear that we would all meet again over the garden wall, as easy to become planed off into the shavings rustling about us.

I was about to escape back to my Number 17 when Anador again rose hugely in my way, accompanied this time by a small, neatly shaped, widely smiling blonde woman of what is politely called an indeterminate age, a miniature transposition, I thought at first glance, of her own physical elements, indeed I would have said her anagram if I did not on a second look observe in the woman beside her the more dainty waist, the longer neck, the whiter wider smile offered with an assurance more accustomed to conquer. Now that I have had five years during which to compare mother and daughter I know, too, that her eyes were twice the size of comically peering Anador's, and that her tropical complexion, her daffodil hair and her eggshell skin, all quite absurd in view of her presumptive age, bridged with both art and zest the poles of time in a way that poor Anador's wind-blown cheeks and virile Viking hair never could. Anador introduced me:

'This is Mr Younger our next-door neighbour whom I mistakenly thought I had met years ago in Number 118. Mr Younger, this is my mother.'

Having said which she was at once sucked back into the scrum by her duty as hostess to two late guests while I and Mrs ffrench began uttering polite 'How d'ye do's?' after which she said masterfully, 'Come and see a self-portrait that Anador did when she was twenty-two. I gave it to her today as a house-warming gift in return for a portrait of me I had done by a friend from Zanzibar when,' this coyly, 'I was rather younger than I am now. Every year we exchange these two portraits. This way we save money and neither of us gets tired of the other's face.'

Thereupon, to my annoyance, she turned her back on me and walked away from me into an adjoining room to her right, clearly assured that I would obediently follow her – as I did. I told her long afterwards that she reminded me at that moment of a miniature Queen Victoria, who, reputedly, whenever she wished to sit down, at no matter what moment, in no matter what corner, in no matter what palace, just bent her knees and sat down, assured that the Chamberlain of the Chair would be there to slide her chair under her descending bottom. I followed her obediently into the empty room off the two crowded reception rooms. There she took me masterfully by the hand and led me to a corner out of sight of the door, though not out of sound of the roaring cacophony beyond it. She halted under Anador's frowning self-portrait, turned about, threw down my hand, and with a glare like a searchlight from her bulging pomeranian's eyes she addressed me furiously.

'Bobby! Where the hell have you been these last six months?'

The exhilaration of her touch ran through me from that soft, warm, padded hand. What was this? A messenger from the gods? The touch of their spurs? All, at the moment, I could observe was how elegant she looked, for all her angry excitement, and long after I have forgotten the touch of her lips and the precise timbre of her voice it is this elegance rather than any other of her bodily excellences that I most clearly remember, her inspiriting capacity for losing herself at any moment in the moment's maximum excitement without losing a minimal jot of her natural poise and cool grace. Now that she is gone from me I think I do know why the fates allowed me to re-experience this one single, blissful part of my old life. They restored her to me as a lab test, their way of amusedly observing how an adult human faces a similar, indeed almost identical challenge for the second, third or fourth time.

I have no hope of recording the overwhelming variety of impressions that Ana ffrench made on me during the five years that followed that Sunday morning and afternoon. Memory, longing, desire, passing floods of happiness, rare abrasions, ultimate loss have clouded the momentary actualities of those years. How could I possibly be objective about an unrecognised woman, remet at noon, remarried before twilight, remembered fully while the clouds turned to darkening roses over Dublin? Besides, I am writing all this that I have so far written five years after her last five years and my first, remembering chiefly the unconsolable sorrow and immeasurable desolation of a shattered heart, until last night when I became the lover of Anador Longfield who may, I do not know whether to hope or hate the thought, refract my blinding memories of her matchless mother. It is not that time or any other force would diminish Ana ffrench but it has disembodied her. I have elevated her to a star, so that when I look up at the skies at night it consoles me to say, 'That star – or that one – or that one is Ana.'

At forty-five Anador perfectly suits my fifty-five. What will happen as she grows older and I grow younger is something that, for the moment, I dare not consider.

Still, if I am to record even in an approximate way the order of my life with Ana ffrench I must make some effort to re-evoke her.

It would be a simple, if not very helpful, matter to signalise her after the manner of The Lovers' Passport: Profession: *The Pompadour's.* Place of birth: *She said London, I sentimentally insisted on Heaven.* Age: *Older than the rocks.* Hair: *Usually blonde.* Eyes: *'Do you know, my love, that your eyelids are always lowered just below the Plimsoll mark of your pupils?' Iris, the colour I once saw described by a romantic Irishman as that of a thistle flower just when it is opening. General effect, lecherous.* Beauty: *I have heard a less pretty rival compare her face to that of a small pig.* Not a bad description. Whenever she made a cross face at somebody I was often reminded of a small pug. But her greatest attraction is not to be described – her zest, whether it poured from her twelve-inch smile of welcome or from her snarl of fury at some experience she deemed worthy of her attention. I used to think that when she was in one of her more lively moods a seismograph a thousand miles away would have oscillated as wildly as for an earthquake in the next street. At the same time anybody who was not on her side might have been forgiven for labelling her dismissively as another of those face-lifted ladies who had been the flibbertygibbets of the decades between the last two Last Wars. It would have been a neat judgement, and wrong. Without speaking a word she could impart her excitement at being alive, simply I think by her certitude that whatever interested her was of universal interest, though no more than the sun beaming upward from behind a light-edged cloud, or a colt racing around a field out of sheer high spirits, or a raindrop caught on a child's outstretched tongue, some new scent, some old book; and her reading was a *mixum gatherum* justified only by 'I like it!' Jack London, Agatha Christie, Jane Austen (she knew every smallest character in the canon), William McFee, Angela Brazil, Pope, Ouida, Malraux, Ring Lardner, Ballantyne, Forster, Kipling, Saint Exupéry. You might think that anybody so enthusiastically undiscriminating must perforce be either embarrassing or boring. She often was. But she could enthuse about rubbish with so much enjoyment, and such indifference to the disapproval of the learned, that one could only feel thankful that somebody possessed the art of living happily. Or am I fooling myself? Did I always feel so during those five enchanting years? Now that I have amassed ten full years of clear memory I find that, however clear it may be, it does act on things like a translation into another language. Memory can dazzle, like love. At the end I am at the mercy of both.

When she growled at me that Sunday morning ten years ago, 'Where the hell have you been this last six months?' my reaction was, 'And who the hell are you?' I knew that whoever I was I was not her husband when she moaned, 'Bobby! If you don't kiss me this minute I am going to fall dead at your feet.' She kissed me with abandon. I kissed her dutifully. She drew back, glared at me (the pug's nose glare) and said coldly. 'So that is what has happened? You have lost all your affection for me?' I had no option but to do the honourable thing. I told her a lie.

'The whole truth of the matter, Mrs ffrench, is that I have lost my memory. All I know about you is that you are Anador Longfield's mother.'

In old-fashioned novels people frequently stamp a foot with rage. I can do it, or pretend to do it when sitting, not when standing. I have asked friends of mine to stamp a foot with rage. They all seem to perform badly. It may have been a fashionable gesture at one time. She stamped the carpet. To do so she hooped, clenched her fist and her pretty nose became a sow's snout.

'But,' she bassoed, rising swiftly to a tenor, 'we have known one another for forty years? Ever since I was twenty.' (I noted that she thereby reduced her age by five years if Anador had been telling the truth about it a few days ago.) 'Have you forgotten all those forty years? Don't you even remember that we have been madly in love for the last twenty years?'

Voracious if attractive old creature! I defended myself. I insisted with feeling that I had forgotten everything and everybody. First she glared, then she burst into radiant laughter.

'Everything?' she whispered delightedly and wickedly. 'In that case, my darling, you have come to the right person. I can tell you a very great deal about yourself. Leave it to me, Bobby. I will revive more than your memory. We cannot talk here. Ring me at home at three o'clock sharp. Reggie is going golfing after this jamboree. Let us rejoin the party.'

At the door I held her arm and muttered, 'You call me Bobby. Is that really my name? You are sure of it?' at which she laughed her white gash of laughter as if I had said something witty, and answered, '"Tell me what thy name is on the night's plutonian shore" ', and was engulfed by the high tide of babble beyond us while I slipped away.

Home. A man of minus sixty-five, lunching in his kitchen, in his two-tier flat in a cul-de-sac, in suburban Dublin, his kitchen newly fitted, blue, biscuit and egg white. He sat hunched over his Sunday snack of bacon and eggs, wholewheat bread, unsalted butter and honey, coffee flavoured by chicory, staring out at his newly mown back garden; on either side of it roses, lupins, phlox, and behind them all those dark cypresses against the summer blue.

Known her for forty years? As Shakespeare says, forsooth! His mistress for twenty years? Forsooth! And still so? Forsooth! At her age? Impossible! Anyway why should those fellows Upstairs suddenly send this gift Downstairs, after preventing him for the last God-knows-how-long from making the smallest human contact with his past life? Sadism? 'So, there you were! Trying to do it yourself. If you had only had the wit to kill for us a bird, beast, cock, cow, man or woman, even offer us an ear of corn, a jug of wine, a bottle of whiskey, a pinch of incense. Now, a gift from us. You may proceed.' To be sure, they could still be playing tricks with me. She sounded real, but then if they have invented her she would have to. What fun it would be if she, too, was given a second life and we two were to grow young together . . .

His mind wandered pleasantly.

He woke to find himself uptilting the coffee pot. The dregs were cold. The cuckoo clock told him that he had spent almost an hour day-dreaming. Twenty minutes later he was driving along Ailesbury Road, untrafficked, Sunday afternoonish. He saw only one person, a long way down the road, a strolling Civic Guard, in his blue shirt, because of the hot day. A flag hung immobile from the staff of a foreign embassy nearby. He drove into the gravelled forecourt of 118. At the top of its eleven granite steps he touched the bell in the centre of a door of seventeen panels. Red brick, granite quoins, detached, early Victorian, set between trees in, he anticipated, an acre of suburban peace. The heavy door was swung wide open by her strong, small arm – was she seven stone in weight? A yard of white smile. 'At last!' Her thistle-blue-grey eyes uplooking. Waist absurdly small. Her chestnut skirt flared from it provocatively as a tutu – 36/20/36? – fit for a nubile girl and no doubt attractive to such as had such tastes. She led the way. The calves of a young woman, blonde poll, a suggestion of sandalwood. Impossible to believe she was sixty-five.

Immediately he stepped into her vast drawing room he got the whiff of her generation: great, standing, decorative lamps clustered with chinaware roses like fake, clotted Meissen, vastly flowered curtains, parrots in porcelain, baroque mirrors uttering a perpetual invitation to a waltz that whispered from an invisible source. He wished yet once again that he knew what his own twenties had been like and saw a new moon like a sliver of spoon held under a silver star over the crooked back-streets of smelly Cork. His youth there.

It was a generous room that spanned the house from its front to its three tall, rear windows, ceiling to floor. These windows extended the perspective through the garden he had expected to an unexpected row of ancient beeches that evoked a quondam country estate miles beyond the last gas lamps of a William IV city. Those skin-straining trees blended with some more beech in neighbouring gardens to reinforce the impression of a rural mansion well beyond canals, barracks, churches, walls. He espied a small lake. Chintz. Sporting prints. Large oils. Silver. Two portrait heads in bronze. Longfield's? Three Persian carpets. She held his hand. Only the brevity of her sentences revealed her tension.

'Reggie's gone to his golf. I've sent the maid to Howth for the day. To her sister. They won't return until about ten. We always let the cook off on Sundays. We have the house to ourselves.'

She sat on the settee. He sat opposite her on a chair, the low glass-topped table between them. She switched off the electric silver kettle that she must have switched on when he rang. She gushed:

'See! Everything all prepared. By my own tiny hands. No sugar, as I know so well. No milk either, not with Ichang. Though you, oddly, like it with Keemun. Your favourite wholemeal biscuits. You observe, Mr Younger, how I pander to all your tastes?'

She poured from silver to china. The longer he looked at her the more handsome she grew. She led him to chat about various teas. Putting him at his ease? Not when she smiled crookedly at him and remarked that he had not forgotten about teas. Startled, he said 'Apparently not'. She showed him two birthday gifts she had received. He recognised and admired a Georgian strawberry dish, about fifteen ounces.

She saw him looking at an old oil painting of clouds, sea, a white beach, two cows at their ease on the reedy foreground, and said,

'I got a new frame for it. I think it suits it better, don't you?'

'I do not know that particular Hone,' he said. 'But it is a Hone.'

'If you can tell a Hone from a haystack you have not lost your memory.'

He considered her viewpoint.

'Yes, I do seem to retain my professional knowledge fairly accurately, and that, as I found on a recent visit to London, includes,' he glanced back at the Hone, 'the arts. For some reason especially the arts. In the National Gallery . . .'

'The Gozzoli?'

He stared, she laughed, 'I'll tell you later, go on.'

'Some places and events remain with me. Others are a fuzz. Living people not at all. Which includes myself. I am not wholly sure of my name.'

She looked hard at him.

'No name, no person. No person and you wouldn't care about a name. You are so much a person to me. I don't believe you. What *is* your name?'

That direct, stinging manner. In what other existence?

'Recently I thought I was J. J. Younger. Now I think I am Robert Bernard Younger. B.B.'

'James, as you must well know, was your twin. You are Bobby. He was killed last December in that plane crash in the States. Why are you fooling? You must know that! He went out there!' She softened. 'Or did that give you a bad shock, Bobby?'

'Could I,' he avoided, 'have had a wife who died in that crash?'

'Christabel Lee died over twenty years ago. You and I became lovers after she died. Bobby, you are being very tiresome. You must surely remember something. Are you listening to me?'

I breathed a sigh of relief. If I had had any doubts left about that damned dossier this was the end of them. I felt like a dog scrambling out from under a smother of hay. I had a last question. Was I really a journalist too? She laughed again, mockingly, affectionately. She patted the settee firmly. 'Come over and sit beside me.'

'You were twins in so many things. He covered sport. You covered,' she intoned the list with relish, 'the theatre, cinema, painting, literature, sculpture, ballet, architecture, music, wine, food, ceramics, discs, books, quartets, grand opera, musical comedy, brass and reed bands, jazz. Not all for one paper, of course. Over your wandering life. I liked it best when you were on the Manchester *Evening News*. You did cinema. The number of times we held hands in cinemas! Manchester is so convenient. So near, so far. I invented an aged aunt in Manchester. Auntie Roberta. I told Reggie she was full of money. When I invented her I made her seventy. That was in '46. She has to be ninety now. A couple of times Reggie has asked, "Is that old aunt of yours still alive?" Hoping for her cash! But we had such lovely times everywhere, you and I, after the war driving around Yorkshire and Lincolnshire in that little blue Morgan of yours. Secondhand, I agree, but even so. You always had elegant tastes. An elegant sort of fellow. I like handsome men, well-dressed men and rich men. There was only one big thing in which you differed from your twin brother. He was not so attractive.'

Wiles? Familiar? I said I was sixty-five. I nearly said 'in reverse'. She dismissed time. We had met when I was twenty-four and she eighteen. (Blast it! Now she had knocked off seven years.) 'You haven't changed, not by more than that one small wrinkle there,' touching the corner of my mouth, seductively.

Never shall I forget that sentence. It contains the essence of her. Unchanged. But a wrinkle is observed. Not the truth, not a lie. She never knew the difference between the actress and her part: behind both, the mystery of her reality. She reigned a kingdom bounded by fantasy and actuality, yet never limited herself to either. All self-makers do it.

Silence. We kissed again, this time to her satisfaction. After that, more silence. After that all I retain is the wide view from her upstairs window over the garden and the beeches. A bright, wide feminine room. Carpeted in maroon wall to wall. And thereafter lying silently in her bed side by side, all passion spent, lovers who could between them clock up one hundred and thirty years – and half as many again to come for me.

Truth does not gleam like a trout at the bottom of a pool. She gleams only when she surfaces.

'Ana! You are not making up any of this, are you? Have we really known one another for forty years?'

'Forty-one. Since 1924. June the second. I was eighteen. I was engaged. You were thinking about getting engaged. To your Christabel Lee. I got married seven months later. You got married seven years later.' He heard the bubbles of submerging Truth. His marriage certificate was dated . . . But that was his brother's! Truth sank twice for shame. 'We met in London beside one of the fountains in Trafalgar Square, the one called Emma, not the one called Horatio.' An extemporised invention? 'Don't you think theirs was the most touching love story in the world? Emma Hamilton in love with a sailor who had only one eye and one arm? Would you still love me if I had only one eye and only one arm?'

She nudged me. I was trying to remember when did Nelson lose his arm.

'Would you?'

I was thinking of fountains.

'Of course I would. Just the same!'

'Supposing I had only one eye, only one arm and only one leg, would you still love me?'

'A horrible thought. I'd hate you to be so blemished.'

'But would you?'

'Naturally, yes, yes, of course I would.'

(It fitted with the diary. After Italy. And C. who was Christabel Lee whom I ultimately married? But in whose diary was that for God's sake?)

'Would you still love me supposing I had only one eye, only one arm, only one leg and only one bosom . . .' Her laughter shook him. 'Anyway, that is where we met. Lots of people meet there, but not many Londoners, just as you don't see many Venetians feeding pigeons in the Piazza San Marco or Romans throwing coins into fountains. I'm a Londoner born. So I know. But do *you* know? Oh, dear, have I to tell you everything all over again? That my father was a doctor. Irish. Transplanted. Lapsed Catholic. Like me. The only reason I was by the fountain was that I was feeling lost. Like Emma? I was wearing my engagement ring – this one – that I had just been given by Reggie at lunch in the Café Royal. Like him to choose the Café Royal, conventional and convenient, sure of a quick cab to Charing Cross. He was dashing off to some medical pow-wow somewhere. He is Irish, of course. But Prod. His father was a bishop who knew my father at Trinity. Looking into that fountain I got a sudden flash that I had walked into a nest of people whose fathers and mothers knew everybody else's fathers and mothers and that he would always be dashing off somewhere to persuade all those people who knew all those people to tell other people that he was madly busy making pots of money and climbing to the top of the tree which he was and which is where he is. I had been wandering around London for hours in total misery. I was looking into the water of the fountain thinking "My God, what have I done? How can I get free of it?" Though mind you, Reggie was very handsome then, a tennis champion, and a rugger blue. The first time I saw him dashing around the tennis court he made me think of a Newfoundland chasing a butterfly all over a flower bed and I wished I was both the butterfly and the flower bed. Besides, the day I asked him to marry me he forgot to say yes but he swore he would show me the whole world. I thought of Japan and cherry blossom, rickshaws in Singapore, Paris in the season, big-game shooting in Africa, Maugham's Africa, Conrad's Malay and Java. I was mad about Conrad then. I discovered that to Reggie the world meant the Côte d'Azur where I had gone every May since I was ten with my father and mother. My God! How sick I am of the bloody Côte d' Azur! So I looked at the young man standing near me, weeping into the fountain, and I wondered would you marry me if I asked you.'

'I was not weeping into any fountain! I've never wept into a fountain in my life!'

'If you have lost your memory how can you tell? I liked the cut of your jib so I picked you up. I was always picking men up though I generally found that all they had was just a jib and you can't sail very far with just a jib.'

'I bet you don't even know what a jib is.'

'Reggie is commodore of his Yacht Club. I could sail you across the North Sea. Anyway jib or no jib, that was how I managed to lose my virginity at sixteen.'

She glanced sideways at me. I kept my eyes on the ceiling. I was wondering, 'My God, what have I done?' And, 'I am supposed to be a man of experience.' I said:

'Did you find out why I was feeling lost?'

'Yes. You were wondering whether you ought to get engaged. We discussed engagements. They made for a certain fellow feeling when we went into the National Gallery and sat down to talk about Life, and Love and Ideals, and Experience of Life, and Courage, and Truth, and Honour. You told me you were a journalist. You talked about Germany. The Allies, you told me, had just agreed to evacuate the Ruhr, a part of Germany, you kindly explained, that had been occupied to make the Germans pay up for the war. This, you said, was the end of the war. In 1924! You said it was also the beginning of the next war. I was enthralled. I had never heard of this man you were talking about – Adolf Hitler. He was apparently in prison at the time. You were the only young man I ever picked up who talked about anything but himself. I fell in love with you right away.'

'But you had only just got engaged to your husband!'

She hooted.

'You only met me, or so you say, two hours ago, and look where you are now. In your skin. In a strange woman's bed.'

'Where was I living in 1924?'

'In London, but you said you were going to move to the Colchester *Evening Gazette*. I remember that because you enchanted me by saying that 'at the moment' you were covering Europe for the Cork *Examiner*, but that presently you would be covering the arts for the Colchester *Gazette*. Your brother Jim was in London the same day. He was covering sport for a paper in Newcastle. It sounded awfully exciting. I never before knew that any journalist could cover anything. I felt I was being taken to the heart of Fleet Street. Just to check I said that we might as well have a look at the paintings and I remember deciding that whatever you knew about Europe you knew a lot about painting, because when you were not looking I saw a tab under a picture saying Gozzoli, and just to test you I said, "Hello, I bet that's a Giorgione", and you said very loftily, "Probably a fake! I'd say it is a late Sassetta. Besides all art aspires to the condition of music. Pater on Giorgione. Could you hear music when you look at that thing?" Giorgione! You were very toploftical.'

'You have a memory!'

'Just a little tape recorder. So you see you can rely on me when I tell you you covered the arts for the Sheffield *Telegraph* for two years.'

'Did I?'

'After the paintings we went for a drink in a pub behind the gallery, near Irving Street, and you looked across at the Garrick and asked would I like to come to a show. Your brother, the chap on the Newcastle paper, had two stalls for the Aldwych that he got from the Literary Editor of *The Morning Post*, a man named E. B. Osborn who didn't want to use them because he did not think the thing worth notice. It was a farce by Ben Travers with Tom Walls and Ralph Lynn, so I said I would if you would let me stand you dinner in Soho, and we had a fight about that and in the end we went Dutch on condition that I paid for the wine along of my being the daughter of a wine merchant.'

'But you have just said...'

'Yes, I know he was a doctor. But I had to have my way with you somehow. I chose a Pontet Canet. You see, you can trust my memory absolutely.'

'But can I trust you?'

'You can check. We dined at the Commercio in Frith Street. I had *Tette di Vacca* which I thought meant calves' brains and turned out to be four cow's paps laid in a row like white sausages on the plate. You asked me what they were and not to upset you I said they were sausages and I ate them milk and all. We held hands all through the play, and I enjoyed every word of it and I felt it was the most miserable night of my life because if you asked me to marry you I would, and I knew you would not because of that stupid cow of a girl of yours. So you saw me into a taxi for Victoria and the last thing I said to you through the window was "I'll remember you for ever and ever", and you said the same, and it was five years before we saw one another again.'

We lay looking silently at the ceiling as if its wavering brightness were the lights and shadows of our youth sauntering across the sky.

I saw a young man of twenty-four leaning into a cab on the Strand saying to a girl that he would remember her too for ever and ever, and the cab hauling her out from the kerb and driving off for the Embankment and Victoria. Would she have sat in the District Line all the way to Kew Gardens thinking happily, 'What a day!' or chuckling, 'If Reggie only knew!' or, 'I believe I really would have if he'd asked me', or, 'Nice! But! Ah! Well!'?

In this way for the five heavenly years we had together after this so late reunion, I would again and again make her recover the past like an archaeologist repiecing some ancient gapped mosaic floor troughed like the sea by sinkage. Not that I did not check, from habit, and to increase my pleasure. Result:

'Well, there is our fountain! Now, can you any longer doubt me? This was our old home in Kew, after we moved out of the Old Brompton Road. I used to take the District Line here every morning to school near Sloane Square. The Francis Holland School for Girls. No, not Catholic! My mother was a devout Cat but my father was not. He'd given it up. He gave up Ireland and half his name. He was born a MacCarthy but in England he chose to practise as Carty. He was tolerant. He let me be whatever was convenient from time to time. When I went to school with The Faithful Companions of Jesus near Isleworth I was very Cat. It was one of my great attractions for Reggie, a Prod specialist in Cat Dublin. His pious patients could say, "Well, his wife is a Catholic." You,' stroking my shoulder, 'are some sort of Cat. Look! There is our Aldwych Theatre! Why don't we have tea at the National Gallery at *our* table? But, ochone, ochone, the old Commercio is gone.'

It was on that very first afternoon, lying beside me, staring at the ceiling, her arms behind her head, that she mentioned Nice.

'It was funny this morning at Anador's sherry party when I pointed you out to Reggie. "There's Bobby Younger back, we haven't seen him for years!" He only half-remembered you. He said, "When did I meet him?" I said "Nonsense! Or are you pretending you don't remember that night in Nice?" He said, "Of course I remember that marvellous night in Nice, but what had he to do with it?" Total black-out. Admittedly he was on an unholy bender there. And it *is* thirty-five years ago. Now he is next door to an alcoholic. And then Anador introduces you and you have forgotten *me*! Really! Do I collect nut cases?'

'Tell me about Nice.'

'1930?'

Listening, my head close to hers on our pillows, Truth once more wearily bubbling up and down, it struck me that one of the joys of her talk would always be the perception of the moment when her kind of what-occurs would suddenly become an aria distantly related to its opera's libretto. Not that she was ever deceived or wanted to deceive me by her imaginations and inventions. Indeed the only firm difference between us was that it was not until I had enjoyed her opera to the full that I would try to wind its coloured kite to the grass, and a fat lot of good it did since what was at issue was never her destination – only her approach to it, not her facts but her style. So it worked out on that quietly adulterous Sunday afternoon with, on the road outside, a bored Civic Guard in his blue shirt, and Japan's red circle a limp oval, and only a rare car passing.

'It's so lovely to have you back. I was beginning to be afraid you had caught some disease. Such as religion? You were such an old puritan long ago. But you have learned a lot since then. We both have. Kiss me again!'

'Tell me about Nice. And why was I there in 1930? And why with your husband? And why was I an old Puritan? Why do you say I have learned a lot since then?'

'You used to be, but you are not. It took you years to "sing away sorrow, cast away care". Don Quixote. Book Three. Reggie and you? In Nice? In 1930? Even that has gone? Even that? Surely not that?'

'I am sorry if it is important. Ana! This morning I heard somebody address a man with grey sideburns as "ffrench". I was told that he was your husband. It was the first time in my life that I ever saw that man.'

This is the point where the unfolding of the scroll began. Japanese, from right to left.

'The first time you met Reggie was in 1929, two days before Christmas five years and a few months after you met me at the fountains. You met him in my awful house here in Dublin, in Fitzwilliam Square, my father's wedding present to us, inspired by Reggie. Before I married Reggie I had lived for eighteen years in our honest, middle-class, suburban house in Kew Gardens. By comparison that pretentious house in the Square was a horror. It was a fake. It was calculated sentimentality and snobbery – typical Reggie-ism. It was that phoney house more than anything else that bust up our marriage.'

I turned my face towards hers on the pillow.

'You are still married to him.'

'In name. He said he loved the Square. So suited to his profession. So appropriate, dignified, traditional, pure eighteenth century. It inspired confidence. He insists that security, stability and inherited wealth are marvellous tonics for pregnant women. All meaning that no Dublin specialist who wanted to climb to the top of the tree would dream of putting up his brass plate anywhere but in the Square. Can you even remember F. Square?'

'It is one of the most perfectly preserved eighteenth-century squares in Europe.'

'On a postcard. But try living there with flights of stairs and no lift. No central heating. Dry rot. I called the loos the igloos. Kitchens like dungeons. Cockroaches scuttled when you put the light on. In my ten years there I must have put two hundred maids through my hands. Freezing attics. Damp basements. It got a bit better after Anador came and insisted on a lift, central heating and an intercom telephone. It cost! But I told Reggie I would leave him if he didn't do it, and that, of course, was the one thing he could not afford. It was bad enough his being a Protestant. In Holy Ireland. Especially after the Holy Terror began. The Holy Terror was my greatest ally. Holy Mother the Church gave me total power over

Reggie. At my merest whisper of a divorce he used to go white with fear – it would ruin the only thing he cared about, his precious career. Of course none of those improvements had been done when you visited me that Christmas week of '29. No remember?'

'No remember.'

'We sat close to the fire and drank hot grog to warm us. It was about five o'clock. I suddenly got up and stood at the tall window with my hot glass in my cold fist and looked down across the street into the garden in the square. One street lamp. Fog. I could barely see the railings around the garden, but not the trees in the garden . . .'

Later on, knowing her better, I would have smiled in anticipation. Lights dimming. Applause for conductor rising. Conductor's baton rises. Overture. Curtain rises. An upstairs drawing room in a fashionable Dublin Square. Time, 1929. Ana ffrench stands by the window, holding a glass. Roberto is seated by the fire. She begins her famous aria, *Si ben mi ricordo*:

'I thought, "If my marriage were a ship and he were a passenger on that ship he would hear what I hear. A far foghorn moaning. Waves booming on rocks." For me it was a terrible memory. And you recall not one word about Nice?'

Roberto rises and stands beside her. The duet begins.

'Alas, no.'

'No more than if Nice never happened?'

'Oh? No! Yes. Wait a minute. I seem to see a picture. Was it a photograph? It wavers and is gone again. I thought for a moment that I saw a floating image of you, my love, and a harbour, and a yacht slowly sailing out to sea, at night, under the moon . . .'

She moves her hand, lays it on my cheek softly, speaks sadly.

'Let us dress. I need a drink. Fasten my bra, will you? There is, I perceive, one fact I have to accept. That since that afternoon when we first met by the fountain so long ago you now remember nothing about me. About my life, about our life for forty odd years. Extraordinary! We both need two drinks. I am going to put a match to the fire downstairs. It may be summer but I suddenly feel chilly and grown old. *A Toccata of Galuppi's.*'

Or that, as far as I can remember, is the substance of what was said in that bridal bed. We put on our clothes and went downstairs. I put a match to the fire and while she blew on it with a little, antique fire-bellows I, rising from the lighting of it, felt so dizzy that I had to hold on to the mantelpiece to steady myself, bewildered for the first time – that is the first time to my knowledge – by that which is, of all questions pertaining to human relationships, the question nearest to the unanswerable: 'What has this appealingly shapely, vivacious, warm-tempered woman seen for so many years in this old man in this mirror who is now once more her lover?' I asked it of myself time and again afterwards, in various forms not, I most strongly assure myself, *not* because I ever felt submissive, or humble before her maturity and her attractiveness, or fearful of being enthralled by her bewitching power, her blend of feminine elegance and ferocious passion, her natural humour or practised grace. I asked the question *only*, and again I stress the only because of the light the answer could throw on the scope and nature of my own qualities during all those obliterated years. Now that she has died I know that I shall glimpse the answer only when I am grown old enough to be again the sapling that appealed to her in her sapling days, young and old enough to have accumulated a remembered past.

It was still bright in the long garden which, facing west, retained the daylight longest. We both chose whiskey. Seated before the fire I gathered from her that when we met in that Christmas season of 1929 she was still childless and I had twice become dis-engaged. After it we had exchanged Christmas cards but little more, a book from me, a biography of Lady Hamilton; a comic Valentine from her; a couple of shifty letters. Up to that year my cards had come to her from places in the north of England, or from London where I generally spent every Christmas with my married brother Jim, then on *The Post*. Her cards had always come from Dublin and Fitzwilliam Square. But in '29 my brother had temporarily exchanged his job on *The Post* for a job on *The Irish Times* so I had been able to stroll around that Christmas to her house and drop my greetings into her letter-box. That afternoon when she returned from her last-minute Christmas shopping she had rung me and I had come at once, through the mist, and we sat before her fire gossiping over a hot toddy until just as she was telling me why grog is called grog – after an eighteenth-century English Admiral named Vernon called Old Grog because he wore grogram breeches – she rose and walked over to the tall window overlooking the all but invisible Square, stood silent for a while and then spoke over her shoulder to me.

What she really said, as she now remembered, was, 'London.

The Thames in fog. Battersea. Chiswick. Richmond. You give me the *mal du pays*.'

When we remeet people after a long separation we often say, 'You haven't changed one bit.' All we mean is that we see behind the veils of time what we had always seen and, ourselves ageing and changing, are comforted by illusions of immutability. In all those forty odd years between the fountains and this Sunday afternoon in Ailesbury Road she must have greatly changed. Yet, when later that evening I asked her to show me photographs of herself at fountain-age and she produced a heavy album I was astounded at the objectively little change that had come over her in those four decades. Indeed, I began to tease her, though affectionately, by telling her that she was Faustine who had sold her soul to the devil for eternal youth, and I was the more impressed because I now had reason not to fear but to welcome change in myself. She had changed a little, of course, if only in her fashion of dress and her way of doing her hair, as those pictures shewed, and I noticed the long sleeves she now wore to hide the vulnerable elbows – having in my mirror noticed the drawn and twisted skin of my own arms between elbows and armpits – and the circlets of pearls about the neck and the loose gold bangles falling down over her corrugating wrists. But if that was all she had changed in forty round years, how very little she would have altered in the five between the fountains and the Square, still, I have no doubt the same youthful, exquisitely shaped figure, her blonde hair still cut short in the fashion of the Twenties, standing by a tall Georgian window, looking out through the dusk at the closed garden of her past.

'The *mal du pays*? That was what I said to you over my shoulder that Christmas Eve, but what I was hearing was Reggie downstairs in his surgery with a patient. It was Lady Breffny. She had been a MacMahon before she married. Of simple origin, she took on grand airs after she married. She was having her first child. Reggie was marvellous with women like that, sympathetic, reassuring, charming – he can be a great charmer for the requisite period of time. I am sure that in those days a great part of his charm for those pregnant women was that they sighed for this strong, tall, vigorous, athletic handsome, kind man who had married a woman who, unlike them, could not give him a child.

'I came back from the fog to the fire and sat down and said to you, "I want to divorce Reggie." You were shocked, not because you were a Catholic and did not believe in divorce – as I say, so far as I could see you did not really believe in anything then and,' with a sly smile, 'less later on – but because I had to explain to you that if Reggie ever did agree to a divorce it would only be on the condition that I would pretend to be the guilty party. You said at once that he was a swine. I defended him. After all, Reggie is not a wicked man, just a bore about everything except sport and his job, and the only reason anyway why I gave a damn about how the divorce would have been run through would have been what my mother and father would feel at seeing me cited in an English court and in the press as an adulteress.

'At this you really blew your top, I heard her car starting below in the Square and the hall door thudding, and Reggie bounding up the stairs. I introduced you as a family friend. He charmed you at once, in fact he took quite a shine to you, had a quick drink with us, excused himself, said he had to dash off to some ritual Christmas Eve celebration at the club.'

'I wish I could remember what he was like then.'

She loked across the room, gestured towards a painting. I went over to look at it. Knee length, at a desk, the right hand reclining on the desk, the left on the arm of his chair, the head turned to look at the painter or the beholder, smiling slightly, quizzically, also somewhat arrogantly. Fair hair, blue eyes, jutting lower lip, high complexion, a sufficiently handsome face. For a moment I thought it could be an Orpen, but suddenly remembered Orpen's brilliant student, Leo Whelan.

'When was it done?' I asked across my shoulder, still held by my admiration both for the painter and his handsome subject. 'A Whelan, isn't it?'

''35. Yes. Whelan was very fashionable at that time.'

I returned to her side.

'Very impressive.'

'That day you first met him here, you were so impressed by him that I was amused, but neither annoyed nor surprised when you turned to me after he had gone with, "A divorce? He seems all right. What's wrong?" I waited to let the door thud again and his Bentley whizz away, then I said, and you were the first and only person in my life to whom I said it, which shows at what a low ebb you caught me that Christmas Eve, I said, "There is nothing wrong with him – apart from being a bit of a bore – except that he is not a real man. And I want babies." That was, of course, where his weakness became his strength. He knew I could never say it in a public court.

He knew that I knew that it would destroy him as a gynaecologist, above all in Dublin.'

Can all this be true? Impotent? That powerful man I met this morning in Rosmeen Park? There is Anador, her grown daughter. She is still living with him. Unless Anador is not his daughter?

'When you got back to Colchester you wrote, and I wrote, and after that we wrote to one another fairly often. My mother fell ill that February. I had to go over, you came down to London, we dined at Shortt's pub, near us in Richmond. You came over here the following Easter. Reggie took you out golfing once, and when he heard that you had done some sailing at the Royal Harwich he was all for your joining his crew in mid-May to sail to Nice. I begged you not to go with him – it had been a bad winter for both of us over that divorce, I was afraid he might start using you the way we both had begun to use all our friends, as a buffer between us, him at one end of the table, I at the other, our guests between. I knew you were already half in love with me. I did not want to see you getting involved in any way in the unpleasant side of my life. So I was delighted when you said you could not sail to Nice with him, though you did promise, whether for my sake or not I could not know, to visit us there for a couple of days around Whitsun.'

'Us?'

She took up her album and riffled it until she came on the picture she wanted – Reggie and herself and a younger man standing aboard his yacht in harbour. An incandescent sun, the two men in whites, she in a white pullover and creased white slacks. They were all three laughing. I recognised the young man. Later Anador's husband, Leslie Longfield. She looked so young, so happy, so zestful, so fetching. Now I know it was all pose. Her laughter was characteristic. On stage. Curtain up. *Carpe diem*. I failed – it was an important detail – to ask who took the photograph.

'Us? Yes! It was his last gamble. His sentimental idea that a second honeymoon might patch things up. That photograph was taken on the *Regina* the day we arrived, four days before you turned up. Those four days we did nothing but argue all day long ding dong. I was set on a divorce. He was frantic with fear. The evening you came I met you in the foyer of the hotel, the Royale. I told you that you had come just in time for a quick aperitif, a bath, a change and to join the two of us at eight for dinner. You met him coming out of the bar, already as drunk as a wheelbarrow.

He had been drinking non-stop for three days. He grabbed you at once, dragged you back in and . . . Bobby! You actually don't remember what he said to you in that bar?'

I shook my head. She rose, went to a desk in the corner of the room, unlocked it, took out a long, pale blue envelope, returned to sit near me, extracted from it a letter of several pages and handed them to me. I recognised my own handwriting. Closely written flimsy pages. She said, 'I came on it last month in a pack of old letters. Your first love letter to me.'

I read it in silence. It was dated June, 1930.

Darling Ana,

I adore you. I am writing this on the Calais–Dover boat. Dusk is falling. I suppose it was a long journey up from Nice but I dozed much of the way (as you may imagine, I needed the sleep), and whenever I was awake I was in a confusion of thought which it took me all day to clarify, so much so that when I now try to recall even one sparkle of my journey up through France I become aware only of a floating background of fields, trees, villages, towns peopled at every point and moment by you. How could it be otherwise? I still smelled of your scent, I still felt the warmth of your body in my arms, I was still floundering in the swell and slop of your husband's improbity. Now that I have gone over everything said and done since you greeted me in the foyer of the Royale, now that last night has been filtered clear at last by daylight and distance, I find that what I want to talk to you about most urgently is not so much about my love for you as our common situation. We owe it to one another to say to what we stand pledged. For me, I throw my very last card, my ace of hearts, into your lap. Do you pick it up? Are we promised to one another for ever and ever?

But wait one moment. I must first, in justice to myself, forestall any reconsiderations you may have been forming about me since we parted early this morning. I am terrified lest you might have meanwhile been tempted into comparing my apprehensions for your honour and happiness during the months since that evening in Dublin last Christmas – the sea fog creeping over Fitzwilliam Square, your grog glassed in our hands, you standing by your tall window, your husband's swift appearance and disappearance, your despairing confession, my repulsive words – the gentlest was *swine* – for his readiness to throw all the public blame and shame for a broken marriage on you – and now a bare six months later I come into your hotel bedroom, not devotedly, not even hopefully or expectantly but in the basest possible role of pseudo-lover at that same swine's behest.

Ana! I went to your room solely to sustain you in your splendid disregard for this common, purchasable world, to encourage you against its timid conventionalities, to defend your right to live freely on the supreme heights of your vision of life. If you do not believe me in this we are both lost.

Remember especially this, that when your husband dragged me into a corner of that bar last night I had no premonition of the thing that had been growing in his mind for days. When he began to reveal his odious plan to me I felt, as I very much was, like a man who, just arrived in a strange city, in an unfamiliar hotel, suddenly finds a house crumbling inescapably on his head. I was knocked to the ground by the blind brazenness of his triple betrayal – you as victim, me as catspaw, himself as inventor of the whole rotten thing. I have never seen a man made so impenetrable by self-absorption. I do not believe he heard one word of the thousands I poured over him, pleading, insulting, mocking, imploring, during the next hour. The sole crumb of half-reason, it was no more, that I extracted from his crazed mind, Dublin's most distinguished gynaecologist, hooped over me there in our remote corner, everybody else, bronze backs, black ties, linen jackets, chattering cheerfully over their cocktails, was his answer when I demanded, 'Why don't you hire your own perjurer, your own assassin, to be known politely as the correspondent? Why choose *me?*' He was outraged. Insult you? Humiliate you? His own wife? Ask you to tolerate the presence in your bedroom of a purchased stranger! Whereas I, an old friend of the family, a reliable, honourable man of his word – all I would have to do was just sit there, reading a book in an armchair, the maid in the morning would come in, knock of course first, give me time to sit on the side of your bed, a bit tousled, then testify in the courts. Finally I demanded, 'Have you or have you not put this whole thing to Ana? And, on your oath, has she or has she not agreed to it?' He was swearing that he had mooted some such procedure to you, that you had not absolutely rejected it, and that he was going to put it to you clearly and finally after dinner, take it or leave it, now or never, accept it or go back to your struggling G.M.P. of a father in his grubby house in Kew on your bare feet if you so wanted, when he was interrupted by a bell-boy at his side with a note from you that it was eight o'clock and that in five minutes with or without us you were going into dinner. As he wambled upstairs to change he uttered an inimitable word: he was going to spend the night on his boat so as to leave *the stage* clear for me.

As I escaped out to the Promenade des Anglais I threw a glance into the dining room. You were at your table in a bay window, elegant as always, in smiling conversation with an aged wine waiter. Cars glittered past. Pedestrians had grown fewer. I must have wandered unseeingly for miles westward and back again between the half day and the half dusk, up and about the back streets, avenues, boulevards of Nice, fagging myself on the hilly roads beyond. Twilight had long dimmed the Baie des Anges. The lights had germinated over the city. A lighthouse beamed from the port. I recall a remark of Jean Giono about Provence, that he had lived there for sixty years, adding *Je le connais pas.* I can say I was in Nice for twelve hours. I did not see it. I sat a long while in some public park. Took shelter in a couple of pubs. I suppose I ate somewhere. In a despairing moment I went up to the Gare Centrale to ask about a night *rapide* for Paris: a slow lift of eyebrows, a down drop of eyelids, a shoulder moved an inch. Was it there three women in a group accosted me and jeered at me? It was midnight before I surrendered. I had to know what had happened meanwhile between you and him. But when I got there I did not want to wake you if you were asleep and I took it that he was lying drunk in his boat. The night porter informed me that there had been three telephone calls from Madame ffrench, the last at 11.20, and he handed me with the key an envelope directed in your handwriting. When I tore it open I tore the enclosed page, put the two halves together on his desk. *Dear Bobby, He has driven to Monaco for the night. I have agreed. My room is 351. Ana.* Number 351 was at the end of the corridor. On the sea. I knocked.

I went over to her garden window. Above Dublin the tops of the clouds were flat as plates and as pallid, the undersides suggested a first faint blush. I tore open my tie to breathe, turned for a moment and looked at her and on the instant, across the years, shattering all the prescriptions of the omnipotent gods I burst into remembrance. Her eyes large and sensual as a cow's by nature were now twice dilated. That night when I opened her door she had looked at me over immense horn-rimmed glasses, comical on her tiny nose – she had been reading. Bare shoulders, banks of pillows, creamy lace, a single sheet rounded by knee or haunch, a bedside lamp. Only she. I even remembered the name of her book: *The Galley Slave*, a cookery book for campers, yachtsmen, bachelors. 'Hello, Bobby,' she had said, in seemingly complete self-command, 'have you been taking the air?'

I whirled from the Dublin roof-scape and said, 'I remember how wan you looked.'

At this she jumped up and hurled her whiskey into the grate, glass and all, it went up in a blaze as her voice did. She whirled me around by my arm to face her.

'And what about you? You were as white as peppermint, you were trembling like a schoolboy with his first woman, and I loved you for it because it meant that you were afraid both of yourself and me, and angry with him – his good, honourable, reliable friend of the family, a man of his word, a loyal chum, the one man he felt he could trust. If I looked what you call wan, it was from knowing what you had been through for the last four hours, torturing yourself out there in the dark over the question that came out of you like a cork from a champagne bottle, leaning your back against my door: "Ana! How *could* you?" I told you very easily why I had agreed: because he was not only blind drunk but mad from drink and exhaustion, worn out by days of quarrelling and arguing, terrified of the damage I could do to him in his profession in Dublin, hating me venomously. I told you that after that dinner we had come up to my room and he had thrown me on the bed – I showed you the blue bruises on my neck and arm – pulled out the filthy, black, snubby revolver that he always kept in his boat for God alone knows what juvenile dreams of piracy, mutiny, sharks, whales, clicked it open, showed me two nippled bullets in the chambers, one for me, one for him, shoved its muzzle tight into my belly, roared now or never, take it or leave it, my way or this way. Choose!'

She calmed. She returned to the fireplace, one hand on the marble mantelpiece, one embroidered toe on the fender. She looked at me along the line of her shoulder.

'As that letter tells you, I agreed. So far.'

'So far? How far was so far?'

'May I have my letter? No! I don't need it. I have read it so often I could recite it for you by heart. You put it into the form of players in a play. "*Me*: So far? How far is so far? *You*: So far as to promise to tell you when you returned to the hotel that I had agreed, and to ask you to come. After that it would be up to you to stay or to go. *Me*: Why did you promise even that much? *You*: Have you ever had a madman boring a gun into your belly? He was quite capable of pulling the trigger."

'If I had challenged him to go on, to do it, he would not have believed I meant it. I had not tamed him then. A couple of months later, driving beside him in Ireland, he kept nagging at me about something. Nag, nag, nag like a bully. I shouted at him to stop or I would throw myself out of the car. He haw-haw-hawed mockingly at me. I pulled the door open and threw myself out. I was not badly hurt, I rolled down a grass verge into a pond. He was terrified. I sat back in beside him and ordered him to drive home and to shut up. After that I was the boss. But not that night in Nice. Besides, there was one other thing that I did mention to you then: that in some inexplicable way I felt sorry for him, that marriage is a bond that is not always easy to break, that even between such disparates as Reggie and me there can be some happy memories. And there was one last thing which I did not mention to you and which was the most important of all: that between his going and your coming I kept asking myself over and over what above all other things is most dear to me in life, and I finally decided that it is freedom, and I saw a keyhole to freedom – in you. And that is how it has all ended. I am, I have seen to it,' she finished savagely, 'that I have ever since been free. Thanks to you.'

'Thanks to me?' – in bewilderment.

She gestured towards my letter.

'The last three lines of page four.'

I read them out:

'When you said that about you and Reggie having happy memories I thought I had better go. This might, after all, be a very intimate thing between a man and a wife. I said I thought I should do nothing to help break their marriage, that I should go. At once you grasped my hand and cried, "You must not go, I am afraid he may come back." '

A toy log tumbled from her fire. I went and stooped and laid it back with her tongs. I was trying, half kneeling there, to get back again to that midnight bedroom across those thirty-five years, but it had all suddenly faded the way a radio may fade because of some technical fault or interference over the ether leaving one looking at a dumb machine. After a longish silence:

'What happened then?' I asked the warm ashes.

She smiled dryly.

'You stayed. I had arranged a little round table for you by the window with a small reading light. A bottle of Irish. It even pleased me in a silly wifely way to have left a tube of Reggie's Alka-Seltzers for you and to have put a cosy little armchair there in a green tweed upholstery. "Now," I said to you sternly, "we must both try to sleep." I put out my bedside lamp and waited, looking up at the ceiling at your spot of light. You removed your shoes, peeped between the curtains, and I knew what you were seeing because I, too, had peeped out a lot before you came. The tall lights along the empty Promenade des Anglais. Whispering wavelets. In the port the riding lights on a few invisible masts. *Le phare*. Presently you crept past the foot of my bed in your stockinged feet for, I knew, a couple of Reggie's Alka-Seltzers in long drinks of cold water in the bathroom. On the way back you paused. I closed my eyes.'

'Ah! Yes, yes!' I interpreted. 'I can see it, your fair hair on your bare shoulder the way I have seen it today, so light a child's breath could lift it.'

'I opened my eyes. "You can't sleep?" you sympathised. "Dreams," I whispered. "I am afraid of them." We kept looking at one another.'

'A single sheet rounded on your haunch?'

The telephone beside her rang. 'Hello, Reggie, where are you, though need I ask? The nineteenth hole? Not at all, I am fine, though I do wish old man you did not call me old girl. Nice of you to ring. Dinner? Oh, I suppose the usual, at the airport restaurant, where better can one dine in Dublin on a Sunday? I do wish they would keep the clubs open on Sundays. At seven-thirty. Don't be late. 'Bye.'

As if she had not been interrupted:

'You went back to your little green armchair, tore off your jacket and tie, and put out your reading light. I could hear you creaking, twisting, curling, crumpling. Later I again heard you at the curtains. "What are you seeing?" I asked across the room. Cupping your face against the glass, you said you could see the lights of a yacht moving out of the port. "A marvellous night for a cruise in the bay," I suggested, thinking of the lights of Nice, Cap Ferrat, Monaco, Monte Carlo. "Just us two. Away from all this."

You said suspiciously to the window, "Did he really have a revolver?" I refused to answer. "What," you persisted, "is he doing in Monaco?" "Drinking? Or at the casino. Des will look after him." I explained about Des, a clerical student from Dublin, his father a rancher, said for some reason to be a young man with a great future. Something to do with family connections, the usual Irish dynastic stuff, a wit, a good horseman, a trencherman, said to be a brilliant student, the third man of our crew. You went back to your chair. I lay awake, thinking of you over there in your dark thinking of me in my dark lying with my hair over my shoulder in a white bed with one white sheet. Time passed, as they say. I was aware of your little reading lamp being lit. Then I heard you come creeping over to me. I gazed up at you. You gazed down at me. Now or never? You knelt. I did not stir. You rolled back the corner of the sheet. You said, "Your knee is like a white cup." After that . . . Well, I know we did sleep then, and then we whispered and whispered – as if there were anybody to hear us – and then we talked and talked but I only remember of all our talk that you said you could not face this man whose trust you had betrayed, that you must clear out of the hotel and out of Nice by the first train at six o'clock, that we must meet in London, and that I said, "Yes, yes! But write at once or I won't believe it is true".'

She received my letter back from me, calmly slid it into its envelope, stood up and completed the Nicean story.

'A maid, as ordered, came in at seven and looked eagerly around. I said, *"Il n'y a personne"*. She shrugged, eyebrows up. I fell into a deep, dreamless sleep. Reggie came in around ten o'clock and shook me wide awake. He was shaved, pomaded, talcumed, scented, fresh as the morning, in whites, full of gaiety, delighted with life, eager for a bit of a cruise, carrying the green duffle bag that he stuffs with sailing gear. I said, "Bob Younger has gone back to London by an early train on business." He looked at me, puzzled, said, "Who? Oh! Didn't he dine with us last night? I'm afraid, old girl, I was a bit sozzled last night. All I can remember is driving to Monaco with Des Moran, Father Des to be, Monsignor Des, Cardinal Des, Pope Desmond".'

'He threw himself on his back across the foot of my bed and began to kick his heels and laugh and laugh with sheer joy of life – the man really has, he even still has, the constitution of an ox. As I looked at him in astonishment and, I can admit it now, in fear that he had gone clean off his head, he sat up, leaned across me, dragged open the round mouth of the duffle bag and started to pour all over me thousands of bank notes, English singles, fivers, tenners, franc notes of every size.

'All for you, darling!' he roared, and laughed, and beat them and threw them in the air. 'I won them at the casino. I made them close up shop. Fifty thousand pounds! And every penny of it yours. And I have no least recollection of winning one penny of it, or of anything except standing champagne all round. Drunk as Bacchus! Fifty thou. Do you realise what that means? Properly invested you are independent for life. All that nonsense we went on with about divorce! It's all over. Live your own life, old girl, and let me live mine. I shan't bother you. You can travel, enjoy life, cut a dash, bring your mama over to Nice at once, do the old girl all the good in the world ...'

I suddenly realised that she was looking under her eyebrows at me, not so much steadily as guiltily. Or was she a mirror of the sense of guilt in me?

'So you see, Bobby, I again accepted his offer. Not at once. But I did take the fifty thousand pounds in the end.'

She handed me the envelope of the letter that I wrote on the Calais–Dover boat.

'I got your letter two months later. In Dublin. It had wandered.'

I looked at the pale blue envelope. It bore several re-directions. I had addressed it to *Madame ffrench, Hotel Royale, Promenade des Anglais, London*. She received it from me.

'Probably the word *Anglais*, plus the white cliffs ahead of you, and your exhaustion made you write *London*. Not every post office clerk in London has heard of the *Promenade des Anglais*. There must be a score of Royal Hotels in Europe. The wonder is that I ever got it, at all. After six weeks I gave you up. You had probably regretted the episode. You had once told me you had a girl of your own. I was not going to come crawling to you. Why should I bust up your life? I was just another tumble to you. And I was pregnant.'

Her voice was not sixty years old, it was the voice of a young woman hardened by experience. Determination had put a spot of clean glitter into each eye. Her jaw was set.

'I did a lot of deciding in those six long weeks. If I had only waited another two weeks for your letter I would have understood what you too had been thinking. Now it was too late. I had taken the money. I was going to have my child. I decided I could protect my child, lead a life of my own, put Reggie in his place. All of which

I have done. The last I heard from you was from London, a printed invitation to your wedding on, I regret to say, a grey and silver card. It came three months after Nice.'

My mind refused to take it, my body could not absorb it, I had no measure for it, I had no hand, act or part in this. It was a fable, a fantasy, a myth, an opera to do with somebody else, or something else. And she was laughing at it all, a triumphant, mocking, Carmen laugh, though I was not too beside myself to be unable to understand why she laughed, and mocked – I must have looked all I felt; nor was I too much beside myself not to note that she was laughing without one jot of bitterness.

Half of this is, of course, retrospect. For the unmasking moment, I wanted to ask three questions at once. The first one I almost shouted. And how egotistical it was!

'My wife?'

'Christabel? She was blinded and maimed by a flying bomb, in London. Later she died of its effects. You told me so in '45 when, it is hard to believe, such chances must rarely happen, we met again beside the fountain in Trafalgar Square on the night of V.E. Day. Twice you let me slip through your fingers. The third time you held on to me. That night. In your little flat in Chalk Farm. The gods have been good to us. In the end.'

I could not ask my third question. It was a dozen questions around one central question, which was: 'Was it really too late – even then?' It would wait. Somehow she imposed reticence on me. We did it to one another. It was our unspoken compact: silence in love's name.

No sooner was I back in my bandbox of a house that night, so small after the spaciousness of Ailesbury Road that it seemed no bigger than two railway carriages superimposed, than I put my palms before my face and began to sob for my faceless, unremembered, once loved wife, poor now beyond a farthing's worth of recollection from a lover who, no doubt, had years ago welcomed her with the rubric of all lovers – *Incipit Vita Nuova*. I thereby learned that my second birth had its price, among other prices, in a torment unknown to catechumens – namely the grown man's awareness that no present joy is ever quite the same thing as memory will later make it. It may be, poor ghost, that I now feel for you much more tenderly than when you lived; still, how many well remembered fellow shades can boast your power to be forgotten with tears?

Have I seen her face in my album of photographs? If so it has said no more to me than my toothbrush. Yet she has since visited me eloquently in my dreams. That first night, having gone tearfully to bed, I at once fell sound asleep until I became aware of the dawn chorus of the birds around four o'clock. I slept again, embraced by her, faceless as always, and she stayed with me hypnotically for hours. Her wavelet did not dry on the sand until I told my dream on the telephone to Ana the following afternoon. I told her that in my dream I had been sitting alone in a railway carriage stranded in the middle of the great, flat bogland of central Ireland, aware that before the rest of the train had uncoupled from me in its onward race I had had my masked wife as my sole companion. In her lap she carried a baby. From this illusion I woke, doubly deserted, cast out, abandoned by my Jocasta. When I told the dream to Ana she laughed and said, 'What do you know about your father?' I said I knew nothing, but gathered that he may have been a bit of a drunk. 'Which,' she observed, 'makes you so sober?' Is it always a *masked* face that I may expect to meet in an empty carriage halted in an empty steppe?

I knew, of course, that if I were to ask Ana the name of the church printed on the grey and silver wedding announcement that I had sent her she would, with her phenomenal memory, remember it. What would it profit me? I would travel there, and, as with Castletownroche, find this scent, too, gone stale, the trail a trick. I could never expect from her the total and literal truth about any part of our common past. Such as Anador. If I said, 'Why didn't you tell me', she would say, 'But I did . . .' Or, 'Why should I?' Or, 'I had my reasons.'

If my dubieties about this or any other of her memories finally disappeared it was not, I must make clear, because I was under her domination, but for a simpler reason. I went to my bookshelves one day, all my books neatly arranged, by subject, in alphabetical order – I am, it is clear, a most methodical man – and there was the book I was seeking. *A Farewell to Arms.* First British edition. I opened it at page one and saw the green reading lamp, heard the wavelets of the Baie des Anges, as soft as her breathing. *In the late summer of that year we lived in a village that looked across the river and the plain to the mountains. In the bed of the river there were pebbles and boulders dry and white from* . . . A page of light blue, torn in half, edged outwards. 'Dear Bobby, He has driven to . . . room is 351. Ana.' That scrap of paper, surrounded by all the little or the much that she had told me, finished my longings to remember all that I had been forbidden to remember. I would never grasp from my past more than a few broken beads on a string.

I did once, of course, and nevertheless, in the third year of our reunion try to round off all with my third question – the last but one – that I had kept at bay for so long.

'Why was it, Ana, too late even then? I know my letter wandered, it came late, but if you wrote even then I would have come flying.

Her answer was Ana-ishly haughty.

'By the time I got your letter I was no longer in the mood.'

What could you make of that? Except that the intensity of her suffering had frozen part of her heart. The frost could have happened in one night. Knowing her as I now do I would say it happened in one click of her finger and, after that, there was no return. She went forward into life as Mrs Reginald ffrench, and let everyone look out henceforward for her pirate's flag. The day I asked her that question she laid her soft, padded hand on mine and said gently, reading my mind, 'And you, Bobby? How did you fare?' I replied with the final question, 'How did Reggie take the news that you were with child? That should have bust up everything.'

There I underestimated her skill and her decisiveness, but I also saw the floodlights blazing, the conductor's eyes raised, the great chords. *Si ben mi ricordo* . . . Why should I tell him? I planned it otherwise. Ah! Roberto! *A qual partito m'ha ridotto!* 'On my way from Nice I stopped in London and telephoned Daddy about my "happy" suspicions. He sent me at once to consult a gynaecologist friend in St Thomas's who was able to telephone him before I got back to Kew that afternoon. He met me with a kiss, a laugh, a joke and a proffered glass. "A little ffrench?" So happy, and Mummy so radiant that I made up my mind at once, there and then, about what I must do. I wrote to Reggie that night and unfolded a marvellous plan. I agreed to drop the idea of a divorce only if I could adopt a baby in London that I would present to Dublin as our baby. He must at once announce to Dublin that I was *enceinte*, and leave it to me to handle the dénouement next March. But that was all he might tell anybody, and I was not to be seen in Dublin from December on.

'He was overcome. Much too delighted to bother about details. He saw himself at the centre of a glorious picture. The childless gynaecologist's barren wife delightfully pregnant, her ailing mother hoping to live only to see her grandchild. An end, a beginning, a death, a birth, embalm, bring forth, night, sunrise, fulfilment, pride, and, I have no doubt whatever – profit! But for me what an *imbroglio*! To him I must appear as flat as the palm of his hand. To Dublin we could play the old comedy of pillows. To my daddy and mummy I must be as round – no trouble there! – as a barrel. But since they could not be told the whole truth, I forbade them to tell anything to Reggie. They were bewildered. I insisted. When they still demurred I became a tempest. I had, I wept, dashed too many hopes already. I invented three miscarriages. He must not be told one word until the baby was born. I swore I would have another miscarriage, then and there on the drawing-room carpet, if they did not swear by Almighty God not to tell him. They did swear, though Daddy did have to say, "But Reggie will want to visit us. He will see for himself. Dammit, he is a gynaecologist!" I told him to leave that to me. I had already solved that problem. I went back to stay in Dublin until October wearing a maternity corset that was like chain mail. Then I told Reggie that Mamma was so ill that I must take her for the winter to Nice. When he wanted to join us there in November I made Daddy tell him that his mother-in-law had hepatitis and that he owed it to his Dublin patients to keep away.

'There was another frightful crisis in December. Daddy decided, very naturally, that he would like to spend Christmas with us in Nice, and told Reggie, who at once naturally wanted to come too. I had 'flu. Reggie said he did not care. By the grace of God the German ambassador's wife was due to have her first in Dublin around December 20th and developed complications. From that on it was pure Russian roulette. By mid-January I saw that Mamma was really failing and I should bring her home to Kew. In fact this threw Reggie off completely; he was a birth doctor not a death doctor. She died in February, in Kew. I was up against the ropes. And I was as big as an elephant. There was nothing for it but to confess the whole truth to Daddy, so there he was, the poor lamb, confronted with the death of a wife, an impotent son-in-law, an adulterous daughter, the forthcoming birth of a bastard, and remember that I had sisters and a brother in and out of that house every day. I prayed so hard that February to St Anne to help us! And by gosh she did. On St Valentine's Day Reggie asked me on the telephone from Dublin would I mind if he dashed off for a week on March 1st for a medical conference in Turkey. I begged him to stay as long as ever he wished, I would keep in touch, as if, anyway, that raging egoist could possibly have resisted the *réclame* of being entertained like a pasha in Smyrna at the Hotel Buyuk Ifes. On March 2nd I had my baby, prematurely, and would you wonder? On St Patrick's Day the three of us returned to Dublin, flags flying, bands playing. I think if I had asked him at that moment for a Taj Mahal to hang on my bracelet he would have ordered two.' She looked ironically at me. 'He gave me the usual pearls.'

The conductor tosses down his baton. The curtain falls in a great scarlet swish. A cloudburst of applause like a storm of hailstones big as slates. My Scheherazade could entertain even though it meant the cuckolding of a husband at the very moment when he thought he was enriching a wife. But if she rarely gave him quarter, she did give him value. 'He does not care tuppence about me,' she once said to me. 'I am just one of his possessions to show off, like his boat or his Bentley.' Thanks to his Monte Carlo windfall she made his name as well known as a folk hero's throughout Ireland, and beyond it wherever people are interested in horse racing, which was what she went in for. She had winners – I wish my brother Jim were alive, he could tell me the facts about them, and as I have long since discovered true memory is dressed not in feelings but in facts which add up to 'experience', balance, a woman's or a man's depth, their responsiveness, the way they look at or through you. It was Ana herself who made me see this by suggesting foolishly that I should keep a proper diary lest I have another lapse of memory – I had probably been pestering her once too often about our clouded past together. I did begin to keep a diary, but after a year I threw it away. I found that I was recording not facts but too many impressions, not enough of those small actual details that alone contain and define.

Just recently I was confirmed in the rightness of my decision when reading the memoirs of a foreign diplomat who had lived in London, as I did, all through the war. On page after page I found myself looking in vain for those testifying details with which, I am sure, his official reports would have been packed, for he was a shrewd observer of English life in all its features – persons, places, institutions, intimate social manners, and it is, after all, the vocation of such men to observe such things accurately and record them persuasively. I notice that whenever he permits himself any unusual degree of personal feeling in those memoirs they at once begin to dissolve into hazy Monetish impressions. Here is an example, resulting from a telephone call from a woman friend suggesting that if he really does want to see the roses in Regent's Park he must come at once because their season is almost over. His record of that moment begins briskly. He lays down the telephone, he puts away the Foreign Office boxes in the safe, he locks up the files, we see him taking his hat and umbrella, we presume a word to his secretary or an encounter with one of his Counsellors on his way out – every detail has its self-germinative effect – he emerges on Whitehall, or Pall Mall or wherever his office is, hails a taxi, directs the cabby to the Park. Thereafter:

> As we walked together I seemed to see the flowers through the lens of her sensibility. The whole scene, the misty river, the Regency villas with their walled gardens, and damp lawns and the late September afternoon weather blended into a dream – a dream in which these were all symbols soaked with a mysterious associative power – a landscape of love. A black swan floating downstream in the evening light – the dark purplish-red roses whose petals already lay scattered – the deserted Nash houses with their flaking stucco colonnades and overgrown gardens – all were symbols speaking a language through which by some miracle we could understand one another.

True? The swan is true. The flaking paint is true. For the rest, a phial of memory's magic has been poured over actuality, detaching a mood from its context, so lifting it that it becomes isolated, above life. Did they not discuss, say, the war news? Or what each was proposing to do that evening? Did he not prod the ground with his umbrella? Or say her frock was becoming, or she observe that his tie was crooked, or worry about his cough? Memory has idealised life, shedding it into literature. As a trained reporter I have to distrust the whole process. I remember the sound Hemingway formula – write it down on the spot. Or can emotion be recollected in tranquillity? My foot! Reconstituted, yes. Recollected as it was? Never. 'True feeling,' said Stendhal, 'leaves no memory.' Which is the fact of the matter? I, a man reborn without a memory, wish to believe that feeling is like the rain that seeps into the earth, lies there invisibly feeding the life that grows above it. Call it memory, knowledge, experience, what matter so long as it lives, sways in the winds, gives life to others.

Ana contradicted her own way of living when she gave me that short advice about keeping a diary. Having paid heavily for her feelings when young she inflated them into fiction as she grew old in the deliberate intent of extracting the last whiff of pleasure not out of that Then but out of this Now.

At times she took this insistence on the Now much further than I could bear, as when she said one night, while we were kissing passionately again and again, 'You will forget every kiss I give you.' This infuriated me (a) because how did she know? and (b) because it meant that *she* could forget *me*! Now that I look back at our happy years, feel her essence and praise her name I cannot remember the touch of her lips. I know that she was right so to live as to have plenty to remember as a play, to forget as a fact.

Reggie never forgot because he never really participated. He ate and drank with others, convivially; he did not live feelingly with them. Being with him was like sitting in a train when another train is travelling in the same direction on a parallel track, now moving ahead, now yielding to slide behind, crowded, diverse, multiple yet, as a train, one. What was this restless, busy, fractured man's unifying principle? I believe that it was his sense (or illusion?) of superiority. He was an aggressive Anglo-Irishman, a left-over colonial preening himself among the inferior natives. Not that he would ever have been such a fool as to utter a word that might suggest his contempt for the rest of us, but he demonstrated it competitively as tennis champion, rugger blue, specialist, yachtsman, proud of his skill, strength, endurance and courage, the stoic Brit line, the stoic Brit symbol, and always so keenly as to be, however anachronistic, ultimately admirable and enviable.

It was only after she died, and he and I mourned drunkenly together, that to my astonishment I became aware of sides of him that she probably never even suspected – such as his tenderness and his grace. I discovered both the afternoon he flicked my flank by calling me 'a journalist' and I returned the flick with 'muscular Christian!' meaning, I explained in response to his angry challenge, a man who believed only in his Red Indian biceps and his Red Indian conviction that every man should be ready to die like a gladiator. He looked at me with a shattering gentleness and said, softly but nobly:

Why should any man bemoan
A fate that leads the natural way?

Or thinks himself a worthier one
Than those who braved it in their day?
If only gladiators died
Or heroes, Death would be his pride.
But have not little maidens gone
And Lesbia's sparrow, all alone?

'Who wrote that?' I demanded, astounded that this man whom my lost love had derided all her life should have in him this unsuspected side. He laughed lightly at me, making me wonder if he had always secretly known about her and me. He said, casually:

'It was written by the man known to journalists like yourself as Buck Mulligan. A Christian, a gentleman, a scholar and a judge of fine liquor, known to the rest of us as Oliver St John Gogarty, M.D., F.R.C.S.I., doctor, specialist, senator, athlete, wit and poet. I think he had Catullus in mind. 'My lady's sparrow is dead, the sparrow, my lady's pet.' *Passer deliciae meae puellae.* Soppy? I suppose you could call it that.'

'You read Latin?' I asked respectfully.

He enjoyed my surprise for a second but he did not attempt to exploit it. (An Irishman would have. Perhaps an Englishman. Not one of these admirable cross-breeds of ours who have most of the virtues of both races and few of their faults.)

'Not really. I had a good classical master at Stonyhurst whom I liked. Even still I sometimes pack a Loeb in my travelling bag for old times' sake. I never open it.'

He had given out the poem finely and bravely, six foot one, broad of back, hooked of nose, his upper lip overlapping his lower like a lid on a box, his right eye white-circled like a blackbird's, glaring slightly like a man possessed. Less than six months previously his sparrow and my sparrow had died.

He was to outlive her by another three years exactly. He was drowned on the 8th November 1973, her death-day, while recklessly attempting to sail, alone, to the Isle of Man in an October gale, aged between seventy-four and five. On the afternoon of the day when the news came that his battered yacht had been found on the coast of Antrim it happened that I was invited into the bar of his Yacht Club by a mutual acquaintance who was an experienced sailor. Apart from the elderly gentlewoman serving us, we were the only two in the bar. The harbour heaved. The lighthouse on the east pier was already licking grey waves. Dusk navy-blued the sky. In the distance across the bay, the first lights of Dublin.

'Even with a full crew,' my yachtsman acquaintance said, 'it was suicidal to take a boat out in a gale like that,' holding out his glass in libation to the gale. 'But to try it alone? At *his* age? The man must have lost his senses.'

I nodded, meaning that he had lost his wife. I admired his faithfulness to his faithless sparrow. I did not blame myself, condemned to life and loss. If I, like him, were to try to commit suicide, I supposed that I would not have been permitted, that is, supposing also that I wanted to die – at the same moment glancing at the clock to check how soon I should leave for an assignation with her majestic bastard daughter.

'Of course,' my host said with a sigh, 'the truth is he didn't get on with the wife.'

'Really?'

'She flew her kite a bit too often. All Dublin knew it.'

'Do you think he knew it?'

'Reggie ffrench was no fool. He knew everything. If it was not for his daughter, the girl who married that fellow Longfield . . . Oh, well! And in spite of everything, he adored that crazy wife of his. When she died he seemed, somehow or other, to let everything go. He just cast off.'

Guilt buzzed about my ears. Before I had time to call for two more elegaic whiskeys, I suddenly found myself wondering exactly when my Ana had decided to cast off. It came to me that there may have been two temptations, the first in the summer of '68, when, at the age of sixty-eight, she was unfaithful to me with L.L., and the second climaxing just before the Christmas of '69, when – I realised it only at that moment in the Yacht Club bar – she must, unknown to us all, have felt disaster in her midriff. The Crab.

The first occasion was entirely due to my own folly.

One summer Sunday afternoon, very like that quiet Sunday afternoon of our first re-meeting in '65, I had turned my head on her pillow to find her staring at me as if I were an object. I looked at her in the same considering manner. I could see no change in her. Naturally (Or have I recorded this already?) I had long since observed the rows of pearls five deep about the swan's neck, the sleeves nowadays always below the elbows, but what a man knows and the lover chooses to observe are two different matters, although I can and do testify to the unflawed perfection of the rest of her body, especially the lovely curve of flesh from her shoulder to her haunch, which I was just then admiring, smooth as a creamy side of beef hanging in a butcher's shop, freshly killed, still tepid, ready for the oven.

'You have changed,' she said coolly. 'Even Reggie, and he is normally the most unobservant of husbands, remarked on it last week.'

She frightened me. Could 'change' be the first word of a summing up? Was she the one who was changing? I was sure that she had always been fickle. I became wildly jealous. Was she being unfaithful to me? I sat up.

'Changed?' I demanded. 'Compared to when? 1924? 1930? 1945?'

She also sat up.

'Of course not since 1924. We were not lovers then. Compared to the time,' she lowered her eyelids below the Plimsoll line, 'when we became lovers, twenty-three golden years ago, on V.E. night, around twelve-thirty a.m.'

'Tell me at once the ways in which you think I have changed.'

She lay back.

'Let me count the ways. One telling way. At the beginning you were full of curiosity about me, my friends, my childhood, my whole life. It was flattering, although when you stopped being inquisitive I felt much happier – it meant that you had at last decided that your beloved could do no wrong. You were content with me and would be constant. Recently you have become curious about me all over again, as if you were enjoying a second youth. Or, no? We were not young when we became lovers. A second middle-age? Or call it a second prime. It is not that I mind, but I do wonder *why* you have changed.'

I decided that this was not just another of those games when lovers go caracoling about one another on globes of fantasy. I took her seriously. I became obsessed with the problem of how to find out if either of us was changing. That night I decided that the only way was to consult some friend who had known us long ago, best of all some man who might have observed her in her younger days when she was green in judgement, and at once thought of Leslie Longfield, still my neighbour, although uncertainly because he had looked a mere boy in that long ago photograph of him, Reggie and Ana aboard that yacht in Nice, laughing in the blue sun, arms about one another's waists. Would he have been more than nineteen then? Still, if he only had known her since 1930 I had only met her twice before that – for that evening by the fountains, and on that

Christmas Eve in her Fitzwilliam Square house. I had met him several times before the war and her not at all, when writing small pieces about his early exhibitions. I had liked his work, which was then young, fresh, full of promise. Once, during the war, when he was doing camouflage for the R.A.F. I had run into him in some pub and given him a night's shelter in my tiny flat in Chalk Farm – in those war years hotels in London were jammed and everybody dossed down where they could. Those were our only links. He was merely a Rosenkrantz. Still, we had shared in the past, we had liked one another, and I knew nobody else more suitable for my purpose. It was easy to get him to invite me to look at his latest work in his studio in town:

'Tell me,' I said casually halting before a green head of Anador that he had done when she was about twenty and he was about forty, 'who do you think changes the quicker, men or women? For example, since we all first met – in Nice was it not? – long ago, which would you say had obviously changed the most, this child's father or her mother? When was it exactly that we met?'

He looked incredulously at me.

'We met,' he said coldly, 'on June 10th, 1930. As you must know as well as I. The answer, of course, to your question about changing is old Reggie. I say as much when I describe him as "old" Reggie. Nobody would dream of speaking of "old" Ana. She has not changed an iota. Look over here at this head of her that I did for her fortieth birthday. As far as age goes one could hardly tell which head is the younger, the mother or the daughter. If I were to do the same today, Ana at sixty-eight, Anador at thirty-eight, you would of course notice the disparity but you would not be so struck by the difference. But . . . Poor old Reggie?'

I explained that I was thinking of change in another context.

'The change we suffer in our characters. Wouldn't you agree, for instance, that Ana has become much more gentle, more tolerant and kind of recent years? Of course,' I said, a little too portentously perhaps, 'I do not remember her very well from the 1930s but I have the feeling that she used to be a rather wilful young woman then.'

He laughed in such an eloquent tone that I felt the snake stir inside me.

'Ana was always kind. And always wilful.'

The bronze heads around us listened. His smile was oblique, twisted, slanting. I felt I was being pushed. I had to come clean:

'You mean men? A honey-pot for the bees. No doubt. But, hang it, at sixty-eight! Surely that is all gone with the wind.'

He became cross.

'Age cannot wither. She never cloys. She is one of those raddled old erotics. She hungers those she feeds. Whether she feeds those she hungers . . .' At which point he ran in the knife, suddenly cold and English. 'You must know perfectly well, Younger, that I was madly in love with her in my teens. I know that after the war she loved you. I was jealous of you. There is no need to shuffle about it now. I do not love her any longer. I outgrew her years ago. For all I know you still may be hooked. I will say this for myself, I never trusted her. You may. It was always one of her greatest charms to be a dissembler. Or to play the part of one. I have never decided which she is. You may?'

I was enraged by the fellow's cheek in joining his callow years to her salad days. Still, so peerless a woman would naturally have attracted scores of admirers. The thing that most enraged me was that to marry the daughter he had had to discredit the mother. I could never have delivered any such verdict on Ana – a faith, I told him, that marked the great differences between age and youth, at which he laughed so scornfully that I at once challenged him to find the least flaw in her, the smallest frailty, to detect in her the slightest note of faithlessness.

'I dare you to extract even one kiss from her to prove it! Though not more than one! I won't allow two. More would dishonour all three of us.'

I was assured that he would fail. Besides, I laughed, I merely wanted to dispel a passing jealousy, which I knew was ridiculous, but which, I did not tell him burned me at that moment as if I were Les Longfield, aged nineteen, still smarting from the first betrayal of his life at her hands. The more I begged him the more he begged me to have sense, to be my age, to let well alone, and the more he said so the stronger I pressed him.

'Just try her!' I shouted. 'I challenge you!'

I felt like a knight defending the honour of his lady love.

'A kiss from my mother-in-law?' he mocked. 'A maternal peck? Will the cheek do? Or must it be on the lips? This is childish! Stuff your challenge!'

'I know you, Les, as one of my oldest friends. This is a favour that I would not dare to ask of anybody else. You are an honourable chap. You are a mature man. What I am asking you to do will be a mere joke to you. The merest formality. A good-humoured experiment. Come on! Be a sport. It's only what I might call *une façon d'embrasser.*'

At this, at last, he took me seriously.

'You can't really suspect? I mean at her age? And at yours?'

I smiled sheepishly, trying to play a cool man-of-the-world role as well as the role of the knight burned with feelings of loyalty for his beloved.

'Surely we both know the answer to that by now? What would you at nineteen have thought of somebody getting married at fifty-five? Well, you have done it, so you know! What is the difference between love at fifteen and twenty-five? Or between thirty-five and forty-five? Or your fifty-five and my sixty-five? A mere ten years. Love outstrips time.'

'Which means that you have always been jealous? I would never have thought it. It also means that you will not become any the less jealous if I fail to kiss Ana. And that if I score as high as three kisses, or four or five kisses you will go mad with jealousy. Be your age, man. You are as happy now with Ana as you ever will be.'

Staring at him I overflowed with the joy of a discovery so simple that I should have made it fifty years ago: that I had been born, lived, still was and if I were to live five times over always would be one same, single, substantive, seamless, passionate, romantic man. The tree grows and grows, and remains the same tree. Nothing changes. I so revelled in this image of myself and of her that I had to have the final proof of it. I explained it to him so forcibly that he gave in and we easily devised a double assignation at his house, semi-detached, as house agents euphemistically say, from mine. The summer was so phenomenally hot that it was quite natural for him to stroll out with my Ana into his garden while I invited his Anador, a born gardener, into mine to advise me about my Romneya poppy. To make the invitation seem more plausible I told them that I feared I was becoming allergic to its great white blooms.

As I stood beside her under those lofty flowers risen four feet above her yellow hair, a forest of white petals each as wide as two of her palms, crinkled like paper, in each bloom a central ball of gold pollen, bee-sucked, wasp-plundered – they sank into its gold like helicopters, rose thigh-nectared – I could hear Ana and her son-in-law murmuring beyond the party wall.

'It was your mother who gave me this plant as a gift three years ago,' I said to Anador, and saw her with Leslie's eyes, yellow-haired, cheeks too pink this warm summer, handsome, powerful in her prime, and as she turned her head from me to peer into the Romneya I was once again delighted by the contrast between her delicate profile and her androgynous body. I could see that while she might not have seemed at all attractive when young she deserved to be appreciated a hundredfold in her maturity by some experienced, perceptive man.

For a moment I was distracted by the burst of Ana's warm, tenor laughter across the wall and Leslie's echo in double bass. As Anador went on talking knowledgeably about three kinds of Californian poppy I was alerted by a total silence from next door. To interpret it the better I tried to draw Anador from the poppy to the dividing wall but she was supporting one of my finest blooms in her broad palm – I confess to a weakness for strong feminine hands – one wrist, I noticed, dusted orange by the pollen, saying, 'I suppose the only cure for an allergy like yours, Bobby, will be some antihistamine to calm your tissues. No?' she asked in surprise when I switched my head to the continuing silence over the wall.

'Your wrists are as dusted,' I said hastily, 'as if you were a bee gathering nectar.'

She had the merriest laugh, it was extraordinary how handsome she looked when she laughed, and, though on a much larger scale, how very like her mother. I ceased to listen, looking.

'Don't stir!' I begged her. 'I want to call them to look at my Romneyas,' and as if to call them I stood up on a little rockery I had built against my garden wall. There they were in the centre of the lawn, locked, kissing, mouth to mouth. They kissed four separate times before I returned to Anador.

'What on earth is wrong?' she asked.

'Your husband is kissing your mother!'

She laughed, stopped suddenly, her head sank sideways, heavy with embarrassment. I could tell by the timbre of her voice that she was lethally hurt.

'I thought you knew,' she said. 'She was his first love. And Ana would kiss the nose off a donkey.'

The semblance of her reality had been shivered. Her large hands were wandering in search of a becoming gesture. I walked away to hide my tears of rage at not being young enough either to throw my arms around her, or to jump over that wall and knock that unfaithful bastard into bits. I came back to her, embellished the truth, breathing it beside her ear, tremulous as a schoolboy.

'Anador! You are a very beautiful woman. If only!'

She stared at me in surprise. Then, her broad palm held up my jaw to her mouth. She kissed me clumsily, like a girl of fifteen, once, twice, three times, four times. Then she sobbed beside my face . . .

From the pier's end the lighthouse circled the tossing waves. I tipped my liquor with my finger and dropped the drop on the counter. 'A libation?' he enquired, and did likewise. I raised my glass (to her), he his (to him). O God! If only we could really live all over again, snatch love from the fountains in our youth as I snatched it in Nice, lost it, snatched it from the fountains again, and lived to hold her on and on into my dwindling age. No pattern except repetition? No lesson, unless it be that the gods are chance and we who snatch it do their will. I recited the Gogarty poem for my drinking chum. He smiled.

'Reggie? I heard him reciting it a couple of times. His one poem.'

It was a girl of fifteen who in the end made her shake out her sail indignantly beyond the harbour's mouth: her American grand-niece, Lalage Kang – an unusual name (Korean? Japanese?) – the grand-daughter of her sister Lily ffrench who had married an American gynaecologist of that name in 1925, and gone to live in Plymouth, Massachusetts. I had not realised how old we all were until I heard and met this monstrous girl.

It was Reggie who by chance brought the Kangs into the family circle by dashing off to his medical conference on the day I first met Ana in Trafalgar Square. At the conference he met Jake Kang and insisted on showing off his beautiful fiancée to him in Kew. There Jake met Lily ffrench. Their son Seymour Kang married a true blue Bostonian named Peggy Davison and wanting to give this monster of a daughter, Lalage, a London 'season' wrote to Reggie for advice. The 'season', Kang shyly suggested, could be a preparation for his daughter's possible presentation at Court, plumed and gowned, having been, of course, properly coached and, he modestly suggested, vouched for by the Lord Chamberlain. Reggie put it to Ana, who generously opened her breast to the viper:

'The silly man should know that that sort of stuff is over and done with long ago. This is May. Tell him to send the girl to us. I'll throw a few parties for her. Run her around what is left of Europe. A spot of art in Paris. Antiquities and fashion in Rome. Work the embassies, Irish, British and American. July is always a nuisance but we'll do something. Have her here for the Horse Show in August. Your lodge* in Kerry for the shooting and fishing? London in September–October, the ballet, the opera, plays. Hunting here in November. We can give her the six months of her life. Is there anything special the girl is interested in?'

Reggie consulted the letter from Boston.

'Her father says she is interested in music. He mentions that she had been studying the violin.'

'Fine!' Ana cried. 'She can attend the School of Music. The Royal Dublin Society has lots of music, hires some of the best quartets in Europe. Come to think of it, why don't I hire some of them to play here? What a splendid idea you have given me! Reggie! Why don't we have a quartet of our very own? Have musical evenings? I will set you up, Reggie, as the most cultured doctor in the whole United States of Europe. Send her father a cable at once. Or ring him up!' She halted in her gallop. 'Wait! Is the girl bright? Is she good-looking? I don't want some ugly duckling moping dimly around my drawing room every day.'

Reggie was able to produce evidence.

'Her father sends a few snapshots. You know the way Americans do that sort of thing. Our home in Concord. Americans don't have houses, only homes. Thanksgiving at our home in Cohasset. Lalage here. Lalage there. The child looks pretty enough.'

Ana examined the photographs appreciatively. The girl might be quite an addition. It could be fun showing her around.

She proved to be a refulgent blonde beauty – long Rapunzel hair, soft as surface water, eyes Capri blue, tall, nubile, and though only just turned fifteen poised, eager, aware, giving promise of a woman's figure, perhaps even a woman's power. Ana took to her at once, ready as always to appreciate every new experience – a new scent, a new martingale or snaffle, a new foal, a new dance, play, cocktail, gadget (from electric toothbrush to portable bidet) a new song which she would gaily sing in her cracked voice to her embarrassed guests. (Those songs! They dated her to the year, not that she would have cared. *My British buddy/We're as different as can be./He thinks he's winning this war/And I think it's me./But I'm in there pitching/And when the job is done/And when the war is won/We'll be clasping hands across/the sea.* That was Irving Berlin and the 1914–18 war. She kept up to date though.

*That 'lodge'. A broken-down cottage. But Reggie had to have his hunting lodge.

She knew her vintage Vera Lynns. *There'll be blue birds over the white cliffs of Dover tomorrow/Just you wait and see!* She knew her 'Forties and after. Tommy Dorsey songs, Paul Western, Frank Sinatra, tunes from *Pal Joey. I could write a book about the ways you look. Do you ever miss me as I miss you . . . Couldn't sleep,/ And wouldn't sleep/Until I could sleep/Where I should sleep/With you . . . When you're alone/And miles away from home/Remember somewhere,/Somebody cares about you.* I think she was right when she sang that fizzle about being 'bewitched, bothered and bewildered'. *Vexed again, perplexed again, over-sexed again.* And yet along with all that frivol she did want that quartet, she knew what real music was. When she was dying she would listen over and over to that gaily haunting Cimarosa concerto for two flutes and orchestra on her stereo, and at the end of her trial by pain she asked Reggie to have the organ play Bach at the Requiem Mass before her funeral. In every way she fought the boredom of age! She hated to see Old Reggie succumbing to it, drinking too much before and at dinner, saying fumblingly, 'Go to Paris? But we've been to Paris!'; or waking up suddenly in his armchair to say, 'In my thirty-five years as a gynaecologist I count that I have delivered twenty thousand, three hundred and fifty-three infants,' or, 'Winston Churchill once said that he had drunk as much brandy as would fill the railway carriage he was travelling in. He was cross when his secretaries worked it out and it proved to be impossible.' Twice when his chin sank on his chest in his armchair after dinner I hatefully saw her go over and kiss his forehead. Besides each time she did it it reminded me that I too must once have had a married life.

Their lovely, young American girl acted like a blood transfusion on the ageing pair of them. Ana started at once on what she called 'My Five Month Plan' whose climax, she declared gleefully, would usher out the last midnight of '69. The Grand Tour began almost at once – London, Paris, Venice, Florence, Rome, Naples. Reggie sailed to Naples to meet us in that charming and select little Yacht Club at Santa Lucia set in what are simultaneously the most picturesque and beggarly surroundings in the world, islanded in floating melon peel, coiling oil, dead dogs. Of his crew I only remember a young medical student named Looney whose zany gaiety lived up to his name but who, Reggie later assured me, was the most reliable anaesthetist and mariner he ever had. I naturally compared him with the Leslie of long ago. From Naples we sailed to Capri, Porto Vecchio and Nice where the men slept aboard and Ana, Lalage and I slept in the Hotel Royale.

'Exorcising?' my old lady asked me happily as we signed the register.

I forget how July passed. I know that the girl was back in Dublin for the Horse Show in August and that she then went off to join friends of her parents in Scotland for the Twelfth; whether she shot anything I do not know but I feel certain that when she got back to the States she would say she shot 'bags'. It may be that I was jealous of Ana's blind admiration for her. They were like crossed fingers. They seemed to enchant one another. It was as if each were the perfect image of what the other hoped or had once longed to be. I suspected that the girl was a natural flatterer, and to be done with it she was. Worse, I found out later that she cruelly mocked Ana to her friends. A bitch. I was glad when she went to Scotland, and after that to meet her parents in London. I regretted her return in October, actually to get in some hard riding in preparation for the hunting season, theoretically to do some 'study', meaning that she was at last prevailed on to take her violin from its dusty case and begin practising with Signor Luca Pollice.

Luca! He marks the date and, I believe now, the occasion, however innocently, of my loved one's undisclosed – perhaps she did not even disclose it to herself – decision that her time had come to 'give up'. Luca was the sole outcome of what Reggie called her 'dotty duchess' dream of having her own private string quartet. After a great deal of formal searching and private enquiries it was I who, by chance, came on him one afternoon in September when I chose, at the last minute, to drop into the Royal Dublin Society where a quartet, hitherto unknown to me even by name, was playing a programme largely composed of eighteenth-century Italian music. The programme notes told me that the father of the first violinist, Luca Pollice, had been the viola of the famous Flonzaley Quartet, whose playing I had enjoyed several times in London in my twenties. I went behind after the performance to meet and thank him. He indulged me so far as to join me for a martini at his hotel in memory of his father and we got on so well that by the third martini he became relaxed and expansive. He was forty-three although his hair, apart from two scrapes of grey over each ear was as smooth and black as a billiard ball. He was as eager as a boy. An American citizen, home in New Jersey, barely five foot two, having wife trouble.

'She is so jealous that she is even jealous of my violin, I have to lock it away from her. "That filthy round thing you snuggle under your chin!" '

I asked him would he like to lead his own quartet.

'Of course! Yes! Every violinist's ambition is to play solo. But at my height?' (It had never occurred to me that height matters to a soloist, but he insisted on it.) 'Concert business is show business. When I began my career my agent made me wear high-heeled shoes!'

He was such a charmer, as well as a fine violinist, that I hastened off to Ana with the news of my discovery. The upshot was that she met him the next morning, liked him on the spot, decided to enlist him, set him all aglow with the dream of leading his own quartet (her occasional fief, but generally free), and, after months of complex negotiation with his agent by letter, cable and long-distance telephone she had him back in Dublin in mid-October either to bring matters to a head or to agree to abandon the whole thing. He came as her guest, all his expenses paid. She could guarantee three solo performances in the houses of her friends and, in addition, a generous fee to give her niece Lalage some violin lessons. Only a woman of her charm and force and a man of his pluck and generosity would have got even that far. He had no certainty that The Pollice Quartet would ever be born; his agent and his colleagues were furious at having to find a substitute for him at such a busy time of the musical year; his wife was convinced that he had concocted the whole thing as a cover for an intrigue in Dublin. He must have seen inside two minutes that the girl Lalage was not a serious student, and that Dr ffrench (who had mocked the whole scheme from the start) disliked him intensely.

It was on the Wednesday afternoon of the first week of November that I invited myself to afternoon tea at Ailesbury Road, a dry, hard day, cold enough to guarantee the ritual fire of turf in the entrance hall. Good hunting weather. Lalage, who had turned out to be a reasonably good horsewoman, had already been out twice (the Ward Union, and the Bray Harriers), with Reggie, although at sixty-nine he was really getting on a bit for hunting. The truth is that he could not resist showing off his pretty American niece and he was at the age when it seems necessary for certain men to keep on kidding themselves that they are not finished as athletes.

As I handed my hat, overcoat and scarf to a new and not bad-looking parlour-maid and followed her piano-leg calves down the hall to the drawing room I heard from the library-study to the left of the hall the girl's unskilful bow accompanied by Luca's gentle pizzicato to simulate the viola or 'cello and keep her in time. Both of them stopped abruptly. I heard Luca's patient voice and the girl's less patient voice in a brief exchange, a memory that even now pangs me with its echo of an erstwhile, a bygone content: the big front door closing on the cold of winter, a plane's turbines dwindling over the Irish sea, a motor whistling past; a whole second of geological slide from our day to the century of *Eine Kleine Nachtmusik* come back to me via a similar dusking afternoon sixty years before in Cork as I walked after school out of town under the elms of the long, quiet avenue, gated, suburban, gaslit, that we called The Mardyke for my regular piano lesson with old exiled Teodor Gmürr, foreknowing that he would begin as always with the same injunction: 'Today we play like thee drops of water falling into thee fountayn': meaning, he had once annotated, some favoured 'fountayn' in his native Innsbruck.

Before the maid opened the door of the drawing room and announced me the night music had begun to plink again in the library. From her desk at the end of the long room Ana turned to look at me over her horn-rimmed glasses, rose smiling, ear cocked, held my right hand in her soft right hand while her left hand rose, ringed, bangled and wrinkled, for silence. I held the door ajar, she listening, I thinking yet once again how smashingly beautiful she must have been when I first saw her forty-five years ago by the blown spray of those London 'fountayns'.

The music paused. I closed the door and sat beside her on the settee, shocked by the sudden awareness that she was even still a woman of the rarest beauty. Of course she did not possess the crystalline beauty of that stupid girl calmly murdering Mozart in the library-study. Unlike some similar handsome chit Ana could not rely on shining pupils, outlined lips, carved nostrils, a petal skin, a firm form. Naked, she would droop. The beauty I treasured in her was of that rare material, Youth matured by Time; unless we are obliged to consider nine-tenths of the world's women plain in order that only gaudy girls may be judged pretty. Would we think an unweathered Venus de Milo more lovely? The victory this ageing woman had won over time was her indifference to it. She was elegant even when doing nothing, just sitting, her hands crossed sedately on her lap like a good child, or a dowager grandmother at a party, listening; or simply when walking across the room, her tulip head poised on its ravaged stem, her shoulders folded like wings. She had the supreme gift that no woman under sixty can command: she was one of those who have lived.

Qui ont vécu. I heard her use the phrase more than once. It was her greatest tribute to women who do not just accept life – who ride it, get thrown, remount. Looking at her that afternoon I wondered if she had really had in her youth a great many of what I in my far off youth used tremblingly call 'experiences'. I remembered how often I had tried to pump her about it and always been, with her usual reticent worldly wisdom, deflected – so that I was more than troubled that afternoon to hear her suddenly begin to murmur smilingly about youth, dreams and love. Was it because of the little night music?

'Young people do right to dream,' she said. 'But it is a mistake to try too hard to make dreams come true. I married too young.'

Irritably she rang the bell for the tea and biscuits, and begged the maid to be so good as to ask Miss Kang and Signor Pollice if they would like to join us.

'I did not sleep well last night. In Kew, when I was a girl if I wanted to invoke sleep I used to think of the lily houses in the Gardens, damp and dark, with the sacred lotus flower asleep in its warm pool. One night I made up a silly poem. *Kew tonight is like a zoo/The lotus groans, "I'm all askew"./Tiger lilies moan and mew/Each gaudy flower a parakeet/Screaming in its tropic heat./The monkey puzzles pound their feet,/Nepenthes jabber as they dine/On flies that whine inside their wine./All Kew tonight is like a lion/Roaring down the District Line.* Ah!'

The girl had entered, smiling, beautiful, self-proud. She wore a pale green Alice band about her brow, her hair waterfalling to her hips, her beauty flawed only by her all too obviously knowing that she was unflawed.

'Lalage!' Ana stretched out her regal hand. The girl accepted the benevolent invitation and sat close to her. 'But where is Signor Pollice? You look unusually pleased, today, Lalage? Any special reason?'

'Mr Pollice is telephoning Milan.'

'Milan? Why Milan?'

The girl smiled and shrugged – both slyly.

'Did the lesson go well? I am sure you played splendidly?'

'I played very well,' the girl announced with a certainty that pleased Ana and infuriated me.

'It is beguiling music. The little music that sends one to sleep. Did you know that the Elector of Saxony commissioned Bach to write special sleep-music for him? And paid him with a gold chalice filled with gold coins?'

The girl nodded but – obviously not knowing – said nothing. I became, and I could see that Ana also became aware of a certain uneasiness in the air.

'Was Signor Pollice pleased with you?'

The girl lowered her head and glanced sidewards at her grand-aunt with a further slyness that further alerted me.

'He was *very* pleased with me!' she laughed.

'You seem very sure of it. Did he compliment you?'

The girl's mouth trembled, her shoulders shivered, her head fell back, her laughter broke, and went on and on, unmusically.

'Why do you laugh?' Ana asked quietly, in a tone that, I knew, foreboded.

Lalage answered heedlessly, triumphantly, pitilessly.

'That old guy kissed me! He actually kissed me! He must be at least forty!'

Ana's neck slowly ascended.

'Were you upset?' she asked softly.

Lalage scoffed a 'No!' that prolonged itself into a bitingly nasal, scornful transatlantic trisyllable like a cat's mew. 'I just gave the old fool a slow burn. Imagine it! Kissing me! Me! He implored me not to tell you.'

The face that I had just been thinking of as indestructibly beautiful wizened, its voice became proportionately softer.

'In that case, Lalage, why have you told me?'

'I just couldn't keep it in. He looked *so* old! and *so* stoopid! You should have seen him crawl!'

At that moment the maid entered with the message that Mr Pollice said he had to leave now.

'Ask him to come in for a moment, Molly.'

I made to rise and go. Her 'Please!' was a command. The three of us waited in a silence that, I thought, began to make even the girl uncomfortable. Luca came in, laid his violin on a chair, his hat on top of it, and stood looking uneasily at the three of us.

'Do sit down, Luca,' she bade him. Then: 'Please tell me frankly, Luca. Is what my grand-niece has just told me true?'

He spread his hands, sighed, nodded sadly.

'But, for heaven's sake, why?'

What a nice chap he is, I thought, watching him turn towards her window to look with sad-comical eyes at the sunset, the bare beeches and the folly of mankind.

'It is a sweet little tune,' he mused. 'And she was playing it so godamn awfully! As she always will. I felt sorry for her. Very sorry. It was a *moment de tendresse*. As if she were my daughter, my baby, peeing on the floor.'

A gasp from Ana brought my eyes around. She was in a blow-winds-and-crack-your-cheeks rage – a rage against the dying of the light, an old woman beating the door of her prison cell. I knew that pug face of old, its naked anger.

'And, so, all Dublin can now break its sides laughing at the lot of us? At you for being such a softy? At me for an old fool dreaming of owning my own quartet? At this child for banjaxing everything? Don't you know that at one whisper in this city the camera is under your nose, every eye as close to you as your coffin, laughter in their eyes and murder in their teeth?'

Luca threw out his hands imploringly.

'But nobody need ever know about this!'

'You idiot! This girl could dine out for a month on it. And would!' She turned to the preening girl. She was polite again, in calm control. 'Lalage! It is five o'clock here. It is morning in Boston. I shall ring Boston straightway and explain nicely to your mother that I observe, most regretfully, that you have become bored with Dublin, that you are longing to be at home for Thanksgiving, and that I shall find you a seat on a plane tomorrow either from here or from London, now, kindly go to your room and pack.'

The only accurate word for the girl's response is *aghast*. Horror stuck in her like a bat clawing her fair hair, or some wet, horrid, crabby thing from the sea. She broke into a wail:

'But, Auntie Ana, there is the meet at Sallins tomorrow, and the big dance at Carton on Friday night, and I promised Jonathan Ganly. . . .

'Kindly pack!' her great-aunt commanded. She got a savage look. She returned it. She was obeyed. To Luca: 'I will, of course, pay your complete fee, and the cost of a plane ticket to anywhere you wish. Rome, Pittsburg, Milan, New York. It is a pity our plan has come to nothing but now, of course, that you have made me the laughing-stock of Dublin it is quite impossible. Thank you for everything, Luca. It was a nice dream.'

With a shrugging gesture from the wrist, American-cool, he took up his violin-case and his hat, and went his way. The female fool followed him.

Ana emptied her cup and mine into the tea bowl, rinsed both, refilled them. Her hand was not trembling. She was as handsome as ever. I disliked her intensely for that steady paw. After all it was I who had involved Luca in this punctured dream.

'As you know,' she resumed, 'the Botanic Gardens at Kew face west.' I followed her eyes out beyond her beeches.

Half an hour ago those western clouds had been buttered by the last of the sunset; now it was lighting-up time all over Dublin.

'I used to think the sun beyond Isleworth sank over the edge of the world.' Another silence. 'Some day, darling, you and I must go back to Kew and look at that giant water lily from the Amazon. When I was growing up it used to put sexy ideas into my head. The heat, and the damp, and the dark. I am afraid they have left the door ajar? Thanks. I feel the cold air from the hall.'

Before I clicked the door shut I heard Luca comforting the weeping girl. The thermometer on the jamb read 72°.

'Sometimes I used cross on the ferry to Isleworth. But it was much nicer to follow the towpath into Richmond and have tea at The Maids of Honour. That was the name of a pastry that was supposed to have greatly pleased Queen Elizabeth when she resided at the palace in Richmond. Or, if it was the summer, I might watch the cricketers on the Green. I once made up a silly poem about Kew. It was a hot night, I could not sleep. Shall I recite it to you?' She recited it, exactly as she had done five minutes or so before. When she had finished it she said, 'I am afraid I must send you away now, Bobby. I have a rather private call to make to Boston. I'll tell you all about it later.'

I had never before seen her in such disarray. An imperial army in full retreat. Her Waterloo.

That month she went into St Vincent's for tests. She came out saying laughingly that it had been a waste of time, the results had all been negative. Reggie gave her six months. She nevertheless held her big Horse Show garden party as usual that following August, but she had to retire to bed even before it was over and she did not leave the house again. On the 8th of November her tortured spirit walked around its street corner. The traffic halted. The traffic passed on. Two months later I ran into an old acquaintance of hers just returned from a business tour in the United States. We chatted. As we moved off he said, 'Oh, give all my wishes to old Reggie. And of course to the charming Ana. We all know she's immortal.'

That November of 1970 is five years ago now. What did I, in younging from sixty-five to fifty-five learn from her? Not love – I had always known that. Despair? Of course – the blood-money of memory. Even in Arcady death is always with us. Besides despair? Its opposite: courage. Marry the two and you get the stoic blend. I can hear her: 'Forget and rejoice.' Something else? That there is such a thing as perfect love even though my famous experience, my worldly wisdom, my cool reason all tell me firmly that I might not have found her flawless if I had lived with her every hour, day, week, year, like poor old Reggie, for forty-six years. I loved her. My frozen past life tells me that love contains desire. It is not contained by it, nor is it what it outlasts. I loved her. We discovered absolute trust. My years laugh that trust, limited by the human capacity, is never absolute. I loved her. And she me. We freely chose one another. An outsider might scoff that we met three times, years apart, before we 'chose'. I have learned that every such choice is a happy surrender to destiny to prove it. Any more? Only the wish that I could live it all over again! Every minute of it. I loved her.

She was superb. She was infallible. She was funny. She was tender. She understood things so well. Can there ever have been any other woman like her? But what folly all this is! I am merely revealing myself, not her. She represented life at the peak of livingness . . . I give up. I have no words. I must stop writing.

It is, of course, possible that she really was exceptional. As possible as the first daffodils, the pink of my almond tree, my forsythia that is the colour of Anador's honey-yellow hair as she walked past my window just now, her head bare to the sun. How noble her mother's daughter always looks! March is going. My tenth birthday gone. Ana is ivory in the clay. The daffodils sway. Soon, summer. When Reggie's will has at last gone through probate and his countless creditors are at last silenced – How extravagantly those two lived! – Anador and Leslie will take over that beloved house in Ailesbury Road. Shall I ever pass it again? Climb its steps? Ring its bell? I close my book. My life is finished. I shall write no more.

A Note on Sequels. I once thought of a book that some bright chap might write – a book to be called AND AFTERWARDS? The retired Prospero becomes known far and wide as a doddering bore. Hamlet recovers from his duel with Laertes and is known to every girl within a hundred miles of Elsinore as a homosexual. Oscar Wilde had a terrible story of how Christ crawled out of his tomb to live on in exile as a humble carpenter – the only man who knew what a lie all that Christ-is-God fable had been; how other carpenters on the job noticed that he always kept his hands covered; and how steadfastedly he refused to go to meetings addressed by the fashionable evangelist Paul; and did not Anatole France write a story about a retired proconsul, named Pilate, pulling his ear and muttering, 'Did you say Jesus Christ? I do seem to remember an odd-ball fellow of that name.'

But what do I have to do with sequels? I shall write no more.

Postscript: I have written all these pages to know myself.
Question: Have I discovered much?
Answer: Who does, ever?
Question: Fie?
Answer: It's not nothing to discover even that much! If I want to know myself I must naturally first define my scope and my limits.
Question: And have I done so?
Answer: Not yet. Shall I ever? If not...

Postpostscript: A date, June 1971. Seven months after Ana's death I created a job for myself. I had to. My life was empty. My income (unearned) seemed to be purchasing less. I have persuaded Leslie Longfield to go partners with me in a little art gallery. The directors are Leslie, his wife and me. I put up half the money. Leslie has generously agreed to put in one or two of the most prestigious pieces in his French collection. It consists of two rooms over an auctioneer's in Anne Street. Inevitably it is called The Anna Livia. It is a wonderful cover for my affair with Anador.

PART TWO

Anador

1970–1990

November 13th, 1990. My life is at a crisis. This morning we buried my bewitching, beloved, betrayed Anador.

Alea jacta. Where the hell was that rivulet that once divided peace from war? Surely we? Yes. Twenty years ago, driving on our informal honeymoon from Venice to Rimini. A piddling stream now called Fiumicino. So, she has recrossed her Rubicon, but not into the trees. Restless, revisiting shade, you once frequently outshone every shade. But one. If there is any lesson that I have learned more firmly than another from you and from Ana it is that man should be born, live and die awake.

Middle age has stolen on me. Anador did not notice it until her fifty-fifth birthday when she said crossly one Sunday afternoon from pillow to pillow, 'You've changed!' So had she. One does at fifty-five. What should I do? Dye my hair white? Their celestial immortalities told me that to avoid scandal I should change my residence according as I younged. Immortals, they had forgotten age and death. All but two of my original neighbours have now gone around their corner. And it was so convenient for us both here with my ladder sloped against her garden wall. By the time she and Leslie finally moved into Ailesbury Road I had become too accustomed to my little house to leave it. Not that I was insensitive. I used to carry a walking stick, limp whenever I remembered to, wear spectacles of plain glass, complain of secret ailments, try to look doomed. A waste of time. All these pensioners around me, bond holders, coupon clippers, rentiers, septuagenarians, octogenarians are as jealous of one another's salubrity as a bevy of old bullfighters, a brood of quondam boxers, voiceless divas, superannuated bishops, throneless kings, jowled movie stars twirling their thumbs, rereading their morning papers, peeping through their lace curtains, studying the oracles of their bowels, contemplating the future of their immortal souls. Sadly? Not at all! In this small enclave I sympathise only with our one atheist. Me. No future for him. For the orthodox? Great Expectations. Under the trees. In arcadia.

I accompanied her daughter to her funeral. Nana, unlike her mother, will never be described as beautiful, not even in profile. She has paprika-red hair and lovely grey-blue eyes but she grew up a rather heavy-featured girl. Still, she has other gifts. Warmly maternal, bulbous, Wife-of-Bathishly witty, sharp and amusing, and entirely fearless, and approaching my age-group. After the funeral I drove her home – this last year she has been living in the basement flat of the Ailesbury Road house which is the final comment on Reggie's and Ana's improvidence. When Anador inherited the house she inherited nothing else. She had the choice either of selling the house or breaking it into three flats. It was disturbing to be alone there with Nana this morning, all the more so because she had disturbed me earlier, in the cemetery, prodding an old sore.

This fog was light then. I could see across the white harvest of Carrara crosses for a quarter of a mile. Now it has thickened, sunk from Killiney Hill to the orange chimney pots around me, the hundreds of coloured TV fishbones all swimming in the same direction. It encouraged us all to light up earlier than usual and then dimmed everything else. My apple tree is a ghost. My tall street lamp is a moon. The traffic's muffled sounds isolate me. The twinges of old unease return. All night I shall hear that damned foghorn off the Muglin rocks moaning basely.

I wish I had earlier taxed Anador about that old troubling doubt that returned to me by the graveside when I deliberately touched Nana's cold hand and she, having swivelled a quick look around the mourners, pressed it affirmatively. Who truly was the father of the woman in that coffin? I have put on record Ana's ambiguous suggestion – it was not a positive statement – about Anador's paternity. I have also clearly put down, trying to clarify it for myself, to do justice to myself, to calm myself, my reason for not pursuing her about it: that only a fool would halt a masque to challenge a fact. I have always refused to believe that she could have deliberately decided that night in Nice to give the most taunting possible reason for divorce to her husband. She would not have involved me that utterly when neither of us was certain of the other. And yet, no matter how often I had gone around and around it I again started to worry over it there at the graveside, always holding on at the end to the one final assurance that if her passing suggestion really had been the truth she would have brought it up once more before she left me, if only to . . .

If only to what? I have come stiffly awake in my armchair. It is one-ten a.m. The bottle of whiskey is low. Coffee cold. The moan of the wounded bull. I have gone to my front window and peered between its curtains as I did that summer night when I looked out and saw mast-lights emerging from the harbour into the Baie des Anges. Is the fog lifting? My street lamp still wears a nimbus such as one sees about the heads of gods in sacred pictures. Life, 'diverse and flowing' (Who? Montaigne?) can often best impress its profoundest truths at its farthest circumference. Ana had always been more truthful than Anador, or me, or any one, when gesturing from her shoulder to the horizon.

I let the curtains fall. Who else could it have been? Who else had been on that sail to Nice? The most innocent question would have sufficed, such as, 'Leslie, who took that photograph of you three on that boat?' Or: 'I'm sorry, Reggie, I can't get away from my paper for that long! Who can you get for a substitute?' Or after Ana's: 'Catch me! Locked up in a boat with two men and a boy, that's all Les is, and the Reverend Des isn't much better.' Des? I had no recollection of him, of ever meeting him but I must have felt something about him, I accepted him so quickly when we did at last again meet face to face at her valedictory Horse Show party and he mentioned Nice.

August 1970. It had been so like her to insist on holding it, doomed though she knew she was, playing the game in her own way so sturdily that she may well have fooled herself that she was on the road back to health; acting the happy hostess, producing smiles wherever she wandered among her guests, supervising her usual lavish hospitality. To those three or four of us who knew the truth her performance was between the heroic and the ham – the red and white striped marquee, the faint waves of brass from the army's band at the not-so-distant Show, her own quartet in the marquee, that is her hired quartet, playing Cimarosa, Offenbach and Strauss, the waiters in black ties and tails waltzing with the high-held trays of champagne, caviar and canapés among the chatterers scattered about the garden at intimate tables, the women in gauzy Horse Show frocks and flowered, flopping hats, some of the men in grey toppers, and I remember two who came in hunting pink. Reggie told me afterwards that before the party ended he had to lift her up the stairs to bed, a retreat, not a defeat, observed by nobody, not even, I shamefully admit, by me.

I was otherwise engaged, accosted by a powerful, broad-shouldered parson or priest, about sixty, ruddy, cigar-smoking, in elegantly tailored clericals who kept staring at me in amused puzzlement as if he were seeing a dot of light at the end of a tunnel. As I looked at him I too divined a light; he was the first of us to name it, heartily:

'Bob Younger by all that's holy! The Côte d'Azur. Nice. 1930. Des Moran. Remember?'

I gripped his outstretched hand. I did not remember him, but knew that we must have met.

'The third man? Aboard the *Regina*? Des Moran?'

Behind me Reggie said over his shoulder, 'To you, sir, Monsignor Desmond Francis Moran. George Cross. O.B.E. Quondam doyen of the British Army's private army of official army chaplains.'

In keeping with the spirit of the day, the music, the sun, the champagne, we embraced, laughingly, French manner. I did not for a moment think of him as a priest; I thought of him as a man of the world. We began to stroll from the crowded part of the garden towards the quiet pool and the white garden seat beside it, exchanging fifteen-word life stories.

'The last time I heard of you you were a promising young reporter in Colchester. Or was it London? What are you up to now? Retired? Although you look damned young to be retired.'

'The last time we crossed paths you were a gay young clerical student. Just about to step over the pillow. Wasn't that the expression? Reggie has just given me your *Who's Who* since then. What actually are you doing here? Working in Ireland?'

'I come to Dublin three or four time a year. I have sisters and a brother. Actually what *do* you live on?'

'Actually I work as a free-lance. I run an art gallery. Do a bit of journalism. A bit of radio. On whatever happens to interest me at the moment. You?'

'*Beneficium sine cura*. Put out to grass in Westminster. I suppose you could call me an ecclesiastical public relations officer. E.P.R.O. Actually what *does* happen to interest you at the moment?'

I looked up the garden. Anador, at the hither edge of the crowd was queening it splendidly over them all – tall, stately, in a long chiffon dress that I considered unsuited to her strength, her waistless figure, her manly brow, her shortish waved hair, her strong hand holding the inevitable cigarette.

I said the word impishly, or compulsively, or as if whiffed by a stray wing of truth shooting across the garden:

'Incest.'

He startled me with, 'Ana wouldn't like this.' His hand dispelled cigar smoke from a rose – her favourite Danse des Sylphides, as I informed him. He gave me a bawdy grin. Did I remember Lampedusa's Prince? He had a weakness for a rose called Cuisse de Nymphe Emue.

'Reminded him in Palermo, his little Dublin, of the smell of dancers' thighs at the Paris opera.'

He paused, leaned back, looked up at the cloudlets feathering one by one before our prevailing south-wester. 'Incest?' he said to them, and speculatively he looked at me.

Champagne-filled, in our primes, under the clouds' feathers crossing the pool, we sat on, he cheerfully enouncing, I cheerfully querying the various diriment impediments of church and state to cohabitation between close relatives. He began with what he pedantically called *raptus* ('Is this what you have in mind?') Or would I prefer the word abduction? The forcible dragging of a female from one place to another for marriage. 'Or better?' He moved on, wryly, to *impotentia*. 'Concerns neither of us.' He considered whether or not a man should be allowed to marry the relative of a discarded fiancée.

'But why on earth shouldn't he?' I asked.

'Public decorum,' he replied. 'A typical imperial Roman idea. A bond is a bond. An "engagement" is a bond. Marriage follows inevitably. One of those many sound secular ideas that the Church has turned into theology.'

'But surely,' I cried, 'you don't believe in it as an impediment to marriage? Or would you?'

'Believe? The word is too strong. Advise? Possibly.'

'Advise something you don't believe in?'

'I might even request obedience if I were so commanded. I have been a soldier. I've seen men go to their deaths on the order of some officer who, they knew, was a bloody fool. You've got to have discipline, you know.'

That observation left an impression on me. (Had I always been a man of order?) I dared not press him to come to the point. He came to her at his ease.

I was to find him on many other occasions a good talker, a good mimic, one of the best raconteurs I have ever heard, though never in better key than during that half hour at the lily pond, enjoying the sun, the subject, his whiskey, the muted chattering floating down from the house, though what I most appreciated in him was that whenever he seemed to want to expand on some aspect of his subject, instead of weighing in heavily on it he merely invoked some rum detail that made the whole thing laugh at itself expansively. So, instead of giving me an elaborate account of Napoleon's skill in dismissing the Empress Josephine with full ecclesiastical blessing he simply threw a cynical smile in the direction of the unfortunate blesser, the then Archbishop of Paris. Instead of going into details about the mess Napoleon's brother Joseph Buonaparte made of his efforts to get rid of his wife, Miss Paterson of Baltimore (U.S.A.), he mentioned the total bewilderment of the Patersons at large. He skipped Marconi's ingenuity in persuading Rome to annul his nineteen-year-old marriage with Beatrice O'Brien, the daughter of Lord Inchiquin of Dromoland Castle in County Clare – barely mentioning that the young woman had loftily not bothered to tell her poor local parish priest about her intentions with the result that there were no banns. The old priest dozing over his grog by his turf-fire on the windy Shannon's shore as naturally made no fuss about such a trifling omission.

'It was a doze that started an international social, political and theological scandal whose echoes,' Des laughed comfortably, 'still groan through the corridors of the Vatican.'

He waved a horseman's hand.

'Incest? It is not really a moral question. How, for example, could it possibly matter a damn either to church or state if some Englishman wants to marry the sister of his dead wife? For one thousand, eighteen hundred and thirty-five years Celts, Angles, Saxons and Jutes had been doing it and nobody said boo. Then in comes the Marriage Act of 1835 and it becomes a crime. Seventy-three years later in comes the Deceased Wife's Sister's Marriage Act and it becomes lawful again! Did you ask, "Can the laws change?" Why not? And you and I have to obey each time or become anarchists. You and I belong to a capitalist church. We believe in its power and respect its property. Rules and laws about marriage, adultery, incest and so on spring from the urges and pressures of tribal power and property. Each time those pressures change the laws change. I agree that now that contraceptives can be bought from public slot machines in the shadow of the Vatican it matters far less to any propertied man or woman who his or her consort sleeps with.

Meanwhile, the law is the law!' He sighed. 'Life and religion were much easier when there were no laws at all. Christianity had its Golden Age when it was dreaming of heaven in the catacombs. Since then? A bureaucratic mess of dolly statues, silly miracles, pietistic devotions, gaudy churches, feast days and fasting days, a mafia of canon lawyers. Do this, do that, do the other! Argue, argue, argue! As if God alone were not enough to keep a man in silent wonder all his life! Give me some little white-washed country church in Calabria or Connemara with nothing in it but the silence. Give me that and you can have all the lordly cathedrals in the world.'

That was it. Thinking back to it I see now where he got his strange blend of mockery and scepticism, crudity and delicacy, courage and compassion. No man of his feeling and intelligence could have gone through years of war in half a dozen countries, seen men, women and children reduced week after week to the contents of a butcher's barrel – and I would not be at all surprised to hear that he had himself killed his man in battle – without developing a grateful acceptance of life as a good investment – an annual return of ten nights of star-scattering rockets for every ninety days eating dry-as-dust powder. An Epicurean. A Stoic. A heaven-aiming martyr working inside the drawn bounds of the way things are. How the world's rebellious egoists, wits, visionaries would despise him. His whole mind, his pleasures, even his memory were dominated by his vocation. I would, did that day ask him something about his campaigning years. I found that he was dismally uninteresting about such key struggles as El Alamein and Caserta. The next minute he was enthusiastic and vivid about a hammering day after the hounds in Galway or Tipperary; quoting aptly from Dante (it would be Dante); evoking triumphantly a stormy night sailing in the North Sea. He was a brave man, but a man of peace; he showed it by his way of attaching to the end of each frightening war story a little tag like a price label on a tapestry at a sale, a tone of voice that so reduced its value that one heard it tinkling away down a chute to the top of a pit of all those other deflated doubloons of history that some divinely appointed slot machine attendant has to spend his eternal life wearily lugging away in a bag to the melting pot of oblivion. But why did he remember one thing and not another? If, I gradually realised as I got to know him better, I knew the answer to that problem I would have his nature in the palm of my hand. It lay in his choice of what islets of fact he permitted to rise above the vast, all forgetting sea on which he was sailing through the waves of this world to his God-alone-knew-where.

Just as I was beginning, that August afternoon, to think of him in this way – a delicate, devoted, dangerous, mystical, adventurous, sophisticated influence, not unimpeachable, always refined, always sensitive, I heard him say to me, 'Well, Bobby? Whose cousin, mother, daughter or sister among all that lot of chatterers up there are you proposing to fuck?'

At the time the word was not a commonplace. It was coarse. I record his word not because he was a Monsignor, not because this was old-fashioned Ireland where some men, I found, considered him an indecorous priest, but simply to remind myself that the earthiness of his ways was an indication of the unearthiness of his life. There was, indeed, coarseness in Des Moran, but it was never to be segregated from his compassion for his suffering fellow-men packed into this insufferable world. The secret of his nature was that whether he was enjoying himself on the hunting field, or risking death on the field of battle, or doing his job as ecclesiastical P.R.O. in some well-equipped office in Westminster, he did not give a damn about this world. He saw life as St Paul's shadowy enigma. In death he would face its reality. I can see why men might think him crude, even venal, even hypocritical. (Women were attracted by him – the attraction of the unattainable?) His motto was – Endure, adore, enjoy.

I did not answer his blunt question and he did not repeat it. Then:

'You presumably know,' he said, as if feeling that his moment had come, 'that Anna ffrench is dying? I want you to persuade her to die a Catholic.'

This took me back to the trivial round of where and when and who we were.

'I certainly will not! Why on earth should I? Mrs ffrench gave all that up years ago.'

'Because you two have been lovers for the last twenty-five years. You are the only man in the world she will listen to. You have to do it. I have seen a power of men die. Some few did not care about the blankness waiting for them but most of them did, and they died more easily in the hope of another life waiting. You have loved her alive. Don't you want to help her to die? Or do you love your precious principles more than you have loved her?'

'How do you know I loved her?'

'Forty years ago. That night in 1930. Remember? Until you

came she was an actress playing a part. After you came she became her lovely human self. A child could have seen it in her eyes. It was I who drove Reggie to Monte Carlo that night. He was so pixily secretive that I knew something queer was up, and so drunk on the way back that he never stopped blathering. For about a week after you left she went on glowing. As the days and the weeks passed the light went out of her more and more. Her honeymood lasted exactly a month. When it ended she became a bat flying her kite into every night wind. As I have good reason to know. I did not see her again for years and years after that. It is one thing for a clerical student to toss his hat over the moon. It is another thing for an ordained priest to disrespect Our Lady of the Heavens. Or for a soldier. Or a poet.' He grinned mockingly at himself and me. 'I quote you Baudelaire on the only men worthy of respect – the priest, the killer and the artist. Today is not the only time I have seen her since then, but it very nearly is. The war broke up so many attachments, including hers to that Longfield boy who in the end married my daughter.'

He had shocked me a third time.

'Your daughter? You have no proof that Anador is your daughter!'

He banged his chest with his fist.

'I know it in here. I tried everywhere for proof. I even got a copy of the birth certificate.'

'What did it say?'

'What do you think? "Reginald ffrench." '

I burst out at him. I lashed him where his flesh was already raw.

'You are boasting. She could have been mine. Or Leslie's.'

He responded with passion:

'She didn't bother about that boy until it was over between her and me – for all the little that "it" ever was. And do you think that if the child was his she would have let her marry the runt? Or that if she had been yours you would find her sexually attractive now? Or that if she were not my daughter I would feel so warm towards her, so responsible, so torn by compassion for her dying mother? For Christ's sweet sake, and I don't say that name blasphemously, talk to Ana. You owe it to her. We both owe it to her. You and I both know calmly that this is the end. She will not see another August. Next year will be your first year without her.'

I said that he should talk to her himself. He drew his big hand over his face. Cobwebs of agony.

'I have tried to. She rebuffed me. What happened happened when I was young and wild. It gives me no claim on her in my old age.'

Disturbed, he rose, strayed into the crowd. I followed. Separated I, with Reggie's encouragement, went to her bedroom to say my thanks for the garden party. Though much made up in the modish orange-yellow of the period she was pinched, grey and hollow-cheeked. Des Moran was right. She would not see another summer. She received me graciously. With affection she compelled me to sit close to her. That was the moment when she said tenderly, 'I wish you could die before me, you will be so unhappy if I go first.' It was, I perceived, a command not to take her imminent death for granted. She was refusing to cross the river until she damned well had to. The next thing she said was as disturbing, still not a crossing of the river, but almost that:

'I observed you talking to Monsignor Moran. I want you to do something for me, Bobby. I want you to do two things. You were born a believing Catholic. So was I. I want us to finish our lives together as we began them. Whichever of us survives it will help him to live without the other. Is this something I ought not to ask of you?'

I assured her, lyingly. She was pleased. She said she would trust Monsignor Moran to hear her Confession. The garden party had almost completely scattered. I listened through the open window for the faint music of the Army Band but could no longer hear a sound. The gay day was done.

'The other thing,' she said gently, propped up against her lace-edged pillows, her hands wrinkled, quietly folded, 'is, would you please collect for me a hundred Seconals. The pains have begun. Reggie, being a gentleman, would have to refuse me.'

I at once enlisted Anador who got a prescription for five Seconals from Reggie, changed the five to fifteen and filched five blank pages from his prescription block. On these I copied the original. By visiting three doctors each about alleged insomnia we procured sixty more capsules. We were squirrels of death. I am sure that her wish to die a Catholic death was not another Puccini aria – I am sure she really did think it a serious and honourable way to die. On a later visit, towards the end, I dared to ask her what 'God' meant to her and was humbly impressed by the force of her (patently sentimental) celebration of 'Somebody kind and loving who will look after me'. However, at these celestial altitudes the ground is less than solid and what chiefly impressed me was the sad feeling that 'looking after' her was the one thing I had never had the chance to do. In the end one accepts whatever anybody one is fond of accepts. As she had once said, the beloved can do no wrong.

Since I have been writing all these words in the continuing hope of uncovering their author's 'true character and disposition', as Montaigne puts it, I must lay all my actions, however embarrassing to me, on the table. During my beloved's final weeks of life Anador and I met virtually every day, sometimes twice a day. We were her most frequent visitors after Reggie. I did not at that time make a 'pass' at her (the word is borrowed from fencing) though I confess, I was often tempted. Not that if I had yielded a tolerant person would have seen anything reprehensible in a harmless flirtation inspired mainly by my sense of death's cockroaches creeping from their holes. Nor do I think anybody would denounce me for having gone on soliciting the same harmless consolation after Ana died, and after her Reggie, after which the home next door to me was emptied and put up for sale. (It was ultimately occupied by a young professor of physics and his wife, and two excessively active children.) Nevertheless, on looking back at that first miserable period, I fear that it was chiefly Reggie's clinging friendship and close observation that restrained me. I held out until he too went. By then, time retiring from me and advancing for Anador had brought us so close that on her next birthday she was forty-four, I only eleven years older, and . . . Well!

I have something else to charge against myself. That you did thereafter insensitively pursue your overtures on many occasions where you should not in decency have pursued them, within the bounds of a house that must have evoked the most tender memories; that you felt troubled by this, and that you never once let it deter you. All you can say for yourself, I gather, is that you felt more shattered than triumphant when you at last found yourself in the same bed in the same room of the same house with your dead love's daughter. 'Where now,' you felt like asking her, but did not ask her, 'is all this devotion, this faith, this one true love above all other loves which each of us has so long been elevating to the other as the sole road to lasting joy? How right,' you wanted to say, 'Einstein was in saying that happiness, well being and pleasure are pursuits worthy of a pig!'

I now know, beyond all self-deceiving, that I deliberately made myself fall in love with her. What there was in her, what it was that she possessed that I so wanted to be part of I do not know – something certainly that called out to me, but I shall never know whether it was her strength, portrayed in the shape of her body, or the emotional vulnerability of a passionate woman always on the edge of overpowering feelings and emotions. I am not aware – an ignorance of no meaning in any human being – of any special or unmanning weakness in myself or of any special vice of hardness or coldness. All I knew, and know is that she had something I needed and that I decided quite consciously to pursue it in her until we became one person. I paid for that pursuit. For over fifteen years I have been turn and turn about burned and frozen by its icy ecstasy. The fact may be that Anador was the tormenting image of her mamma by being her matching antithesis. I can believe that the image looking at her out of her mirror every day not only halved the size of her face, as all mirrors do to all faces, but by transposing shadows, flipping lights, evoking memories, actually reproduced something of her mother's elegance if not daintiness. But whereas Ana had been a realist who, all through her life, had figure-skated up and down the river in search of romance, Anador, though just as romantic from her earliest years – as I must record in a moment – had picked up somewhere or other a sixth sense of reality, from what she liked to call 'my little green man on my shoulder', whispering such warnings as, 'Careful! This ice is thin', or 'Not here! This is a dangerous current'. To which she would at once agree. 'Fatal!' she would cry gratefully – and make straight for the calamity, survive, ponder, and (frugal like all artists) put the experience into her paintings.

I had not paid much attention to these paintings until I fell in love with her. Then I realised that while at first glance all her images seemed slight, light-hearted and gay, they in fact depicted a chain of disaster: three small boys in harlequin clothes falling off an elephant, a hooting storm upsetting a merry youthful picnic, a pair of baby hands in the sky gaily shaking a pepper pot and a salt sprinkler over a baroque cathedral, a gaily coloured Children's Zoo with all the cage doors open. The symbols became transparent after we became lovers. Her work, overtly realistic, though not without its zest of fancy, was wholly related to one dreadful common subject, the betrayal of all childish dreams. Every one of her youthful characters sees visions that invite instant destruction; girlish dreams that have never had a chance to do more than waver in the wind like smoke. She was at once the young heroine and the grown avenger, unillusioned about illusions, strong about weakness, ruthless about the pitiful. That I say this says nothing about the so-sayer except perhaps that, so much older than her, I must have broken my pitcher many times at the same stone cistern. In that knowledge I who had been the full ally of small Ana's fantasies became the challenger of big Anador's. We lived in a state of undulant fever, for ever chasing the bitter sweet of uncertain love. We quarrelled often. We came together again tempestuously. Doubles? Too alike? Bad for marriage, fatal for breeding.

My mistake, my stupidity, was not to have seen earlier that she (perhaps everyone) lives only when divided. Her undertow of emotion – i.e. her volatility, her excessive imagination, her other worldliness, her romantic nature was both her enemy and the defence of an apparently contradictory, in fact complementary She, a highly practical woman in a tailor-made suit cut as by a razor's edge to her androgynous body, shrewdly peering eyes (she was too vain to wear glasses) cool and X-raying, a vigorous laugh (she had a hair-trigger sense of humour), a fist that looked capable of knocking down a horse, a type that no stranger would have thought a dreamer or a *larmoyante* yet who, caught off guard, could brim, overflow, bawl like a lost child.

This Jana image – my importunate impression of her from our first encounter years before – was finally driven home to me by a simple, even a comical, thing when she visited me in the Gallery one morning and I took her out for a coffee in Grafton Street. As we were about to part she remembered that she needed to buy a zip-fastener in Woolworth's, I a kitchen gadget – a tea-infuser it was – so that by chance we found ourselves fumbling at the opposite sides of the same row of shelves. As I searched for my tea-infuser I threw a sideward glance at a small boy to my left, obviously poor, staring at some attractive bows of pink hair-ribbons, such as a small girl might wear on a pigtail, taking one down, putting it back again, hesitating, staring, held, fascinated, glancing up the aisle, again handling a ribbon, again staring, leaving me in no doubt about what he was tempted to do. At the same moment I became aware that Anador across the aisle was also watching the comedy. The idea came to me to buy the ribbon for the urchin, but I felt it would be a sentimental thing to do and, in any case, I was more interested to see what would happen.

What did happen was that Anador came swiftly around the end

of the shelves, crouched on her hunkers and said sweetly to the child, 'You want it for your girl? Here is twenty pence. Go ahead! Buy it for her.' The boy unhesitatingly grabbed the two coins and ran. An alarm bell screamed. A store detective raced to the door and nailed his victim. Anador and I strode after them. Blazing, she said, 'You leave that child alone! I gave him the money to pay for the ribbon.'

The man turned on her.

'You keep out of this, madam. We know this brat. He's a pincher. We've thrown him out of this shop three times already.'

'But he has the money! He was paying for it!'

'He was making for the street with the goods in one fist and the money in the other!'

Customers and attendants closed around the four of us. Six cross voices entangled. The boy wailed. Anador's dignity disappeared. Half an hour ago, ten minutes ago she could have been the Countess of Killarney. Now her face was blotched by rage and pity. I was aware of dentures, her nostrils dampened, she shook uncontrollably, her voice was unsweet. I, the only male there except the store detective, intervened to say to him with an oily sympathy, 'You are absolutely right, but you will never be able to prove it. Take my tip, I am a lawyer, boot him out.' Which wisely and forcefully he did while I led big Anador away, raging and sobbing at me for being a cold bloody prig and a stinking bourgeois snob, a bastard unfit to call himself even a yellow journalist. I lured her, still blistering, into the Shelbourne Rooms for a drink and, in due course, thence across to the Green where all of a sudden she gave out one of her boisterous laughs at the sight of a duck in the nearer pond slowly turning upside down to search for something in the mud and I knew that one of her romantic fits was over and that her powerful green man's commonsense was in command again – until the next time.

'Change everything,' said Voltaire rebelliously, 'except love.' As if love does not above all powers most swiftly change. I know I should have observed sooner that her mutations were as essential to her permanence as its phases are to the moon, but I am glad I did not. The exploration of the continent of Anador was a long, slow, if sometimes painful joy, and what gossipy pleasure is more relished by lovers than telling lies and remembering? And when did you? And where did you? And did you too . . . ? Relished and sorely needed in those years after Ana died when I knew less about her daughter's nature and beginnings than I knew about my own.

In search of her source I used to drive her up to those rolling hills whose nearness to Dublin is one of the city's great attractions; up to some forested slope above some Guinness-frothed mountain loch, some empty stretch of beach yellow as her head where we could flirt and whisper. On one such long, warm May afternoon – it was in 1975 – after picnicking above Luggalaw Lake she whispered away so many veils of years that I suddenly became aware, in delight, that I was holding in my arms not a woman of forty-four but a zestful, dreaming girl still in her first teens.

'I lived in that Fitzwilliam Square house for six years, a vast square of rosy houses, each a big box of bricks, all alike tall and level, with long narrow gardens at their backs, mostly neglected, ending in crumbling Georgian mews with classical pilasters, pediments and tondos – the one to the left of ours had a dished tondo with a bust of somebody who by now has, I'm sure, become absolutely anonymous to the world and time. Looking in that direction from my lofty bedroom during summer's daylit evenings, I would see the backs of other houses and the whiteness of clouds moving *en masse* over more roofs, over the canal, over the Liffey, out to sea. Those roofs of Dublin were a lake of blue and grey water. The other way, in the front, from the windows of my schoolroom, or Nanny's room, I looked into the green garden at the centre of the red box, a place hidden in the street from everybody by railings, shrubs, grenadier trees. My nanny, Denise, a Breton, would bring me down there to play with my yorky, Grump, slowly unlocking the gate – only residents had keys and hardly anybody ever made use of them except, maybe, some lone nursemaid on a bench reading beside a pram – relocking the gate again with a click behind her.

'I hated Denise. She was a selfish old thing. She fooled Ana to the tips of her ears.'

(To be noted: this child never remembered 'mummy' or 'mother', always a third person – 'Ana'.)

'Whenever Ana went off to the races, or any day-long thing, leaving me with many hugs and kisses in the sound, safe hands of my dear Denise for the day, my safe, sound, dear nanny would as like as not tie me by a long chain to the hotwater radiator and go off into town for a gossip with a crony, or an hour's shopping. She had that one splendid quality – her gossip. And there was plenty to gossip about in nanny-world. I was what I call a banisters child, leaning over the banisters high up, like I suppose lots of other children in other grand houses all over the world, in my white night-gown, peering down at the grand guests arriving, with Denise leaning beside me whispering scornful remarks about each new arrival. Four years ago when I visited her in her home in Nantes, where she went when she retired and survived the whole war – I found a small old, very old woman perpetually bent in two at right angles as if from leaning over too many banisters all her life. All she wanted to talk about was Dublin.

'"Ah! The old days! The Dublin days! The Dublin nights! The cabs lining up in the Square. Madame was always so gay and so lively. A ball of fire. Always laughing. How she loved a party! And, oh!" she leered joyfully. "The men! The men! I forget their names. That young man. A sculptor. Was his name Lester? Once, just before the war, a tall man. I heard he became a great figure in the Church. A French painter. A black doctor, shining like a billiard ball. He painted too."'

'And yet, I went out of my way, years after she left us, to visit her. Why? I think it was because she was part of Ana's play. And anybody who was...

(By the way I must bear in mind that the name Anador was Ana's invention. Like Anabaptist – somebody baptised all over again. Anador – somebody to be adored again. A joke in honour of its creator.)

'I should not be surprised if Denise was not the trigger that caused me to be shot down to a country convent school when I was getting on to ten – we had moved to Ailesbury Road by then. She had got on Reggie's nerves. He despised her. He said she was a gossip carrier. Ana put it more frankly. She said, "The child is beginning to take notice." *Notice* as the echo of gossip. "Did you notice her hat? Did you notice who he was talking to all night?" When she said I needed to be sent somewhere to school all I grasped was the word "sent", as if I were a parcel, or a dog or a weanling filly. Their conversations on this theme went on for weeks. Ana refused to send me to what she called some scrubby Irish boarding school, run by nuns, inspected by priests, smelling of incense, washing soda, shopkeepers' daughters' unwashed underwear. Reggie suggested a boarding school in England called Battle Abbey, but Ana downed that one – the battle of Hastings, the defeat of England, a Stink Port, good for the lungs, the poor man's Brighton, and anyway "the poor child" would be miserable out of Ireland, and there *was* a war on. What about a Dublin day school? I felt like an unwanted thing. Reggie would not "dream" of a Dublin day school – no place for a girl to learn how to be a lady. It took me years to discover what he had meant by that last extraordinary word. Then he confessed a bit mawkishly that he had wanted to protect me, that he was thinking of colleagues of his who stupidly took their daughters skiing in smart resorts like Gstaad, or summering in jet-set places like Eden Roc or St Tropez. "I was not going to risk my little girl with *those* sorts of people." I asked him, wide-eyed, if he thought the daughters of *those* sorts of people frequented Dublin's nun-run day schools. He glared at me with mad, blackbird, Evelyn Waugh eyes and said, "I bet even nuns go skiing in Gstaad nowadays!" He really was a bit crazy.

'Just as I was beginning to feel totally unwanted by everybody he remembered that he had a cousin "or something" who was head of a school run by *La Sainte Union du Sacré Cœur*. A very well connected eighteenth-century order, very refined, most cultivated, French, controlled strictly and directly from France itself.

'Ana asked him where this paragon of a cousin had this paragon of a school.

' "It is," he said proudly, "In Banagher, of all places."

' "And where," she asked coldly, "is this Banagher-of-all-places? In the wild west somewhere? Where your famous Ancestral Home is? Didn't we visit it fourteen or fifteen years ago? I remember a wreck of a place. All ivy and hens. And how can you have a cousin who is a Catholic? You never told me you have a cousin who is a Catholic. It's not like you, Reggie, to be so modest about so saleable a possession! You always parade me as a Catholic. You persuaded me to bring up this child as a Catholic. And, anyway, this is another scrubby, nunny boarding school. I won't have my Anador locked up day and night in a beastly nunny boarding school. Half starved. Sleeping in a dormitory. Freezing with the cold...'

'Reggie lost his temper. "I am indeed referring," he said haughtily, "to the old ffrench home situated cosily near the town of Banagher on our side of the River Shannon." ' (His "our" made me see Green Indians roving nightly on the other side of "our" river.) ' "It is true that we did briefly visit it soon after our marriage. My sisters were somewhat unprepared. The house is not a wreck. It is an impressive eighteenth-century mansion. As for the Reverend Mother's religion, there have always been Protestant ffrenchs, a sad relic of pre-Emancipation days when only Protestants could legally inherit property, the result being that the boys were generally reared as Protestants . . ."

' "To inherit the earth?"

' "And the girls as Catholics . . ."

' "To inherit heaven. In convents?"

'He trumped her ace. "To counter the evil effects of the French Revolution! And as for being locked up in what you so disrespectfully call a nunny boarding school the whole point of my splendid idea is that Anador would *not* reside in the convent. She would live in comfort and elegance with my two sisters, her Aunt Mon and her Aunt Mar, and be driven every day to the Sacré Cœur by the groom from ffrench Chase, or ride there on horseback. I do not suppose," he said smugly, "either of you knows why my ancestral home is called ffrench Chase? Or even what a Chase is. It is a large, unenclosed, privately owned tract of land reserved for the hunting of wild game. As in Chevy Chase."

'I was watching Ana. As all kids watch the eyes of elders at that age. I knew by the way her face lit up at the bit about me riding on horseback into the convent that, as we used afterwards say in the Sacré Cœur, my seal was doomed. An iceberg began to grow in my belly. She was off full cock about how I could learn French from the good sisters, mix with other well brought-up girls from the other Big Houses in the county, go to dances and parties there, learn to ride properly, follow the hunt, play hockey and tennis, learn deportment, all as if ffrench Chase were a seventeenth-century French *château*. All the same I remembered later how she also looked hard at Reggie and said, "She must, of course, be a *paying* guest."

'She always knew the real score.

'Once upon a time there was a stop-and-turn-back train from Dublin to Banagher once a day, a branch line off the main line out of Dublin to the West, laid down in the pre-automobile age merely because there was a distillery there, an occasional cattle fair and the first bridge across the Shannon after Lough Derg. Today there is no railway. I suppose less than a thousand people, men, women and children live in the town. A mere spot on an alluvial plain of hundreds of sodden square miles flat as a billiard table. Perfect for wandering caravans. Tinkers with their drifts of donkeys. Smoky fires visible miles and miles away.'

(As I looked down at her that day, lying on her back beside me on a grassy patch between the purple heather and the peaty earth, with far below us that tiny lake of Luggalaw, black and froth edged, her blue eyes full of the sky and of her childhood, her throat loaded with pearls, her great ear rings, her bangled wrists, I thought, 'Jesus! You *are* a Romany! A wild bird caged.' I said, 'It all sounds even more cut off than Castletownroche.' She wanted to know where that is. I said it was where I spent my childhood – 'But go on about your pigtail years.')

'I was met at the station by the ffrench Chase groom, a little, old retainer named Gussy with a tuft of white hair coming out of a hole in his cap, holding a hairy horse drawing a buggy smelling of fish, straw and manure. We drove out of Banagher, jog, walk, jog, walk to The Ancestral Home. We went in past a gate lodge, Gothic, peeling, smelling of woodsmoke, laurels and long ago, up a winding avenue rutted with pools of pink rain. The house was a whirl of rooks, shrieks of blackness against the sunset. Aunt Mon was on the steps. She could have been Gussy's mother. She wore a black woollen shawl. Behind her was Aunt Mar cowering from the cold inside the hall. There was enough space time between them and Reggie for a dozen ffrenchs. When they choked me with their smelly embraces I began to cry – it was such a joy after selfish, scratchy old Denise to be petted over and fussed over, and to look over their shoulders out through a front door so wide that you could drive a car through it and see woods, and fields and pink skies and imagine wild animals rustling or gypsies untackling under the trees before the night, instead of Ailesbury Road, long, clean, empty and silent, with its one bored Civic Guard.

'Aunt Mon and Aunt Mar lived like any provincial Russian landowner around 1830 except that he might own two thousand, or two hundred, serfs and they had only poor Gussy. They had no cook. No maid. A slop named Hannah came in twice a week. But they had a co-los-sal tea ready for me, they must have spent all day preparing it as if I was one of the starving children of . . . Where? India? Spain? Tibet was always good for a starve. Abyssinia? They stuffed me. "Tea", please notice, not dinner. They had sunk to all the simple, homely, rustic, unReggie-ish ways of the town of Banagher. I ate! Oh! I ate! *I ate!* It was the kind of meal that every child of ten dreams of. Cakes, cream, chocolate, brack, tarts, jam sandwich, boiled cake – Scrumptious! – hot scones, dropped scones, crumpets . . . When I could not eat another crumb they laid me out in a great armchair of cushions before a piled up fire of silently blazing peat and began the questions.

'As I sprawled there exhausted from eating, my tummy like a drum, tired after the journey – two changes of train – but deliberately keeping myself wide awake, I found at once that they had not laid eyes on Reggie for eighteen years – he had not even let them come to his wedding – apart from that one day when he and Ana "called" for half an hour. For twelve years they had been no farther out of Banagher than the market town of Birr, ten miles away. The last time they went to Dublin was 1910, on legal business. All this time I was casing the joint, it looked super but I had to be sure, this was where I might have to live for quite a while to come. That "while" actually stretched out, largely thanks to the war, to five gorgeous years. Before I half-crawled upstairs to my bedroom that night, I knew the ropes far better even than Ana, brilliant though she was, to have been able, sight unseen, to guess their poverty and loneliness. ("She must, of course, be a *paying* guest.") Within a week I was gone as wild as a duck in the reeds of the Shannon or a hare in its form in the woods of ffrench Chase. Reggie's memories of The Ancestral Home had become over the years pure fantasy. There may have been some basis for them when he was a boy, before the First World War, but now, with two of his older brothers killed in that war, three sisters married out of Ireland, father and mother gone, and a new war blasting away all over the world, the Irish Land Commission had taken over the arable land, and only the house remained. I never heard of anybody shooting anything there but rabbits. Even I, a child, could see that the timber was falling on top of itself from neglect. During the war the woods vanished, cut down for firewood. For the first time in my life I had friends.

'My pals were Molly S. Silkin, the postmaster's daughter, who had a vocabulary that would have made bits of Babel, whose father knew and freely divulged the most intimate secrets of the countryside, which she as gloatingly divulged to us, who did not fully understand them; or Una Pee Whelehan, the daughter of Jay Pee (P for Publican) to distinguish him from Jay Vee (V for Vet.). It was Una who first introduced me to whiskey, at the age of eleven – nothing in a baby bottle was safe on her father's shelves. Later I heard she ended up as a nun in an enclosed order, the Poor Clares, I believe. Or there were the two giant Fallon sisters, Florry and Fanny, who, by fourteen, were already powerful oarswomen, champion swimmers and divers. Nobody in Banagher spoke a word of French. The nuns were all farmers' daughters. All I ever rode was an old cast-iron Pierce bicycle, Irish made, vintage 1900. Of course, one whisper to Ana and she'd have shipped me down a first-class hunter within twenty-four hours. But was I to betray Una Pee, and Molly Ess-Ess, and big Florry and fat Fanny for a horse? It was bad enough that on really downpouring days Gussy and Aunty Mon and Aunty Mar insisted on my being driven to school in their dusty old buggy. I dare not refuse it – with Gussy standing out there in front of The Ancestral Home and Mon and Mar leaning out of their windows under umbrellas to see me off, and in the afternoon he would be at the convent door without fail to collect me back again, to the hooting cheers of Fanny and Florry and Una Pee and Molly Ess-Ess.'

'What did you do there?'

'Do? What do you mean by *do*? You mean what was I up to? I was up to the one joy of Banagher that stupid old Reggie never mentioned. I was in love. With the river. I swam it, rowed it, fished it, and before I left I shot over it and sailed it, in a Shannon One design, centre board, the kind with a single mast stuck through a hole in the forrard thwart. The Shannon was once, B.C., a god, the great highway of the west, a forest frontier, smelling its slow way, a dragon-sized worm, out to the Atlantic.'

(How right I had been to call her a Vikingess! It is what she should have been.)

'Why were they called Aunt Mon and Aunt Mar?'

'This was explained to me that first night. Aunt Mar said that Mar was short for Mariana in Tennyson's *Mariana in the Moated Grange*, the poor wight who was always looking out the window for her lover who never came and was always sighing *My life is dreary if He cometh not; I am aweary I would that I were dead*, which Aunty Mar, fat, bulby and old, said very mournfully, and then winked in order to make me laugh. Effortlessly I always did. Aunty Mon said Mon was short for Monica from *The Confessions of St Augustine*. Reggie said this was nonsense, that she was named Mona after an ancient Irish queen. I sometimes wondered afterwards were the poor old things sex-starved. Anyway Reggie thinking of protecting his dear little girl from the sexy jet sets of Gestadt or Eden Roc was out of his empty little mind. That first week-end was so warm that Gussy had to take the three of us on a circular tour to show me the country. Inside an hour I was shown three ancestral homes, that is the front gates of three ancestral homes tied up with barbed wire, in one of which there had been a murder, in another a suicide and the third had been burned sixty years back, all for something so mumbled that even at ten I knew it had to do with sex. Anthony Trollope lived for a while in Banagher and wrote a novel called *The Macdermots of Ballycloran*. Sex? Wild savage stuff! And small wonder. Do you know that dreary, empty flat country at all between Lough Ree and Lough Derg?'

'No. It does not sound very exciting.'

'Actually no! To me lovely. *So* lovely! I can still evoke that first Sunday in September. Soft and sunny after a night's rain. The air as sweet as water in a well. Trees heavy with fading leaves. Every sound dulled. A whole cloud-sky moving slowly from the west. Space. I had been long in city pent. If you look at any of my paintings you will find that they all have lots of air space. A watery land. Cold in winter. There is a poem about the ruins of Clonmacnoise, which is only ten miles down-river from Banagher as the crow flies. "In a quiet watered land, a land of roses, stands St Kieran's city fair." Every red-nosed winter Una Pee used to recite it as 'In a quiet watered land of noses'. The river winds so slowly that it has looped out scores of river-islands. In the winter, floods. Oxbow lakes in summer. On the Grand Canal the locks that raise or lower the level of the canal a bare foot or two are as much as fifteen miles apart. The roads straight as bullets. From my bedroom window I could see a couple of low hills off to the east and a couple of swellings away off to the south west. The locals call them mountains. But it was upward I used always look. At space.

'My aunts left me to myself. They loved to hear the smallest, latest thing I was up to, but they were far too proud ever to ask. They would suck every word I chose to tell. They were living through me. Exciting? No! The word is content. Even still whenever I am upset or cannot sleep I cozen myself back there, into the arms of the river, to a silence rustled only when my boat suckles the shallows, or brushes beside blown reeds, always *brown* reeds where there will be three feet of safe water above the mud. I am lying too low to see over the banks but I can smell the invisible meadows. Through my sleepy eyelashes the clouds float and I float off to sleep.

'I suppose I could say, I sometimes do say that my seven years in Banagher were the happiest years of my life. Not true. If it were true it would mean that I must have lived a very odd life ever since. I have experienced far deeper, far richer and far more varied happiness, but Banagher was my first unbroken happiness and anybody who wanted to make me forget it now after it is gone for ever would have to cut a lump out of my brain and halve my heart. And you ask me what did I *do* there!'

'Did you ever tell any of this in this way to Ana? Did she guess?'

'Guess? She knew! She visited. She was appalled. She said so. But when she saw the terror in my eyes she understood. Ana, as you well know, was a warm, passionate woman. And a very intelligent woman. A remarkable woman. If this was what I wanted, so be it. Just as if I did not want a horse, that was up to me, but if I would really like a sailing boat . . . I got it immediately. She met Una Pee, and Florry and Fanny, and Molly Ess-Ess and she said to me, "Poor things! Typical Irish. All up in the air. No future. They'll end as nuns." She was one-fourth right. I spent all my holidays with her. Because of the war we could not travel, and anyway I was not ripe for it, but after the war she took me everywhere. To Rome, Florence, Munich, Naples, Athens, Paris. To Bayreuth for the revived Wagner festival. To London – theatres, galleries, opera, films, the lot. When I was at Trinity she let me have a little flat to myself. And let me go afterwards to Paris to study painting. I am grateful to her for lots of things. But more than anything else I bless her for leaving me to ffrench Chase, and to the one street in Banagher that slopes up to the old Church of Ireland rectory, and to my river god. I was rich in Banagher.'

(Rich with a wealth of memories I can never have.)

'Did you never go back?'

'When Aunt Monnie died, thirteen years ago, I was in Paris. I flew back for the funeral and I wished I hadn't. Everybody I knew was married elsewhere or gone into a convent. Aunt Mar was bed-ridden. The house drained to the dregs of "ould dacency". Gussy crippled with arthritis. I'd read of old houses like that in Russia before the Revolution. Lost in the vast, remote Russian grass-lands. In the deep South in America. They are probably to be found everywhere. Killing themselves to keep themselves. Crumbling into shabbiness like an old hat. It was my year of fate because it was during that return to Ireland that I met Leslie. While we were on our honeymoon Aunt Mar died. Reggie inherited the place but he could not do much with it except install a houseman and keep the roof on. That did at least keep the house intact.'

'Why did he bother?'

She gave me a twisted, turned-down smile and said something about the way old homes tie ropes of ivy around people.

'I bothered. You do not know that when Reggie was drowned it descended to me. I was finally told last week that it is now fully and legally mine. I at once drove to Banagher to look at "my" house.' (Whereupon her eyes became moist.) 'At what Ana used derisively call The Ancestral Home. I am proud to own it. Although the rational side of me admits that one should never go back. That nobody can live early happiness twice over. But I shall get over that,' she said in her resolute way. 'I shall both forget and remember. I am always planning to put a few rooms into a decent condition and spend the summers there. It was my childhood. I am grateful to it. I love it! You must have grateful memories like that from your childhood?'

Had I? All I could summon up was a river I had once known somewhere, or had read about, a small tributary of her Great River flowing through my mind somewhere in Limerick. Or was it in Clare?

'I have nothing,' whispering, our breaths mingling, 'to match your river god, except a river that flows like yours into the Atlantic, strolling aimlessly, silent as a darting trout or dragonfly, but now and again as noisy as a salmon leap, sun splashing, the white bodies of boys diving, juvenile boastings, screams, challenges. Roads as straight and limestone white as yours, as many hundreds of square miles of flatness to the north and south, with a reed-bordered, mud-edged tidal estuary like your god's before he enters your sea.'

'I wish I knew you *then*!'

'How I wish I knew *you* then! Would you,' I asked, 'like us both to be as young as that again?'

I was aware of a tautening of her lower eyelid, a warning peer that I was coming to know well. She rolled on her back. A cloud rested in each eye. She decided angrily.

'No! Now is always better than then. The lovelier the past the more you have to pay for it. Why the hell must age always betray youth?'

This angered me. I could not afford to believe it. I told her she was talking rot. Lots of people are at least as happy old as young. If she had dreamed too hard or soft when she was a girl that was her look-out. Idealists are always cheated, and often soured. She had had her fun with her river god. Now she was turning him into a banana skin to make me fall wham on my backside. Vulnerable man-woman-girl she so often fell over her own feet and went wham, as she did that day on the hills when I rounded on her, and, her wet cheek against mine, our tide and river met in a bore of such violent passion – hers was of a shatteringly unexpected animal ferocity – that, since passion can notoriously be single and selfish and true love is always twofold, I remained unsure for months afterwards of the purity of my feelings for her. I became sure only on the day when, the least expected and least desired catalyst possible, her husband, killed every consideration in me except horror at seeing her dignity threatened by his venality.

I have the exact dates from various documents. Ana died on November 8th, 1970. The Anna Livia Gallery was opened seven months later, June 1971, with Anador, Leslie and me as directors, offering for sale six pieces of his sculpture, ten of Anador's pictures, about twenty paintings by five younger Irish artists and three impressively expensive items of European sculpture from Leslie's private collection: namely, a Giacometti bronze, a Modigliani bronze and a six-inch Degas wax model or *abbozzo* of a ballet dancer. The sale of any one of those last three items could, we knew, keep us afloat for a year even if we failed to sell another thing, and that is virtually what happened for the first two years, whereupon Leslie brought in another Giacometti and another Degas.

Now, everybody in the world who is over thirty must remember from his earlier years some moments of unmanning shame that sting every winter like an old soldier's wounds. I suffered one of those unforgettable wounds of shame the morning – it was Monday, August 7th, 1974, Horse Show week – I opened a letter from the client to whom I had so happily sold our first Degas the year before. He wrote that he had since moved to Washington and had shown his figurine to experts in the Smithsonian. They satisfied him that it was a fake: Degas never used that kind of material. What did I now propose to do about it? I remember looking slowly across the room, or across the salon as Leslie like to call it, at our new Degas. As I looked at it I thought that indeed no artist is so easy to imitate as the artist who has developed an idiosyncratic style. Anybody could now produce a plausible Picasso, Giacometti, Modigliani, Wyatt, Pollock or Dali. I looked at our second Giacometti. They say about such things: 'A schoolboy could do that!' He could not 'do' that, but an adept sculptor plausibly could imitate that.

I telephoned Leslie at once. He did what I expected him to do. He became emotional. He said furiously that he had been the one who had been deceived when he bought that Degas in Paris in the first instance. When I asked him what we should do about our American client he said it was a classical case of *caveat emptor*, and that if the man wanted to fight the case in the courts the directors of the gallery must stand shoulder to shoulder in mutual self-defence – meaning me and Anador.

That was a bad autumn. When I told Anador a great blush rose slowly from her jaw to her eyebrows like a glass filling, drops of sweat came out on her forehead, then her glass emptied, her face as quickly became grey as death. She wavered and had to sit down. In that instant she surrendered to what must have been a long suspected truth about Leslie. She said:

'There can be no court case. I have a small personal income. I will pay back the client.'

After a great deal of argufying she allowed me to pretend to Leslie that I was holding off our client: that way we might not wholly avoid painful scenes with him but we could reduce them.

'But will he believe us?' I asked.

She looked at me stonily.

'He believes whatever he finds most convenient to believe. The more important question is whether you can continue to work with him.'

I shook my head, took and held her hand.

'The important question is whether you can continue to live with him.'

She looked at me dully. (She always looked a little stupid when she was feeling either solemn or passionate.)

'I am lucky. My poor, dead aunts must be watching over me. I shall go to live at ffrench Chase until the autumn. Then I shall see.

She said it quite simply; she had, unlike her mother, no thespian art – too honest for that: all the same I had heard an invitation.

She took bodily possession of ffrench Chase that week. I drove her there with her red-headed child, Nana aged ten, who revelled in the whole camping-outness of the adventure, and I stayed with them for a week helping to get three rooms and the kitchen into some sort of decent order. It was such a glorious August that we suffered no discomfort. Nearby Ballinasloe and Birr were good towns in which to shop and eat. Returning thence at night, when the darkness concealed the tall old house's age and neglect except where our sweeping headlights exposed a stuffed window or an outhouse's crooked slates I used to feel that if she could live there, even intermittently, for ten years, she might make it into a real house, if never into a real home. But during that rapturous week neither of us looked ahead so far. Perhaps only the child may have dreamed some such dream.

She stayed there until the late autumn. It was never to become her second home but it was to be her constant retreat while her husband lived. She almost developed a blood relationship with it, partly because of the ffrench connection, partly because she had been so happy there when she had been a schoolgirl. It was that autumn she decided to send Nana to the same school. I had some of my happiest days in the uncosy old house.

Happy? 'Happier then?' asked Mr Bloom, speaking for all mankind. 'Happier now?' I still have the love letter I left her on the night of my departure that first August when we were at the peak of our mutual adoration. It is an enchanting letter and she was enchanted by it.

> My beloved, you will find this little letter when you retire to bed tonight, folded in four on your pillow in 'our' room, and you will smile at it won't you? I long for that smile from those dear, beautiful eyes that have wept so many tears. Sleep, my own dear Anador. Dream that I love you. Dream that I am lying at your feet. Dream that you are my love. Dream that I cannot exist without you. Dream that I am thinking of you. Dream even that I am writing to you, and that before you fell asleep you found this little letter and woke to find your dream come true, I kiss your tiny feet and your great eyes. Your adoring Beebee.

I am a cautious lover, never putting an address on the page, the name of the beloved, or my own. She might well be enchanted by it – it was written by Victor Hugo to his life-long mistress Juliette Drouet. I remembered the gist of it from a book I used to own in my old life, *Love Letters from Many Lands*. After all, I thought, it is the spirit of a letter that matters. I could never hope to write so well. Later I read about Balzac that he often sent his women love letters that he took from his own novels, and sure enough when I read his *Louis Lambert* there was one such. I sent it at once to my dear Anador. And there is another, also by Hugo, that has later to come back into my possession. It still remains tender and intimate even though I adapted it to a certain local occasion to give her a special meed of pleasure:

> My love, I am still shaken by the memory of last night in Moran's Imperial Hotel in Kilkenny when I, Beebee, again became the happiest and proudest man in the world. I will confess to you that until then I had not felt to the full the joy of loving you and being loved by you in return. This letter and envelope will appear to be a communication from the Irish Inland Revenue Commissioners, which is fitting since it really and truly is the equivalent of a legal statement on the present rich state of my heart. This document will accordingly hold valid for the whole of my mortal life. Any day, any hour, any minute that you choose to present this document to me I hereby solemnly promise to surrender the aforesaid heart in the condition in which it now is at this glorious hour filled with one love only, your love, and with thoughts of one person only, you. Signed at Dublin, this day, at 4 p.m., the 14th July, 1878.

I signed it 'B.B.' and added the following, 'As witness to this document I hereby add one thousand kisses.'

I failed to change the year to 1978 from its original date. She teased me about it. 'Just a century out!' I laughed. 'It makes our union a century longer,' at which we started kissing all over again.

How happy we both were in those years!

In this manner I completed the quartet: Leslie Longfield, Anador Longfield, Des Moran and Bob Younger – three men once in fief to her mother, now in fief to her daughter as respectively husband, father and lover. Each of us would, I may suppose, have at some time or other asked himself the same question about the others in a different way: the other two, 'Like mother like daughter?'; the priest, 'Thank God he is too old for sex, the old lecher, though he may not look it?'; I, 'Used she once to cry on Leslie's shoulder?' – each ready to question the others' loyalty to her, yet allowing every such flux of jealousy to melt in the mutual compassion of fellow prisoners.

It would have been hard for me not to realize and easy for me to guess how much Des Moran must have suffered for years at not being able to watch his child grow: first in FitzWilliam Square, a 'banister child' whom at least on one visit – her nanny Denise's memory – he would have seen looking down at him through the well of the stairs if only he had looked up; separated from her by his war years in France; then by Africa, Italy, Germany, while she was flowering as grossly as any tinker's child beside the Shannon. Still, the war may have been a kind of balm too. She and her Shannon would soak into the desert, dry in the ghastly heat of Sicily, be forgotten in the slow slog north through Taranto, Brindisi, Bari, the white dust that would cloud every miserable, battered, stinking village on the bloody crawl to Rome. That would be in 1943, she twelving, he passing middle age, more than half way to his biblical three score and ten. He would live longer, get more glimpses of her, yet never recoup her lovely, ignorant years in Banagher. She would be just as elusive when rising out of that first girlhood to exchange her reedy, lake-wide, duck-whispering river for Dublin's black-walled rivulet, Banagher's one bridge for crowded city bridges and streets, her rustic convent of the Sacred Heart for classical Dublin's Trinity College with its perpetual gaggle of noisy young men and women. He would see nothing at all of her in London, Paris, London again. He and I had good reason to be jealous of Leslie Longfield who for years had possessed all of her.

As for him, it was only after I fell in love with his wife that he could have had more than a purely professional interest for me, as in the days when I was an art-reporter. (I never called myself an art-critic.) In fact Anador had been my mistress for some ten years before, one July day in London, on some journalistic business, I was reminded of him in the British Museum by a smallish Greek statuette or monument called a double Herma or Hermes. It depicted two antithetical heads poll to poll, possibly, as I later gathered, Aphrodite or Venus backed by Hermes or Mercury, that handsome, ankle-winged, cunning, contriving, thriving, trading rascally message-boy of the gods. This pair, I also gathered, had produced Hermaphroditos. Staring at that figure of opposites conjoined I saw again Longfield's tidy, lithe, aggressive, muscular Jimmy Cagney figure, a light-weight boxer with the dreamy left eye of the artist and a sharp fleck of malice blinking aggressively in his right eye. (It is the right eye that always gives away a man's operative character; the left is the unchallenging, sociable, public eye. I never look at it.) Standing before the male face of that Herma it occurred to me that this might be exactly the side of Les Longfield – contriving, circumspect, wordly-wise, almost too proficient – that had drawn into his web my trustful, warm, unsuspecting Anador, totally unworldly, but oh! so avid to be a woman of the world. 'You will look after me?' I could imagine her saying it to him in one of her more defenceless moments, and to be fair to him so he did, on his own ultimately unbearable terms and I have also no doubt, enjoyed doing it, seeing himself as hero of the battle of *Ars Contra Mundum*. Yet, he did have that other side of him, the left-eye-side; sensitive, emotional, nervy, porcupinish, vulnerable and on occasion as near to tears as his wife. (Both sides had come out in the affair of the Gallery scandal.) A split? Cloven? Twins? Was it in this manner also that Anador excited me? If so what split in me did she betoken? Who could tell me? I went to the telephone, rang Ashley Place and invited the Monsignore to dine with me that night. Happily he was free.

The Charlotte–Percy Street area, like the whole region north of Soho, is at its most agreeable for dinner on Saturday in midsummer, the sky whiter, the place quieter, the daylight longer, offering if one reserves a window seat a cool feel of *plein air* café life. My guest was in perfect harmony, strikingly so, with his great height, his grey-streaked temples, his brilliant grey eyes still black lashed, the triangle of reddish-purple glowing under his Roman collar, his American-type cuffs and gold links gleaming in the pink lamplight, so that even the antique waiter who tended us was enchanted to have a client who had a bit of the 'class' that had, so long ago, first made his restaurant famous.

This was not, by any means, my first meeting with Des Moran since our Ana died. So far as I knew he had never omitted, during his familial visits to Dublin to hail me at the very least on the telephone; more likely – while Anador still lived next door – for an unannounced late night visit to Rosmeen Park after he had visited her, when we would talk and drink until the early hours of the morning – he hated sleep, perhaps feared its dreams? Or – after she moved over to Ailesbury Road – we might discuss a bottle of wine together over a dinner in town. This London evening was part of that sustained, if uneven rapport which, over the years, had developed its own ritual. First, there would be polite enquiries about everybody's health; then Dublin gossip and Westminster gossip; political affairs or religious affairs ('How is your theology these days? Tory, Liberal, Labour, Communist, Curia?') Not until these matters had been attended to, the second bottle of wine broached, the pair of us unbuttoned and unburthening, would I hear the regular sideward reference to Anador, and deflect it yet once again with something of his own tactful obliquity. Then finally, would come his usual direct question: 'How about her marriage to Leslie? How's that doing?' a bluntness that always touched me, and far from tenderly – not because my answer was always the same ambiguous affirmative, and not because I knew that it always would be so, but because I had never dared to be so blunt with her. Fear of her answer? Foreknowledge of it? Not entirely either – a memory, rather, of my solitary approach to Ana about our possible marriage:

'Why on earth,' I had said that day to her, 'do you continue to put up with a marriage that you so clearly find unsatisfactory? You are in love with me! You are not in love with Reggie!'

The reply had come instantaneously, not cruelly but with the certainty of somebody who had been calmly adding it up.

'He is a base.'

In that sense she was wise. It is why women marry.

As I once reassured my Monsignore about Anador's marriage I had to stop myself from striking the table with my fist, furious at not having hit earlier on an association that I saw blindingly at that moment only because I had by chance been re-reading my favourite Henry James, *The Wings of the Dove*. As I recalled it, I felt a secret complicity with the most painful of the various sub-implications of James's ironic title, that which describes his wealthy, dove-like, dying heroine as 'an angel with a thumping bank account' and speaks of her 'bejewelled wings'. My mental association was with Ana's scornful remark about Reggie – I do not say against Reggie because most of her remarks on that quarter were contra rather than pro – after she presented him with the jewel of a baby daughter. She had said, with a sniff, 'He gave me the pearls'. Which she was nevertheless pleased to wear and which Anador duly wore in her turn. Leslie a base? Certainly it had been some sort of *mariage de raison*.

Des received the answer to his ritual question with a sanguine elevation of his glass and I have no doubt that he would as usual have relaxed for the remainder of the evening into his regular blend of impersonal ideas and personal gossip if the secret reason for my dinner invitation, together with that image of empearled doves – an elegant specimen of those luxuries was throating in contralto at the table next to ours – had not spurred me to approach the matter by sounding the contrapuntal masculine note on marriage. As I matched his vinous elevation I said that we were both men of the world and unguardedly went on:

'After all, Des, your Leslie is not the worst possible son-in-law. He *is* a base. He does provide! In fact I gather he has been selling well recently, especially in the United States. As we say in Ireland of a good husband, he keeps bread in the bin. You agree?'

I must give *Il Monsignore* his due: his reactions were instantaneous.

Des: (*Calmly twirling his glass.*) '*My* Leslie?' I was very interested the other day in the way *my* Leslie talked about *your* Jimmy.

Me: But my brother Jimmy died years ago. In '65 actually.

Des: (*Calmly.*) He said your *son* Jimmy. Who called himself 'The Emigrant Boy'.

Me: (*Blacked out by that word 'son' the way you can be by a fall, or a car crash, waking, recovering, but hazy.*) My son? This is interesting. How did he meet him? Where? When?

Des: When he was showing some of his sculpture in a four-man Irish show in Philadelphia two weeks ago. You know the way Irish Americans follow the flag. After the show, this grey-haired man came up to him, said his name was Jimmy Younger and asked him if he had ever heard of an Irish journalist named Robert Bernard Younger. Des said you used to be his next-door neighbour. At this the man said the most extraordinary thing, he said 'I think he could be my father.' I 'think'?

Me: I see. (*I could see also that Des was peering closely at me.*)

Des: Les didn't know you had a son. No more did I. What tickled Les was that the man looked old enough to be *your* father.

Me: (*Trying to scramble from my knees.*) America takes it out of them.

Des: I am surprised that Les didn't mention it to you. Or did Anador?

Me: The Longfields live further away from me now.

Des: Your son did not write to you about this meeting?

Me: (*He could not hide his eye of a bird, head cocked, watching for the least stir of a worm under the grass. I dared not risk a second trap.*) I am not the best correspondent in the world.

Des: Les felt sorry for the man, he seemed so confused. Talked one minute about his father having fought in the Rising of 1916. That would be either you or your older brother would it not? Were you even alive then? Or more than a boy? The next minute he seemed to be suggesting that he himself was born in 1916! Then he talked about being sent from London to Ireland at the age of four for the duration of the war. Did you engender a lot of children in your burning youth, B.B.? Or has this chap a lot of fathers?

My mind ran to Ana. Had I kept this even from her? I could not have kept anything from her! Had she kept it even from me? She well could – mistress of a reticence that we had consciously respected the more to respect one another, a reticence for which I was now paying.

Des: You're a very secretive chap, B.B., you never even told me you were married. Was there a divorce?
Me: She was a victim of the Blitz. 1941. First blinded and maimed, then died.
Des: I *am* sorry.
Me: I could blame myself about the boy. But what could I do?
Des: (*Relenting.*) Families breaking up? It is one of the saddest and commonest tragedies of war. I gathered the boy was lucky to have somebody – Your eldest brother Stephen? – in the United States to sponsor him after the war. Well, your son apparently has a son himself now, named Bob after yourself. Bob the second. Bob two. Bob you.

Stephen? A third brother? That Des and Les had had a long session on me I knew when he leaned across and patted my arm. I was still in shock. A bomb had exploded behind me. It was as well that our old waiter came between us just then because my reaction to his kindly pat was rage. He had pulled the pin out of that Mill's bomb just to watch the effect on me. By the time the old waiter had gone my wasps were down to a neutral humming. I did a lightning calculation.

Me: I do think it bad of Les not to have told me.
Des: (*Slyly, innocently – the two faces are not dissimilar.*) Perhaps because there was so little to tell you that you did not already know?

After a pause during which I tried to face in his eyes a dozen whos, whys, hows he said, 'Say it, old man!'

Old man, old chap, old boy, old chum? How bloody English! Say what? You spy! Say, 'I remember nothing'? Say, 'Old man, what you don't know is that I have bartered my memory for a Faustian youth'? And I wondered, 'Or do you? Do you know more? Guess everything?'

Me: Des, it sounds like another life. I had almost begun to forget it. The truth is . . . that child . . . of course . . .

I have put down the word: *unburthening*. There is suppression and confession. One involves the other as lies do truth. Priests, who can absolve others but not themselves, confess to other priests. We all need somebody in whom to confide our lies. Love's release. Fear's victim. All the rest is mere cognisance. 'Yes, I knew of him/her.' One can only be free as the air by unballasting. Looking out of the open window across pallid Charlotte Street at a closed stationer's shop, a Greek restaurant, sidewards towards where Bertorelli's used to be at a heap of rubbish bins waiting for the morning, I had to confide in him. He wanted me to. It was his vocation. Anyway what he had said about a son and a wife had created in me as well as fear and suspicion a deep, sad yearning like a nostalgic Count Basie fall out, or some old, high wailing Gershwin number played straight on the tenor sax:

Me: You see, Des, the dates were against us. I got married in 1930. Right? The year, 1930, was our year of fate. Mine as well as yours. Here's to it! (*The two elderly gentlemen at the window tables raise their glasses, exchanging sympathetic smiles.*) He was our first, and as it proved, our only child. God sent him in '36. Right? We doted on him. Dear Christabel and I. God rest her. The war. The bombs. Her poor, dear eyes. An absurdly beautiful baby. I insisted on naming him after me. Bobby. Bob Two. *Where did you come from baby dear? Out of the everywhere into the here*. 'Back of the North Wind?' Fair to begin with, brunette later, great eyelashes dusting his cheeks, hair curled. I have many a time and oft looked at old photographs of him and his mother. He took after her. When he was nearly five his mother went completely blind. She was never to see him again. *Thou cam'st a little baby thing that made a woman cry*. She lingered only a couple of years. My brother in Dublin said, 'Send the kid over here!' Imagine my feelings. But what else could I do? I visited him in Ireland every single year. The war ended. I could not rear him. My brother Stephen, as you heard, took him. I am not pitying myself, but it is all over now, I am an old Tithonus, an old Lear, a blind Tiresias, I can be frank with you now about that wild, cheering V.E. night when I met Ana ffrench again beside the fountains in Trafalgar Square. We were all drunk, I was a widower, it was fifteen years after the Baie des Anges. Did that man in Philadelphia talk about his mother to Leslie? Would you like a brandy, Des? Would you prefer a Benedictine?

Des: Thanks. Both. I rather think he did mention her name. You must ask Leslie. I suspect that your son ended by regarding your brother Stephen and his wife as his parents, and America as his country. I am sure Les will tell you all about him when he gets around to it.

Me: I am sure he will.

Des: Les did say that this man remembered London not at all but Ireland quite well. There was mention of a famous Younger Conference after the war when you three brothers foregathered in Dublin to decide what to do with him.

(I knew that voice so well, I was allowed from my childhood to remember that voice, the sympathetic, probing detachment of my father confessor. I kicked for touch.)

Me: Des! I had no future, no home to offer the kid. I remember my brother James laughing to me at that meeting after the war, 'Bob, when that child grows up what are you going to do with him? He could not bring even a male friend into that two-roomed flat of yours.'

Des: (*Dryly*.) Especially since you and Ana had by then come together again?

Me: (*Passionately*.) Dammit, Des, I was no longer young.

Des: (*Smiling. Hot and bloody Africa, Sicily and Italy lay behind that cool smile*.) Younger's last choice? A second life? Or a son?

Thoughtfully sipping his brandy he looked across the dusty, summer street to the waiting rubbish bins and the black plastic bags. A marmalade cat nosing amongst them. Upstairs in a wide open window a young man in a white chef's hat and white jacket taking a breath of London's cool night air. Our window, too, was open. Des waved an idle palm to the man and the man idly waved back. Des looked at the cat.

Des: When cats stop having kittens do they think, 'I'm getting old'? To think that that handsome daughter of mine is now turned fifty! Handsome? Well, what do you think? Sometimes very? Sometimes not at all? Perhaps you think she is a beauty? (*Needling me? Just how much does the bastard know about Anador and me?*) And what character she has developed! A splendidly masterful woman. Very like our Ana, don't you agree?
Me: (*Flattering him.*) Children take after masterful parents.

Immediately I said it I realised that one of Ana's attractions for me had been her bossiness. Anador is capable of being bossy too if I did not stand up to her. Intense, scornful, bossy, super-sensitive.

Des: Time flies and its effects elude us. Why, by the way, did you bring up Leslie earlier in the evening? *My* son-in-law as you called him.
Me: (*At last seizing my chance to ask my question.*) I just happened to begin to wonder recently about Anador's attraction for such different kinds of people.
Des: (*Laugh.*) Such as yourself?
Me: (*Laugh.*) I am naturally interested in her mother's daughter. What was her attraction for Leslie?
Des: (*Grunt.*) Her attraction for everyone is her bodily vigour and her mental delicacy. Did you ever watch her when she is painting those delicate fantasies of hers? I did once. She did not know I was watching her. I saw beads of sweat gather on her forehead. That woman paints her dreams the way a stone-cutter cuts. (*He sniffs rudely.*) Not at all the way her husband works. He is not a sculptor. She is. He is an interior decorator. Too light. Too graceful. An attractive boy. A weak character. He drinks far too much. And he is calculating. I distrust his honesty. Has he any?

I did not rise to his fly. He knew all about Leslie.

After we parted and as I walked, absorbed, unseeing, unhearing, through Soho's dirty dimness, across the blare and brightness of Piccadilly, down past Shakespeare's statue in Leicester Square and the National Portrait Gallery towards my hotel on the Strand I was reassessing. Another brother? Named Stephen. A son. And again the ghost of Christabel Lee. I had long become inured to my blankness about her – five completely happy years with Ana, five alone, those past ten tumultuous years with Anador, so much else interwoven. A son, mine and not mine? Living, married, with a son of his own named after me? A Bob to whom I am an old, mentioned grandfather, probably dead? They must all once have had a curiosity about me. Yet, how much had this resurrected son whom Leslie met really known about a father he could hardly, if at all, remember? Des had said it. He remembered London, meaning me, not at all, but Ireland, meaning J.J., Bridget, his virtual stepmother, quite well. Had I never written to him later, as he grew up in America? Or had they told me not to? If he were to travel to Dublin now in search of me what more could we tell one another than the brief little we must once have known, the so very, very little compared to what he knew of his American life, what I know of Ana and me, Ana and Reggie, Ana and Leslie, Ana and my spying Monsignor, Anador now and me.

I must keep on my guard with Des. He is fond of me, but he distrusts me. He will, in his theological detachment, his humane compassion, tolerate my hanging around his daughter for as long as he is assured that her marriage is not in jeopardy. If once that marriage bond, to me now contemptible, lying, absurd were seen to be in danger from me I might at once expect thugee treatment, the garotte, the cudgel that twists it tighter and tighter about the throat.

I reached Trafalgar Square, descended to the nearest fountain and was encouraged by the smile of a certain familiar star in its still water to smile back in turn at the heavens, back too to my night's guest hopelessly asserting Heaven against Love. And yet I had to admire his courage. He could only assert. I knew. His Christian God had given him no proofs. My pagan gods had. He was gambling that when he met his end his God would not have another last trump up His sleeve. I knew that I would never die. I would simply vanish.

I must make no bones about him, chewing him like a starving dog over a dry bone. He liked me and he spied on me but he did not strike until the end and that and then, I am sure, between a sigh for a friend and a laugh of victory over his friend's devil. I am not sure when precisely first he began to suspect my secret, probably that afternoon of Ana's final Horse Show party, at the sight of an ageing man who had supposititiously lost his sex as he had lost his religion – by not practising either – casting goat's eyes at his statuesque daughter. It would have been his mystical eye, his vocational eye that would have stripped me, seen me as in some form or another a slave of Satan. A man of reason would have baulked at so tall a fence. The man of God would have soared over a thing so commonplace as a compound of heaven and hell. After all I remember poor old little Pope Paul VI on the radio long ago telling the world that the Devil was daily walking up and down the earth. Waving his tail? And did not that exquisite mind, John Henry Cardinal Newman, believe in flying angels? Only if you believe in God can you believe in Satan.

It is of the essence of the modern novel that the writer is an interpreter not a recorder – anybody may record – and we who attend to him are collaborators in his guessing and hinting game. I who am neither author nor audience, who am the main character, who was so to speak there, I know. I do not know when he began the hunt but I do know a couple of the approaches that took him over the last fence.

One of them was the trivial affair of Anador's night-gown. This was a night-gown that she tried to buy at Harrods one morning about a year after that dinner with Des in Charlotte Street when she and I were on a jaunt together in London. She was still in full bloom, around fifty-four, not one of her great pink petals yet gone with the wind that flings roses riotously etc.; though to a sharp eye hers were a trifle wide and dishevelled, proposing that age when another older woman may enviously say, 'Darling, you look wonderful, who is your surgeon?'

I could have told them her secret. It was her mother's trick – though not played at all so well – of treating life as theatre. The Russians were always good at it. It is a common Irish gift. The Germans know it but always ham it. The Americans sell it canned: supermarket stuff. The English disapprove of it on moral grounds. The Italians excel at it, always parading before their mirrors, cutting a fine dash. It is a gift that can produce the most noble actions, the most heroic sacrifices and the most frightful folly, but it does keep one young. Not that, even so late in our story, I clearly saw Anador in this way apart from intuiting that the most common source of her frequent freshets of tears was her sense of dramatic frustration whenever life refused to play. It could be why she still liked to paint her handsome pictures of disaster – the artist in her still realistically saluting the enemy of her dreams. It took the night-gown incident to make me understand all this – not that it made me love her any the less, indeed, it may even have made me love her more, if less often.

She had a one o'clock appointment for a lone luncheon with the Monsignor – I was naturally not supposed to be in London at all – which allowed her time to drag me with her around noon to Harrods. It was only when we got there that she explained that she wished to buy a night-gown. I at once felt cross with her, then yokelishly embarrassed, then more cross with myself for feeling embarrassed, and still further embarrassed by the thought that if she had been glowingly young and slim I might have enjoyed those moments when she coyly held up another and yet another pinkish, greenish, midnight, buttercup, chiffonish wisp by its shoulder ribbons against her great Viking body, glancing smilingly for approval from the impassive saleswoman to me, who only became fully aware of the depths of my discomfort when I heard myself furiously whispering to her between those pinkish flimsy folds, 'You know you have no waist!'

The next instant the saleswoman on turning back to us with a wildly scarlet gown found her customer weeping in a hiccuping wail, clutching up her bag and fleeing blindly before me through the crowds like a kleptomaniac pursued by a house detective. At the door she climbed into a cab that had just relinquished a customer, banged the door in my face, and was whirled off to Hyde Park and her lunch at the Serpentine restaurant. Des always tried to do her proud, and the Serpentine is a restaurant that goes down well with all teenagers, especially at mid-term.

When she returned to our hotel in the afternoon her storm had subsided. No, he had not mentioned me. But I observed that old Eagle Eye had nevertheless been on my tracks again – he had probably observed something of her residual perturbation, and become proportionately suspicious:

'Did you know, I never did, that the old boy is my godfather? Anyway he has just told me so. Surely Ana would have told me so. Do you suppose he is lying? But why? Has he a crush on me? He asked me twice was I troubled about anything. Do you suppose he meant sin? Or did he mean money? Was I well? *Quite* well? We talked a lot about Dublin. You? No, but without his asking me I did mention that I had not seen you for quite a long while. That may have been a bit of a mistake because when I said that our Nana saw you once or twice in the Bailey pub he looked a bit crookedly at either me or the pub. He straightaway began to probe me a lot about Nana. Come to think of it, it *was* a bit of a third degree. Though a godfather may, I presume, have a grandgod-daughter. I had to remind him that she is still a mere Trinity student. "Sweet Seventeen".'

Here she laughed her hearty Irish laugh, put on a rural Banagher Irish accent.

'He r-r-rumbled like an ould volcano! Rrrumbled and grrumbled. "She looks more like twenty-three. Damned handsome with that red hair of hers. Buxom. Vigorous. Gay. Fling her cap over the moon while you'd be looking about you. You will want to watch that girl, Anador. It is a very dangerous age. Girl? She is a woman. Nowadays girls are nubile even in these cold climates at twelve!" I love old Des when he starts blowing off. And I can tell you this – old as he is he can be very attractive sometimes!'

I grumbled that certain other ladies might agree with her if they were still alive. Secretly I was thinking that if he had been observing Nana Longfield with disapproval I ought to have a look at the girl.

By chance I saw her in the street a month later coming from a lecture at Trinity. She was laughingly saying goodbye to a young man, and even if I had never known her – and I had so far known her only as anybody may 'know' the daughter of a house he visits – I would have looked admiringly at that laughing head, a fawny paprika expressive of flaming youth. I walked on, she caught up with me, passed me by. I kept pace with her for the length of Lower Grafton Street, past the Provost's House to where the WAIT sign of the traffic lights halted her. She had nothing of her mother's virility, or of her grandmother's elegance. She was broad of hip, heavy of shoulder, firm of calf, maternal rather than youthful as she stood at her relaxed ease, her hand and weight on her right leg, giving out by that casual equilibrium a sense of open easiness, frankness, *disinvoltura*. I was on the point of asking her – it was just gone noon – to join me for a sandwich and a coffee or beer in Davy Byrne's, but I decided against it. It was one thing to be drawn, as I had been by Ana, first in my forties, again in my sixties, to a woman of my own age; or to impose myself on a grown woman as I had done in my fifties on Anador in her forties. It would be a very different matter to become the laughing-stock of a university student of seventeen.

All the same that first delighting image clung, even though (whenever I again saw her in Ailesbury Road) I defensively adopted the attitude that when Des spoke of her as buxom he would have more accurately said bottomy. But everybody's vocabulary veers and hauls before the winds of feeling, so that while I would – at that stage of my interest in her – not have demurred at the word 'fat' (once I heard unmoved a woman, a very thin woman, speak of her as 'gross') – I presently began to think of her lavish flesh in terms of the torsos and limbs of Rubens or Tintoretto. In like manner while I was still pretending to be merely amused by her I would not have minded if I had overheard somebody saying she was tow-coloured, carroty or ginger. As the seasons passed however and I took notice of the extraordinary blue of her eyes – the irises of most blue eyes are, like the blue plume of the *fleur de lis*, modified by fleckings, whereas hers are blue to the horizon – I found myself transported by the contrast between their inexorable blueness and the glow above it. Sunset? Fiery? Russet? Gold? Autumnal? How could bare words cope with what had ultimately become for me the symbol of an allure beyond definition? As desire had already transformed her weight into wealth, her eyes and hair now became twin metaphors for the powerful yet graceful Maillolesque peasantry of the meadows, blue streams, clouds, thyme, mint, fennel of Roussillon, with the great peaks of the oriental Pyrenees lifted against the purest azure sky, vibrant with sun, life, energy. When, later, I confessed this fantasy to her how she laughed at me! She was not at all like that – her joy was to lie on a sofa and be fed cream-filled chocolates; which joke, I decided or hoped, was just her love-born metaphor. Both our minds were playing juggler's tricks with unacknowledged passion.

The game I went on playing with her until she was well into her twentieth year proved to be no joke. Though it was a game that our passions went on happily playing with us both. Forty. Twenty. We acted out the parts of wicked man and innocent girl courteously, delicately, dangerously, Old Man wryly admiring. Unattainable Virgin happily basking in her security, amused to discard her normal suspicion, dubiety, hesitations, cautions. Eve may have been like that. Nothing to fear! And Adam right about the sequel. What young woman in Eve's circumstance would not have tempted? What man not encourage her to tempt? Besides, I could fairly describe my circumstances as extenuating. The word means finely woven, diminished, narrowed, thinned down, as my circumstances certainly were whenever her mother was in the flat above us. Only after dusk could I safely visit the one unseen by t'other. Even so

Anador once caught me emerging from Nana's door. I said I was merely handing in a promised book. When promised? What book? Another quarrel.

As I look out of my Rosmeen window now I think my circumstances were like this gauzy fog which blurs everything distant and lends excitement to everything close up. Time, my tyrant and slave, was filling her sails as well as mine. She had always sworn that as soon as ever she could, she would abandon Dublin for London or Paris as her mummy had done before her. (It was comical and charming to hear this bursting young woman call her stately mother 'mummy'.) But once my amazon tasted Paris or London? I knew the old song, *How can we keep 'em down on the farm once they've seen gay Paree?* On the other hand our converging parallel lines meant that in the long run time was on my side, provided that I saw to it that when she did take off she would carry with her from me no such sounds, smells or memories of the dreary Irish boglands as had inoculated her 'mummy' decades ago.

'She shall,' I decided, 'remember me as her first intimation of the great, wide world.'

Then a few visits to her in London or Paris and . . .

I do not believe that I had ever thought as brazenly as this in my lost youth, not because I remember – Damn it, I remember so little that *is* or might be worth remembering! – but because I still feel certain twinges, certain aches intimating unknown chances that I muffed, certain might-have-beens of the sort that make young people blush for rage at three o'clock in the morning and old men cry, 'O God! If I could only live that all over again!' Well? Well! How did I behave this time? Did I carry it off with the skill of a young Frenchman? Or not? I think I behaved just as well, that is if it be agreed that every Frenchman is a rationalist about everything except his erotic emotions and as big a muff as everybody else about these. I forethought carefully. I foreplanned. And I buggered it all up. I thought, for example, that it would be clever to use the great gap between our ages as a provocative challenge. And so it might have been if she had not suddenly chosen to stop being a girl. She grew as slim as her bone structure would allow; her neck rose arrogantly from her shoulders; she achieved height and dignity; immanent womanhood, calm assurance breasted her bud. I was outflanked. I had no time to remanoeuvre.

I first observed these dismayingly delightful changes in her at a garden party in Ailesbury Road that Anador and Leslie insisted she must have to celebrate her coming-of-age a week before on Midsummer Day – it virtually coincided with Anador's fifty-fifth birthday. I was formally invited. So, of course, was our *éminence grise*. Nana resisted the whole idea fiercely, gave in only because Anador wept the usual floods, then, cursing obscenely, put on a long green frock ('I feel like a bloody frog in this rig-out!') and assumed a fat-girl gaucherie that, she guessed, would give a sentimental pleasure to the older guests and vastly entertain her younger friends. Her act did not last long. As her guests passed on to be welcomed by her father and mother she gradually tired of it. Her right hand behind her waist clasped around the arm of the left, her rosy head wheeling restlessly, slowly on her high neck, her blue-blue eyes glinting, she became an athlete poised before the race, balancing easily from foot to foot, ready to greet the world, eager not merely to engage another country but to challenge all life. It was one of the most touching and exhilarating transformations I have ever seen, a girl taking final command of herself as a woman.

'Ah, yes,' Monsignor Des sighed, following my admiring glance. 'Youth! Youth! Eighteen at last! Come of age!'

He looked even more distinguished than ever, those grey wings of hair, his height unabated, carrying a silver-headed walking-stick, and he was the only clergyman I have ever met who in his old age adopted a monocle. He was to outlive Leslie only by a year, as Leslie was to leave us six months after that party.

'A godchild lost,' he grinned. 'A godwoman found. How is your lumbago?'

I had months back complained of an imaginary lumbago, also of a weak heart and an enlarged prostate.

'I bear with it. I have to watch the old ticker pretty carefully too. No excitement. Not much liquor. And you?'

'Less m.p.h. every day. A stately figure is she not?'

'Amazingly so! For one so young. It is what is so wonderful about her.'

He glinted sharply. His voice edged.

'I was referring to Anador in case you have in your dotage forgotten her name. Ana's child. The mother of that girl Nana.'

Still spying? Smelling brimstone? On whose behalf now?

It was, I recall, a Tuesday, sunny and warm, a pet June day. Within two months or so she would have left Dublin. I could not take my eyes off her. His Reverence let me look and then he pulled the trigger.

'Poor old Leslie is for it, he won't last a year.'

It was not his words but his sheriff's voice that made me look at him.

'You seem to be very sure of it.'

'Anador confides in me.'

(Did he stress the 'me'?)

'What?'

'Leukaemia.'

His eye held me. If anybody asked me before that moment whether an eye can hold one I would have said, 'A journalist's verb'. After that frightening moment I knew what it is to be instantaneously held, stopped dead, immobilised by terror as if, at night on a dark and apparently empty road, one felt an invisible figure stepping alongside and stopped, unable to stir. I knew what he was about to say. He said it:

'She will be a widow within a year. She could marry you then. She is only fifty-five.'

I moved away from him rapidly.

God, Jehovah, Jupiter, the Almighty Father, ruling all things, all people. *Only* fifty-five? In a party of young who cared for neither gods nor fathers! He kept trailing me. Even as I dodged him I caught the phrases from the conspiratorial side of his mouth. 'Very attractive still.' Or, 'Take good care of a man, yeh know.' And once, to my rage, 'Like to like for God's sake!'

With what joy I found Nana floating up to me with, 'For God's sake keep that bloody old sky-pilot off me, I think he wants me to enter an enclosed order of nuns! Is he nutty?' Later I saw Anador listening to him with an impenetrable smile. I did not dare to engage Nana further. I watched her from a distance, noting with pride that she was always surrounded by the largest group of merry young. I suppose it was, in their eyes, a 'smashing' party; plenty of champagne, the waiters waltzing around them with salvered glasses of it, though I did at one point think that Ana ffrench would have done it so much better; but then Ana ffrench had always commanded a bigger overdraft.

'Mind you,' from the monocle at my right ear, 'Leslie was never what you might call a . . .'

I gave him my shoulder, caught Anador's smile twenty yards across the grass. I walked over to her still noble figure.

'Enjoying yourself, Mr Younger?' she hoped humbly.

'Very much, Mrs Longfield,' I conceded sympathetically.

The westering sun sent a blade of light through the trees to a nest of age under her left ear.

'My child is very much the young beauty this afternoon, don't you think, Mr Younger?'

I glanced sidewards towards her.

'She is a nice girl. No longer a child.'

'I was in some doubt about saying it to any of our old friends but I do think age sets off youth, don't you?'

'And the other way round?'

Whereupon I thought of a lovely poem of Victor Hugo to Judith Gautier about how much age and beauty have in common, a star in the east and in the west, in the bright sky, over the dark sea and I wandered again towards Nana's star just as she was wandering towards me.

'Your good mother has just been saying that you do not look your great age.'

'I feel ancient. My life is over.' She leaned sidewards to brush a fold of her green frock that swayed between us, and growled secretively, 'I'm bored stiff, my key is on my window-sill, drop in there for a jug of black coffee when this funeral is over.'

The reverend monocle joined us.

'Are you free for dinner, B.B.? There are certain things I want to discuss with you.'

'That would be no better than a sermon. I have a date. In fact,' looking at my wrist, 'I must leave at once to keep it.'

Waiting downstairs in her flat, I recalled that love poem of Hugo's to Judith Gautier and began to translate it into a letter to her. As I wrote I kept hearing young voices outside, laughter, goodbyes, footsteps, now and again a departing car grinding the gravel of the drive. I had barely completed the translation – my first love letter to her – found an envelope, put the letter into it, addressed it *To Nana* and slipped it into her letter box when she came, laughing like a zany, flung herself on her sofa and informed the ceiling that she thanked God that the unspeakably bestial business of being young was at last over. I started to whisper lest we be heard through the window by anybody else passing down the steps. I said I regretted to hear her say so, that I preferred her as an eager virgin, at which she haughtily glowered with her eyebrows.

'I have had my fill of virginal youth. It is why I have refused to go wassailing elsewhere with my young friends tonight. I wanted to chat with some world-weary old chum like you.'

In three months' time she would have many world-weary young chums. I asked her what she thought so appealing about London or Paris. She answered at once:

'Any place where nobody will know me, where I can be just myself, alone all alone on a wild, wild sea.'

'Would you hate it if I paid you a visit in London or Paris?'

'Ah! You are different, Bobby. One of the few people in this city who has never treated me as a half-wit.'

She leaped up, went to a bowl of apples on her round table, seized one, threw me another, went off chewing into her bedroom to change, returned in slacks and a tight pullover, and lay again on her settee, patting it imperiously to indicate that I should sit beside her. I smelled wine. It was the Irish June light, still bright as day. I am a gentleman. I was brought up in colonial Ireland to believe that all life is divided between cads and gentlemen. Only a cad would take advantage of a tipsy girl. I told her I was taking her out for dinner. 'We must put some grub into you. You've had too much fizz.'

She whispered, eyes and ears upwards, 'Then wait! The Moran bird is taking my father to dine at the club. Sit closer. Talk to me about Paris. How shall I set about looking for a flat in Paris? You were an international journalist. Before you came back to live in Ireland did you have a flat in Paris? What a life you must have had in Paris! Did you travel everywhere?'

'Everywhere. London. Paris. Rome. Stockholm, Madrid. Vienna. One follows the news.'

'Throw me your apple. Try mine.'

I did, and got a flash of remembrance of her grandmother bossily taking me by the hand into a corner of her mother's breakfast room to ask me where in hell I had been for the previous six months. She went on chewing, I whispering until we heard yet another car on the gravel. It was a taxi. We heard three voices on the top steps and the front door go plunk. We peeped out and saw Anador and the Monsignor helping Leslie into the taxi. Anador did not join them. Instead she took her Mini and drove away, presumably to dine with one of her guests.

I do not know precisely what Des and Leslie discussed at that dinner, but from what happened later I now know that they discussed me. I might have guessed it sooner if I had been more alert when I asked Nana two days later whether she had got my letter and she laughed and said, 'Oh, your nice crumpled old letter.' I failed to heed that word 'crumpled'. In fact I never suspected any interference with our correspondence during the following two or three months during which I must have written her a dozen letters, although several of them did seem to be delayed in transit. Unknown to me Leslie was intercepting them and copying them. With a dying man's avarice he told nobody, refusing to relinquish those secret morsels of passion until he should feel his own carriage and pair slowing to a halt at his last street corner.

We drove up the hills to The Lamb Doyle's, high over the distant lights of a city blessed better by the blaze of the midsummer moon out over the sea. After dining we drove along the flanges of the hills, paused, got out and, arms around one another's waists, looked down at Dublin and the wide bay again.

'Will you sigh for these lights in Paris?'

She shivered her rejection of Ireland, her lust for France.

'I shall be seeing the lights of Paris.'

I mentioned that the lights of Paris are made of millions of the same sort of electric light bulbs.

'But nobody,' she riposted, 'will ever call Dublin *la ville lumière*.'

'The road of the moon across that sea?'

'The same moon in the Seine.'

'You will never be able to forget the Liffey. Your mother has never been able to forget the Shannon.'

I felt her shoulders shrugging disbelief and released her waist. Not yet. Perhaps not ever? At her party she had seemed so sure, teetering on the edge of her diving board, that I had felt airborne by the sight of youth in all its certainty. Overlooking this sea that lay before us, feeling the warmth of her young body, her faith, her resolution, I recalled those famous frightening lines about the world 'that *seems* to lie before us like a land of dreams'. I became a brother protecting his sister, an old man his daughter, and surely there must have been occasions when even Don Juan was cooled by the recollection of opportunities taken that had been better lost. The zany streak in her – reminding me of the heydays of her grandmother and her mother – suddenly threw her arms wide open.

'I want to swim away into that moon!'

'Let us drive down to it!'

We did, though Glencullen, into the cleft of the Scalp's tumble of black shadows and headlight flashes, through the woods of the Glen o' the Downs down to a level ebbtide simmering on Greystones' beach. It was too early in the year for seaside visitors, too late in the night for village strollers. Alone with her there, hearing no sound but the repeated scrape of the retreating tide and our feet crunching away from the dim lights of the village I was suspended between hell and heaven like that night-bird winging low over the surface of the sea beside us. We stopped.

'Well?' I said. 'There is your sea! I dare you!'

'Turn around,' she ordered, 'and don't turn back until I call out.'

I obeyed. Minutes later I heard her wild shriek, whirled and was doubled up with laughter. The savage cold of the Irish Sea, cold even in June, had reached her thighs. Gasping and cursing, the splendid bottomy creature dived and swam strongly out. I watched in wonderment and admiration, heard her on her back shout at the moon, then turned and walked back up the gravel to the shelter of the railway bank where the sand gathers between the vast concrete blocks of the breakwater. I lay there until she joined me, dressed, large, lank-haired, teeth chattering, cursing herself for her folly.

I took off my jacket, threw it over her shoulders and for a longish while held her shivering in my arms. Dressing, she did not say a word. As we walked back to the car and drove back to the city she was silent. All my efforts to get talk out of her failed to produce more than a dull 'Yes?', or 'No?', or 'So?'. I gave it up. I halted a hundred yards or so from Number 118 and looked at her. For a moment she stared sullenly ahead, then opened the door, paused with one foot on the pavement, looked back at me and spoke. She has by nature a very soft voice; this time it was more than soft, it was a little girl's voice.

'Thanks, Bobby.'

'For nothing!'

'I admire you greatly.'

'Admire? Why not? But "greatly"?'

'For not making a pass at me.'

As she walked away I wondered in dismay if Greystones were not one of those lost chances, those might-have-beens that I would later bitterly regret. Then, with a gasp, I understood. The girl had realistically plotted that encounter on the beach while I was thinking moodily of her land of dreams. She had wanted me to make an amorous pass at her there. Had I, she told me long afterwards, when we became true lovers, she would both have been compliant and had no further interest in me. As it was I had established a degree of unattainability to match her own. Some of all this I blissfully and clearly saw as I drove away from Ailesbury Road and headed for Rosmeen Park. Tomorrow morning, perhaps already, she would be reading my letter-poem with a smile of loving complicity. I had, or at least I deserved to have won her. The upshot of it was that before she left for Paris each of us knew that there was nobody of whom either was more fond than of the other.

When I visited her in Paris that October we proved it rapturously. That autumn and the whole year following was our perfect year, apart from Anador's growing suspicions of every woman in Dublin and Leslie's decline, though in the end he was not, as in my literary flourish a while ago, permitted to descend sedately from his carriage and disappear with dignity – instead he slipped on a tiny piece of banana that Anador was slicing for his breakfast cereal in their kitchen and smashed his skull against the edge of the gas-cooker.

Have I been making more old bones? I hope not. I have already recorded what happened between Nana and me this morning while the gravediggers were moving through the fog with the flowers and immortelles to lay them on the boards across Anador's as yet unfilled grave. (They always wait for the mourners to depart before shovelling in the resounding earth.) My hanging hand touched Nana's hand hanging beside me. When she pressed it I prayed that we might again become one. I was so utterly alone – Ana gone, Reggie gone, Les gone, Anador now gone, and last of them all my hound of heaven, Des Moran: friends, lovers, even collaborators, to each of whom Nana and I were both in deep debt.

How deeply indebted I did not know until I found out that not only had Leslie been intercepting and copying my letters to his daughter, but just before his untimely death he entrusted his copies to Des with (Des would say it to me) death's pale bile on his lips. The line of fate might have halted even there if Des had not so madly wanted to make me marry his Anador and abandon her Nana – a folly that only a celibate would have proposed, with Anador now approaching sixty, I ending my forties, and Nana in the full blaze of her first womanhood.

At first all he did with those accursed love letters was to ruffle their pages at me behind Leslie's back, as when one day he visited me just before the Christmas following Leslie's death, greeted me cordially, sat in my favourite armchair with a big book on his lap, and began to roast me slowly.

'What's the book?' I asked as I poured him his usual large Irish.

'It is a life of Victor Hugo. Have you read it? By Maurois.'

'Yes. It must be nearly forty years old. It came out in the 'Fifties, didn't it?'

'Its interest is eternal. A great poet, an insatiable womaniser, a patriot, a liar and a rascal.' He opened it at the first of a few inter-leaved slips of paper, fixed his monocle, and leered at me. 'Listen to this. I find it vastly entertaining.' Calmly, amusedly he read out a love letter of Hugo's to his life-long mistress Juliette Drouet.

> 'Beloved Juliette', or, to be sure, beloved any woman of the moment, 'you will find this letter when you wake up, folded in four on your pillow, and you will smile at it won't you? I long for that smile from those dear beautiful eyes that have wept so many tears. Sleep my own Juliette.' Or any other lady of the moment. 'Dream that I love you. Dream that I am lying at your feet. Dream that you are my love ...'

My belly curled. It was my first intimation that my letters had been stolen. I remembered that letter well, my very first love letter to Anador, laid on her pillow the night I left ffrench Chase after spending a week there helping her to put the place into order as a summer residence. As he quietly read on I felt a second horrible fear. Had I sent that same letter to Nana? I had written so many letters to them both. How right Corneille was: if you must lie be sure you have a good memory. Whose letters had he, where, how got hold of them? When he had finished he gave me the under-eye-brows smile of a sly inquisitor, drew out another marker from his book and smiled even more happily.

'This one is a real beauty. It is in verse. Our gallant Victor, after betraying his beloved year in and year out, is astonished to find her not only a trifle upset but jealous! What does he do? Conquers her all over again with a ravishing poem. And I presume you know that "ravish" and "rape" are twin words?'

As he read it, with a mock passion that made its fraudulence doubly flagrant, I remembered its occasion. It was a Hugo verse with which I had tried to pacify Anador the day after she surprised me leaving Nana's flat.

What, you jealous? You? O why
My soul's delight, heed every passerby?
Immortal planet! Queen of the crowded sky,
My adoration of whose light can never die,
What if I dallied with some fledgling Anador?
Must my goddess moon heed every wayside flower?

As he read I decided that he – no! that Leslie had rifled Anador's portfolio. There would normally be no telltale names, no addresses or signature – but there would be my handwriting. I surrendered. I confessed that, yes, once, or twice, twice, yes, I had expressed my admiration for Anador, 'for your daughter', and that I had leaned somewhat on Victor Hugo. He must know how sentimental ageing men can be? He would, I was sure, understand.

He understood sufficiently to rise, produce from the tail pocket of his clerical frock-coat and hold aloft a bundle of letters that, he declared, proved far more, and ordered me like a Hildebrandine pope to rid myself at once of my ridiculous infatuation for 'the girl' and marry her mother. Furiously I defied him. Anyway how should I gain by his nonsense? I hurled a splendid 'Publish and be damned' at him and showed him the door. He pestered me for weeks and weeks.

That Christmas when Nana came back from Paris he was waiting for her in Dublin. An hour later she was in my hallway, pale with rage – she refused to enter beyond it – retailing their encounter:

'"To your own mother!" he laughed at me, and threw your letters into my lap. I glanced at the first two or three of them and laughed into his face. "Father Dezzy," I hooted at him, "they are all to ME!"'

'To which he said?'

Silence. Then, coldly:

'He just pointed out to me a poem you sent to me when you were sniffing around my petticoats. He observed that it was another Hugo job. As if I would not have known it anyway, I haven't been studying French Lit. for nothing. It contained one charming line out of your own clever little head. Remember? *What if I dallied with some fledgling Anador?* And you called me a wayside flower.'

'And you said?'

'I told the truth of course. I said I had known since I was thirteen that you and my mother were in love. Ever since you came down that June night in '82 to ffrench Chase when I was there and slept next door to her room and you both kept me awake half the night quarrelling like the corncrakes in the meadows. Did all that go on after me? As if you would tell me! Don't try! That precious poem about me as your wayside flower was dated only a few months before you swore eternal troth to me in Paris.'

'Anador was ill. I would have done more than that for her. I loved her once.'

'Your precious Monsignor was pleased to tell me also that my mother was a bastard. Is that true?'

I wavered for speech so long that she shouted it at me.

'Is it true?'

'Why should he want to tell you that?'

'Is it true?'

I nodded. I again asked her quietly why she thought he spoke of it. She did not hedge – she had guts: to break her spirit – and to judge by her staring eyes he nearly did.

'Who was my mother's father?'

'You mean who is your grandfather?'

'Yes.'

'All that is known is that your grandfather was not your grandmother's husband.'

'And why could that much be known?'

'Dublin speaks with a common voice. A very common voice. It is a town where everybody is known to everybody. That is what they mean by a man-sized city. He was a Dublin joke. The impotent gynaecologist who delivered others but could not himself deliver.'

'Christ!'

Meaning how happy she was to be living now where everybody does not know everybody – or not at least since, say, the days of The Revolution. By the way her brows darkened I guessed that Des had gone further.

'Did he tell you anything else?'

'He suggested that bastards run in families. That I also might be one, and that you might be my father.'

That piece of savagery gave me a sour pleasure. So this particular Christian can fight like a savage beneath the polish of his sanctified centuries. Ends and means?

'I first met your mother one morning in March 1965. I assure you that I did not at once assault her. I did not know her. I was in love with somebody else. You are Anador's daughter. Your father was Leslie Longfield.'

I could feel her entire body melting, relaxing, reasserting the individual existence that His Sanctitude had tried to destroy.

'Shall I,' she said with satisfaction, 'tell you why you and Anador were quarrelling that night in '82 in ffrench Chase? Because you were never in love with her. Remember what Balzac said about love? That it is not a feeling – it is a situation. We don't fall in love. We enlist in it. Once we are in the army we have to act as if we really liked it. Nor was she in love with you. With both of you it was an act you deliberately wrote into the Human Comedy. You were both liars.'

We were still standing in the hallway of my little suburban house. In the railway cutting a commuters' train hooted bleakly as it pushed off either to Dublin or to the sea.

'All right,' I conceded. 'What happens now?'

'Now?' she demanded haughtily. 'Now, I am your wayside flower, and you are a louse, and a liar and a shit, and,' with a groan, 'I shall probably never be able to forget you.'

She did not bang the door.

Forget? If it be admitted that memories like hers and mine flow on and on under busy city streets and asphalt avenues I can truly say that I did not forget her for one moment. It was the most nauseating Christmas of my life, the most cruel, empty, solitary, deserted. I did not have even the comfort of an enemy – Des Moran, struck by 'flu and virus pneumonia, went into hospital and died inside a month. He had been my wicked angel, my saintly Satan twisting everything I said and did. His stoic sanctity had invented my evil. I had committed none. I had told a few small lies that gave pain to two people who had been dear to me. I had botched everything because I had accepted the world as the gods gave it to me, just as he had accepted the world as his faith invented it for him. In my disarray I looked about me for allies and found that I had not a single friend – only acquaintances in plenty; but no man opens his soul to every other man, no woman to every other, and those who devote their lives to the confidences of love have no friends. As I sat there during those festive weeks, in my silent room, in my suburban house, I found myself so down-beaten as to open my old photograph album, mine or my late brother's, once again searching face after face for some warm current of recognition. I had slipped a picture of Anador into it, and several of Ana. These two smiled, laughed, posed, were snapped unaware only to torture me. Surely some other face *must* be of my forgotten wife? I had an image which matched no image in the book: somebody frail and elegant and very young, induced, I think, through her names Christabel and Lee, by Poe and Coleridge. *She was a child and I was a child/In this kingdom by the sea,/But we loved with a love that was more than love –/I and my Annabel Lee –/With such a love that the winged seraphs of Heaven/Coveted her and me.*

Glumly I restored the album to its place, saw *Love Letters from Many Lands*, drew it out and opened it under the rubric, HUGO. A few scribblings on the margins still remained legible. *And if some fledgling Christabel and if I were to pass an hour and if I dallied with some daffodil Christabel flower hour stars April wayside flower.* On the page of Contents some letters had been allotted three commendatory stars, some two, most one. After some names there was pencilled the word *bum* – such as Napoleon, Edward VII, Crippen or Oscar Wilde. But Eleanora Duse and d'Annunzio had been appreciated. I closed the book with a shake of the head. There is indeed an observable pattern in nature. Proving the consistency of the creator of life?

It was during that Christmas period that the dreams began, in anxiety or frustration. *Nessun maggior dolore* . . . No misery greater than the memory of some happy yesterday. Ana beside me, laughing and gay, I as happy, then waking to Nothing. Anador's monumental figure, her strong hand, her vigorous laugh. I never dreamed of Nana. An old dream came back twice that year: of a train halted on a boundless moor, or rather, as it dissolvingly became, one carriage of a train that had gone ahead, the carriage empty but for that one figure sitting opposite me, a woman, shrouded, or masked, my only wife. If only I could live it all, meaning all, ALL over again how I would squeeze every moment dry!

It was as well for me that I was isolated that Christmas. Almost a year passed before I was to hear about how much I had escaped thereby: all the painful colloguings that had gone on through that holiday between mother and daughter, their fine balancings between compassion and reproof, infected all by Bad Faith, that is by their suppressed longings to have the tooth out, lance the boil, be done with it, to say 'You were a fool, we were deceived, you were dishonest, I was silly.' By the time I heard of it I had been chastened by misery and could calmly say to her though, and it will 'always' be so, still curling with shame, 'No! Not that way! Not Anador!'

'Your grandmother yes. She would have let it all out, and with vigour. Not Anador. She could have exploded to her husband, even to me, but never to you. Misery in a shrug or secret tears. In public never more than an eyelid quivering for "If one had more sense", or "One should have guessed." "One". Never "you". Never "I". Too proud. Anador was always too damned proud.'

Nana was to report that they had both behaved themselves, that their most explicit statements came when Anador slowly turned a wedding ring on her finger, and Nana replied with a stare at her throatful of pearls. If only (Nana's most savage comment) they had had the guts to blow it all away with an explosion of laughter, not, most certainly not that, not making peace with the villain of the piece but with their own cowardly duplicity. After all, each of the three of us had been deceiving somebody else. 'Face saving!' Nana insisted furiously after I had driven her back from Anador's funeral to her old garden flat on Ailesbury Road, adding inexorably lest I use her phrase as an escape hatch, 'You bastard!' and adding truthfully to that, 'You did not deserve either of us!' As I watched her ample figure bustling around her red-tiled kitchen-cum-living room (originally the Ailesbury Road basements had been servants' quarters), making Irish coffee to warm us after that foggy graveyard I was in no position to reply. The floor overhead, so familiar so much lived in, so much loved in, was at last empty.

'And don't think I have yet made my peace with you,' she said severely as she handed me the hot glass implying by that 'yet' that there could be peace at a price: conceivably that which Anador had as eagerly desired as her mother had haughtily rejected? Not that Nana would be explicit about her terms – she, too, when it became her, could intimate silently. Her wishes would come, if at all, as a tone of voice, a lingering backward look at some old college chum met in the street with her small daughter, a reference to marriage as diplomatically distanced as it would be applicable near at hand. Friday's footprint.

And why not? God knows what I now have is a house not a home. A circle of friends? Who needs them more? Colleagues? Is she thinking of a job for me? At my present forty I am about ready for one. (I could imagine my employer saying amiably, 'No reason why you shouldn't look forward to twenty good years with us!' and my thinking, 'Or thirty if you don't mind employing an ancient of ten?') Nana was looking at me uncertainly.

'Bob! Last Christmas one of the things Anador said to me was "And such an old man, too." How old really are you?'

The question had not been asked before. Ana and Anador had been sufficiently self-conscious about age not to want to raise it. After a flicker of fear I remembered that there was now nobody living who could calculate that, mathematically, I am ninety. Could I dare say to Nana, 'I am forty.' I thought, 'It is the truth!' and straight away I knocked fifty years off my ninety.

Me: Heaven help me. I am fully forty years old. Almost twice your tender age.

Nana: Vanity box! Leslie used to say he first met you when you were twenty.

Me: Pfoo! Leslie was always exaggerating. He probably confused me with my brother J.J. Leslie was a vague creature. Do I look all that old?

Nana: You look young enough to populate an ark. What does age matter anyway! The most attractive man I met in Paris was a painter of sixty.

Me: I am a youth compared to him. I really am forty. You can trust me.

Nana: (*Sucking down the last of her whiskified coffee and leaving an enchanting little moustache of cream on her upper lip.*) Trust you? I wouldn't trust you, you worm, for five minutes. Perhaps after all what I need is a younger man who couldn't trust me? (*Her eye and ear suddenly cocked.*) See who that is, would you?

Me: Who is what? (*I had heard nothing but her threat.*)

She: (*Eyes out and up to the main hall door.*) Youth knocking at *the door. Ta-ta-ta! Ta-a-a!*

I went out and looked sideupwards to the hall door. A handsome young man, broad-shouldered, enlarged by the fog, looked down at me over the cast-iron banister. Brown-skinned, blue-eyed, bareheaded, white-toothed, high cheekboned and with that egalitarian American manner that can in a moment annihilate the entire Atlantic Ocean and centuries of European class-consciousness.

'Hi!' he said amiably. 'My name is B. B. Younger. You live here?'

My grandson.

'What name did you say? And whom do you want?'

'I am Robert Bernard Younger. I am trying to unearth some family history. My father was Jimmy Younger. My grandfather was Stephen Younger, from Castletownroche, in Cork County. I am looking for a Mr and Mrs Longfield. A Mr Longfield met my father, Jimmy, a couple of years ago in Philadelphia. He said he knew a Younger who lived near him in Dunleary, Dublin. I have rung that house and this house a dozen times this morning and got no answer.'

'Mrs Longfield was buried this morning. Mr Longfield died last year.'

'Too bad! It all meant a lot to my father and my grandfather Old Stephen. It means a lot to me.'

The moment stays. Faint throbs in memory's stethoscope. The hearts of more old men trying to remember. A silent road. A fog wispy in the bare trees, a dampness of air not worth calling a mist wafting from the sea and shore. It dimmed my spectacles. It was probably dimming every window around the circle of Dublin Bay. I knew about links. A fog-drop from the ivy on the iron railings above me exploded on one of my lenses. I took off my spectacles to dry them while still peering up at him.

'So you are on the tracks of your family here in Dublin?'

'I am looking for information about Youngers anywhere in Ireland.'

He would visit Castletownroche, find my name in the parish registers, born ninety years ago. And that would only be the beginning. Behind me Nana. Sandalwood. They looked at one another, down approving, up welcoming.

'Bring the man in,' she said in her hearty way. 'Do come in. Down this way. It is a rotten, foggy old morning.'

He skipped down the granite steps. We, inside now, heard the gravel crunch as he approached.

Basta. Typing all night. My fingers calloused. She said last night, about my 'crisis', 'Write it all down'. All in one second a man wins or loses, is born or dies, falls in love or out of it. One year is thirty million seconds. In sixty years your heart throbs two billion times. Art and Memory leave too many things out. Let me contain the essence. The scent of a dead love in sandalwood. A mass bell. 7.15 a.m. or 9.45 a.m.?

I have just dragged the curtains open.

Sun! Blue morning! Sleep? But not under the trees. Age! Love! Life! Youth again!

PART THREE

Nana

1990–2024

That morning of Anador's funeral as he skipped down the eleven granite steps in his elegant Texan cowboy boots and crunched towards us on the gravel I had whispered to Nana, 'Let's get rid of him quick, he's just another of those Irish-Americans fondly searching for long-lost forebears.' She did not because she had not my bad conscience. He came in. I had to say, 'This is Mr Robert Younger, Miss Longfield. I am B. B. Younger,' and he eagerly hand shaking, saying smilingly (he held her hand longer than necessary), 'I think it may have been your father, Miss Longfield, who met my father, Jimmy Younger, in Philadelphia a few years ago. And, sir, I am delighted to make your acquaintance. You must know all about the Younger family, especially our American branch.' She invited him to take off his overcoat and sit down, offering him Irish coffee, switched on the coffee pot before he could do more than half demur and bustled to get fresh glasses. I had to put up with it. It was her way with everybody. Open. Warm. Guiltless. Friendly.

He responded to her warmth by remembering his manners. He lived in Dallas, Texas. He did have a place in Florida too. More accurate to say he was based in Dallas, he travelled so much. An engineer. Mining. Married? No, adding a 'Not yet' with a grin. He scarcely knew Europe. His work took him elsewhere. He had been to Paris, and listened. She apparently got more out of it than he did. But then she would know the language. She tried hard to sell him Paris. He tried amiably to sell her Mexico and Mayan ruins. Nor was this a European holiday. Far from it! Which gave him his opportunity at long last to mention the Youngers of Castletownroche and turn his attention to me. I forestalled him at once.

'I am afraid I am going to be of very little help, Mr Younger. I know so little about our family, apart from my father, and he is dead this thirty-five years.'

'Where were you born, sir?'

'In Castletownroche.'

'Then you must know all about our old Stephen, my grandfather, and J.J. and B.B.!'

I shook my head. He frowned.

'But,' Nana cried to me, 'you *are* B. B.'

I smiled that away – it was only twenty minutes ago since I told her I was a mere forty years old, and I had been ready for all this ever since that dinner in Charlotte Street when Des Moran produced my 'son' Jimmy, and his 'father' old Stephen. I had gone over the ground so often and so closely that I could now produce a genealogy plausible enough to satisfy any normal questioner.

'I am,' I agreed with Nana, 'B.B. But I am not our American friend's B.B. Your B.B., Mr Younger, was a generation before me. It is this way.'

I explained sympathetically that, well over a hundred years ago, in this small village of Castletownroche in Cork County, there had originally been two brothers named Younger who owned a tavern – he would probably call them saloon keepers. One of them never married. The other did and had three sons, Stephen, J.J. or John Jo, and B.B., Robert Bernard – all, of course, dead now. 'Those are the clan you are interested in, and I can well understand your interest – they were after all your American family's Irish ancestors.'

'To my father Jimmy and my grandfather they were far more than just "interesting". They regarded them as three heroes, three great Irishmen, three great fighters for Ireland's freedom.'

'Were they really?' Nana asked in an astonished voice, handing him his cream-topped glass of whiskey and coffee. He turned to her.

'Old Stephen was always telling us about it. Over and over again. How they fought the British in 1916 in the central Post Office here in Dublin – I saw it only last night, the first place I visited on my arrival here.'

Nana was looking at me. Incredulously? Appealingly? Wanting me to help this vital, handsome young man who was challenging now one, now the other of us? I insisted quietly:

'Whatever your grandfather told you, Mr Younger, or your father, about any Robert Bernard Younger it could not have been me. As I have good reason to know. I was born thirty-four years after 1916. The B. B. your family has been celebrating must have been my father.'

'Even so,' he hooped in his excitement, 'your father must have told you all about us over there just as my grandfather told us all about you over here?'

I felt sympathetic. I said so, I knew those deceptive memories, but I shook my head.

'It was a long time ago, Mr Younger. To modern Ireland 1916 is a frozen memory. Something writers try to defrost in history books. You must see the real picture. In 1916 your B.B., my father, is a boy of sixteen. What the lad thinks is going to be a glorious rebellion against the whole might of the British Empire breaks out. He plays his modest part in it as a despatch rider, a Boy Scout, what in those days used to be called one of the Fianna Eireann, those young warrior heroes of the old sagas. The boy is hot with dreams of glory. He experiences the actual crudities of bullets, blood, looting, curses, death, flames, fear, dissension, cowardice, desertion, defeat. I often heard him cursing and muttering about it. It may be why he married late and died comparatively young.'

The American gazed, troubled, at me. I felt I was making it pretty vivid. A journalist can make anything vivid. I went on:

'Your grandfather spoke to you of three fighting Youngers. I suggest that he exaggerated. I am sure that J.J. took no part in that Rising. In fact, like most Irish people here he disapproved of it when it broke out. Anyway you must remember that years before that Rising those three boys, Stephen, J.J., and B.B. were the scattered sons of a bankrupt pub. The father and uncle who ran that pub were gamblers, at first in a small way, later on a ruinous scale. When the pub had to be sold Stephen stayed with his father, J.J. was sent to a genteel aunt in Cork who reared him as a nice, well-behaved British boy, B.B. was sent to Dublin to an uncle who, my father told me, was an old Fenian, which was how he got drawn into the Rebellion.'

'Could this uncle still be alive?'

'After three-quarters of a century? The upshot of it was that J.J. became a British journalist. B.B. remained hard-up for years after the Rising in Dublin, the typical impoverished, disillusioned, embittered idealist. Then a crowd here calling themselves true blue republicans got into power – ever since the 1916 legend became super-sanctified there has always been some crowd here calling themselves true-blue republicans. They remembered their 1916 boy-hero and gave him a job as a journalist on one of their newspapers. It was then that he married. In the 'Thirties. My uncle, J.J., got him into the British press. Colchester, Manchester, Leeds, *The Evening News*. He was happy there. He died in Colchester.'

(I was sorry I said that: the journalist's hunger for the small graphic detail. Drawing on my own dossier. But what matter! If he went there he would no more find a firm Younger trail than I had done.)

'You,' he probed, 'also became a journalist?'

'Yes.' And to confuse the trail further: 'But I wandered, too. Leeds. Durham. Yorkshire. London.'

(I was sorry I said that, too. Suppose he started searching the marriage registers of Somerset House, which I had been too discouraged to do? No more details.) 'As for Old Stephen, your grandfather, I know absolutely nothing.'

Nana was looking sympathetically at our guest. He had fallen silent, possibly thoughtful, more likely – I thought – rebellious, in which it turned out I was wrong – he was a bit more sceptical than I then knew.

'You,' she said to him in a kindly voice, 'got your story of your forebears from your father, Jimmy?'

'Of course. From Jimmy Younger. Who got it from Old Stephen. I remember the old man rolling it off like a gramophone record every Easter Week and every 17th of March without fail. His wife used to leave the room when he began at it she was so sick of it. The anniversary of the Rising and St Patrick's Day.'

I disremember what our visitor and Nana talked about after that. I was frightened by the results of my own imaginings. I had turned myself into my own father, rediscovered myself as my own son, and here was my real grandson fiercely making imaginary cat's cradles with his weaving fingers. I had finally denied my wife, his grandmother, Christabel. At the same time I felt proud of myself to have silenced him long enough to win me the one day and night that I needed – I had realised it immediately I saw him – to win Nana again. I became aware of the two of them colloguing earnestly head to head and saw that I might well have won no more than a battle. I was sure of it when, risen suddenly on his authoritative feet, he said:

'Why don't you two pleasant people come to lunch with me right now in my suite at the Shelbourne Hotel? I've got my car outside, I have the feeling that I can still get lots more out of you both about all those Irish Youngers.'

I did not want to go but Nana did. While he was bringing a great creamy Mercedes into the driveway and she was making up her face I reminded her that she had said that she preferred 'older men who know their way around'. She laughed mockingly that she also liked younger men who pay their way around, and although I knew her to be incapable of any such calculation I resented this young fellow's air of blatant success. I even resented his placing her beside him in front and placing me, the presumed authority on our precious family, behind. On the seat beside me lay a black leather binder with a card in a little slot on the cover bearing the typed word *Youngers*. I flipped it open. 'Contents. 1: Dublin. National Library records. Genealogical Office, Dublin Castle. 2: Castletownroche. 3: Cork city. Church registers of births, marriages, deaths. Cork Historical Society. Mortician's records. Vintners Association. 4: Newspapers and periodicals in Ireland or Great Britain. 5: Record Office, London. 6: Clubs. e.g. Old I.R.A. Gaelic League. G.A.A. Medals, decorations, Old I.R.A. pensions lists.'

I flipped it closed. All this implied previous research in America, money already spent, and still more to be spent on his behalf there and in Britain after he would have left for the United States.

We had lunch in the drawing-cum-dining room of a second floor suite in the Shelbourne, its tall windows facing south across St Stephen's Green and out beyond its bare tree-tops over Georgian Dublin's roofs, still damp, spread under a tent of cloud. The sounds of traffic in the street below, having no opposite houses to resound against, was defused. The furnishings were unmodern, the rooms high, bright and large. A turf fire glowed under a Bozzi mantelpiece. Aperitifs, the ordering of lunch, a long-distance business call from Houston, chat about his lavish quarters filled the blank in our acquaintance for a while. His father, Jimmy Younger – the name was always uttered as if it were of international repute (as for all I knew of his profession it possibly once was) – had always advised him to stay in The Connaught in London, The Crillon in Paris, The Bayerischer Hof in Munich, the old Minerva in Rome. Places with an air. The Shelbourne in Dublin. But I was interested only to find out why a whole suite in Dublin? It became clear as he talked – expansively, like any successful third generation Irish-American adventurer – willing to show off, careful never to boast. Old Stephen had studied metallurgy and metalliferous mining at M.I.T. There were mentions of mines in South America, in Africa, in the Middle East.

'And what better could I do in my turn than the same?' To Nana: 'Would you like a 1970 claret with the steak *minute*? It is said to be a good year.' To me: 'You knock me a bit off course telling me that B.B. was only sixteen at the time of the Rising, we had always thought of him as older than Old Stephen, old enough to help young Jimmy during his bad months between Dublin and New York. Could the old man have meant J.J.? The younger brother?'

'He may have got confused as he grew older.'

Our host slowly turned the stem of his wine glass.

'That is why I am here. I sometimes think he might well have been confused. Jimmy Younger sometimes thought he was very confused. The way you describe young B.B.'s experience in the Rising gives a possible clue. Do you suppose Old Stephen might also have suffered some kind of postponed shock from that same disenchanting experience?'

I lifted and lowered redundant palms like a boy floating on a bicycle.

'And so I really am the last of my clan?'

'It seems so! The last to remember and to forget.'

He drew in his chin at that word, bridled angrily.

'Forget! The first place I went last night when I arrived here was to Moore Street and that great pillared General Post Office in O'Connell Street, the H.Q. of the rebels in '16. As I stood there I was remembering Old Stephen telling us of his last look at the flames pouring out of its higher windows as he ran for his life down Moore Street. As he ran he passed the body of The O'Rahilly lying dead on the pavement after signing his name in his own blood on the wall. Down side lanes. British bullets whistling after him. In through that lucky, half-open door, shutting it behind his back on the racing boots behind him, panting, facing the dark staircase, revolver cocked for friend or foe. On the first floor, lit only by the sky on fire, on a tumbled bed was a whore and a Brit soldier. On the second floor a boy-child in rags sleeping rough in a bare corner. On the third floor an old dying woman. On the top floor a room, humble, clean, candlelit, and a colleen of surpassing beauty praying on her knees for the rebels, glad to help him, save him, love him, bear him a son for Ireland's sake.'

The foreign patrol tramped back slowly to their quarters along the street below. Khaki pygmies. A sleepless night of love. A lucky escape at dawn. Down to the docks. A boat about to cast off for the Port of London. A bribe. A stowaway. Sailing down the Liffey to the open sea. Behind him Dublin seen through a port-hole glowing to the clouds like a rising sun. A love lost. A son found. A battle lost. A country born. Shit!

I threw a questioning look at Nana. Joy poured into me when she lifted her eyebrows and lowered the corners of her lips. I could hear Old Stephen wheezing his preposterous legend to his Texan clan. And yet! He had lived. He had been. But who and what had the old imposter really been? What self had he invented out of pipe smoke and rye for a real man aching for a real past.

There was a longish silence. Then I asked quietly how Stephen Younger could know that he actually had fathered a son, that Easter morning. Bob Two looked out of the tall window at the farther Green, contemplating, I assumed, the time-magnified image of his ancestor. Then, to my astonishment, dismay, and embarrassent his head sank back between his shoulders and he let out a peal of laughter that revealed to me that I had been making a fool of myself. And what a fool!

I had been, for a few moments, seeing traditional sanctity and loveliness, a terrible beauty born, hating this old liar's pinchbeck image of its actual blend of concern and defeat; whereas to this young man 'great fighter' meant any kind of fighter – his own, his father's and his grandfather's kind, exploring, risking, freezing, burning, enduring, chancing, gambling, cheating, persisting by every conceivable means to Success, which was where he got the cut of the jib that he now presented to the world about him: a world far removed from the dimly depressing ancestral images I had brought away from my one glimpse of a mottled pub in a village as silent as a fish. A second later and I saw that I had once again misinterpreted everything. The man was laughing with delight in the livingness, the inventiveness of a preposterously splendid ancestor.

'Venus and Mars!' he hooted. 'That was old Stevie's motto from start to finish. And he began early. Twenty, he said, when he fathered my father in the smoke of Dublin, sailed away down the Liffey for England and America, though to believe his whole life-story, even if he had never fought in the Rising he would have had to get the hell out of Ireland anyway p.d.q. A wild man from the day he was born.'

A liar? Old Stephen a liar? Of course he was a liar! But what a liar! And not all liar!

'If I believed he was just that would I be here today? I am satisfied, whatever anybody else says, that my father Jimmy was his son. How did he know? He and she had taken note of one another's names. He told how he paid detectives to search for her in Ireland and England. One finally located her in London. Like to see a picture of our Irish grandmother?'

He drew a cabinet sized photograph from a pocket in the black file that lay on a side table near him, and handed it to Nana. She broke into a zany laughter.

'She is like Olympia, the weight-lifting woman in Duffy's circus.'

She handed it to me. The woman was elephantine. I asked, 'This stupendous creature?'

I handed it back to him, infuriated. That hippopotamus my wife?

'It could be anybody!'

He nodded. My thought was, 'But where did they get the name?' I know where. From my young Jimmy, arriving in the U.S. with a pink label dangling from his coat button. ('*My name is . . . My destination is . . .*') remembering scraps, a dog, church bells, kids in his street, red buses, an Uncle James, an Auntie Bridie, the other man they called Beebee who occasionally came for a day. So many things to be overlaid by the nice, dainty dancing name – uttered by whom? – that stuck in his head: Christabel Lee.

'That picture,' Bob the Second said, 'is the only family document Stephen had. Of course, it is a fake. It could be anybody. All Old Stephen said was that one of his researchers in London produced it.'

'But, surely,' Nana sensibly intervened, 'your grandfather Stephen must if even only once or twice have written to his brothers in Ireland or in England?'

'He said he wrote. But who knows? Exile does strange things to the mind. A man needs all his energy to live one life. Few men have the energy to live two. One cuts one's losses. And then, suppose he did write, and was answered, did he keep the answers? Old Stephen had a great misfortune before he died – in fact in the very month in which he died. A fire. It was confined to his study, but he lost all his papers.'

I made myself ask what year that was, well foreknowing the answer. Anno Dominorum 1965.

'Yes,' I said to the incoming waiter, 'I would! A large brandy.'

Over it and the coffee I got around to imploring him fearfully not to go to Castletownroche, not to persist in futile researches. His reply cut the sod from under my feet. He had no such intention. After seeing Moore Street how could he expect more from Main Street? He would leave Castletownroche and all the rest of it to his researchers. He turned to Nana, gently lifted her hand again.

'Would you like to be my chief researcher? I know I could trust you? You go to Castletownroche for me. Yes?'

'Why me?'

He just looked knowingly at her, took up the photograph of the alleged Christabel Lee, glanced at it, threw it aside contemptuously, and gave us both a pleasant discourse on identification.

There are, he proposed, only two modes of identification that deserve the name. The first involves the utmost particularisation of the person concerned. Height, weight, bodily particularities such as moles, warts, wounds, eye measurements, blood pressure, cardiac details, blood count, I.Q., dentist's records, legal documents, all confirming one another. The second mode of identification depends on Repetition or Continuity, or Tradition. No document can equal the human memory. A passport can be forged. A baptismal certificate can be stolen. All they tell us is that at some time a boy or girl was born, or christened or married in the name recorded by that or this certificate, but how can we know if the claimant to that certificate was the person therein mentioned? We cannot know until by repetition over many years that boy or girl becomes accepted by everybody as the boy or girl indicated on the document.

'Repetition is Continuity is Tradition is Memory is Truth. Let me tell you a story about Jimmy Younger.'

He had been searching somewhere in western Anatolia for the site of some ancient silver mines, referred to, quite incidentally, indeed irrelevantly, in, of all quite likely places, a tourist guide to Constantinople ('and beyond') by, if I remember rightly, a Turk named Demetrius Coufopoulos, published in London some time around 1890, which Jimmy had picked out of a barrow in Charing Cross Road for tuppence. Coufopoulos, or whatever his name was, was obviously dead. Jimmy set off with a couple of his assistant engineers to find the mines himself, and spent a lot of time, trouble and dollars in a carefully prepared, obstinate but futile search. His colleagues told him to give it up. Jimmy pondered and remembered an old theory of his father's that wherever you find any revered monument, from one of those votive thorn trees in Ireland that his father used to talk about, full of rags tied to its branches, beside a 'holy' well, to a temple in mainland Greece or in Magna Graecia, you can be damned sure that there is some tactical or economic reason for the choice of site. 'Fellas!' he said. 'We've been looking for the wrong thing. Let's look for a monument. A votive altar. Or a tiny temple. Any such thing that those old Byzantine miners or their bosses would have run up while they were on the job in some remote place. Let's forget maps and look for memorials.' They started to search again and ask again. They found it. A small, overgrown, crumbling temple. Bang beside it was the mine-shaft. Where were you born?'

The question was shot at me. I answered wildly, 'London.' Far and impersonal?

'Of course! You told me your father married there.'

Had I said so? I nodded.

'That is an extraordinarily interesting story,' I fended, "about the mine-shaft. But what could possibly be the Youngers' votive altar?'

His story about the Byzantine miners had also gripped Nana. I could tell it by the way she stood up to a mirror and tidied her hair.

'Did you really mean that about me being your researcher?' she asked him in the mirror.

To her: 'Certainly I meant it. You are obviously the type who never gives up.' To me: 'A Younger memorial? One never knows. What about a gravestone? I would say the key to the whole thing is a gravestone to Bob One.' He looked at me. 'Your father.'

She ignored me. I was thinking of my gravestone. She said: 'Old Stephen did have papers. Didn't he even remember any of them?'

'I have got to come straight with you, Miss ongfield. By the way, what is your name? If we are to work together I can't keep calling you Miss Longfield? Nana? Nice name. Call me Bob Two. Well, Nana, the fact is . . . I hate to say it, but the fact is Jimmy Younger sometimes felt that Old Stephen was as you,' glancing at me, 'say getting more than a bit confused. A little hole in his memory here or there. Inconsistent details in the same incident.'

'Such as?'

'Dates that did not fit. For example Jimmy would know sooner or later that if he arrived in the States as a mere child in 1946 he could not have been conceived on the field of battle in 1916. At that stage the old man, I gather rather sheepishly, had to admit that that union in Dublin on the night of his escape had been a misfire, and that it had taken him a little bit longer than he had said to discover Christabel Lee, but that as soon as ever he did he went tearing back to England where he found her still unwedded and brought her back with him to Texas. Five years later she presented him with a boy child, Jimmy, but, alas, she died in childbirth. That was about the time the child was sent to Ireland to his grandparents and duly returned to the States in '46.'

Bob Two looked hard at me. I said, 'I see,' as I did not, as nobody would, as he saw, and as Jimmy before him would also have seen. By that time we were all feeling relaxed – Irish coffee, aperitifs, two bottles of claret, the brandy. There had been no moment of truth. Nana roughly said:

'No papers. Birth? Marriage? Death? Where was Christabel Lee buried? Did Jimmy locate *her* memorial?'

'She was cremated. So he said.'

The Green was clear. The fog had lifted. The horizon of roofs was now as sharp as knives.

'Where are the ashes?' She asked it sharply.

He looked as sharply at her.

'Jimmy Younger always kept them in a Chinese type of vase, sealed, in a glass-fronted what-not in the corner of the living room, among a number of curios and precious things that Stephen had collected, silver, gold, enamel, oriental lacquer, ceramics, bric-à-brac.'

'He got the ashes from Old Stephen?' He nodded. She brought the session to a close by saying, 'You could have them analysed.'

He looked long at her, tapped her shoulder, said in quiet approbation, 'I knew you were my kind of girl,' rose from the table, and handed her his black file. We all shook hands and agreed to keep in touch. After I had closed the door behind us I remembered that I had left my umbrella on the chair beside it and reopened the door to retrieve it. He was standing, his back to me, his hands deep in his trouser pockets, staring out over the Green. He could be thinking of any number of things but I felt jealously certain that I knew what he was thinking of. I retrieved my umbrella and quietly closed the door between us.

Nana and I taxied back to Ailesbury Road. There I at once put my arms around her and implored her to marry me. A strange thing always happens to her when her feelings are stirred: her blue eyes seem to go dark, fixed, sightless, or to penetrate to some vision beyond normal sight. I seemed to be talking to somebody who was not hearing what I said while I pointed out to her that, after all, she had had her fling, in Paris, London, Paris again. I knew I was much older than she was but she had said, 'What does age matter, anyway?' I already had a fairish income as a property owner, but inside a week I would get a real job. I would work myself to the bone for her. We would make a lovely home. We would travel. She said neither yes nor no. She went on looking through me, although when I asked her if she had come to dislike me she shook her head strongly.

'Let us wait, then,' I begged her. 'Now that you are home let us see more of each other.'

I released her, and I saw her eyes become blue again and focus on me.

'Yes. Let us wait. I am at home, for a while at any rate. After all I have promised Bob Two to take charge of his investigations when he goes back to America.'

I spoke on a sudden impulse. I offered to help her in her enquiries. After all I was a Younger, one of the family. I could drive her all over Ireland and England where I knew all the relevant places so well. And further afield if it turned out to be necessary, in Europe, even in the States. She thought all this an excellent scheme. I suggested one proviso – that she should not tell Bob Younger that I was helping her. She let out a laugh of mockery, amiable though hooting – her laughter was never hurtful – hopeless, rather, as if life were to her, as I now know it is, an unfailing fountain of happy despair.

'He won't mind as long as he knows that I am the boss.'

'Are you saying that he does not trust *me*?'

'He will trust you as much as I do. He does not want me to trust anybody. I don't believe he even trusts himself.'

Her tone was regretful, that of a young woman who ached to get and give belief but who would rap its every coin on the counter ten times before giving or accepting. This desire for absolute, total giving and taking I had already experienced jubilantly with Ana ffrench; never with my insecure Anador, overtly so strong, inwardly so insecure. As I looked at this young woman's crystalline blue eyes I heard the two lines from *Love in the Valley* – '*Love that so desires would fain keep her changeless,/Fain would fling the net, and fain have her free.*' Who wants a netted woman? Love is war. Eros has his camps. In that emulatory hunters' spirit we began our chase hand in hand after, it transpired, me. I admit that I deceived her thoroughly but only, it seems now, that I might the more completely undeceive her at the end.

I had to do this for as long as Bob Two would not go about his business or hung around threateningly. He did go to London for

Christmas to stay with friends, if outsize business men ever have friends. Left alone she did give me some but not all of her love, only loving comradeship, her total trust withheld so exasperatingly that for a time I began to fear I had another vacillating Anador on my hands. When he returned to Dublin I saw much less of her, and suffered deeply from her evasions. He went back to Paris and we lived again in gaiety and affection. When he returned once more we did our best together to keep him entertained, but my fear got in the way – he was all too plainly taken by her. Besides he was often pathetic, a lonely man with no intimates but us two. I did, with the double purpose of helping him and relieving myself, introduce him to a few sailing acquaintances in the Royal St George who helped him to break into the American diplomatic and business sets. When they got him provisionally accepted as a country member of the Kildare Street and University Club he was as hugely pleased as a boy, he wanted so much, or seemed to want so much to 'belong' in Ireland. I could not help telling him that he would get a far greater sense of belonging if he were to join The Confraternity of the Sacred Heart in Castletownroche. Why had I said that? Was I hoping that the gods might of their goodness produce a collision between his Mercedes and a blue truck a mile outside the village? He did go there, but with her, and came back safely, bearing only one fact more than I had found there: the birth date of Stephen Younger. It may have been a close shave – some lesser god-in-charge deciding that mercy might thicken the plot.

I soon began to think that he would never go back to the States. And why was she staying in Dublin? Or why did we not start our travels in search of his origins? She could disappear completely for a week and if I asked her where the devil she had been, what doing – Didn't she know I would feel both lonely and anxious? – she would just glance at me haughtily from her lidded blue eyes and say, 'Searching'. I, of course, could think of only one reason for her absences, although he too had his own way of vanishing solo, and then, when I thought he was at last gone, I would see him in the street, once wearing black glasses, either not noticing or pretending not to notice me when I raised a hand in salute. Once she did come back with a discovery. She had located in a cemetery in Cork, oddly called The Botanic Gardens, a headstone to one James Younger and his beloved wife Bridie; and from the cemetery records she had assembled their data, homes, origins, dates, the one 1870 to 1946, the other 1875 to 1945. I at once saw the significance of the dates, as when I tested her I found so did she. She was quite open about it:

'This is very close to where our Bob Two's father, Jimmy Younger, begins. Sent, you may remember, to his grandparents in Ireland until after the war ended in '45. Bridie Younger died, we observe, in '45. Her husband died the year after. What to do with the lad then? Old Stephen said he then took him – "naturally", he said, since Jimmy was, he claimed, his own son by Christabel Lee.'

'You believe him?'

'I don't think anybody any longer believes Stephen's fantasies, but it is a question of proof. Only a part of the proof follows from that headstone to his grandparents.'

'How do you know those two Youngers on that headstone were who you say?'

'I checked the records of the Compulsory Vaccination Act of 1863–79. The grandfather had been duly vaccinated, in the town of Lismore, on the Blackwater, fairly near, as you know, to Castletownroche. I spent a pleasant couple of days there enquiring about the Youngers. I thought I might also look up the records for the vaccination of a child called Jimmy Younger in Cork.'

'He had never been vaccinated,' I said compulsively.

'What did you say?' she pounced.

'I asked a question. He had never been vaccinated?'

'My hunch was right. His grandfather had the child vaccinated when he received him into his care. The certificate, dated 1941, gives the name of the boy as James, the child of Robert Younger, of Number 10 Sheffield Avenue, Fulham, London. Vaccination performed by one Patrick Hayes, medical officer.'

I did not dare enquire further.

Even when Bob Two did go off to the United States she still went on scratching around the Genealogical Office and the Custom House. Building up whose tree? Only in March did she decide to extend her researches further. Can love be obtuse? She later told me the simple reason why she had delayed – he had not decided to trust her until he actually saw his family tree growing under her hands. Then he did open a generous account in her name at the local branch of the Chase Manhattan Bank and told her to spend just as much as she wanted for travelling as far and as long as she thought 'profitable'. (Business men can also be obtuse.) I remember how she looked as she told me this: brooding, a gentle but positive glare in those crystal eyes, the soft lips pursed, but not enough – there never was enough – to flaw the gentleness of those swollen lips whose suggestion was always of a secret inner temple, an unspoiled world of girlhood searching, trusting, hoping for faith past and to come. This shone out in her fully the time, months later, I asked her how she could spend so much time on the life-lines of forgotten people. She did not laugh. She smiled at my folly, or was it at her own?

'I want to make a long five foot line of lives, going back and back. I have already gone as far with the Youngers as your great, great grandfather. Did you know how they got to that part of Ireland, to that little village in County Cork from Cornwall where they originally came from, I don't yet know how long ago, maybe centuries ago? They were salaried land agents to the Dukes of Devonshire who had the big castle at Lismore down the Blackwater from Castletownroche. It has been held by a Lord Castlehaven, an Earl of Orrery, the Great Earl of Cork, who was a young fellow-my-lad named Boyle who came over here in the sixteenth century with nothing but a signet ring and a cheque-book and made a fortune. Before him Sir Walter Raleigh had the land. The Earl of Morton had it. Away back in the seventh century it was a monastery when the Danes rowed up the Blackwater to sack it. The last family to have it are the Dukes of Devonshire, Cavendishes, their fifth home in these islands. Your grandfather and your grand-uncle somehow got hold of a small farm of land due west of it near the border of County Cork.' (She meant my uncle and father, those two sixpenny gamblers on flies spotting their pub windows.) 'Your grandfather set himself up with a brother of his in that general store and public house in Castletownroche. I had a special interest in this because somehow or other Castletownroche reminded me of the town of Banagher, and the old ffrench Chase house where I used to visit as a girl when my mother used to stay there. Or should I say,' with a wicked look at me, 'used to retire there to be *alone*? I like to have a picture of things going back and back, a lot of memories, traditions, a family, a line, any line, even if it is not my own line. This search for the Youngers has put me in search also of the ffrenchs and even of my grandmother Ana ffrench's people in London.'

To all this I listened jealously, wishing that I knew one-tenth as much about my past and, under the sway of her interest in her people and his people I began to realise with full feeling, for the first time, how important it was for Bob Two to find out everything he could about his father, Jimmy, and I at one and the same moment wanted to give him Jimmy and did not want him to have my son, a branch in my tree, a nest of me. So, when we did set off on our travels, first to London – we stayed in the Cadogan Hotel, where Wilde was arrested – it was as much to look again at Ana's place in Kew as to look for further records of the Youngers in Somerset House, though she also began to ask me questions about where I lived in London and why had I not married, and did I not want a family, and where in London did my brother live, and all this curiosity pleased me at the same time that I discouraged it lest she should come too close to my buried me, for what should I or any man or woman be if everything were known and we had no private darkness at all?

'I begin to see,' she said to me one day, 'what a pleasure it must be to write a biography and to come bit by bit, word by word, letter by letter on the inner lives of people who had before that been a mere name to you. I thought it very strongly yesterday as I went through some letters my mother got from various intimates in her hey-day.'

Here she again looked at me slyly-wickedly, obviously meaning that I had written some of these letters, and a great ache came into my heart to realise that I had already begun to form a small mortuary of clear memories, Ana in Fitzwilliam Square, Ana by the fountains, Ana in London, or in Kew long ago, Anador in Banagher, or on the Wicklow hills, and I asked her had she found any old photos of her mother and her grandmother; but I was relieved that she was able to produce none of Ana that I had not already been shown when she startled me by saying:

'I have come on some personal letters to Ana. Even a love letter,' she laughed, 'of sixty years ago when she and my grandfather Reggie used to spend summers sailing in the Mediterranean. She must have been a high flyer in her time. Judging by her pictures she must have been very pretty in her twenties and thirties.'

'I wish I had known Ana ffrench, I mean your grandmother.'

'I must show you one letter that will specially interest you, from a lover of hers away back in 1930. An extraordinary letter. Concerning a plan for giving her husband faked evidence for a divorce. It was written to her by your own father, Robert Younger. Did you know that your father was once in love with my grandmother?'

How the gods must have laughed at us over their port and cigars. It took me a long while to decide finally that while I thought I was escorting her she was conducting me, that while she gave the impression of being fascinated by family lines, her own, Reggie's, her father Leslie's, Ana ffrench's, Bob Two's, she was puzzling over my ignorance of my own. She had a hunch. She had not worked it out. But she smelled fish. In any case there is something oddly old-fashioned, young and romantic woven into her otherwise ironical and mordaunt nature that on the flick of a trout's tail transforms her into one of those romantic, rebellious, soulful often put upon, even frustrated young women of the 1840s and '50s that one meets in novels of the time, especially Russian novels, saying things like, 'I want to know what the storms of life have done to his soul, what convictions he has, what his deepest views are, what he will become, what life will make of him', which is not a modern way of thinking at all; so that even if she had not had a practical interest in me in relation to the job she was being paid to do for Bob Two she would still have become deeply interested in me as a person. A natural curiosity about other people's lives? That also, to be sure, but behind it something far more powerful. What, in the '60s and '70s we used to call 'commitment'? Something stronger still that I can only describe as a mastering desire, hot as lust, for total life-involvement.

She behaved, and looked, very much that way one showery evening in late April when her last combings through the registers of London's dead in Somerset House brought us out to a vast suburban cemetery beyond Richmond-on-Thames. The only human being in sight, a workman, told us with a dry smile that it contained 46,000 dead. Its central avenue is wide, straight, and empty. I could see why such cemeteries are called fields of the dead – acres of white Carrara unbroken except for an occasional granite weed, a macracarpa dark as a churchyard yew, few rosebeds beside the avenue, silence. The suburban traffic along the farthest boundary was silent as it was ceaseless, and heedless. Beyond the boundaries red-tiled roofs. Once I did hear a sound – an invisible plane above low clouds presumably making its approach to Heathrow airport. Nana would only say that she was looking for a grave in the Catholic portion of the cemetery but would not name its occupant until she found it among the Bertorellis, Landowskis, O'Hagans, Devlins. I got the feeling that I was being deliberately led, being deliberately surrounded by watching shades. If so they seemed all the more watchfully uncommunicative because a desolate yellow glow to our right indicated the approaching death of the sun in a sky whose lowering foretold a storm about to invade London from the coast. We halted at last on either side of a grave plainly numbered 17, in a section clearly marked 23R. There one last drift of yellow light touched a headstone of black marble whose carved inscription in gold read as follows:

Here Lie the Mortal Remains

of

Christabel Younger

of Richmond, Surrey

1903–1941

and of

Her Loving Husband

Robert Bernard Younger

of Castletownroche, Ireland.

May They Rest in Peace

I found myself silently reciting *Father who art in heaven/Thy name praised/Thy will done/Below as above./Give us bread to eat today/Forgive us our debts/As we forgive our debtors/And save us from the devil.* The twilight sank through the ground on the features of a tall woman, a poplar or aspen whose leaves shake in the littlest wind, her blue eyes fixed upward on me, her smiling mouth wide and white, not a vision but a body, so hot, smooth, odorous, loving, touchable that only my main force held me from falling on the hummock of grass above her. A bell tolled.

I looked in apprehension across the grave. Nana was staring at me from within the oval of her kerchief like an alerted blackbird. From that moment I was certain that she knew but was afraid to accept my secret. Then, as suddenly, blood flooded her face and in her self controlling, powerful, clear headed way she mastered herself.

'Hoopla!' she laughed. 'I suddenly understand what happened. Your father did what, as Anador told me, her father did when his wife died. He put his name on her tombstone. "May as well make one job of it," he said bitterly. The irony of it was that they found his wrecked yacht but they never found his body. So even his tombstone lied! You notice that this stone does not give the dates of your father's birth and death?'

'He died in 1965,' I assured her.

The bell tolled.

'That,' she said cheerfully, 'is the bell ordering visitors to let the dead sleep in peace. Let the living go and have a drink at the nearest pub.'

We had left the side path and were walking slowly along the main avenue leading to the entrance gates when she turned her head to look back. The light was so deceptive and there were so many spiky monuments that I could not be sure whether the solitary figure standing back there was looking at the grave of my wife or at one hard by it, but the outline was familiar. She gripped my lower arm and drew me to walk on quickly to the gates. We glanced about the virtually empty car park and there was the cream Mercedes. As we walked on in search of the nearest elegiac pub I asked her coldly whether she did not want to talk to her friend.

'I did not even know he was in London.'

'Is one allowed to ask if you have met him in London before this?'

'I have not met him this time or any time in London. I saw him once by chance on The Strand when I was leaving Somerset House. He was on his way in. I do not believe he spotted me. I have the feeling that he is dogging my footsteps. Always checking up on me. I tell him I am going to Manchester. I see a man like him in Manchester. I tell him I have been to Colchester. Sooner or later I find he has either been to Colchester or sent somebody there.'

'Why in Colchester for heaven's sake?'

'Because you said in the Shelbourne Hotel or somewhere that your father died in Colchester. He got the idea that you might have been born there.'

'Why should my father matter to him.'

'He wants to know every single detail about his forebears. He wants proof of everything. His finger in the wound. It is an obsession. I drew him up a chart as long as a Chinese *kakemono* on a wall. Still he is not satisfied. I protested to him once about it. I said, "I tell you everything I find out." He said, "I can't help it." And just for that once he seemed pathetic to me. He said, "Look, I don't want to have this feeling that I must live a life that's closed at both ends. I know it's closed at the far end. I hate this feeling that it's closed too at the beginning, that I don't know what is was before me. Living between two walls. My birth and death. It is not enough. It's not good enough. It is like being an illegitimate. To be always wanting to know Who? Why? When?' She halted, looked up at me. 'I should not have said that.'

'Why not?'

She drew me onwards. We reached the pub, sat in its dim lounge bar before two whiskies. We had just got there in time. The earth darkened, the sky trembled, the rain from the coast exploded in a summer cloudburst on the cemetery, on the pub's windows.

'Well,' she said glumly. 'I am finished with this job. I can't do any more. Not for him. He says I can but I don't want to.'

'What else does he want?'

She looked at me under her eyebrows.

'He wants to find out all about you.'

'Such as?'

'What I've said to you. When you were born, and to whom. It is the one blank on my *kakemono*. He wants to see your birth certificate. When I point to my *kakemono* and say to him, "He comes in here somewhere," he gets furious. He must know exactly. Well, I'm not going to be either your coroner or your midwife.'

'Ask me!' I said. 'Ask me anything. You can believe me utterly.'

She shook her wheatsheaf head and said, 'It is not a question of anything. It is a question of everything.'

'What is this bloody everything?'

She looked through the speckled window. She looked at me and said it:

'Your birth certificate.'

'Why?'

She looked out again at the battering rain, and resolved. She dipped the tip of her right forefinger into her whiskey and slowly drew a wet line on the white bakelite of the table. She let three drops fall on it at intervals and patiently, almost insultingly patiently, she explicated:

'Number one. Stephen Younger. Yes? Two. J.J. Yes? Three. Robert Bernard. Right? All three born in Castletownroche, in, respectively 1895, 1900 and 1900. Local parish records. An R.B. marries one Christabel Lee in London, in 1930. Somerset House records. In 1936 – S. House again – they have a child, Jimmy. Jimmy is sent to his grandfather James in Ireland, date uncertain but presumably in 1941, by which latter date his mother has died. Register of the Cemetery Board. This Jimmy is known to be in Ireland in the care of his grandfather James Younger in 1941. Vaccination certificate. The boy remains there until his grandmother and grandfather die towards the end of World War Two, whereupon, late in 1946, he is sent to the United States to his uncle Stephen Younger. American immigration registers. The boy grows to manhood. In 1960 he marries one Anna Saxe of Dallas, Texas. Records of the Health Department, Registry Division, city of Austin, Texas.' Her wetted finger drew down a perpendicular line to mark another generation. 'In 1961 he has a son, christened Robert Bernard Younger, to wit our friend of the cream-and-coffee Mercedes who is at this moment either peering through the window at us disguised as a policeman or has been serving us our whiskey disguised as a nun.'

She spread her palms. Between them there hovered an interrogation.

'So?' I challenged, feeling whole cemeteries yawn, as Hamlet said and as a million hack journalists like me have said after him. (Imagine any journalist being able to invent an image like that!)

Her smile was as apologetic as an executioner's. Down came her axe.

'So where do you come in?'

'You tell me,' I said, laughing my boyish laughter.

She lowered her eyes to the table and slowly wiped out Stephen Younger.

'Balmy!' she said. She next wiped out my twin, J.J. 'Childless,' she said. Without lifting her head she placed one pointing finger on his twin B.B. – that is on me and from under her red eyebrows looked at me.

'That is one place, Bobby, where you could have joined the Younger line, but only if you were now about ninety-one years old. Or here, as an older brother of Jimmy Younger, but only if you were now about fifty-seven years old. Or you could come in here as an older brother of Bob Two, but only as an American citizen approximately thirty years old. Of none of these births have we found any record and Bob Two has in his thorough way employed one of the best trained genealogists in Britain, an old lady named Amy Poinsett, solely to search for any document anywhere that would demonstrate your existence between 1930 when your father B.B. married Christabel Lee and 1936 when Jimmy was born of that union.

'Why stop at '36?'

'Because Bob Two is only interested in the next of kin of his father. Such as a brother of his father or a son of his father older than himself.'

I opened my mouth to ask a question. She answered it before I could speak:

'Bobby! Do you think he is going to all this bother and expense merely out of curiosity about his relations?'

'Pfoo! All these sentimental Irish Americans...'

'Flying in from Texas on the least hint of a discovery? Scattering money like grass seed? Employing researchers in America, me in Ireland, Mrs Poinsett in Britain? You have him all wrong, Bobby. He is third generation American. And Texan. He is not ghetto Irish. He has not got their ethnic obsession. He is away up, and out, and rich and on the loose. He is only marginally interested in his forebears. And he is not in the least sentimental about them. Insofar as he gives any other impression,' she glowered at me, 'it is an act, performance, a mask!'

'For what?'

She spoke as patiently as to a schoolboy.

'To hide his real concern. Which is that his father Jimmy Younger died intestate and a widower. He left no will. Amy Poinsett told me so a few days ago. If you were either a younger brother of the late Jimmy Younger or an older brother of his son Bob Two you would be next of kin, and entitled to inherit a lot of money.'

'Who do you believe I am?'

'I could believe that you were, as you told me, born forty years ago. But since you have named no father, and no birthplace, and we can find no corroborative documents I should in that case also have to believe that you were born out of wedlock. It is the kind of birth for which complete records are rarely available, beyond the name of the mother – Smith, Jones, Tompkinson, Murphy, what you like; the Record Office is chock-a-block with them. Unless you can produce verifiable details of your earliest infancy, and the name of some identifiable relative other than an adoptive father I must believe that you have emerged from out of a void. Who said it about lost memory? "An aching void this world can never fill". Otherwise...'

Her candid eyes left it to me to speak. I dared not. She laid a tender hand on mine, looked out, said, 'Rain stopped!'

The storm had moved away northward. A cool gleam of sun caught the pools it had left behind. The road shone. We were almost completely silent on the way back to the Cadogan where a message waited her. Would Miss Longfield please urgently contact Mr R. B. Younger II at the Connaught Hotel. I dined alone. She returned late in a mood between rage and regret. Miss Poinsett had unearthed two Youngers whose dates could conceivably fit, though she was, imaginably, sceptical: one in Newcastle-on-Tyne and the other in, of all places, Ostend. To accommodate Miss Poinsett she had unwillingly agreed to follow both lines of enquiry. He wished to accompany her northward. He would drive.

When I saw her again in Dublin ten days later, her attitude to him had changed. He had charmed her. Newcastle had not been bad, Ostend had been awful, she had enjoyed guiding him around Paris. It helped that both the trails had proved, as old Miss Poinsett expected, dead ends. In other words I was no threat to him. I was not in his pedigree. Christabel Lee had died, on my own showing, years before I was born. I was much too young to be the elder son of Jimmy Younger who had married years after I was born. To show his appreciation of her work Bob Two had given her a present of a handsome gold wristlet watch and had invited her to visit him, at his expense, in Texas in June. I had no chance to probe her about this generous (?) offer. In fact we had no conversations at all during her stay in Dublin, she was too preoccupied with other things – preparing her flat for letting, putting it into the hands of estate agents, gathering suitable, and winter, clothes for Paris where she wanted to resume as quickly as possible the studies that had been interrupted by her mother's death. Within twenty-four hours she had come and gone and I was alone again in Rosmeen Park with my fears, suspicions and, at times, near despair.

It had seemed to me during her hasty passage through Dublin that an ominous change had come over her since that day at the cemetery. There had been, or so I felt, a new kind of light about her, like that nimbus or glow that surrounds my pavement lamp whenever the fog seeps up from the shore and from my window I see this glow rather than the central bulb. She had about her a new temerity, a suggestion of hardihood, of abruptness, boldness, audacity, something like the intensity of a horsewoman facing a long, rough gallop over double ditches and five-barred gates, a touch of the rash, reckless, heedless, accompanied at the same time by an in-withdrawn air as if there were a very private battle going on in her between, perhaps, her past and her future, between the person she used to be and what she either now was or was resolved to be. Under what stress? Was I responsible? Or he? Or was it just Paris? She gave no hint. I naturally guessed, wrongly as it proved, that he had asked her to marry him and feared that, at best, she had postponed the decision – whence the idea of Texas in June.

My main hope was that it would have been unlike her not to have told me so frankly. All I knew was that she had come and gone like – it is an inappropriate image for a woman of her strength of body – a bird in flight, and that this swift coming and going left me with the black feeling that this was an End, that I had either been deliberately neglected or quietly rejected. And yet, those twenty-four hours had had their lovely side – the sight of her eager activity, her youthful self-absorption, her concentrated activity even if all this young bustle was also a sight that made her continued presence all the more desirable and her departure all the harder to bear. Sitting alone in Rosmeen I felt purposeless.

And then, quite unexpectedly, he solved everything for, as the sequence of events turned out, all three of us. He rang me one morning, shortly before noon, from Collinstown airport to say that he had just arrived in Dublin and would be in town for a night or two on his way home to Texas. I at once invited him to lunch at my club. I met a very different Bob Two – subdued, more friendly, not at all bumptious but, expectedly, as vague as ever about what he was up to in Dublin. He did talk in a large if random way about Irish mining, which could have had some basis to it, but if so the matter did not occupy much of his mind or time during that after-noon and the next. Indeed all his talk was so random that at one moment I got the queasy feeling that he was going to ask me if I would become his 'chief researcher' in Ireland and that the subject this time would be Nana Longfield, so often did he advert to her; indeed so often that I soon found it embarrassing that two adults could be held together by one sole idea, which was not even hinted at for a second by either of us, if, that is, the idea of marrying Nana Longfield could be considered the same idea for two men of such completely different origins and different experiences as a one-time Irish journalist who had spent half his lifetime pottering around with provincial British newspapers and a young American mining engineer leading a high-pressured life all over the world. Apart from Nana I could not see that we had anything much in common.

So, after that opening lunch we drove, at his suggestion, up beyond the Dublin hills talking desultorily and it seemed to me aimlessly during a prolonged tramp over the Wicklow moors. (We passed, I observed, the little hollow where Anador and I had first made love.) On our return to town he insisted on my dining with him. We met the next day after lunch for another rural tramp, dined at a country inn, adverted many times to Nana, and in the most impersonal manner to marriage, always as a subject of general interest, and said our goodbyes outside the Shelbourne. By this time we both knew what was in both our minds, though I was baffled as to why he had paused in Dublin just to talk to me about it. I understood when he rang me on the airport telephone the next morning, though only at the last moment when he hung up on a manly, 'Well, goodbye Bob, and may the best man win.' In his relations with her he had plainly come up against an even more forbidding barrier than, he must have divined, the forest that now stood between her and me. He had halted in Dublin solely to measure his chances against the differences or similarities between us. In a burst of joy I kissed the receiver. She had been unable to conceal from him the warmth of her feelings for me.

I understood more. I understood that what held us both at a distance from her ever since that stormy April afternoon at the cemetery near Richmond was nothing so solid or identifiable as a barrier, or a word, or a wall. For me certainly and I think also for him it was a growing awareness of a sweet delicacy of perception in her, a sensibility more powerful than either of us had experienced in any woman before we met her, and I am not forgetting her super-sensitive mother and the penetration and the sensibilities of her splendid grandmother. This dimension had showed itself clearly in the way we had built her up in our talks as a creature of such courage and fineness that I now know how right I had been to have been reminded by her earlier of those nineteenth-century heroines whose unbreakable honesty made the men around them seem weak and petty. It had been made plain too in the effect we both had on her over the last few months. He had begun well. He had shrivelled before her perception that however pleasant he might be as a companion he would always use her gifts in the way he used everybody's gifts – as so many chips on the green baize of success. On the other hand she had found me so secretive if not actually deceptive that I could now win back her trust only by an honesty as total as her own. In those last two wondering, wandering days he and I had half-perceived and half-created a woman who was more than a woman – an ikon, a figure on one of those great Byzantine mosaics of Monreale, Palermo or Ravenna, modelled on some once-breathing human creature, subsumed as an essence that would henceforth mean to me the bodily presence called Nana.

Now that I have been her lover for so many years, known all the joys and absorbed all the abrasions of our marriage, did I greatly exaggerate that morning as I laid down the black receiver, seeing as I did so our young American ruefully picking up his brief case at a final importunate call to board his plane for New York and Texas? Who can tell? The woman a man least knows is his beloved wife, mistress, daughter. We are all deceived by closeness, custom and above all imperceptible change.

I waited. When she chose to give me a signal I would have to decide how much of the total truth I could dare to tell her. I sent her a birthday card in June with one line: *Happy Birthday, even if you are spending it in Texas!* By return came a coloured postcard, the photograph of a café and some trees in rue des Archives where, I was to find, she had perched herself in a quiet third-floor-back two-room flat. The card bore one line: *In this glorious Parisian sun? Phooey! Ever. Nana.* That word 'Ever' brought me face to face with my problem. What truth could I tell anybody that would not be received with the conclusive rebuff of a horse laugh? I was once more on the point of evading her challenge when I found the way out of my quandary by worming my way into her own.

I had got as far as flying to Paris. I had called on her. We were enjoying a cassis outside a café at a corner of rue des Archives. I had in vain been trying this road and that to the entrance of her citadel. I tried once more:

'Tell me again,' I said, 'tell me once more of the time you first, as far back as you can remember, took notice of my existence.'

'But I told you all that long ago? When I was thirteen, that night in Banagher. I don't think I can have been more than thirteen. Yes, of course, I was thirteen. June, my birthday.'

(A child of thirteen. Anador forty-nine. I fifty.)

'Tell me once again.'

'Late, near midnight, you arrived in Banagher, down from Dublin, or west or whatever. It must have been at least midnight because I was asleep, in the room next door to Anador. You woke me up, the pair of you with your quarrelling. I fell asleep. You woke me up again with your love-making. I dozed again. I woke up again to the sound of more quarrelling. I could not stand it. To hell with this I thought and got up and stole down the stairs. I unchained the big door, turned the big key, got my bicycle and rode to the river and my boat.'

I saw the summer night. The poor waif would probably have first sat on the stairs with her fingers in her horrified ears. We two would have heard no corncrake from the moon-balanced meadows, lying uneasily or turbulently in our anger or passion in that ancestral bed in that lofty bedroom high over the great plain stretched silently all about us, and that child of thirteen shaking out her sail on the Shannon to get away from us into her own first bewildering longings and wonderings. One had to relate her flight to the delicacy that was her natural birthright and that would become her permanent strength, too strong by far for fastidious withdrawal or easy denial, the core, as I now know, of her own inborn belief in an ideal life where there need be no discordant deceptions, no doubts, nothing but the clean, moon-bright truth. She had seen enough of clouded truth already as between her mother and her father – I never did hear her say anything good about her father – and now here was more confusion between Anador and me; as, these many years after, still more shuffling between me and her, more dissembling, more bad faith. Not that there has ever been any place in her life for romancing. She loves living too much for that sort of evasion. Idealist in mind, a realist in body, spontaneous there as a mare on heat, a tigress, roe, fish, bird, brute, pig's mate, without a fleck of that inventive prurience which is the least excusable of man's multifarious adulterations of the pure flame of love. A driven character. Delicacy always ready to rebel, but rebel good-humouredly, because always ready to take up arms in defence as well as rejection, and never afraid to chop and change. This new coin is good, this new coin is false. A woman to whom somebody would always be wanting to say, amiably, 'Nana, one never knows where one is with you!' Did she know herself? For if all this be agreed, what was her constant, her compass, her consistency, her fixed star?

This was the moment when, outside that café, the noisy traffic as ignored as ignoring, I began to feel a key softly turning, and, now that I have lived so long with her I know that it did turn at that moment on her secret tabernacle, hut, temple of the numenous, the intuitive, the inexplicable, the spirit that whenever she is driven with her back to the wall she describes as The Something Else, meaning her otherwise reticent devotion to that extension of life that people vulgarly call religion – 'vulgarly' because all they mean is some organised sect or institution – cherished in her passionate imagination, but not shared by her passionate flesh. Her flesh anchors her firmly to the earth, that is to say to all men and women – chiefly, she would be the first to agree, to all men. In this harmony of her flesh and spirit, outside that busy café, over our heads the too sweet ache of the Mendelssohn, I found my sole ground for hope. Such a woman would never say of my piece of truth, 'Ridiculous!', or 'Do you take me as a fool?' She would quietly say, 'It is just another bit of the miracle of life.' Triumphantly, therefore, I told her in a few flourishing phrases about her gift for seeing all life ever since childhood, eyes wide open, as a miracle.

She replied with a look that made me see that I was yet once more making a fool of myself.

'You oversimplify. All my life I have been going to London to see the Queen and all I ever seem to have done there has been to frighten a little mouse under a chair. "Eyes wide open?" What were the four main events of my heaven-directed childhood? Ana ffrench died when I was three. I felt and remember nothing about it. But Anador told me I had bad nightmares for months after Reggie's death. No wonder. Storm night after night, the battered *Regina II* found, his body never given up by the sea. I was old enough to be distressed, in the way a bird gets distressed when a magpie hovers over its nestlings, by the quarrels that rumbled through Ailesbury Road over that gallery scandal. Later, of course, I coldly understood. My father had simply been selling forgeries. I came nearest to "eyes-wide-open" when I was sent to Anador's old boarding school in Banagher. As you know I mostly resided there but I also lived in the old ffrench Chase house with Anador whenever she took off from Ailesbury Road.

'But,' she hooted, 'I did not really open my eyes until I had been there some four years. Four years! I am sure my very wide-awake chums in the town and its rustic environs must have thought me a proper city mug. Angey O'Connor, Saucy Canty, Hanny Bolger, Minny Molloy. They did their best. As when they told me what it meant to be "after" somebody. Saucy was mad after a young Guard. Minny Molloy was out every night after Kruger Casey the butcher's boy who lived with his half-deaf mother, our housekeeper, in the gate lodge. I was sleepwalking. I did not notice that what they were politely trying to tell me was that you were after my mother. In the end it was a nun who woke me up.'

'About me and Anador?'

'About what you call the miracle of life.'

I pounced on the nun. This thirteen or fourteen year old girl inflamed by enthusiasms poured into her by some sweet young *illuminée* in the empty middle of Ireland. Turning her glass of cassis on the marble table top she recalled her nun.

'A cracked old thing. I only saw her once, when I sat beside her in the train going down to Clara, where I used to catch the bus for Banagher. I had been up in Dublin to my dentist. This ancient creature was returning from a family funeral to her own convent in Galway. My kind father seeing her alone in a Non-Smoker put me eloquently in her care, and her flatteringly in my care, kissed me dramatically, generously gave me a ten pound note (one knows what that was worth then), sent his best, best, best love to my mother and left us two looking warily at one another.

'For some miles she prayed, slept, started asking me questions about myself, then began to talk solemnly and prophetically about the Acropolis. She must have been nearly as old. I had seen pictures of the Acropolis. I suddenly think that Banagher school may have been a very good school – it had a good history teacher and lots of pictures of everywhere and everything. My old nun kept on saying that the Acropolis was coming and that all would be revealed. She assured me that St John the Divine could not be wrong. Then she probed me about my father who had seen me off at the station. Why only my father? I explained that my mother spent the summer in the country, painting. I was an only child. This pained her. She had six sisters and two brothers. I told her where I lived, and the why and the wherefore. I even told her about our friends and visitors, including you. How kind you were, in spite of your age, visiting my mother and me in ffrench Chase so often. As I was only just thirteen I thought and said that you were ancient. She took my hand in her yellow hands and she said, "Child! The old ones are the worst." I remember she said *wurrst*. No! Wurrssst! With a lot of spit to it.

' "Beware of that man. He is after your mother. If she is a beautiful woman he is the Devil's servant."

'Of course I knew then that the poor old thing was off her chump. After? My mother? An old man? Like you? She said, "We must pray for a miracle. Pray that he will fall dead in a fit or be knocked down by a car." And she gathered up her long string of beads and prayed all the rest of the way, mumble, mumble, that you would die in a fit. Still, for the first time I began to see, anyway to feel what it could really mean for a girl to be after a boy. But a grown man like you . . .

'I was staring out of the window at the fields floating up and down when she stopped mumbling and said something extraordinarily wise. She said, "God help us all, it's a crazy worruld." I said a Hail Mary that you would vanish harmlessly. That, I said to myself, would be a nice miracle. But two weeks later there you still were, knocking at the heavy hall door, waking the rooks, and the nun's word "crazy" suddenly spoke to me from the sky. I told you the rest. Well after midnight, sailing on the river, a duck clucking in the reeds, the half melon of the moon in the water, yellow – or as Saucy Canty always used say, the *yallow* moon – two yallow moons, each transparent, the one in the sky inside a pink halo, and I knowing that you were lying on top of Anador, and that this is a crazy world, and that there are no miracles, and that no one would tell me the truth and I'd have to find it out for myself. And . . .' she said briskly, holding out her glass for a refill, 'I have never since had any reason to alter my opinion on these matters'.

'But,' I ventured gently, 'you do still believe in other dimensions, in what people call another world. Where things are decrazyfied.'

I took a sour pleasure out of watching her shuffle.

'I know there is Something Else. But life in this world is like playing Scrabble with an incomplete set, or half a jigsaw, so I don't know how to fit scoundrels like you into it.'

I took her hand. She glared at me and insolently asked me if I was about to make a declaration. I threw all my chips on the marble.

'I challenge you to fit my true story into your jigsaw. And I bet you won't have the guts to try.'

'Go on!' Eyes darting at the challenge.

'Ten years or so ago,' I lunged and felt the suck of her flesh under my knife, 'you were shocked when you saw me with Anador. You thought me ninety. Be shocked now when you find me courting her daughter when I really am ninety. In fact, to be exact, I am ninety-one and a half. I am the third Younger brother. I am the grandfather of your American friend, as I believe you suspected, and feared, months ago. No other dates fit. No other records exist. I am nobody else. Born in March 1900. At no other time. In no other place. My piece of the truth about life, if you have the courage to accept it, is that we are all experiments of the gods. I am an experiment of the gods. They fixed it that I should die like Lazarus when I was sixty-five and be born again, still sixty-five, from that point down-growing, back-growing, un-growing so that at this moment I have down-passed forty and will go on younging like this until I am a youth, a boy, a child, become a baby in the lap, until I am seconds old. Then swoosh! Now, tell me I am mad. Or a liar.'

Her blue eyes had grown dark with excitement. She looked unseeing at the traffic in the street. A film of calculations unrolled in her eyes.

'Tell me all about it,' she ordered gently. 'Every detail.'

I did.

When I had finished we had four saucers each before us. Her eyes had cleared, become sky-blue, widened, smiled. Her hand fondled mine. I had not foreseen an acceptance so gentle. I was reminded of St Theresa's 'Let nothing disturb thee, nothing affright thee . . . He who has God lacks for nothing.' I have never seen such serenity, nor ever her again so unperturbed. The world fell away from us. If all the tanks in the French army had come rumbling down rue des Archives at that moment neither of us would have seen them.

'You mean,' she smiled, 'that in ten years or so from now you will be dwindling from thirty and I shall be coming up the course to thirty-five? A pleasant age for a mature marriage. And ten years after that I shall be near forty-five, and you will be?'

'Near eighteen.'

She clapped her hands, opened her gullet and laughed so joyously that three young men at the next table looked at her in admiration, she had taken on such a sun-burst bonus of beauty from the zest of her laughter.

'Eighteen? And forty-five? What *will* the neighbours say?'

Never before have I admired her more. I stared at the miracle of her reality.

'And I had expected you to say either that I am a liar, or hallucinated, or that it is really a miracle! You have said neither! You believe me!'

She shrugged one shoulder, smiled wryly.

'Miracles can happen. But they don't. As for believe? You forget that what I am supposed to be is a student of philosophy. I can accept, accede, assent. But what and how far? Belief is a tall order. If I ever do believe you it will be only because your story is so crazy as to be plausible.'

'Meaning what?'

'Meaning what Tertullian meant when he said that the idea of God is so absurd that it has to be accepted. *Prorsus credibile est quia ineptum est*. Even my shining intellect has to suspend judgement on one or two things! This world is so patently absurd that purely rational explanations of it can satisfy nobody. There can be no rational explanation of the fact, if it is a fact, that you are ninety-one years old and look and behave like a man of forty? For instance, at ninety, so I am told men have long ceased to be sexually potent, and as we know, Mr Younger, this is not at all true of you.'

'You mean I can prove the truth of nothing else to you?'

'You can prove that you are alive. As plausibly as you can prove the truth of a great many other similar trifles. Prove it, that is, for all practical purposes, which practicality ought to be and generally is enough for everybody else except the kind of philosopher who while scratching his own bottom all day long loves to make fun of such popular fancies, caprices and illusions as that it is indefectably certain that anybody has a bottom. Mind you, the world is full of illusions. I cherish one or two about you. And you, I am sure, about me. You could easily be under the illusion that you got a message from Olympus. It might be a hangover from a dream. On the other hand there are limits also to the value of so-called evidence. I have tried hard to track you down to your birth and have always hovered finally in a great fright over the date that would make you the age you are. On the other hand remember your American friend's story about his father telling his mining engineers in Anatolia that what should count most in a search such as theirs was the persistent evidence of ancient monuments. But there is your monument in Richmond announcing that you are lying underneath it! Mining is one thing. Death is another. So is birth. You have persisted too damned long and look too young against all the evidence of countless generations about the inevitability of decay. Here you nevertheless are! When such a case arises we can only take refuge where we can. As Sherlock Holmes had it, when all possible solutions fail we must seek for an impossible one. What seems crazy may be sane. The crooked be straight. Like a crook's kiss – such as yours – which, in my view of the world, old wise crone that I am, is much more likely to be reliable than the kiss of some honourable slob who, poor fool, firmly believes in something called eternal love. While I do not understand what happened to you ninety-one years ago I can, however provisionally, accept that it could happen. In a word I believe *you* now. Kiss me. I will believe your story is a fact when I am fifty and you are twelve, and look it.'

We left the café nose to nose like any pair of lovers oblivious to everything but themselves, talking earnestly about youth's courage and age's defeatism, love, marriage, children, food, clothes, God, Right, Wrong and, of course over and over about Honour, Loyalty and Truth. We might both have been seventeen so serious and happy we were. I cannot remember where we wandered. We paused, I know, at cafés to rest and drink. We must have dined somewhere. Or did we? I told her everything (nearly), though as for genealogies she was now far less interested in mine than her own, chagrined to the point of temper to think that if she had known her pedigree in her teens how nicely and slyly and persistently she could have roasted the old Monsignor! When I told her how I had loved Ana ffrench in the last five years of her life, and apparently had loved her for twenty years before I began life all over again, she was at first so convulsed with laughter that to the amusement of passers-by she had to lean against a tree for support – 'I am in love with a man who was in love with my grandmother!' – and then became so curious, indeed so inquisitorial that from long habits of secrecy about my past I concealed from her (at least for the present) the fact that I am putting it all down in a Memoir.

The next morning I awoke in her bed alone. It was almost noon. My head was woozy, my heart pounding from too much liquor. A note left by her said 'Everything in the refrigerator including Alka-Seltzer gone to a lecture you dear drunken slob meet me at the Café Assassin at 5. N.' I lay for a long time gazing at the ceiling, triumphantly happy, my joy overflowing its brim, except for certain looming fears, chiefly three. (1) What would the gods have to say to all this? (2) If one whisper of gossip about me were to escape beyond the pair of us then our happiness was over: within hours we would have the world's press, radio, television, medical science, mobs from every country howling at our door for the secret of second life. (3) In spite of her sanguine amusement at the thought of herself aged fifty and me aged twelve must she not sooner or later feel depressed at the chasm of the years first narrowing then widening and widening between us? I dared to no more than glance at the complement of this possibility – that I also might come to regret the dividing years.

In my halcyon [*sic*] days as a journalist I would blithely [*sic*] write at this point of time [*sic*] that my feelings may easily [*sic*] be imagined when I saw her approaching the Café Assassin around five o'clock. My feelings cannot at all be imagined. I found myself suddenly tossed about by a whirlwind of astonishment, admiration, tenderness, awe, triumph, fear, desire, humility, vainglory and an all over sense of the presence of the incredible and impossible when I saw my future wife emerging from the foam of that Parisian pavement; feelings that were as suddenly chilled when she received my kiss coolly and ordered her *cassis vin blanc* with a disturbingly preoccupied air.

'Was the lecture no good,'

'I didn't go to it. I wandered. Remembering your past and wondering about my future.'

'Wondering? What? About me?'

'About Christabel Lee.'

'Oh, for God's sake . . .'

'. . . and the first real love of your life, my grandmother Ana ffrench. You see, Beebee, if I am now to accept as possible, or as likely, or even as a fact that you are who you say you are I realise that that long letter to Ana ffrench in 1930 about a night spent with a lover in Nice, and about her half-crazy husband and their proposed divorce, was written by you. Thinking to myself about your love-making that night and then about your sudden marriage on the rebound to Christabel Lee made a lot of things fall into place and raised a new question.'

'What new question? Anyway all that was in another life!' She surveyed me ironically from under her eyelashes.

'Whose life? Lived all over again? I think it is sensible of me, you must agree, to have a special interest in my predecessors in your affections. After all, here is a woman, your dead or vanished wife, who might have become a very close relation, a late grandmother-in-law, your grandson Bob Two's grandmother, were it not that my wisdom or folly, or the grace of God, or the lack of it threw me into *your* treacherous arms instead of his.'

Whereupon in that buzzing café she recaptured from the summer just gone those days when she had flown into Dublin and out of it within forty-eight hours, leaving me who had been so close to her for so long with an uncomprehending sense of having been summarily snubbed. Taking up her *cassis* she revealed all. On her way back to Dublin from Paris she had paused in London, and spent a night with her genealogist friend and colleague Amy Poinsett. At the name I slowly lowered my glass to the table and listened carefully, keeping one eye on her brief-case from which she was slowly withdrawing a long packed envelope. In a thriller novel she would be withdrawing a small black gun.

'We chatted, of course, about The Younger Case. She always refers to her commission as "cases", says it adds a touch of romance to her work, makes her feel like Miss Marple. Most of her tasks, she confesses, are mechanical, performed quickly and forgotten quickly, but for some reason The Case of the Missing Younger never seemed to her to have been quite "polished off". A small part of it stuck with an especial stubbornness in her mind as unfinished business: to wit, The Case of Christabel Lee. She was both amused and frank about this minor obsession. While saying to me that if I ever adopted her profession I should never neglect these odd little obsessions, which occasionally open up an unexpectedly golden lode, she also admitted that part of the attraction of The Case of Christabel Lee lay in its euphonious title. Born in Richmond, she thought, married in Richmond, buried in Richmond. A local girl?

' "To be sure," she agreed, "Richmond has since become a widespread suburban borough, with a population of say 200,000 people. But in 1930, when Miss Lee was married, an old directory gave the population of Richmond-on-Thames as a mere 37,791 and that would have included a large proportion of the new environs of the old town. It even still has the air and remnants of its one time rural remoteness – now destroyed, of course, by motor cars, buses and the London Underground railway, and Greater London spreading far out and around and beyond it. Yet it even still has its village cricket pitch on the Green, its ancient Commons, its old pubs, its village church with tombstones of the seventeenth century, some of its old houses, its mayor and council, and of course its great park and Tudor palace."

'Anyway, Amy Poinsett thought that in 1930 it might have still been the sort of place that would have had its own little local paper, news sheet, gazette, or even "Parish News" where, by chance, a local girl might rate a passing mention. The tennis club? The archery club? A church fête? True to her form and to her profession old Amy followed her hunch and, sure enough, there was such a local paper in 1930; in fact it had been there since the early 1870s – The Richmond and Twickenham *Times*. Weekly. Every Saturday. Twopence. Circulating in Richmond, Kingston, Surbiton, Norbiton, Twickenham, Brentford, Hounslow, Chiswick and eleven other places. Trust old Amy to list them all. See! Her letter. "Full to the brim," she says, "as a pocket mirror of the happy faces between the two Great Wars, more cosy, companionable, gossipy, villageous than you ever could guess without looking at its grizzled old pages in Richmond's Public Library." Any local event so important as a wedding would be at least recorded. Indeed page two of the *R. & T.* was (Amy again) "a confetti of weddings" under such bright captions as A SPORTSMAN'S WEDDING, TWIN SISTERS WED, A LABOUR PARTY

WEDDING, UNIQUE DOUBLE WEDDING, COUSINS AS BRIDESMAIDS, SO that when "our reporter" attended your wedding to Miss Christabel Lee (of St Margaret's-on-Thames) in St Elizabeth's Church in some retired part of Richmond known as The Vineyard, we may safely envisage the young man's, the doubtless *very* young man's bursting pride and excitement as he pencilled the startling headline FROM CONVENT BELLS TO WEDDING BELLS. Three months before her marriage, he explained, the bridesmaid had been a nun.'

The waiter removed our empty glasses. I gazed as wildly at him as if he were Banquo's ghost. Nana smilingly indicated to him that we would like to have the same again.

'In fact,' she resumed, 'he did not report the matter quite correctly. Christabel Lee had not been a nun. She had been a postulant. Even so such a marriage, in 1930, must have struck the readers of the paper as most romantic. I presume that I am to take it, Bobby, that you have no recollection of this striking event? Has it ever occurred to you that this bad or lost memory of yours is a symbol? That you must always have felt a bit lost, unattached, uprooted or unrooted, not belonging, a born exile? You became a physical exile when you left Ireland. Yet even exiles attach themselves to other people, sometimes to other exiles, or to people whom they change into exiles, preferably when those others are young. Ana Carty later Ana ffrench, Anador ffrench, me, Nana Longfield. How old I wonder was Christabel Lee when you first met her? How young?'

'Ana,' I protested, 'was not young. When we chummed up together she was turned sixty.'

'But when you *first* met her? My mother was not all that young but I always think of her as a girl who never grew up. You can see why this letter of Amy Poinsett upsets me. You ditched that young woman for my mother. You ditched my mother for her. Christabel Lee joined something when she entered that convent. You uprooted her. It is not your fault that she died. Nor that Ana ffrench died. Yet you finally ditched my mother, for me.' She ruffled the letter in her hand. 'Why? Are you a natural ditcher? Let's reconstruct. In Nice in June 1930 you are in love with Ana ffrench. In September you marry another woman.'

I held up my open palms.

'Yes, yes, I know, you cannot remember, but surely after you and Ana ffrench met again, years later, she and you must have cleared all that up? And unless you have also forgotten that clearing up, she must have told you when you became lovers again what happened to you both after that wild night in Nice?'

(If I only had had time to read my Memoirs again! Perhaps to excise anything in them that might wound her...)

'She told me that my letter to her, confirming our midnight declaration of love, wrongly addressed, took so long to reach her – nearly two months, she waiting for it week after week, I waiting for her reply to it – that we both became prisoners of our own pride. When I did not write, or appeared not to write, she took it that she had been just another casual tumble to me. I presumed that when she did not reply to my letter I had been just a casual tumble to her. Otherwise I might have telephoned Nice, or Dublin. By the time she did get my wandering letter she felt bitter of me, she had planned her future, and she was pregnant.'

'By?'

'It could have been me. It could have been Leslie. It could have been Des Moran. It could have been anybody, except apparently her husband.'

'So you sought out your old girl, Christabel Lee, found that she, also feeling abandoned by you, bitter of you and of life and love, had presented herself as a postulant in a convent – Amy Poinsett has established it – in Kent. You went there and completely disturbed her. Amy, as pertinaceous as Holmes, or you, or me, driven by her own vocational pride, also went there, and found there – as you in Castletownroche found an old man in his eighties who had known your parents – an old nun in her eighties who remembered the postulant who ran away one night on the milk train to somebody she had formerly known in London, and was presumably found by him the next morning sitting on the doorstep of his flat beside two milk bottles. Like the nineteenth-century Irish gentleman that you think you are you happily transformed her from a dishonest nun into an honest wife.'

It was, I think I may reasonably think, an unusual conversation even for the terrace of the Café Assassin, on Boulevard St Germain, that September 11th, 1991, if only for her old impressive reason that because it sounded crazy it must be true.

'I had to tell you all this, Bobby. Enough secrets have come between us. I have been wondering all day whether to think the worse or the better of you for what you did with that young woman. I did not know you had so much dash in you as to drag a nun by the hair out of a convent and marry her. On the other hand nobody trusts these marital *contre coups*. A second choice always suggests a second best. Then, that stray-away letter to Ana ffrench in Nice! The letter of a man deeply in love, yet you could not wait, you did not seek her out, you put pride before passion. How long, I wondered, before he also ditches me.'

'Me! This ancient of days?' I laughed at myself and gave her what I thought the perfect answer. 'You are my last love.'

It seemed to calm her, but after a moment or two she cocked a slightly satirical eye at me and murmured, 'Younger by name and by nature.' And from that on she became increasingly sensitive to the contrast between our ages. There was that party, for example, on New Year's Eve of 2002 that we shared with a few of her Trinity friends. During it I tactlessly remembered to her that for one tiny second some time between June and the end of the year just about to disappear we had been exactly the same age. 'Our ships passed in the night.' At her sharp look I clenched my fists in anger at myself. She said nothing then but on the way home we drove in silence for about five minutes. Then she said, 'In ten years this century will be ten years old and you twenty. What will our friends feel about that?' Intent on my driving, what with all those Dublin drunks weaving and screaming I could only grunt that the gods alone know. She laughed, elated by the wine, addressed the flitting street lamps: *O temps, suspends ton vol! Et vous, heures propices, suspendez votre cours*. Push in your throttle, Time. Give us time, O Time, to savour our finest years. *Aimons donc! Aimons donc!* The which in the Park of the Gentle Rose we duly did.

They had, indeed, been six of our best years, for by that midnight we had been legally married for over six years. I write *legally* married because the upshot of my primal 'confession' that morning in that café on rue des Archives, capped by a further and final clearing up in the Café Assassin the next day, had been that we threw ourselves into a reckless, joyous, improvident, pre-marital honeymoon that – it seems incredible now, so staid have we become – extended itself into two and a half carefree years spent between Paris, where her philosophical studies were quickly immured by the hands of Time's best gravedigger, Love, and such Grand Tour centres as Geneva, Milan, Lago Maggiore, the high Trentino for winter sport, the Turkish Riviera, Tunis and Egypt for the rest of the winter, then Athens, Siracusa, Palermo, by boat to Naples, on to Rome, Florence and so back to the Italian Lakes where I was permitted access to two of her secreted caves of feeling, prophecy, illumination, life-sense: namely (a.) that her conscience had all these months been intermittently troubling her by her betrayal of 'the microcosm of thought', to wit her vocation, to wit Divine Philosophy, and (b.) that she had accordingly decided in Florence to become pregnant. (Explain this who can: I cannot follow her logic here. If not *thoughts* about 'reality' then the thing itself?). This secret decision she revealed to me at Lake Maggiore, again perhaps with some notion of a gesture towards 'reality' in so far as this had been the place where we began our southern tour and was now the start of our last lap back to Dublin, where since she had given up her flat on Ailesbury Road we settled down in 17 Rosmeen Park. From there she gave birth to a baby girl in March 1994 whom, at my random suggestion, we christened Ana.

It was to be three more years before she was able to resume her studies in her old college, Trinity, and then unsatisfactorily because interruptedly until Ana was old enough to be pushed off to a boarding school in Brittany that a college friend warmly recommended to us. Nana, by then a splendidly mature woman took her degree of D. Phil, at forty-one, and became assistant lecturer in philosophy in Trinity at forty-two. We celebrated that event with a small but gay dinner where I the host (at twenty-one) was the youngest person present. After our guests had gone and we were washing up together I remarked to her that with these friends and acquaintances, new and old, I must obviously begin all over again to disguise my age.

'Your adverb,' she replied, 'is appropriate,' and added that she was also 'obviously' going to find it increasingly difficult not to look like my mother.

After a pensive silence she said, 'I at last admit it. You really are a child of the gods.'

'Incest?' I asked.

'Semi,' she agreed.

'You like it?'

She stroked my hand with her yellow rubber-gloved hand.

Every woman should burk at the word 'successful' as applied to marriage. It is too purposeful, it is a word whose history implies, like 'marriage' and 'marital', a woman who, lucky thing, belongs to a husband. Marriage has no aim or object. It can neither succeed nor fail. It is a declaration of a crazily wild hope that love can live for ever. Has our love lived on, as a perennial does, flowering in season? Looking back now have I learned anything about marriage except the virtue of silence in its time and of speech in its time, but as to when is the time! I have been unwise time and time again; made what at the time I felt sure was a mistake that years later proved to be the pinnacle of wisdom; took pride in something that years later was to be exposed as the depth of folly. About one of my speakings-out, my most explicit and prolonged, I am still unsure whether I was wise or foolish. I did it when she was exactly forty-three, I three months into my twentieth year, and our daughter Ana, a striking and charming likeness of her great-grandmother Ana, sixteen. That June morning my birthday present to my wife was this manuscript of my Memoirs completed to that date. Everything that happened on the head of this gesture, all that was said and done, or not done, remembered or suppressed, should answer my question about the flowering or fading of our love up to then.

She kept my Memoirs for two days and then handed them back to me with, 'Thanks for your trust, Bobby. I have made a few corrections.' Corrections?

Nana's 'Corrections'

What a liar! Not altogether, of course. Who is? A lot that he has written here is recorded history, but always lurking in the wings is the somnambulist, the fantasist, the romantic, visionary, day-dreaming B.B. A man who has committed the fatal mistake of turning his sensibilities inwards. I have on occasion wondered if this terrible gift of a second life may not have unnerved him, laid too great a load on his will, fogged his sense of common realities. He calls himself a journalist and at one point lauds the superiority of immediate facts over idealising memory, but he himself constantly idealises what he does remember. B.B. is midway between a journalist and an impressionist. He has several times boasted that he is not writing a novel, will have no fake suspense, no truth held back for guessing at, no romancing, no dramatics. If we believed him all he wanted to do in this record was to make a television documentary without a script, plonk his recording camera in an empty street and let it whirr. Bull!

A clear example is that scene in the cemetery in Sheen (Richmond), with my gob open at the inscription on the black tombstone indicating that he, Robert Bernard Younger, is lying underneath. That is pure thriller stuff. (Maria Martin. Dracula. Frankenstein. The Rue Morgue.) I was there, true, but not the way he tells it! I had seen the headstone the day before. I brought him there solely to observe its effect on him. Of course he dramatises. As a journalist he has to. It is true that Life is, externally, what the whirring camera records. A blank street. Girl slowly pushes pram. Emptiness. A car passes. Blank street. Two men come walking slowly towards the camera beside a long, high wall. Not much happens in this street? Another girl slowly pushes her pram. When she is gone another car passes. Blank street. Silence. Emptiness. Silence. A third girl pushes pram. A dog barks. So far, all true. But as soon as any of these smallest things happens not in the blank street but on the white screen or the white page every one of us says, 'Aha! Those two men are part of a story. The three prams have a meaning. That long wall is hiding something. Presently it will all be tied up into a pattern, a plot? If it is not we demand our money back.' This happens because when one is writing about something, and not just taking idle pictures of something, it is reasonable to presume that one is seeing shapes of conceptual meaning.

Here one can see B.B. all the time looking at his film in the cutting room, matching this bit with that, contrasting, dramatising, making or faking shapes of meaning. He can't help it, it is his nature, being what he is, whatever the hell he really is! A very small bit of a realist? Or a large 'bit of an artist' as we Irish say of so many of our otherwise rational friends? Or is he both? Wilde did mention that if art is art because it is not life we also notice that life has a disconcerting way of imitating it. Which opens up the old question, 'What is real?' Not that I mind what my old crook does along these lines with other people. That is how my old savage is made.* If, for example, he wants to romanticise about Ana the First, I do not mind – anyway I do not remember (I was three when she died) his Queen and huntress chaste and fair, not, as I have gathered from all sides, that she was either very chaste or very fair. Nevertheless, O.K., let him. Even though Anador told me once that her mother was a ruthless egoist whose only interest in her was to get shut of her. But, then, who was Anador to talk? Or I? If she parked me in the same convent and in the same old ruinated family house on the Shannon while she got on with her painting in peace and quiet, I, while I was finishing my Ph.D., parked my young Ana in a convent school in Brittany where the dear child now tells me that half the kids were on the pill, and all the nuns. But I do most strongly object when B.B. romanticises about me.

Take that famous June night he describes when he drove down at midnight to be with Anador, and I, poor little tiny waif, sat (he says) on the stairs with my fingers in my ears while they made groaning love in the bedroom next to mine. They did squabble, they did make love, but I never sat on the stairs as he imagined so guiltily. For all I know they may have been at it all night long. I do not know because, as he records, I got fed up with them, got out my bicycle and did go sailing on the river, but the part that is pure romancing is the idea that while I was moseying along the river in my scallop shell of quiet I was asking the moon to reveal to

***Note by B.B.* I give the text of her 'Corrections' unaltered but I must note that whenever Nana is feeling affectionate towards me she likes to conceal her emotions by calling me names like 'crook' or 'savage', the latter being one of her most endearing terms. As for the amiable epithet 'old' I was still twenty when she wrote the above. Is this note of mine also faking form? Or *just* explaining? My entire memoirs are an explanation.

me the mysteries of human passion. I knew all about them ever since everything had been revealed to me by that old cracked nun in the train with her St John the Divine, and her Apocalypse-Acropolis and her one shattering word 'crazy'. I had, naturally, tried other more direct ways into the mystery before her. Reggie, and Ana and Anador had left their meed of erotic fiction behind them and I naturally read them all, though it is true that not one of these books had told me anything. I think it was Simone de Beauvoir who remembers in her autobiography that she had, like me, gone through the erotica locked away in her father's bookcase and discovered nothing about the mystery of life until her mother said one day, 'Now, my dear, you must read a good, sound English novel,' and gave her *Adam Bede*. When Hetty went into a wood and came out pregnant Simone (like me with that magic word Crazy) at once understood *everything*. Anyway I had been looking at the telly, and I was not alone that night on the river. I had with me Kruger Casey, the butcher's boy who lived with his natural, i.e. unmarried mother, Gertie Burke, our rural concierge, in the gate lodge. My ears had gathered from his love-lorn Minny Molloy which was the window of his bedroom. It was a small, quartered window facing up the avenue of ffrench Chase. The month being June and the night warm I had found it wide open, put in my head and beheld by the brightness of the moon his white moon-sized backside where he lay asleep naked in his low bed. A fair-sized stone well aimed woke him up. He turned, rubbing his behind, saw me and leaped to the window, too startled to be aware of his nakedness, whispering, 'What's up? Is there some trouble at the house?'

'Kruger,' I begged in the idiom of the country, 'would ye ever come out for a sail in my boat?'

He looked up at the moon, rubbed the sleep out of his eyes, and stared at me.

'Jasus, it must be after one o'clock! Are ye daft? Sailing in the middle of the night?'

'Kruger, I'm feeling lonely.'

I will never forget how quick-witted he was, and how decent he was, meaning how kind.

'Did I hear a car at the house an hour back? And somebody knocking?'

'That was Mr Younger.'

He craned out of the window, looked towards the big house, saw as I too saw through the trees one lighted window. He looked straight at me. I looked straight at him. He looked up at the naked half-moon, and understood at once. (I know now that Minny Molloy and, it would have followed, all the rest of my young comrades, had long known all about 'Mr Younger', but through that blend of delicacy and prudence natural to all country people they never mentioned his name in my presence.) He said, 'You have the bike?' I nodded. He put his long, strong, bare arm out and grabbed my shoulder to inform me in the most considerate manner possible that if I told one word of all this to Minny Molloy he would knock my two eyes into one and tear every hair off my head till I would be as bald as an egg. He then withdrew to drag on a shirt and trousers, emerged barefoot, hair porcupined, to seat me on the handlebars and cycle off wobbling to the tiny harbour where my boat, among others, was moored.

The river that night is one of my happiest memories ever. We swam in our skins through moonlight leaping on water. We doused one another. Shouted. Woke the ducks. All I remember of a one-second picture of Kruger on deck is the sleek line of his side from the top of one hip down, the lean scoop on the side of his boyish buttock down to the side of his knee, a thigh with drops shining. I had never before noticed from pictures in books this highly informative difference between the way the female hip swells and the way the male hip slims. Out of the water he most politely kept his backside to me. We were *Paul et Virginie*. Or, no! He behaved, rather, like one of those 'perfect gentlemen' that one may still read about in English books written in an imperial age that, as I now know, had come to an end a generation before either Kruger or I was born. Kruger's slim hip completed my sexual education that had started with the word 'crazy'. (Correction. That bit, back there, where I mention beholding through his window a bottom as big as the moon. Inaccurate. As two half moons perhaps.)

Authentic detail. That is what I most regret to miss in B.B.'s record. And he is much too concerned about his own sensibilities. Damn your sensibilities, Bobby! Keep them for me – not for your historical record. Take one other example – that scandal at the art gallery when Leslie sold his fake Giacometti to an American. Some while before she died Anador told me in detail all about it. You, B.B., are so upset by the way everybody's feelings are upset that you never mention that you (not Anador) repaid that American out of your own pocket. Surely this was an objective detail that tells us something about you? As well as a lot about the crazy way the three of you ran the gallery. Did you never notice that it affected my mother's feelings about you? Or were you too delicately modest to mention the matter? If so I approve.

I come on your real nature, on you, on the you-ness of the you I love only at such *visible* moments as these in your record. Another is when you share with a friend a commemorative whiskey in the Yacht Club to drowned Reggie, evoking his storm, his night, his wreck, his courage, his misery at the death of a wife who had never loved him and whom he had (you say) never gone to bed with. That is the you I know, your compassion, your penetration, your sense of justice, your warmth, your honest anger against life which I like so much in you, all projected by one tiny glass of whiskey. Or there is the place where the ageing Ana suddenly becomes bitter and savage when she finds that her middle-aged Italian violinist has been kissing her pretty American guest. That is your pity extended into *an image* of age and defeat. Or the place where my powerfully built mother tried to buy a girly night-gown in Harrods and was shattered by your cruel remark that she had no waist. That moment is at the very centre of the not at all nice you exchanging your resentment against the world for her resentment at not having been born an aerial Undine in a Harrods nightdress.

To be sure there have been plenty of philosophers who have held that memory can exist without images. My test for them is: Can a blind man remember the silence of the night? He *can*, but how inadequately! I think of two silent nights, one near Lake Maggiore on our last night in Italy at the end of our honeymoon, one in Banagher when I was a child. You had been to Maggiore earlier, so you told me, alone and young; you had talked to me about looking across a river at the plain and the mountains, about boulders white in the stream, dry pebbles, how the water ran clear, and swift and blue in the channels. That night you had left me alone to go into Milan about some trouble concerning our car. I was alone. September stars. The line of dark mountains unrolled beneath them. One faint, far, tiny star floated briefly down through the sky. If the night throbbed I could not hear. Perhaps a heavenly stethoscope might? It is that speck of star floating down through the blue-black sky that makes me most clearly remember Italy's silence now.

As it made me remember, then, another September night, long before, in Banagher, not cold, not warm, me leaning out of another lofty window remembering in turn that this was the autumnal equinox, and thinking among other things how on the previous June I had been on the river with Kruger Casey one starry night and how the drops had shone on his bare thigh. What had those two silent nights in common? When I left that Banagher window and went to bed and opened my book I barely touched the angle-poise lamp illuminating my book. A faint speck of dust floated down past the light for a second or two and vanished.

In short, Bobby, I want projections not reflections. I want what your eye sees out there at the end of the telescope, not you oohing and aahing, even if your rhapsodies are all supposedly inspired by me...'

Enough! There are several more pages of these absurd Corrections. *Basta!* And more than *basta*. I have given the mare her head. She has made herself quite clear. For a week we argued daily on the head of it about subjects of which I knew nothing, such as Realism and Idealism, or Appearance and Reality. She told me in disgust that I was a Platonist when I said furiously that appearances in themselves are quite uninformative. Appearances? I skip through all descriptions of personal appearance in novels: e.g. 'his nose was long and aquiline like a seabird's beak, his hair was a warm russet, soft and curling, his two small eyes, small as a mouse's, darted when he spoke . . .' All that sort of thing, often for a whole paragraph. What the hell does it matter if his nose was long rather than short, or his hair russet rather than fair, or his eyes small rather than normal? Oddly, the last time I came on that tiresome sort of thing was in some Turgenev story side by side with the remark that the details of a man's face are never so important as what Byron called 'the music of a face'. Whereas what you want from me, Nana, is a photographic record of my immediate consciousness of a place or a face or a fact as it was *at that time*. It is impossible. All we have is echoing sound.

She sighed.

'Give me an example?'

'I'll give you an example from your own experience one day when we were driving in northern Italy. An incident I did not put into my Memoirs. I do not now see you at all as you were that day, but you and that moment remain with me like a piece of music remembered vividly in its long echoing effect. On our way south from Geneva you said you wanted to pass through Grenoble in memory of Stendhal. It pleased my innocence that you had so much regard for that splendid life-loving liar that I acceded at once, though pointing out that the Mont Cenis crossing would be safer – it was getting on into October – because if there happened to be an early Alpine snow on the passes we could put the car on the train between Modane and Bardonecchia.'

She closed her eyes, trying to remember. So did I.

It was not until we had crossed the southern Col du Lautaret, and after it the Col de Montgenèvre that I discovered that she had a second reason for coming into Italy this way. Once over the border, below the fashionable skiing resorts, descending to the plains of Piedmont, indeed within fifty kilometres of Torino she looked up from her map and cried out, with an air of innocence that completely deceived me. 'Ah! The Vallées Vaudoises, the Waldensian valleys! We must make a pilgrimage to one of them!' – and began talking animatedly about those twenty-five thousand breakaway Protestant enthusiasts who fled from the orthodox Catholics of France for safety into these harsh Alpine valleys in the thirteenth century only to be persecuted, and hunted, and killed there like animals by the Roman Catholic soldiery of Piedmont in every generation, until they were at long last given rights as free citizens quite late in the nineteenth century. And yet, so she insisted with passion, they had always been the backbone of Piedmont, and possibly still are the main element of the sturdy idealism that marks Piedmont off from Lombardy, that is to say the best side of old Turin from modern, self-indulgent, cosmopolitan, smart Milan.

Well, we were on our honeyoon. Madly in love. I would have agreed to any wish of hers. We turned off to a little place beyond, if I remember right, Torre Pellice, which itself shelters maybe less than five thousand people, proud to be the capital of those remote valleys of the Waldensians. It had, I observed, one inn, already closed, the season over, boasting a *giardino ombreggiato*. 'Shaded!' In the Cottian Alps, in October! We pushed on and upward into the valley until after several climbing, winding arid miles I halted outside the last village and looked at her enquiringly. The sun had gone down behind the towering Alps. The day was fading. I was thinking of the splendid restaurants of Torino, among the best in Italy outside Rome and Tuscany. I was also thinking fearfully of that single closed inn with its crackling vine trellises. She got out of the car, and to the wide, cold valley and its scattered farms she recited quietly but firmly and to me startlingly:

'Avenge, O Lord, thy slaughtered saints whose bones
Lie scattered on the Alpine mountains cold,
Even them who kept thy truth so pure of old
When all our fathers worshipped stocks and stones.
Forget not; in thy book record their groans
Who were thy sheep . . .'

She spoke the words quietly but her eyebrows glowered and her voice showed that she was deeply stirred. Finished, she looked around for a few moments, then said in a whisper, 'Let's go.' I did not say anything. I had no wish to break her mood with a word of disagreement. I drove on fast into Turin, relieved that we were not to spend the night in some freezing, one-horse Alpine *locanda*.

Nearly twenty years after that night I held up the manuscript of my memoirs.

'Well? Looking back at that incident am I not entitled to think it contradictory of you to expect lots of revelatory images in my modest memoirs and not to have exacted one real image or picture from Milton?'

Her reply did not persuade me:

'Milton was writing a poem. You are writing prose. Milton did not need to describe persons or pinpoint the place. The poem is not about a place or specifically about persons. It is about something the whole world understands – tyranny, brute power, sectarian murder, liberty of thought, any poor defenceless immigrants anywhere wanting to live their own little silly lives in their own harmless way. A Chinese could be moved by that poem just as readily as you or I. A black boy from Zaïre who had never seen snow. A girl from Sri Lanka who had no idea where Piedmont is.'

At that point I believe I pinked her.

'I disagree! When you were moved by that remembered poem you must have been moved by some private half-forgotten things in your own life, perhaps by some private injustice you experienced or observed or by many of them. Life is full of them, not recalled "specifically" but like the poem itself coming back to you like the far off roll of drums, or a horn calling through a wood. Artists never tell us anything new. They can only confirm what we have always suspected.'

In fact, on our honeymoon wanderings down through Italy we went on clashing wooden swords over this business of melodies heard and images unseen; as we well might on such travels where we looked daily at so many things that give the mirror pleasure of the Here and Now, and at so many more fine things concerned with Things Somewhere Else. She preferred the former, I the latter.

When I put this to Nana at the very end of our Italian wanderings she just laughed and said, 'All this means is that you like one kind of picture and I like another. And that is simply because you are an idealiser and I am a realiser. I remember the day in the Uffizi when you thought you had lost me and were going around in a flap from room to room. You had been held by the idealism of the Botticellis. I had become entranced by the reality of the Bronzinos. It is not that I did not know as a philosopher that the supposed antithesis between Realism and Idealism is false. I have good reason tonight to know that body and spirit are one. An hour ago leaning out of that window looking at the stars I added up the months. I am fully three months gone. I am preggers, Bobby.'

I have just taken down the now dusty old black brief-case containing these memoirs from its dusty top shelf in my study in Rosmeen to see exactly how long ago it is since I added anything to them.

I cannot believe it. It all seems like a third life and appears to have been only five years ago. I look at my boyish face in the mirror. It must be true. I do not look a day more or less than fifteen. What did really happen to me in those intervening years?

Having washed the dust from my paws in the pink hand-basin of what used to be my study bedroom fifty crowded years ago I recap:

It was in 1991 that Nana and I smoked our pipe of peace in Paris and set off on our prolonged honeymoon – Paris, Carthage, Dublin, slowly wandering, caught in passion's dream – bearing back with us Ana Two, our first our only child.

For five blissful years, settled into Rosmeen, Nana lived as her mother, our housekeeper, my married mistress. She was quite clear-eyed about the future: 'I will give five years to Ana's life and then I will go back to my own.' Those were our happiest years! Not that either of us did anything that an outsider would have thought remarkable. I did what little I could with small Ana, the shopping, the washing up, the garden, odd jobs about the house, looked after my properties, wrote the occasional article or book review, gave the occasional radio talk. I was absolutely contented. That brings me up to the time Nana kept to her word by resuming her studies seriously at T.C.D.

There was no reason why we should not have moved into a larger house – I was well off – and installed a full time housekeeper, or at least somebody who would be part nanny, part help, but with a vehemence that I at first thought odd but later came to respect, Nana refused to 'make a business of it'. She had come to like these narrow quarters; there was, she said, 'a certain merit in modesty' and since I had been happy pigging along here why start now to get entangled in making a business of the business of living?

She took her degree of D.Phil. five years later, impressing her examiners so much that T.C.D. at once offered her the post of assistant lecturer. She was elevated to the post of full-blown Lecturer in Philosophy in May 2010. She was then forty-three, I twenty. I still not only adored her. I revered her so much that if anybody had asked me that May, 'Well? Do you still believe that your old friend/enemy the Monsignore was right when he said that life is a good investment?' I would have laughed as wide as the full May moon and said, 'Work it out for yourself. Forty-five years have passed since I was (re)born in 1965. Since that March morning what a generous return in happiness I have enjoyed! And I know, that is I *know*, that is I KNOW what no other living creature knows about himself, that I have exactly twenty more years to live!'

Two weeks later I would not have laughed. Twenty years to go, yes – but of what vitality? That night of June 2nd. We had returned home late to Rosmeen from a big dinner given by the Italian embassy celebrating I cannot now remember what one of Italy's many splendid anniversaries, and were lying in bed, in the dark, well wined and dined, relaxing, waiting for the slope of sleep. As a way of saying goodnight I stretched my hand, laid it on her soft amber belly and said fondly, droopily, 'You looked marvellous tonight.' She, alerted, gripped my hand, rubbed it with her thumb and said, 'You looked too bloody marvellous tonight.'

'Meaning?'

I knew by the shaking of her belly that she was silently laughing, but not happily, especially when she let out a long shivering breath and fiercely shook my hand.

'Meaning that you do not in the very least look like the father of a daughter of sixteen. I overheard two women after dinner tonight whispering, "Which is Mrs Younger's husband?", and then saying, "That one? But he is a mere student." Beebee! Our Ana Two must sometimes wonder about you. Last Christmas when she came home for the holidays from Downe House* she asked me how old you were when we got married.' At this point she shook my hand as if we were saying goodbye. 'Beebee! Ought you really be here this summer when she comes home for the long vac.?'

Around 7.30 p.m. the last commuter train rumbles through the railway cutting east of Rosmeen Park. After that the park becomes completely silent. It was well after midnight. She must have heard my silence pulsing. Everybody else in the park would be sound asleep. Again that urgent handshake, that prelude to something like, 'Safe journey, darling, do write to me. Kiss kiss. 'Bye!'

'Next year if she goes up to Trinity she will be coming and going and bringing in her friends all the time. Go somewhere for some business reason while you still look old enough to need to go somewhere for business reasons. Just for the summer? Anywhere. A spot of travel? In Europe, or Asia, or the U.S.A.? Why not Texas? Call on your grandson, Bob Two. He must be around fifty by now. Be your own son. Tell him the Bob Younger he met in Dublin twenty years ago is gone to his rest. I am sure he would love to see you. If it comes to that all you have to do is to show an interest in the Younger branch in America. Then he will think it entirely natural that you should visit him?'

One of my minor afflictions is that I can hear my pulse in my right ear. I could count my pulse for you just by listening to my right ear. I can distinguish accurately between 80 and 82. At that moment I swear it must have been belting like a baby's, which can be as fast as 120 to the minute. Anyway it was going bong-BONG, bong-BONG, and not from drink. She patted my hand sympathetically. But she persisted:

'We can't wait until your two ships pass in the night. You must do something about it. You can't suddenly be plainly younger than your own daughter. What would she think? Feel? The shock . . .'

I surrendered, filled with admiration for her directness, her plain speech. She had waited to the limit. Not that I had been unaware of the problem. For several years I had felt it coming. It was not *my* age that mattered. At that time there was in Dublin a much-liked couple who had been unmarried lovers since she was thirty-five and he was fifteen; she, a pious Catholic, would neither contracept nor abort; she had already had four children by four other

*Downe House was her school in Kent. Kent, not Ireland, for the obvious reason.

fathers and four more by this youth. People laughed cheerfully about it. By being pious she admitted that she was a sinner and that made everything clear, clean, decent and part of the general pattern. Ana's age meant either that I had had fruitful sexual intercourse with her mother at the age of four or that I was not the man who had and that would not be part of the pattern. When Nana had said across the pillows that I must do something about it I knew that the reason I had procrastinated was that I had not known what 'something' to do about it except to vanish like a runaway husband or – and I dared for the first time to put this last possibility into words – boldly declare that I never was her husband. I said it aloud to the glow of the street lamp on the ceiling. I felt Nana slowly turning her face to me on the pillow. I lit the bedside lamp to meet her rage. She was looking at me with an astonishment so purely intellectual, so untainted by feeling that it wordlessly reminded me that there are other intelligent people like Amy Poinsett for whom also genealogy is an exact science. Her look said, 'And do you suppose that the same cock-eyed plan had not crossed *my* mind?'

I put out the light. It would not work either to suggest that Ana Two was an adopted child. Sooner or later, for any of half a dozen reasons, she would have to produce her birth certificate. So, we lay like two recumbent statues on a tomb, each brooding over similar fears, doubts and near resentments, I traded off as a lover for a daughter, fighting away my betrayal, she with as good a right to trace her betrayal back to the start of our acquaintance. At last I let out my bitterness:

'She is my daughter.'

'She is also *my* daughter.'

'Am I to lose her utterly? I want to see her again, and again. And again! And again? Always.'

'And me?'

'I would be lost without you.'

'And what about me without you?'

'If I go,' I challenged, 'how can I be sure you will ever want me back?'

'Of course I shall want you back, you dear idiot!'

'Are you sure I shall want to come back?'

Her hand shot towards me under the sheets, grasped my balls, shook them passionately.

'I shall die if you don't come back to me.'

Wildly, we made lovers' love.

Just the same, she did send me away. Passion and Reason? Divided? Every man and woman alive a collective self-ruled by a collective self? 'Brain and sky, the one the other will contain – and you beside?'

Well? We made our peace. What next? Go I must. But where? Back to Paris? To Geneva, the Italian Lakes, Venice? Become a wanderer around Provence? Hotel by hotel along the two Rivieras, step my way to the toe of Italy on to Greece, across again to Carthage? What folly! Like two ships' bells, echoing one another in a fog, each name evoked its own ghost. As if one cell in my brain were disturbing others around it I recalled that somewhere once while walking through some large white-boned cemetery I saw in the mushroomed distance a lone figure. What else would any estranged lover look like who returned alone to a place that she and he had once crowded with loving joy? I would have to go far away from her to some place where neither she nor I had ever been.

PART FOUR

Christabel

2010–2015

The plane made a bumpy touch down in Boston. Logan Airport. I glanced at my watch. By now Ana Two would have arrived in the airport in Dublin, frugally made her way home to Rosmeen Park by bus and commuter train, helped Nana with the dinner, eaten well and drunk well – I had left her a special bottle of claret – helped with the washing up, curled her legs, long, pretty, reedy, on the settee and ruffling her curls, yellow-white, almost albino, the way she always does when she gets excited, settled down to a long, argumentative, laughing, cosy gossip with her mother. Sixteen? An entrancing age. For the first time, so far as I know from both my lives I knew what homelessness means. Boston's skyscrapers, like all skyscrapers, looked unwelcoming. As I walked towards the arrival hall this homelessness became so intense that I stopped dead, rigid as a statue. I became aware that part of my mind, the lonely part, had slid away from the main stream of my consciousness and was looking back into it reflectively and objectively. I was familiar with the process. Psychologists call it dissociation, and say that it gives a momentary sense of autonomy to our slid-off bit. It may be so. With my belief that every man is a plurality who decides everything like a parliament, en masse, by some highly personal social system of 'checks and balances' I am more inclined to think of dissociation as a revolt, a *Putsch*, a take-over by one obsession, which means that the tributary, the slide-off is given the mere illusion of autonomy. All I am certain of is that in that airport some bit of me that for the moment felt itself King of the Castle said clearly and defiantly – a man hastening past me twisted his head, made an astonished face and strode on – 'I *can* live alone!'

Well . . . Let me remember. Could I?

I liked the cut of Boston and if I had my ups-and-downs there that was not Boston's fault. I liked its good bones, its old face, crooked, wrinkled, self-approving as well as self-deceiving, old fashioned, full of character, as well as conscientious, hardworking, staid, sober and dryly humorous. Its only outstanding vices are those we always associate with old men, old women, old cities – a ruinous frugality and an inordinate interest in the movements of its markets and its bowels, that is to say in its life expectation. Also Boston has the habit of interrupting every discussion about itself by leaning sideways, putting a thumb nail perpendicularly between its two front teeth, closing its eyes and having a quick word on the direct line with God, which is an unfair way of discussing anything with those of us who are less godly. I also much enjoyed the Boston version of the endemic American conflict between fathers and children (often byblows), ranging here between the traditions of the old native Bostonian settlers and the equally old (but far more devious) traditions of Italians, Irish, Greeks, Blacks, Browns, Yellows, together with the accompanying feeling that this place was thereby busy in various special, local ethnic ways, not certainly in the more coherent ways of an established metropolis; more in the way of a peripatetic Fair in some Old World country town – say Hardy's Casterbridge – so that I often felt that I should not be much surprised if I were to wake up any morning and find the Fair Green being swept, tents being struck, an exhausted maid in a mob cap yawningly drawing the curtains of the inn and nine-tenths of the town disappeared overnight. The only thing lacking in Boston then would be cows cud-chewing on the Common.

I liked its ingrown ways and open spaces, its empty harbour, its decayed railroad precincts, its lake-wide river drawing after it an endless parade of clouds over parks, ponds, fens, reclaimed marshlands (heaven for artists, hell for arthritics), greenery underfoot and overhead, hints of monumental boulevards, all so beautifully different to Manhattan's numbered narrows and avenues where one is only reminded of sky when a stray cloud floats past a wall of glass. In New York's name the essential word is New, something fresh and exciting every day. Nobody will ever call Boston exciting or anticipate newness there. On the contrary, like Dublin, of which it occasionally and painfully reminded me, it has the almost untouchable, smellable, visible character that comes with a local tradition stubbornly maintained since its foundation four centuries ago. Whereas Manhattan has changed so often, so fast, daringly, blithely inventively and irreverently that no city of like importance shows fewer marks of its past to annotate its present.

In Boston I lived on the hill in a poky apartment on Joy Street, a block from the umbrella of the State House so that in crossing the

Common every evening from the subway at Tremont and Park, hard by the Old Granary Burial Ground, I had to face uphill towards the Georgian façades of Beacon Street wined by the westering sun. All too often that summer when, my day done, my spirits at the ebb, no rendezvous planned for the night, I would emerge from the stuffy dimness of the subway's maw through a scatter of chattering friends to the still white-hot sky over the Common, half-fearing, half hoping for another kind of tryst at that point where the radial path to Beacon reaches the exit opposite Joy Street. There I knew that I would command a full perspective of the old pink-coated regiment whose suavity protects the dignity of the Hill from the commerce of the valley. Even before I reached it I always knew for certain whether I would or would not see from the bricked sidewalk a translucent shadow passing high over those civic muniments, sense a cloud of tawny hair, a slowly floating shape as florescent as a cumulus, dimly hear her appropriate music far and faint, blending the European years of that continent and this, French, English, Irish, Italian: Couperin, Purcell, Carolan, Corelli, Boccherini, Vivaldi. I would sense rather than hear that music, gay, pure and passionate though always with an underbreath of melancholy in the pipes and strings. I would smell those smells that are as cannabis to every native Irishman, the scent of a peat fire curling up into the sky, blue, white, and moist, the musk of new-mown hay browning in the fickle sun, the tang of grass beaten by hammering hooves exuding its own particular incense to the green sport of life. But whether she did or did not visit me on one of those empty Boston evenings, the ultimate effect was alike: agony at so brief a passage of Love that I could not face the invading night alone. In a plain terror of my poky room I would be glad of any chance companionship. The nearest and most accessible was what I called the pub under the glowing umbrella of the State House where I could be almost sure to meet a few comradely boyos for whom another native drug was always on tap. There I could at best choke the dark in booze. At worst I would, wandering elsewhere, end it with some casual female, always justifying myself with the certainty that when Nana pushed me out of my home and country she must, in her clear eyed way, have foreseen everything. Either way the empty summer sky could beget longing that begat dreams that begat desire that became stink and ashes long before the first dawn chirrup on the empty Common ended the silence of another hot Boston night. In this way another month and another month created between us a manifest sense of withdrawal and an unspoken sense of resentment felt, I fear, by both, desired, I am sure, by neither.

That 'pub'! I have recorded things out of order. I made its acquaintance the day after I arrived. I had come with a few letters of introduction – not that I wanted material help from anybody but that I knew that the two best ways to get the hang of any country are to have the services of an intelligent native guide, and to undertake some slight, part-time job. One of my letters was from a Dublin politician, addressed to a City Father named Bill Hogan, in Boston's State House. Bill was in the conventional sense the most Irish-looking American that I met in the States during the years I spent there. He had the kind of a face that Phiz and Cruikshank made so famous through their Dickensian caricatures of London's poorer classes in the first half of the nineteenth century, many of whom would have been Irish immigrant workers. Bill Hogan had their characteristic long upper lip, broad jaw, crack-in-a-potato grin, comfortable snub nose and vivacious blue eyes set in a ruddy face as beamingly broad as it was long. When I explained to him that I was an Irish journalist who, just to get the general feel of America, wanted to do a bit of part-time radio work, of which I had experience in Dublin, money no object, in fact I would pay for the privilege, he at once, true to his ancestral traditions, telephoned somebody he knew in the local radio station, clapped me on the back with an air that was both reassuring and noncommittal and led the way to this nearby saloon, bar or pub where he introduced me to a cheerfully noisy company with the ancient Irish rallying cry, 'Boys! One of ours!' He had agreed in his office to let me take him some place for lunch. In this hostelry the meal proved to be mainly liquid, passing as easily from hand to hand as if nobody's forefather had ever left Dublin or Donegal. I was handshaken on all sides. The ethnic atmosphere was overpowering. I had never in Ireland felt so strong a sense of lineage. Every one of these men was a modern true born American to within a millimetre of his backbone and there old Ireland stood to attention, tradition at the ready.

After that, meaning at least five glasses of Irish whiskey, I remember of that day nothing of interest until long after the rest of Boston had returned to work and I found myself and four other men alone, if five Irishmen can ever be said to be alone: me, the man called up by Bill Hogan from the radio station – a splendid fellow named

Sean Kershaw with whom or under whom I was to 'work' or pretend to 'work' all that summer – and two teachers of Economics, one from Boston College, one from Tufts and an impressive young man named Sullavan from Pittsburgh, keen, eager and, I gathered, remarkably successful, revisiting his native city in search of as good a job, at least, as he held in Pennsylvania. He made such an impression on me that when Dave left, and then he rose and left, I was astonished by the passion with which the two economics teachers who a moment before had been so amiable with him, even paternal – exploded in anger behind his disappearing back. Why, was the burthen of their muttering rage, why the hell must bright fellows like Sullavan always come crawling back to Boston? He had a good job with Heinz in Pittsburgh, he was on the up-and-up, he could rise to any heights. The teacher from Boston College groaned into his glass:

'I've watched over that guy from the first day I spoke to him in B.C. to the day I wished him luck in his Pittsburgh job four years ago. I guessed his quality.' He gripped my arm; he could have been talking of his son, he was so passionate about it. 'And was I right? Four years more and I betcha he could be a Junior Assistant Vice-President. Another five and he could be running the joint. But no! The same bloody old story! *"Come home, Paddy Reilly to Ballyjamesduff, come home Paddy Reilly to me."* '

Tufts threw up his left hand and with his right threw back his whiskey.

'Back to the womb!' he said to me sidewards over contemptuous bifocals. 'Back to warm, cosy, safe, smelly old Momma Boston!'

'And what,' I asked with a disbelieving laugh justifiable in a new comer to their attractive city, 'is so very wrong about Boston? Or with Sullavan in wanting to come back to it.'

B.C. took over again.

'There's nothing wrong with Boston. It is as fine a city as you will get in the United States. And there's nothing wrong with Sullavan. He is brilliant. But what's wrong with the two of them together is that his brilliance and his Boston don't match. And why? Because he is Irish! And Boston is mother's milk to the Irish, a place where every Sullavan, every Mac and every O, every Jerry and Shawn always knows there's "one of ours" to look after him, pick him up, dust him down, pull a string for him, cover up for him, attend every birth, christening, marrying and burying inside the clan all their lives long. It's a life pattern they've been nourishing for two hundred years. And that place up there!' He was pointing I presumed in the direction of the golden State House dome. 'There is their golden umbrella. Boston is a place where every Irish man's potential is strangled at birth by kindness.'

I protested that Sullavan had struck me as a fellow who could get on very well on his ownio, without anybody to help him. B.C. looked ironically at Tufts and Tufts looked ironically at B.C. Both rose, as if realising in unison that I would never understand. Tufts gently explained, his hand paternally on my arm!

'He cannot do without a woman. That is where they all get caught. If they go away they climb. If they stay they either slouch, or get married, nearly always to an Irish Catholic girl – she keeps them straight – or they drink or they get smothered in local politics. If they come back to visit, or for some reunion with the old crowd it means four time out of six that they meet The Girl, who won't leave the clan, so the poor sucker stays and starts a new line of Liams, or Shawns, or Marys, or Pats and the old carousel goes piping around and around all over again. Sullavan has met his siren. He will stay, and,' turning to B.C., 'all your work is gone for nothing.'

We parted nearer to four o'clock than three. I can honestly say that the only interest I felt at that moment in their protégé was the passing interest any of us might feel for any fellow man caught in a dilemma, although I did see that Sullavan's story could contain the unwelcome warning to every young Irish Bostonian that he might do better on his own in some more challenging city. All the same the incident must have dropped a seed into some crevice of my being. Once or twice during the following months I found myself wondering whether this pleasant city might not be more than a bit debilitating; especially if I had recently been visiting New York where I always felt the enormous human force of some twelve million people exacting from one another the maximum mutual personal response to their city's coldly impersonal challenge lest they all crumple under it together.

Then I would think back again longingly to Dublin, cosy, chummy, gossipy, easy, malicious, neighbourly, a helping hand at every street corner, a treacherously comforting voice at the end of the telephone, a feather bed, every feather a century. Time past. A pastime. A game everybody understood. I had liked it for over forty years. Why now less than then? Because I am twenty. At which it suddenly burst on me that here was something unique that in my ageing dullness I had failed to foresee on that morning of my miraculous rebirth: that whereas any other man or woman as advanced in years as I now am would long since have lost all zest for life, for love, for the pleasures of the body, for adventure of any kind, I – Yeats was right – must more and more lose interest in anything but the sensual. For me now the music of the salmon falls, the mackerel-crowded seas, the young in one another's arms. Perhaps when I too become very, very aged – say when I am five or four years old – I, too, like old Yeats will find all my pleasures in Byzantium, his symbol for "unageing intellect". No wonder I continued to write to Nana nostalgically, longingly. I began to feel that she replied evasively. The passing years operating on her differently. Byzantium? Philosophy? Motherhood? Middle age?

As when I telephoned her in September. Should I, do you think it safe, come home now? Well, Ana *is* still here! Do you think you could bear to wait, darling, until September ends? Early October: would you like, darling, really and truly, to come home now? Well, I had been thinking that I really ought to see those famous colours of the New England Fall. One miserably empty, drunken night late in October I telephoned her. She was dozing, thinking of rising, I could see her rich figure, feel its warmth. To feel it I merely had to hear her voice. Has my pretty Ana written from Kent? Did she enquire after me? Well, not importunately, but she did say what a wonderful summer she had and she regrets that my father 'could not have shared it with us'. I gather that she *is* looking forward like anything to Christmas. 'When,' I commented, 'I must once again make myself scarce?' Well, Beebee, there *is* Easter! You mean what? Well, for Easter why don't we ('we') plan a skiing holiday for her in say Sestriere. Beebee! You must remember Sestriere, anyway where it is, Darling, you haven't forgotten our honeymoon? It isn't a hundred miles from Bardonecchia and our crossing of the Alps that you made more fuss about than Hannibal. Are you all right, Beebee, phoning me so early in the morning? I'm (yawn) sleepy. What hour is it over there? It's so cold here, raining too. Nana! Why are you bringing up Easter? We have not reached Christmas yet. Well, the fact is it did occur to me the other day that it would not be very sensible for you to leave Boston before the beastly November snow if you have to return there for the still more beastly December snow, whereas in Easter – that is if I can persuade Ana to go abroad...

I had not realised before that empty night how moving the human voice can be when unrelated to any planned intent, thinking at large, in the room with one, alone. Hers meant that we still loved, at least at a distance. After that night we communicated by cassette. On other empty nights I used to replay her tapes over and over again.

On Christmas morning the voice from Dublin said, 'It's still raining.' I looked at my window. Tiny paw marks of flecking snow.

Dearest Nana,

These New York streets are lined with levées of dirty February snow, just now a place of more interest that pleasure, an old fashioned city horizontally, a modern city perpendicularly. There is only one really wide street in it, called Park Avenue. Its checker-board side streets are fit only for donkey traffic. In Manhattan there is one large park. I suppose Manhattan could constitute a very pleasant city if it were confined solely to pedestrians and the Underground. All deliveries done by more tunnels? A pity! All that rock! Even as things are I could suppose it a wholly delightful city for the very, very rich who have nothing to do but stroll around the centre, which is quite small, about twenty blocks north-south by three or four east-west. Alas, as things actually are it does awful things to the remaining ninety-nine per cent of its inmates: all agoraphobics, perfectly pleasant in their cells, called offices, but let them out and they become rude, snorting, hasty, aggressive, defensive and frightened as a squirrel without a tree or a cat without a home. I admit that I did this March, around 4 p.m., at the corner of 39th Street and Eighth observe two fully developed males speaking to one another for fully two minutes, and that yesterday I saw a young woman (white) calmly pushing a perambulator near Bloomingdale's! But I had the supreme delight this morning of seeing a handsome gold retriever – unaccompanied! – cock his leg against a fire hydrant outside the Stork Club. These two gossiping men, that young woman with the pram and the retriever could only have been visiting foreigners, as when one day I saw a man and a woman both making for the same taxi, he ahead, hand already on the handle, and he politely relinquished his claim to the lady. I was with a Dubliner who was then working on the *Times*. I said, 'Polite?' He said, 'Or a Southerner?'

I 'guess' all this rush and rudeness comes from their adoration of their great god Ball. Here it is necessary for successful men and women to be always on this Ball. Not, I may add, that when we put these poor agoraphobic Manhattanites back into their safe enclosures they completely relax even there. Gone are those Edenish days when a Mark Twain type of American business man would have leaned back in his swivel chair, put his heels up on the desk, started to chew a cigar, spit and begun to gossip. The golden age of American culture vanished with the brass spittoon. Still, they do from time to time slow down enough indoors to get for a while off their Ball. A man who spent many years working on a magazine called *Time* once wrote a telling memoir about his experience as a slave in that once-famous galley. On his first day he found himself with a (very well paid) gang of Old Timers, part of whose task it was to teach him how to write Timese. Worn out by several intense hours of writing and talking Timese the gang moved out to their favourite tavern. There, after several hours of medical attention, the innocent newcomer nervously suggested to his fellow slaves that it might be time to go back into *Time*. They looked at him between astonishment and sympathy. Then one sighed, 'Ulcers?' May I suppose that more bicarbonate of soda is imbibed between the Harlem River and Wall Street than in any other equal chunk of real estate in the entire history of mankind?

But I am not telling my darling the most important truth about New York. It really lacks only you.

Je t'adore.
Beebee?

Later I had a more interesting piece of news for her. It was that one night, in the crowded foyer of the Metropolitan Opera House, I saw and heard a man saying, 'Hello! Isn't this Bob Younger?' I turned, startled. He was addressing a handsome, greying, upright man whom after some peering and memory-scraping I recognised as an older version of the Bob Two whom Nana and I had had to do with in Dublin twenty years ago. When the first curtain-call separated those two men I moved down the aisle beside Bob Two. In Dublin, for obvious reasons I had not liked him, but my marriage to Nana had changed all that.

'I beg your pardon,' I said to him amiably. 'My name is Bob Younger. My father and mother met you in Dublin some twenty years ago. Do you remember them?'

He at once clutched my arm with the most charming, open, friendly laugh.

'Of course I remember them. Look, if you have time let's meet after the show and have a drink and a chat in the restaurant.'

'Sure!' I agreed. 'Delighted! Let's do that.'

My attention wandered somewhat during the opera – it was Verdi's *Macbeth* – and during the intervals I kept trying to determine why I had formerly disliked him, apart from the fact that he had been chasing Nana. (She still had that gold wristlet thing he gave her.) He had, I recalled vividly, been prying, persistent, insinuating, secretive, although the last time we met, walking on two successive days over the Dublin hills, we had been on quite good terms, and there was his last manly-sad telephone call from the airport, 'Let the best man win.' His absurdly patriotic conjuration of the myth he called Old Stephen – my clasped hands tautened and I stared beyond sound and space at the fact that I did really once have a brother of that name – had been vexatious, and, whether he had believed the myth or not I still thought it stupid. Nana had insisted that it was merely a cover for his wholly pecuniary concern in his father's last testament, but I had always doubted if the matter were all that simple. As a journalist in Britain mixing with other journalists I had always known something that my brief stay in Boston had done nothing to dispel – that among ambitious men patriotic and pecuniary interests can be so interwoven that even they themselves are unaware of their true motives. As the curtain rose on the last act I presumed that Macbeth also thought when he assassinated his king that he was acting in 'the best interests of my country'.

Yet, immediately I saw him approach the restaurant's door, smiling widely, I thought, 'How ungenerous I am! This is a gentleman. He may be tough but decency shines out of him.' His quiet clap on my shoulder was restrained, his interest in me plainly without calculation, his pleasure in our meeting too simple to be assumed. I was the deceiver. While we waited for our drinks I gave him the essential up-to-date family data – insofar as I dared.

'So,' he smiled over his rye, 'she did marry my rival. And she is alive and well, thank God. And I bet still a handsome colleen. I knew it would go like that.'

'Kismet,' I said.

'The will of God,' he said.

'Like should marry like,' I said.

'My own feeling!'

He had not married a Texan but he had married a Louisianian. A pure creole, an old New Orleans family that could trace its lineage back to Spain. Two sons and a daughter. Living now in Dallas, Texas, on a little rural location called Windfall Farm. And I? A journalist? Aha! That was in the family tradition, wasn't it? A lot to be said for tradition these days. He had called his daughter Christabel.

'After her great-grandmother.' He laughed at his twenty-year-old searches into the past, adding a comical 'I hope!' to point his own folly.

But, I thought, nobody can be totally honest without a basis of self-mockery. He had it. A man of integrity. Would I be moving south? Ring him. He would meet me at the airport. I must be his personal guest. When I got back to my hotel that night I retailed it all to Nana, from whom it would evoke an elegaic shrug and a sniffy smile at this craziness of father, son, grandmother.

I went on to Philadelphia, Washington – she sent me a Happy Birthday cable there in March – I was nineteen – and so to the warmer April climate of New Orleans.

It was clammy and foggy, reminding me of an African sirocco. The tankers on the immensely wide Mississippi were wraiths. The temperature was not high but the air was more muggy than Mayish, a genially tropical effect that greatly pleased me. The eighteenth-century Franco-Hispanic remnants, houses, iron-work, courtyards, were such lovely backdrops that one felt deeply grateful that they had been preserved, even if only for tourists. I could always count on eating well. The tempo was restful. I heard some lively traditional jazz there. It did not even matter that I began to feel hovering memories of other elsewheres that had given me a similar sensation of living in an untimely, i.e. anachronistic spectacle. Or rather, did not matter until it broke unexpectedly on me one night that one of those other elsewheres was Venice; whereupon, miserably, I recalled how Nana and I, after enjoying that spectacular city for two weeks turned and glared at one another one evening – it was in the same old piazza where we, like every visitor, had begun our spellbound wandering – and then, no longer hearing the tumtitty-tum of the town band, started to laugh uncontrollably. When we could speak we uttered simultaneously the same thought, in what words I do not remember, to wit – that for two weeks we had been conned, marvellously, delightfully and informatively conned, but nevertheless conned. This place was visually enchanting and of immense antiquarian interest, on that we agreed, otherwise the word most often applied to Venice by visitors and guide-books strips its life down to the bone – the word *pittoresca*, meaning pleasant to picture. I think of the many 'picturesque' photographs I took in that bemusingly lovely city: such as of some back-street canal with washing out to dry, hung above a dirty truck-type gondola moored by some rat-haunted steps, with one scrap of sunlight daringly spying in from the upper right. Picturesque, lovely and dead.

The lasting pleasures I associate with New Orleans are various but never 'romantic' (the lethal guide-book word for the old bits of that city). I still cherish the Tennessee Williams challenges: black life in Algiers, the international life of the Port, the life of the markets, the challenge, not of the Latin Quarter courts but of the busy Criminal Courts, of the University where I made a couple of rare friendships, especially one old historian whose best friends were devoting their lives to recording the last, least echoes of the Black music that crept up the great river to spread through its tributary veins all over the world, threnodies, elegies, dance or festival music, brass band funeral and post-funeral marches that on the discs came up in volume like machine-gun fire in tin huts, which indeed was where much of the best of that music has been recorded. Above all I became absorbed in the unfathomable political corruption of the city and its state.

But such special interests always hold one only in proportion to the livingness of the entire city's response to them. That I did not feel much general response to these keener edges of life in New Orleans is not evidence, but I soon found that I was not alone in this. One incident out of several such comes back to me. One day, when I had been there less than a month I was lunching with two local men, an architect and an engineer. I had not met the engineer before so it was natural for him to ask me the routine question that every traveller must expect to meet sooner or later in all small cities: 'Well, what do you think of our city?' Now it happened that I had met a visiting New York industrialist that morning in the breakfast room of my hotel. Discovering (my accent gave me away) that I was both a visitor and a foreigner, 'Like it here?' he asked indifferently. I said it was all right. He said, 'I've been doing business here off and on for seven years. It's a phoney city.' So when this engineer asked me the routine question at lunch, I replied, experimentally and bluntly: 'It's a phoney city.' The effect on those two men was instantaneous. The engineer leaned across the table, clasped his friend by the wrist, moaned passionately, 'Cary! When are we going to get out of this god-damned place', and, metaphorically speaking, the two of them burst into tears. After which we all three had a pleasant, apparently contented lunch. But when we had separated I went to my room, picked up the telephone and asked the operator if she could locate a certain Mr Robert Younger the Second, of Windfall Farm (I easily remembered the oddly Saxon name) near Dallas, Texas. Her reply startled and informed me. It was: 'You mean Bob Younger? What day is today? Wednesday? Sure, he'll be at home today. Hold the line please.' I held it, calculating that the only country in Europe larger than the state of Texas is the entire spread of Russia from Leningrad to Vladivostock, and that New Orleans is a couple of hundred miles from the most eastern borders of Texas. But then, had he not told me at the Opera in New York that he had married into one of the oldest New Orleans families.

He was at the airport. I had some difficulty in recognising him, open-necked white shirt, white shorts, white knee-length socks, no hat, his hair cropped brassily, black but grey tipped, a small tonsure worn in the poll by the years. The whole picture suggested a tremendous force of energy as he stood up there like a boulder in the stream of come-and-go, concentrating vehemently on his own business, which was to recognise me and to hell with everybody and everything else. It shot me back thousands of miles. He had always been, he would always be ego-centric. His intensity dissolved when he saw me. He shook both my arms, laughing cordially.

'Wanna know sumpn, Bob? You are extraordinarly like your father!'

As we drove off and he talked and talked I noted that his interest in Ireland was vestigial and that his one-time interest in Nana amounted now to a joke. His life had become his work, his family, his wife – he again told me he had married a pure-blooded Spanish creole; almost as good, I thought but did not say so, as a proven Carty, ffrench, Longfield, even Younger. He had brought with him to the airport his two teenage sons, Bob, of course, and Jimmy, of course. At his house, it really was a large farm, acres and acres and acres of it, I met his wife Leonora and his daughter, Christabel, a reedy blonde of about seventeen whose refulgent daffodil beauty reminded me at once of Lalage Kang, that grand-niece of the ffrenchs who had treacherously tempted her French music teacher to kiss her (his ageing *moment de folie*), betrayed him and for her pleasure got shot off at once back to Boston by my then jealously ageing Ana.

Anent my great-grand-daughter Christabel if there is any part of these memoirs whose sole purpose is to record, or confess, the truth for its own sake I insist that this is most patently it; furthermore, I observe honestly, in accordance with this insistence, as I write down the events concerning Christabel-and-me, that I am also writing for my own sake, forward-looking to my fast approaching childhood when I hope to relive in memory, in deep pain but in a deeper joy the singular day when we two fell into glorious and overwhelming love – whatever the hell that word means.

Yes, yes, to be sure, there was, I admit, a hiatus, not long, but nevertheless a clear second of hesitation, a flicker of objectivity between our first flash at one another and the thunderbolt, a pause so brief, so delicate that it is really a little pedantic of my conscience to insist on my recording that at first glance I did not so much 'think' as quarter-feel, 'This is no baby even if she is as unbosomy as if she were thirteen.' Between flash and peal I was already inhaling her heady wine, feeling that first exquisite longing to sip, preliminary to the decision to sip, and the final readiness to drown. For her part, as she confessed to me afterwards, she wanted an older [*sic*] man with more experience of the world 'outside'. I duly heeded that revealing word 'outside'. She had already begun to see her not small state of Texas as a prison.

I must return presently to her obsessive thirst for freedom, whatever that dubious word also may mean! Here I must firmly state that when I did embrace her yoke I was not surrendering to a pretty face, reedy legs, white-daffodil curls, a graceful body. If she had only been that much the result of our meeting would have been no more than a brief, sensual flame; what else could youthful surface beauty mean to a man who had been observing mature womanly beauty for well over a century? I saw only the way those crystalline eyes radiated as if she were a tall, slim lighthouse of gold, wheeling silver light at whatever the winds of life should fling at her. Obviously I was idealising her, turning her – it is easy to say it now when it is all over – into a heroine; and so indelibly that after her, even to a degree up to this day, I am prone to see all American girls in her image of vigorous, wilful, absolute assurance, a self-confidence so fearless, defenceless, imprudent, so abysmally foolish as to make one want to say, 'Look't! There is a manhole open right there in front of you! Stop star-gazing you mug!' Nor was I wholly wrong about her. She had her portable Narcissus pool as they all have. But in this the south (the at first meeting 'dreamy' south) can be most deceptive. She also had behind her the totally opposite southern pioneering tradition, tough and calculating as the far-peering eyes of a horseman identifying a speck two miles away. Indians? Buffalo? Sexually she was abnormally precocious. Kiss the pool, child! Rise! Male approaching. How fetching her airs of girlish innocence could then be, especially then when most in question. Those tight cashmere sweaters; that white-daffodil hair arranged so simply, if expensively, in an airy *bouffant*; her seemingly dreamy, far-off look; even her innocently spontaneous way of jumping or screaming at a rodeo or a ball game; her trick of slowly swinging her jewelled La Vallière pendant above her small breasts.

A born flirt? Patently. (I say it *now*.) But she also had as Americans say, so many real things 'going for her'. She was such a vigorous athlete that my more than five score years could only shake their heads at the sight of her skating at curving speed between a swallow's sweep and a bat's balk, or to watch her diving fearlessly from the high board, riding bareback at a flat gallop in cowgirl rig, hitting the bull's eye every time in her father's outdoor shooting gallery both at arm length and from the hip, waltzing beyond the last moment of an all-night dance as smoothly as when she first floated out on the satined floor. To all this I was specially vulnerable as a foreigner who had never before seen a vigorous young Americaine in action on her own soil and I do not believe that foreigners are ever within measurable distance of an objective judgement about natives outside the natives' air – indeed for all I know her bursting vitality may have seemed extravagant to Americans outside her native State.

I soon saw that I had my own foreign appeal for her and certainly some sort of catalysis did begin to take place between us all in Windfall Farm. One bit of it became apparent within weeks of my arrival. I had come to Dallas hoping to be invited by the Youngers to stay for at most two days. The next morning I was hospitably pressed to stay for a month or longer if I so wished, and this not only because I at once got on such good terms with Bob and Leonora Younger, their two boys and Chris, nor because my invented reason for coming to Texas at all – an invented commission to write four articles for a London paper on American rural life, East, Middle-West, West and the deep South – had fanned a seed of Texan pride, but because my arrival coincided, how opportunely

I did not at first notice, with a domestic tension of some months standing.

It was all too easy to observe that some tension existed but it was virtually by accident that I defined its nature when I rented a car partly to keep up my pretence of being in these parts to collect material for my magazine article, partly not to impose too much on their hospitality. The result was that I at first travelled alone, then with one or both of the boys, then with one of the boys and Chris, finally with Chris alone. On long drives people have to talk. As I won their confidence they talked more and more openly. On top of what they told me I had been rather obtuse not to have seen earlier that Bob and Leonora soon came to regard the intimate friendship between Christabel and myself with indulgent smiles.

I could see why he might well do so, knowing how sound his young visitor's line was: Cartys or McCarthys, ffrenchs, Longfields, Youngers; having met my father in Ireland, fallen for my golden mother Nana, and whatever else he had found out about his own direct line in Castletownroche must have been reassuring since he did welcome me so warmly, even if there always was that one missing link of an untraceable grandfather. It also visibly impressed him that my mother had become a Professor of philosophy in Dublin University – I had elevated Nana's rank a step – and I recklessly mentioned that my father was a chief shareholder in a Dublin newspaper, both fibs given out airily on my first hour in Windfall when I expected to be off their map inside a week. His wife's pleasure in my visit puzzled me a little more until she whispered one day that Chris had been sulky ever since May when, to her sudden rage, her father announced that she was not, after all, to go to Europe in the summer ('A bit soon for you, honey.') in spite, the girl furiously insisted (later to me, earlier to him) of sworn-to-God promises. ('All contingent!' Bob and Leonora insisted). And despite further new promises for next year, this time absolute and ironclad, Chris had gone on being 'sultry'. After all, she grumbled and grumbled, this year was now lost. ('But your daddy must make *proper* arrangements for you!'). And anyway promises performed too late lose all their savour. And she was not growing any younger or wiser. And so on and so forth, while the whole household sighed, groaned, frowned until, lo and behold, into all this contention 'You blessedly come,' an intelligent, travelled, well informed young European journalist, emitting all these daily whiffs and waves of Grand Tour colour and gossip – the which, I may say, I more than gladly did more and more often since it pleased Chris so much and gave me further reason for being alone with her – a new somebody with whom she could plan next summer in such detail that not only was next summer really going to happen but was already happening, map by map, folder by folder, every day.

And it was *every* day! She was insatiable. Her fledgling hunger for the blue sky was as touching as it was obsessed.

'Bobby! Supposing I wanted to live in an apartment in Paris how would I set about it? Are they all scruffy and unfashionable like the ones I read about in Colette and Simenon? How much would a really fash one cost? A mews in London? I saw a woozy repeat of a 'Seventies film with Lollobrigida and who-was-it? – Mastroianni? – set in Rome in a penthouse looking down over the Piazza Navona, the one with the three baroque fountains. Would that cost the earth? If only I was in any one of those three or four colleges in the East that own old palaces and villas in Rome and Florence where they give courses Daddy would *have* to let me go there if I got invited! The way they carry on I have this awful fright and terror that they just want to *take* me abroad with them! Cheese! What I want is to be alone, where NOBODY knows me, to get LOST. But Daddy keeps on treating me as if I was twelve. He keeps on telling me that when or if I ever go to Europe I'll be dreaming of the light of Dallas. DALLAS! What's Venice like in the fall?'

I could have told her what it had been like in the fall of twenty years ago. Dusk. Low fogs. Could not see the inside of a church after noon. Piazza flooded. Closed cafés and hotels, their owners counting their summer gains or losses, staffs gone back into the rural recesses of Cadore to court the local girl or help on the farm, every normally empty church now a going concern (penitence after riotous living), gondolas hooded against the lashing rain, 'half cradle half coffin', the sucking gulp of water on slimy steps of dim canals, nothing to do but drink and make love, the suicide rate highest in Europe.

'It sounds swell to me,' she laughed and I may as well say here as later that it was when I at last got her there to myself alone. In her word, it was 'super'. The pingpong, i.e. the countervailing effect that this exquisite creature had on me extended to (and was enhanced by) the whole life way about her. Even her father's house impressed me: its expansiveness, its luxury, the Olympic swimming pool, the two tennis courts one grass one hard, his three cars, his private plane which he flew himself, and which, he 'promised' me, she could also fly, his private air-strip. And I would have to write a whole essay to re-evoke the omnipresent life feel of Texas itself which affected me in a way directly opposite to Christabel's horror of its provincial enclosure.

To me the supreme power of Texas was its vastly liberating space, its whole, beautiful round-the-compass distance; you did not just see sky, you saw all the sky all the time, a joy that no cooped Easterner can without experiencing it hope to understand. You saw a dwindling straight line of road and at once wanted to say, 'Let's go!' You looked up, wanted that little plane, thought of flying to Mexico, the West Indies, the Pacific. At the dead centre of space, Texas dangles by the twisted string of half a dozen intermediary countries a whole continent to the south of it, baubles to its charm bracelet.

Space does affect space dwellers. After all, the Russian imagination was thriving in and on the expanses of its own vast, melancholy Oblomovist steppes – Gogol, Turgenev, Lermontov, Goncharov, Chekhov – at the same time that the formative generations of all the prairies of America were being nourished to manhood on a similar vacancy. The difference is that whereas Russian space reinforced fate, oppressed the spirit and released a boundless, brooding imagination, American space rejected fate, enlarged the spirit and let loose a boundless ambition. I am thinking of course of that splendid, as-a-colt-new-dropped American spirit of freedom, a stubborn, stupid, irrepressible self-reliance that has flaunted itself nowhere in America more peremptorily, brashly, brutally, selfishly, fearlessly, thickheadedly and idealistically than all over the vast basin of the States of the lower Mississippi between Cairo and the Gulf.

So much about my sucker's relationship with Texas (and Windfall Farm). I thought I had clarified it all pretty satisfactorily until I came bang up against three propositions that revealed to me that our mutual catalysis was working rather less simply than I had been imagining. For one thing I had underestimated the guile of Bob Two; for another I had underestimated the stupidity of Leonora; and I wildly underestimated the egotism of my beloved Chris – until one fine Saturday afternoon in the fall as Bob and I sat by the hard court resting between sets.

He began to probe me about what he called my prospects.

Journalism? That sure was not a very reliable profession? Or was he mistaken in assuming that I had chosen freely not to take an university degree? No? Odd! With a mother who was herself an academe? Here I tried to play it both ways. Well, I had, in fact, done a year at Dublin University, with the idea of going on to the King's Inns and doing Law, but what between my father's financial interest in a newspaper, and my two great uncles who had been journalists, I got drawn into journalism. My ambition was to become an international journalist working out of London.

'Ambition?' he remarked dryly. 'That takes time.'

'I can afford to wait a bit. I have some means of my own.'

'Means meaning? If I may ask the question.'

(I wondered if this was the usual sort of question that fathers of nubile daughters ask of all admiring strangers.)

'Means meaning land, houses, property. Inherited. By European standards I might be called, in a very modest way of course, a man of standing.'

After a lifting of eyebrows, between curiosity, scepticism and that always heartening American readiness to admire and applaud, there came the proposition. Why not resume my university studies right here in the States? He knew people, he had political and educational contacts. He was sure he could manage it in Houston, Texas. Himself, he had gone to Austin, Texas, was an alumnus, had been for four years on the board of governors. Or why not go farther afield? To California? Say San Diego? He had good friends in San Diego. He could speak at first hand for Austin. Chris's first choice had been Houston. Naturally, he smiled, she did not want to go to Dallas. 'They never do want to go to college near home! I didn't.' Naturally I thought best of Houston since Chris would be there. As naturally I did not say so.

'There is always Tulane if you like New Orleans. The world,' he laughed heartily, 'is wide open to you. Just think about it.' As heartily he clapped my back. He was a very hearty Texan. 'If you say yes to the general idea you can leave it to me to do the rest. Trust me. I can manage it.' He winked at me boastfully. 'I can manage anything.'

I thanked him warmly. He probably could 'manage' anything.

'After all,' he laughed, 'we Youngers are a clan. Bound by blood.'

That was the moment when I began to harbour a feeling about him close to distrust. I looked down past the court at the pool. There was Chris doing a double turn into the water from the high board. The shape of a child in a womb. She would be at Houston. I said eagerly that I would think it over. He kept at me, ultimately persuaded me to choose Houston and, I may now presume, heartily enjoyed listening to my grateful thanks while he 'managed' my life at his leisure. He actually got me tolerated by Houston University as a post-graduate from Europe interested to research the history of journalism in the State of Texas. He did not mention the reciprocal and contrary proposition that his wife was meanwhile preparing for Chris. This, about which Chris had to promise absolute secrecy until everything was in order, was the delightful suggestion that she should leave Houston and go to some eastern college in preparation for Paris.

For Bob Two the humour of this contrapuntal *scherzo* was that it was all of my own making. I had, by my constant talk about Europe, infected his child with the illusion that the *Drang nach Osten* ('Go East, young woman!') should be her first step in the correction of her earlier *Drang nach Houston*. New York, Radcliffe, Bryn Mawr, Wellesley, any such eastern university should be every Southerner's first natural step to the wider horizons of Europe if that was what he or she wanted, though what Europe had that America . . . With a characteristic Roman Catholic and conservative prudence he now shifted ground a bit. He persuaded her to go on with her studies (in preparation for Europe) not in an Eastern city but in a mid-east (his phrase) city, to wit St Louis, seven hundred miles from the temptations of New York, named after the pious St Louis IX ('of France'), founded in 1760 something, with two universities, she would naturally go to the R.C. one, a city famous I was to discover for its German beer and orchestra – endless Beethoven and Haydn – its private collections of German expressionist painting, its zoo, its novelist Fanny Hurst, plus a couple of fine remnants of Louis Sullivan architecture in the cemetery, a fine collection of segregated blacks across the river, and Saarinen's fine hairpin monument to St Louis, the Gateway of *the West*. All in all, from the paterfamilial point of view, a prudent arrangement. Keep the young people apart for a while; win time to calculate, to observe as any wise father should; to decide. Ingenious; also entertaining. If I had been the young fellow I looked I would have raged and forced a showdown. That is what Chris wanted to do when she found that we had been tricked. 'I could shoot him!' she said. 'Wait!' I said. Love lashes one into wisdom. I pointed out to her that he had made two mistakes. Absence sweetens love; and the old time romantic sorrows of separation have become a bearable regret thanks to the telephone and the airplane. He lost a daughter. I found one, part mistress, part child, to love, to bring up, to initiate, to set free, with whom to be free myself.

My daughter entered Trinity College, Dublin, in the same month that I entered Houston.

Sex is not knowledge but it is a gateway to knowledge and to deception. Chris in passing through its double gateway cast off her girlish airs so completely that by Thanksgiving Day her parents who had tremulously sent out their baby welcomed back a woman and magnified St Louis accordingly. So did I. In fact – I can write it calmly now after squirming at the shame of it for the better part of three years – she was gulling us all including me. She did a Manon Lescaut on me. She two-timed me. I had proudly thought that when I told her that absence sweetens desire I was ahead of her papa in my knowledge of Woman. So I was, one step. She was two steps ahead of us both when she found that love also increases desire. What a comedy it must have been for her when she and I met that Thanksgiving at Windfall Farm supposedly for the first time since the summer, handshaking politely. She persuaded me not to repeat the performance at Christmas, nor again at mid-term. Spring was coming. 'Think, Bobby, of summer together in Europe!' It was a long time before I discovered that she had not gone back to Texas either for Christmas or mid-term.

That mid-term period I wrote to Nana twice and telephoned her twice from Houston. I wanted to hear about my daughter. Ana Two had had another lovely Christmas.

'You? Well . . . She is very tactful about it – I rather think she thinks we have parted. Besides, she has made so many friends in Trinity it has become her second home. It has been very plucky and unselfish of you to begin a career at that university in Houston. There used to be a very good man in Philosophy there. I think he went to Perth, in Western Australia. That is supposed to be *the* new place for Phil.' Her voice was so serene that I felt myself flooding with longing for her, or, anyway, I would have if at that moment Chris had not unexpectedly put in an urgent call for me on the telephone from St Louis. Yes, yes, I know. Put not your trust in men. In love many women falter; all men. The nursery rhyme says so. *Higomous, hogomous, vimmen monogamus. Hogamous, higgomous, men are polygamous.* It is like cricket or baseball. She may glance now and again about the field. He concentrates coolly. Next please. When my peerless Ana was dying I was already flirting with the idea of Anador. When she was failing I was measuring Nana. Now that Nana is ageing . . .

I skip Houston. It is, I think, a good university. I spent only half a year there and saw little of it. I made what we call friends there, but I have forgotten them. Only one spot in it flourishes in my memory and my affections, its airport, my so frequent point of solitary departure for crowded St Louis and, sometimes without even changing planes, New York, clasping passionate hands all the way for a week-end so 'divine' as to effortlessly forgettable. *L'année de Christabelle*. All its 'divine' details completely gone!

What was her power? An enchanting ignorance? An avidity to know? Those blue and white eyes always staring farther beyond the visible? So much I could perceive. What I failed to realise was that behind the eager, courageous, adventurous, inexperienced girl there was the material also of an avaricious and vengeful Medea, though had I realised it I would no doubt have loved her all the more. Another thing I failed to realise was that in opening the gates of the world to her that is in dispelling the mystery behind them I was destroying a large part of my own. 'Poor boy!' she must have soon thought. 'Is this all it all amounts to?' The revealer of mysteries did not thereby cease to be loved by his pupil, but now how ambiguously! At first her tutor, now her partner to be dropped, betrayed, revenged, felt sorry for all her life. Compassion disguised as desire? Who can like it? Few withstand it. None survive it.

This process that slowly began between Houston, St Louis and New York ran like an express train in Europe. In June they finally had to let her go there alone after, she retailed it proudly, the hell of a fight. They both, she grumbled, insisted on going with her as far as New York, insisted on seeing her on to the plane at Kennedy Airport. Their solicitude touched me even while she laughed at it. Later on, when I found out that she was fooling me too, I was even more touched by their wishes to keep her for ever young, Bob meaning for ever innocent, Leonora for ever ladylike. The only fruitful result of their efforts was that she carefully honoured both their wishes as roles to play. I awaited her plane in London. While waiting at Heathrow, I remember, I telephoned Nana. When after an easy little chat she suddenly asked 'Are you planning a visit to Dublin?' I could feel equally the bodily outrush of maternal solicitude, and the inrush of wifely relief when I answered 'No!'

'How is Ana?' I asked and was flooded by jealousy at the warmth of her prolonged reply to that question...

'I gather,' she went on, and I saw her rich, ironical smile, 'that while you are back on this side of the Atlantic my old friend, dear old Amy Poinsett will be paying a visit on the far side to another mutual friend, Bob Two.'

There was on my side of the Irish Sea a ruminative silence.

'Is she after *me*?'

'I do not think so at all. She just rang me for old times' sake because when Bob Two was writing to her he mentioned you. She did not know, as you and I know, that I had lost my husband.'

'Then is *he* after me?'

'Should he be?'

'If he is not why should he be entertaining a European genealogist instead of an American one?

'I gather that he has become interested in the Spanish end, or beginning, of his wife's family tree. Is there any reason why he should be interested in you particularly? I should not worry, Beebee. She must be a hundred by now, she never met you, she may well have returned from the States before you return there from here. Would you like me to join you somewhere in the continent for a week? Are you alone? Off to Paris, I suppose, Geneva, the Lakes, not the Waldensian valleys, Torino, and so forth. *Lasso me!* Ana and I are spending July in Connemara. Our Wild West. No, she has no interest in Europe. She is one of those young moderns for whom old Europe is a rusty gate through which one looks at a wild garden. She is calling me. I must fly.'

I gave Amy Poinsett two seconds' thought. I was into my seventeenth year. My love was in the sky. Our first European summer held its arms wide open.

'I will send you a card,' I shouted to hold her. 'From where would you like me to send it?'

'From Texas. Poor Beebee! Poor exile of Erin! Ana will be here for at least another two years. She occasionally asks after you. Give my love to...'

She stopped.

'To where? To whom? To what?'

'The lakes. Where I saw our infant star like a speck of dust. Addio!'

'Addio!'

Europe? I should have kept a diary. All I am left with is a jumble of echoing sounds, flavours of sand, sunburn oil, pine-woods, octopi, polenta, tenors, oily water, heat, the smell of her hair after swimming, of bergamot oranges, of liquorice, of dawns in Greece, of marsala, of sandalwood, of superbly curving bays, of cosy small restaurants, of pasta, herbs, coffee smells, of sleep and love in the afternoons, of cablegrams following her like blobs of spring snow. She ceased even to open them. I came on one the other day, in a guide-book to Pompeii, still unopened, to a *poste restante* in Naples, years old. *Hope all well love from both be good Daddy and Mummy.*

We returned deviously, I to Texas, she to Missouri. A few days after her Michaelmas term began I suggested a reunion in New York. She was ill, and was still ill the following week, and the third time. Terrified that she might be pregnant, I flew into St Louis and forced her to disburthen, face to face over coffee in a college cafeteria named The Archives.

'All right, Bobby, I will tell the truth. You have done so much for me, made me so happy, I shall never forget you, you were the first love of my life. But there it is,' she sighed in the sadly wise tones of a courtesan facing another turn of her tide. 'As the poem says, time marches on. Life lies before us! You will meet somebody else the way I have done.' (At, I thought, the tail-end of my seventeenth year? The pre-dawn of my sixteenth?) 'Until I met you I was a bewildered child. Now, thanks to you, I have begun to live as a woman.'

Meaning, she explained eagerly, that on the very first day of her return to St Louis she had met The Older Man she had always dreamed of, thirty-two, handsome, a New Yorker born, a successful art dealer, German-Jewish, divorced. Well, at seventeen a man may meet any danger boldly, fight like a Trojan, be cunning as Ulysses, make bits of any obstacle with a laugh and be laid low by a girl. She laid her left hand softly on mine. I looked down at its diamonded ring. I said to it:

'Engaged! Already?'

I looked at her far-seeing, blue eyes, saw her delicate features, her albino-yellow hair, her virginal bosom that I had so often kissed. If anybody else recounted it to me as his experience I would have expected him to have burst out with something like, 'So after a year and a half as sworn lovers I am kicked out in a single day? You traitorous bitch?' I said nothing. I saw all her beauty melt away, my platonic concept of her die, her lovely eyes, features, hair, childish bosom, become distorted as hideously as a bit of celluloid, a film of happy memories, curling in a smelly match flame. She mistook my shame and horror for grief.

'I don't blame you, Beebee. But you must not blame me. You see, you never did ask me to marry you.'

'And had I? Would you?'

'I might!' she assured me. 'I really and truly might!'

As I gazed into her big, big eyes I saw that I had never loved her. I had merely loved my image of her, feeling that if I loved hard enough I would create her. Otherwise how could I after all my years as a pressman, one of a supposedly cynical tribe, travelled, meeting every sort of man and woman, have been so deluded by a chit of a girl whose only gift, I began to see, was her facility for learning quickly how to compartmentalise the honeycomb of life, decode fact and fancy, simplify the ciphers and ambiguities of love, faith, loyalty, morals, history. How swiftly she had learned! And with whose help? I heard myself saying it in Paris, our first stop after London, when her eyes suddenly flew wide open with the light of revelation as we stood before the Perugino in the Louvre: 'A saint and an atheist, a profoundly religious painter and an atheistical villain.' (I was swiping freely from Berenson.) So delighted was she by this idea of the harmony of contradictions that we hunted him down in Florence, Perugia, Rome. I do believe her whole life changed before that Louvre painting of the naked flute player Marsyas and, calmly watching him, the naked god Apollo who was to flay him alive for daring to be a better flautist. Behind them both the pale gold of the gentlest scenery goes vanishing away in a heavenly perspective of lake and vale and mountain to infinity. That picture destroyed her childhood's unity, that is to say her inherited morality. Thereafter her morality was the amorality of a politician. Not 'I hold', or 'I believe', but 'Our view at this moment is'. She asked me to bring her another coffee.

'Beebee! There is going to be big trouble over this with my father.'

'Does he know?' I asked, suppressing the urge to ask, 'Should I care?'

'He may. Sooner or later he knows everything that concerns him.'

'How?'

'He has X-ray eyes, he has spies and toadies everywhere, he has a nose like a gun dog, one breath is enough for him. I am at a Catholic university, he could pick up one of his cream telephones and talk to the chaplain, the Dean of Studies, the vice-president, the president, anyone he knows at the Chancellery. Within hours he would have a dossier piling up on my Bill Meister.'

'And what will he do then?'

'Nothing openly. He is a politician. Old-style Irish mafia. He will wait for me to show my hand.' (She slipped off her ring and put it out of sight.) 'Then, I should not be surprised if for a starter Billy Meister did not begin soon after to lose a couple of juicy Catholic accounts.'

'He could send you to a university two thousand miles away. Say Oregon!'

'I would not go. And he would never be such a fool as to stretch the elastic so far that it would snap in his face. No! There is only one thing to do. While he is getting on with his investigations we must soften him up. You must help me, Beebee.'

'Why should I?'

'Because you opened the gates for me.'

'Why should he listen to me?'

'You are one of the Younger clan. Irish. R.C. Blood calling to blood. All that.'

So coolly clear-eyed! We had had our happy days. I could hear her saying it soon enough. 'He used to be an old flame of mine.' Now, like a good comrade the old flame must help persuade her R.C. Irish-American father and her R.C. creole mamma to open their arms in delight to a divorced German Jewish son-in-law.

'Let's drift,' I said, and picked up the check. Once outside I went my way with a half-backward half-salute of farewell.

Two weeks later I was not surprised to get a cordial note from her father inviting me to Windfall Farm for the following week-end. (Anyway it sounded cordial.) I was, however, much surprised on my arrival that Saturday afternoon to be invited to join him for an aperitif in his study – I had long been given to understand that this was the one place and the one afternoon of the week when his associates in other Time Zones of the world felt sure to find him at the end of the wire alone and unencumbered. I was still more surprised to find him thick of voice like a man who has already had more than enough to drink. I glanced at his desk. 'Good Lord!' I thought. 'Not still! Not all over again?' as he proudly-coyly gestured towards its scatter of mementoes, memorials, memories – I cannot without irony call them heirlooms, they were so pathetic-ally modest: the same old album in red morocco fit for a royal dynasty, now gold-stamped THE YOUNGERS; picture postcards – I recognised the empty Main Street of Castletownroche; studio portraits of his family; snapshots personally taken, so he assured me, by his grandfather Stephen during his travels in North and South America, the Middle East, Europe as far as the eastern Balkans. There were four printed political handbills dating back to within five years on either side of the 1916 Rising in Dublin. In a small velvet-lined box was a brass military button embossed with the letters I.V., meaning Irish Volunteers, and a spent cartridge case from a Mauser rifle that had been, he said proudly, fired in 1916. There was the rusty head of a pike used in the Irish Rebellion of 1798. The gem of his collection was a stubby .32 revolver allegedly the property of the executed leader of the 1916 rebellion, Patrick Pearse.

'No!' I decided, looking around his functional study for the reassurance of his two telephones, his teleprinter, his dictating machine, the geological maps on the walls. 'Not again? Not still? This is an aberration. These shreds and scraps, real or fake, might once have had some interest for his grandfather, Old Stephen. They have no more to do with the engine of this man's life than a leaky, antique battery lying dustily in the corner of a garage. But in that case why is he dribbling his martini all over them? What is he trying to do to me?'

He slam-shut his album of memories. He looked pleadingly at me.

'Why has my family no interest in these valuable things? Could you believe that my own daughter actually makes fun of them?'

I could. She had several times been highly satirical to me about his 'old rubbish'. I saw more – that one gesture of rejection from his admired, adored, protected, revered first-born – I had so often seen them nuzzling together; she could wind him around her little finger – could knock the certitudes of his life to pieces. Was this bang of his album a translation of his terror at losing her into a defensive rage at her disloyalty to caste and clan? I kept my silence.

'You are a young Irishman. The descendant of Fenian rebels. You can understand what a sacred thing tradition is. Can you explain to me why my family does not?'

Again I could and again I was not going to. Tell him that his saintly relics bored the ass off them? Tell him that they knew he did not believe in them himself? Tell him that if his ancestors had been Polish, Italian, German, Greek, Puerto Rican, Black, British,

Jewish (even Jewish!), Scan, Chinese his dilemma would be the same. Thinking which I fell into an inward fury with him, not because he failed to understand all this clearly – any man might through sentimentality fail to understand it – but because he did understand it quite clearly. He had reverted to that least likeable of all American types the tough tycoon who if it pays will exploit any kind of human feeling to win. For men like those, to misquote Yeats's old play, 'in dreams begins irresponsibility'. Or was I, in my turn, transferring my failure with Chris from my back to his back on the plea that he had corrupted her, even before she met me, with his own brand of double-think? Or, most likely of all was he just another public Will of Steel, another Iron Man who will weep at night on the bosom of his wife or mistress, exhausted by another day's battle with some inner flaw, some secret softness that even he in his own conscience does not fully understand or if he did would still wish to conceal in tears from his last reliable confidante.

I became aware that we were staring inimically at one another.

'Well?' he challenged. 'You have not answered my question.'

I temporised. How tough was he? How ingenuous? Since man is plural he might well be both, and much, much more.

'Ah? To be sure! Tradition? Yes! Yes! In a sense all civilisation depends on it, when it is pure. But we may be certain that it is in practice more often a mixture of the false and the true, alloyed, most often as illegible as some ancient coin that has passed through too many bony hands. Because, Uncle Bob, as we know memories do grow dim. One dawn overlays another. Things do get forgotten. In the end even tradition comes to an end.'

His face tautened into a mask of eyelash-peering murder.

'Odd!' he said softly. 'Your father used exactly those selfsame words to me about the past on November 13th, 1990, during lunch in my suite in the Shelbourne Hotel in Dublin.'

As if I could forget! It was after that lunch that I taxied back to Nana's flat in Ailesbury Road and straightway proposed marriage to her.

'A little before my time,' I smiled, recalling with fresh annoyance his twenty-year-old double-talk about my brother Old Stephen's allegedly glorious youth until this word *past* suddenly became offensive to me, not because it is so often bogus – I always knew it was bogus with him – but for a reason that, on later consideration astounded me: its use was an insult to my country. I had endured my encounters in Dublin pubs with too many other ballsed-up patriots who, having got all the satisfaction they could out of their (?) glorious Past would on the turn of the palm toss it all away with a joke like the men of the world they otherwise pretended to be. Sheep manumitted by the Empire, half-men with the mark of the imperial shepherd for ever indelibly daubed on their backsides. Here he was, an American replica, ready to use any trick to keep his family under another imperial thumb. If I had known Christabel as well then as I do now I would have known that he had bred his match. For the moment all I felt was a furious wish to high heaven that I had been born in some country with few or no memories at all, say some mushroom outback of Western Australia whose sandy tablelands, as an Australian journalist once told me, are Saharan deserts, The Great Sandy, The Gibson, The Victoria, blanks twice the size of all Texas, vacancies where even a dry salt lake is a cartographical event. What freedom it would be to live there within driving distance of a one track railroad halt visited once a fortnight by a Tea and Sugar train composed of tanks of drinking water, a Butcher's carriage, a Social Service carriage, a Grocery carriage, a Dry Goods carriage. They halt, they lower their iron steps for customers, not until the last settler has slowly driven away to his remote oasis do they lift them again and the train chugs slowly away out of level sight. What a joy to be that sort of a solitary, sundered, timeless Crusoe! Yet, even there, I suppose some ancient of days will utter his boring scrap of was-ness. 'I well remember – he-he! – the last kerosene lamp – he-he! – we had! When I think of the smell of it my old bowels turns right over.' Or he will pat some old dicarded cast-iron water pump with a melancholy if also sly, 'Well! Well!' How far back could the oldest resident go? One generation? Far too long! *

I watched my host begin sullenly to gather up from his desk his d.i.y. voodoo set, his lower lip stuck out like a balloon of bubble-gum, his eyebrows like thick black mustachios. His revered (?) I.V. button went into its velveted jewel-box. He wound the alleged 1798 pike-head in green silk. He paused at the revolver that had been allegedly fired during the 1916 Rebellion by Patrick Pearse. He looked defiantly at me as he patted it. (I happen to know that

*At this point the Chairman of the House intervenes. *Chairman*: Is Deputy Younger not describing an Eveless Eden, in other words we are not speaking in harmony with our own practice. *Deputy B. B. Younger*: (Joyfully) We all live by harmonising our contradictions.

Pearse did not fire one shot during that Rebellion. He carried a Yeatsian sword. It was no part of his job to kill. It was his job to make speeches, to be killed, to live on as a martyr, which part in the Heroic Irish Human Comedy he bore nobly.)

I heard a noise outside. He halted in his task. He said, 'Chris is graciously honouring us by her presence this evening. Her mother has gone to collect her at the airport. I am also expecting an old English acquaintance of mine. A Miss Poinsett. They seem to have arrived earlier than I expected.'

So he knew everything? Iron Man? Or Straw Man? I was about to see. A car door banged. Voices were to be heard in the hall. The voices, female, approached. We watched the tentative opening of the study door, half of Leonora's forehead and one wary dark eye. She entered, almost apologetically, conducting a very tall, straight and thin old lady, white haired, dressed entirely in black even to her fretted mittens and her Victorian ear-rings of jet. Behind her came Chris, pallid-eyed, curled hair, darkened eyelashes, green bandana, long-legged green slacks. Her eyes shot with lizard speed to and fro between me and her father. Her raised eyebrows asked. Mine, lowered, replied. Her lip shot forward in determination. The rest went as fast as machine-gun fire.

'Robert Bernard Younger, junior.' He, left thumb in belt, waved a hand between the old lady and me. 'Miss Amy Poinsett.'

She did not take my hand. She leaned towards me, lifted her chin high enough to survey me through her bifocals as if my face were one of the geological maps hanging on the wall. Then in one of those inbred English accents that have never, even in secret, whispered an R she demanded abruptly, 'How old awe you?' I asked her with a smile why on earth she wanted to know. 'Born when?' she snapped. As one who humours an old lady: 'March 17th, 1993.' thinking of that night in Como and the falling floating star that was my daughter come to earth. She turned to her employer.

'There is no need to beat about the bush. I have the pleasure of knowing the young woman who, he alleges, is his mother. It is true that on March 17th 1993 Nana, or Anna, Younger, born Longfield, did bear a child. The child was female. I have a copy of the essential document to prove it. That girl is now in Dublin, a student at Trinity College. This young man is an impostah and a liar.'

Chris had gone the colour of flour, her father the colour of a turnip. He turned on her:

'So you have performed the miracle of being simultaneously seduced by an Irish phoney and a Jewish adventurer. You stupid little fool!'

She and I shouted together, I, 'I am not a liar!' She at him, 'Neither of you know anything about Bill Meister!'

With a maddened scoff he turned away to his wall-safe, shouting, 'I will show you a bit of evidence that will interest you both.' Miss Poinsett left him the centre-stage. Like a minor actor who has said her lines she retired to the wings, that is to a chair at the head of his desk. There she calmly removed her black mittens and began peering inquisitively at his phoney hereditaments. She said as if to herself:

'In point of fact I have met this Mr Meister. In his St Louis gallery last July when buying a life-sized portrait that – so he told me – he had himself painted. He called it *Chris Embattled*. Quite good. Of its kind.' She twisted her head to read the label on the Patrick Pearse pistol, threw open the chamber, observed that it contained four cartridges, made a disapproving *moue*, closed it, went on: 'I bought it for the sum of one thousand dollars. I presume her father still possesses it.'

Chris, mouth clamped, was breathing fast through her nostrils. Her shocked voice became barely audible:

'He *sold* it to you?'

'He was probably hard up,' Poinsett remarked casually to the I.V. button which she was turning hither and over in puzzlement. Bob Two returned from the safe with a quarto envelope. He drew out a coloured photograph and spun it on the desk between the five of us.

'I do NOT possess the filthy thing but that is a photograph of it. The original was signed and dated by him last May.'

We all stared at it, except Poinsett, now engrossed in the Younger family album. The painting was full length, the original was possibly five feet by two and a half. In it Chris stared out boldly at the spectator, left hand on hip, right hand holding a drawn sword bent in a curve against the ground. She wore black knee-length boots and she wore nothing else.

'Last May?' I whispered, struggling to reject the mocking implications of the date.

Old Miss Poinsett leaned back in her desk chair, removed her glasses and gently started to stroke her closed eyes.

'In point of fact, Mr Whoever-you-are, if I do know nothing

about you is not that the whole point of the thing? Nobody does. However, whoever or whatever you actually are I saw you once before today. In Venice.' She turned to Chris. 'You remember those parental cablegrams following you all over the continent?'

Chris said viciously, 'I did not open half of them.'

'You opened one that said, *Have arranged with Chase Manhattan Bank NYC to place to your credit four million lire Banca d'Italia Venice must be collected July 20th. Love. Mummy and Daddy.* It was, of course, a bait. You may even have suspected as much. But it was worth a try on both sides. It was worth only somewhere around five thousand dollars but you apparently found it irresistible. Perhaps you had Mr Meister on your conscience? Well, Venice is an impossible city to do anything in complete secrecy. It is so small. Everybody knows everybody else. No wonder they once went in so much for masks in Venice. At balls. At the gaming houses. Everybody sooner or later crosses that famous Piccadilly Circus of Italy, the Piazza San Marco. I had breakfast there on July 20th last outside Florian's. I could see the eight exits and entrances of the Piazza. Half an hour after the banks opened you both came in, arm in arm, glowing with happiness and, I presume, four million lire. I left. I had seen all I needed to see.'

Bob Two picked up the nude photograph and looked contemptuously at me.

'And you have seen and heard all you need to see and hear. It remains only to inform the Jew,' he looked at Chris, 'that my daughter has been two-timing him with another guy for God alone knows how long.'

He leaned across the desk for the nearer one of his two cream telephones. She jutted her lower lip:

'I am going to marry Bill Meister.'

He lifted the receiver.

'He is already married,' Miss Poinsett mentioned. 'Twice.'

'His wife is a lush,' from Chris. 'He will easily divorce her.'

He began to dial.

'For you? After I have told him all this?'

She leaned forward on the desk on her two hands.

'Who are you dialling? The gallery is never open at this hour. He's not listed in his apartment.'

'Is that so? Then I'm going to dial my old friend Pat O'Hara, the Chief of Police in St Louis. He is the sort of man who has strong views about guys who go around debauching teen-aged girls.'

She did not appear to stir her hand or pick up the Pearse pistol, or aim it or fire it, but there was a mild crack and the telephone receiver in his fist blew in white bits. His right eye closed tight, his left glared madly at her, his underlip slewed sideways, his Iron Man jaw shot out, he grabbed the second telephone, clamped it to his ear. This time she aimed straight from the shoulder.

'Drop it!'

Her mother screamed her name. He dialled smartly. I stared at him. I hated him. I watched her trigger finger, white-knuckled, contracting slowly, and at the last second I jerked my elbow hard under her firing arm. Again the crack was not loud. He looked at her in astonishment. Or was it that he was shocked because she had missed? A line of red slowly appeared along his right temple flecked by a couple of drops of blood such as a butcher's first incision might draw from a creamy haunch of mutton. One drop of blood ran down his cheek. His eyes glazed. He collapsed like a doll across his desk. There from his nose, twisted comically under his face, blood trickled across the mahogany.

I am inclined to think that I suffered a slight but effective black-out such as one may experience when waking up on the morning after some festive dinner unable to remember how it ended or even how one got home. Chris must somehow have induced me out of the house. Had I heard a long scream behind us? I presume that his wife and Miss Poinsett first thought of ringing his doctor; then, Leonora being a Catholic, of calling his priest; later they would call the police. The first thing I clearly remember is the little plane gathering speed along the runway, Chris shouting 'Fasten your seat belt', and the gentle lift from the earth. Then I clearly see the instrument board lighting her delicate but intense features and the stars wheeling sideways about us as she turned south for – she answered me – Houston.

'Why?' I asked.

'The airport. For New York. Chicago. Los Angeles. For the farthest, soonest, quickest you can get out of here.'

'Why not Dallas airport?'

'If we have killed him you wouldn't stand a chance in Dallas. The sheriff and all his men could be out for your blood there in ten minutes from now and if they caught you they'd hammer you into pulp. All I can do for you is give you one hour ahead of them to pick up your cheque-book, your passport, any spare cash you have and scram. But there is one thing you must do for me in Houston –

ring Bill Meister in St Louis, I'll give you his number, and tell him what's happened. Nobody will see that guy's ass for dust when he hangs up his phone. Jews are fast movers. Used to it, I guess.'

'What about you?'

'While they are refuelling me I'll ring home to find out the score. See my priorities? You. Bill. My dad. Me. Whatever happens I fly back home. There I'll play it by ear. Stall off the chase as long as I can.'

'You think fast.'

'Immediately I heard Daddy say he was going to ring his policeman buddy Pat O'Hara in St Louis I knew he was after Bill and you. I pray God in heaven he is only wounded. I can't believe my aim moved more than half an inch from the receiver of that telephone in his fist. When you are aiming direct from the shoulder your arm goes rigid, and you elbowed me up rather than in. God damn you, Bobby, why did you do it?'

I heard my mouth say that I always hated him from the first minute I laid eyes on him. I became aware that she had turned her head to stare at me. I looked down at the line of yellow street lights in some little town below us. Real life, as always, is elsewhere. I was seeing him as I actually first did twenty-two years ago on that foggy morning of Anador's funeral, in Nana's flat on Ailesbury Road.

'What is that place down there?'

'I dunno. It could be Mexia. Or Corsicana. A clear night you could see lights fifty miles away. That could be Waco over there to the south-west. Why the goddam hell did you do it?'

'He robbed me of the one thing I wanted in the world. You.'

'Cheese is priced! It was Bill Meister did that.'

'He sent that English spy of his, Poinsett, after us to Venice.'

'"English"? Are you going all patriotic on me now? I've had it from Daddy about the Irish, from Leonora about Spain, from Bill about Israel, I join old granny Poinsett on the plane at St Louis and all the way to Dallas-Fort Worth she keeps on about how Henry the Second of England never wanted to own Ireland and Henry the Third never wanted France.'

'He is a bully, he is a vampire, he wants to suck your blood, he does not want you to live your own life, he wants to arrange everybody's life, I don't know why else I did it, I did not want you to kill him, I just wanted him out of our way.'

She kept a cool look-out right, left, overhead. A star winked. She said, 'That's just a hedge-hopper out of Waco'. Looking high overhead, 'I bet that's the A.A. jet from Mexico City to Chicago.

'Bobby! We've had a good time, don't spoil it. Don't be a dreamer. What do you want? God almighty, up here in the sky how long does a life last down there? A wink. Sure, I want to marry Bill Meister. Especially now, up here, after all this shouting and shooting when I feel like a winking plane myself. Bobby! We have had our blink. That old witch Poinsett says you are not who you say you are. Is this true? Who REALLY are you? See that, down there? See it moving? That's the train all the way from Mexico City, up and up to St Louis city and Chicago, I want to live in the city of everlasting love the way that train has wanted Chicago ever since it was born in Mexico City. Maybe Bill Meister is just another railroad stop along the way? We would need to live two lives, four lives, ten lives to know what we really want. I hope to God I didn't kill him. He was a good scout. He is a good scout. He had guts. He HAS guts. Why did you do it, you bastard? Why in hell did you do it?'

In little planes there are long silences. In big planes we are sent to sleep.

'Chris! Will I ever see you again after all this?'

'I know why you did it. Because you are an Irish bum. You are all the same. He was the same. He IS the same. You hate life, you resent it because it won't come up to your cock-eyed dreams. He got in your way? He GETS in your way, that is why you hate him but it is not just him you hate, not just Bob Younger Two, it is what he stands for, life as-it-is intruding on your notions of life-as-it-ought-to-be. You are angry with me because I dare to love anybody else but you? Damn you! Before I ever met you I was mad about an Italian. He turned out to be just like you, another guy pretending to be in love with me while all the time he was in love with his own glorious dreams that he called Me. The slob never even kissed me he was so busy adoring me. I love Bill Meister, a Jew, an American Jew, because he has none of that crap about love, he is real, hard, tough, he wants me because he desires me. Okay. Suits me. That is honest. That is true. But you? You don't want to fuck me, you want to fuck my soul. Just like that Italian who kept on telling me I was his Blue Madonna.'

'You never complained before! Ever since I laid eyes on you I loved you, body and soul.'

'There you go again! Can't you leave my soul out of it! And I swear it is all a ploy. Or a cover-up for something. Guilt? You are like my father. If ever a man should be proud of his success he should. But do you think he laughs all the way to the bank? Or the bed? I swear he goes there thanking God for being so good to him, or praying for his Irish dead but for whom *et cetera, ad saecula saeculorum*.'

The sound of the engines. The wind. A big star or planet to the west. Venus? It suddenly vanished. Cloud? Wind?

'You are overwrought, Chris.'

'You Irish are all schizos.'

'I agree. So is everyone only more so. Will I tell you who I am?'

The plane shook as if it had been kicked.

'Spill it.'

'I am my own father.'

She snorted:

'Like the night Hamlet got pissed and met a ghost who told him he was really got by his Uncle Claude out of his mother Gertie which was why Shakespeare left his second-best bed to his wife and wrote that cock-eyed play to tell the world all about it, I had all that crap from a crazy English lecturer in St Louis. He is my father! Dear God, please make him all right. I liked him, I like the poor bastard. He liked me. He likes me. I admired him, I ADMIRE him. He was a real man, IS a real man, I love him, if he lives I'll marry who ever the hell he likes, I wish to Christ I never laid eyes on you.'

The little plane was shaken again. It fell like a broken lift, sailed on again. Lights in the world below us floated by. Darkness. The Gulf. Sheet lightning waved to the south.

'Chris, how can I persuade you? I am who I am and always was, only I was allowed by the gods to grow younger and younger.'

'I am sure, *sure*, SURE it is only a surface wound!'

'Chris! Turn back. I can't let you take the rap for all this.'

'Wanna know sump'n, as they say in Brooklyn, New York, the best Jews are the lapsed Jews and the best Cats are the lapsed Cats. On our summer trip you and I got on fine until somewhere, I don't know where, in Ravenna or Monreale, you suddenly got madly excited by those stiff Byzantine mosaic figures and I said to myself, "It's no use, he's rooted in this stuff just the way my daddy is." You may think different but that, for sure, is the way it is. You are green and Cat to your toe-nails. Like my daddy.

The gusts worsened. She was holding the controls like reins. She said that that glow away ahead was Houston. Once again I asked, 'Why can't I declare it was my fault?'

'The cops would be delighted. The perfect simplification. Forget it, Sydney Carton! Nobody will dare prosecute the daughter of Bob Younger. Anyway, he is not going to die. I won't have it!'

'But I do have to know!'

'Stay in our old haunt in New York, the Biltmore. Sign in as Robert Toberts. Give a London address. I'll send a message.'

She began talking to the control tower in Houston.

I was lucky at Houston. I missed a direct jet to New York but got the last seat on one fifty minutes later to Washington via Nashville, even that barely left me time to drive into Houston, grab my passport and a winter coat and telephone her Bill Meister. He immediately caught the implications of what happened at Windfall Farm, asked no questions, said only one sentence, 'Thanks, I got it', and hung up. I was luckier at Dulles airport. I had time for a sandwich and a drink before boarding a direct plane on to New York. It was around three o'clock in the morning when I checked into the Biltmore Hotel: a quick transit considering the time we had spent flying between Windfall Farm and Houston, the delay there, an interrupted flight to Washington, another delay there, the flight-time to New York, and the final drive into Manhattan and Forty-Third Street. I hung the *Do Not Disturb* sign on the door and slept until eleven – I knew she would not have a positive report until the afternoon. I nevertheless feared thereafter to leave the hotel's precincts, told the telephone operator to have me paged if she got a message for me and wandered around between the news-stand, the restaurant and the bar. On looking back on those hours of waiting I can now clearly remember only feelings of guilt as for myself, and of fear as for Chris.

I can see myself: a young man in a corner of the Hotel Biltmore's lounge, bar, tea-room, restaurant, cafeteria. Outside there is Manhattan whizzing. A seed of private misery in a hotel on Forty-Third Street, N.Y.C. At five o'clock, half drugged with drink, I went to my room and flopped on my bed. I was in God knows what daymare dream about I think a flying fox and baying hounds when the telephone by my head rang. Her voice:

'That you? Don't speak! Just listen. I'm calling from the airport. They could be tapping the house-phone. He is all right. He will live.

He will be well soon again. We are all in the clear. The affair is being treated as an accident. Things were a bit rough here for a while but now everything is going smooth and dandy. There's only one small worry. He has no recollection of what happened. The doctors think he may have lost his memory. I will confirm all this tomorrow by telegram. Thanks for calling Bill Meister. He's where you are at this moment. Please tell him what I have told you. And, Bobby, thanks, thanks, thanks for every single thing. You opened my golden door.'

The sucking sound of a kiss. Click.

So this was what I had been hopefully waiting for? A heavenly emptiness. I had been a fish cast up on the sand by a storm, gasping, flapping the sea-sodden shore, choking, and now suddenly sucked back by the next wave into the blessed, elemental, everyday sea. I put back the receiver, turned my face to the pillow, wept with relief. Does this sound unheroic? It was unheroic. I got up, walked to the window and with my hands in my pockets looked down gratefully at the muted jumble of Madison Avenue. Manhattan, the entire United States, the wide world was again at my disposal! I was free – and after a minute as lonely as Christ or Judas.

Below me in the street a man with a violin case under his arm, and his coat collar turned up. I had seen in the *Times* that Massenet's *Manon* was on at the Met tonight. (It had been *Macbeth* the night I met him.) If I could get a seat I . . . What was this she had said about her Bill Meister? 'Where you are.' In her toy plane she had said, 'Go to our old haunt.' Our? Whose? I recognised the true centre of my feelings yesterday while waiting for her call: not guilt, not loss, not fear but jealousy eating the bowels of my pride, of my self-respect. I imagined the two of them together in this hotel. She had not even bothered to choose another for me. Insensitivity? Duplicity? Perversity? Sarcasm? Triumph? Vanity?

'Can I speak, please, to Mr William Meister. Staying in this hotel.'

The kitten's claws? What an escape I had had! In twenty years what sort of a woman would she be? How many times divorced?

'Hello? Who is speaking?'

'My name is Bob Younger. I spoke to you last evening from Houston from a mutual friend. Remember?'

'I remember.'

'She has just rung me with news which she asks me to transmit to you. It is that all is well. He will recover, almost completely. There is no need for either us, in fact no need for any of us to worry further. His memory has become so impaired that he has no recollection of what happened.'

'So?'

'Nothing. I am doing only what our young friend asked me to do. I was also wondering whether you would care to join me in the bar downstairs for an aperitif before I go out to dinner. A drink to so-to-speak celebrate?'

Silence, i.e. a man thinking.

'Where are you speaking from?'

'The Biltmore Hotel. New York City. Room 253. What is your room?'

'365. Easy to remember. Our . . . my usual suite. I received no message from my . . . our friend. Let us by all means have a drink in as you say the bar downstairs. See you there in three minutes. You will recognise me. I am six foot one. Tall. Grizzled. Oblong glasses, slightly tinted.'

He came in. A handsome fellow, sparse, aquiline, with slightly stooped shoulders as if from a prolonged habit of stooping to talk to people less lofty, more likely from long bending over desks. He was, it turned out, a New York College man, born on the upper East side, his father a small manufacturer but, I gathered, fairly well off. On the telephone he had been so laconic and his enunciation so clipped that I was prepared for an aggressive man and a curt manner. He was quiet, even amiable, diffident without being ingratiating, possibly conscious of being much older than me, already twice married. To him I would seem a boy. His manner would once have been called gentlemanly. He wore a grey suit with a silver tie. His hair was carefully groomed. All in all the ideal answer to Christabel Younger's desire for 'an Older Man'.

Each of us lifted his glass to the other. We spoke without embarrrassment about her:

'I know that Chris has told you that we are engaged to be married. . . . Yes, I can see that it might seem odd to you. A man twice her age. These things, strange as they always seem to others, do happen. . . . She is, indeed, a most impetuous young woman. It is one of her attractions. It is the Irish in her. . . . Ah! But her gaiety is delightful . . . I agree. She has not been frank with either of us. Having thought it over I can see her viewpoint. . . . After all she did not meet Bill until after she had met Bob. She became unsettled. And she had promised to go to Europe with you before any emotional relationship had developed between the two of us . . .

You would have preferred her to speak straight out? About all that? While she was still disturbed and confused? I certainly would not. You say you are Irish. I find that in these matters the Irish behave much more like the way the English behave than the way Americans do. No! I would not have wished to be in any way involved in your attachment to Chris. That could have tied my hands. You see, I do not believe in this English "let-the-best-man-win" attitude, this honourable gentlemanly "fair play" attitude, this élitish idea that "the game is the thing". We had a famous coach here named Vince Lombardi who summed up perfectly the American attitude to every sort of competition, athletic, political, financial, amorous, military when he said, "Winning is not the most important thing. It is THE ONLY THING." Chris plays every game the American way. So do I. And I have won.'

I asked him if he trusted her.

'You suggest that perhaps I have not won? That I merely appear to have won? I do not go along with that kind of dubiety. That is Old World stuff. That is the diminishment of the present by reducing it to a dubious spot in the whole process of Past time moving into Future time. It kills the drama of life. It spoils the vital present moment by clouding everything with what you probably call either History or Philosophy. It makes everything woolly. I live in the Now. I have been married twice before this Now. It is true that I was deceived each time. But I refuse to believe that two unhappy experiences justify total scepticism about such eternal verities. . . .'

'Verities? You are begging the question!' I interpolated.

'. . . as love and marriage. If I did then my next step would have to be an admission of despair. I believe in the truth of the fact of love right across the board.'

He did not say this arrogantly. He spoke quietly, perhaps a little sadly, maybe even humbly and, after all, he was asking very little of life. Perhaps the Lord would bless the end of this Job.

'What sort of truth is it,' I asked, 'that holds good as far as the mountains but cannot be trusted beyond them?'

'All I ask of life is the adventure of living it. I neither ask it nor give it total trust.'

'You have said that two women deceived you. Deception implies trust.'

'It happened several years ago. Now I should say, "I deceived myself." Bad habits live on lazy words.' Bill turned to the attendant barman. 'Two more martinis, Gordon's and Noilly Prat. You know the difference between induction and deduction? The one progresses from the known to the unknown, the other goes the opposite way. In an inductive Sherlock Holmes story the detective has no dogmatic answers until he sees footprints on wet grass, looks at his watch, observes a black cigarette butt with a gold tip, a broken branch low down, is told about a barking dog. Then he says, "We must look for a man of about five feet six, with a limp, a dark complexion, possibly an Egyptian, who passed this way after 6.45 p.m. carrying a heavy weight, possibly a body." This is scientific induction. It is also chicken feed. Good enough for small puzzles; of no use to explain big puzzles like love, hate, fear, greed, betrayal, evil, death, belief, hope, despair. I am an artist. I go along with those prophets who give me dogmatic answers first and then watch me prove or disprove them. It is not scientific but it works to start out by believing that there really are such ideas as perfect love, goodness, evil, trust, charity, to be sought and met in the night, in the rain, in the forests, in the dark. Belief is a way of living. You smile? There never was such a living woman as Leonardo da Vinci's *Mona Lisa*. He created her out of his desire for her. If I had his faith and were as clever, I could make every one of my desires take on flesh.'

I sympathetically toasted his faith, though adding: 'It reminds me a bit of a child saying, "Mummy, please make it come true, make it fine tomorrow for my birthday".'

'You are laughing at me. I do not mind. For me, ambition is the father and mother of happiness.'

Very American, I thought. Very optimistic. And yet was there all that difference between us? Each of us was, as most men are, half-dreamer, half-realist. I told him how much I disbelieve in appearances. That my favourite fable is 'Beauty and the Beast'. 'If only some pretty girl will, for pity, if not yet for love, kiss the horrid beast, his ugly hairy appearance will fall away from him and he will step forth as a shining prince.'

'I'll buy that!' he agreed heartily.

'But there is its counterpart. The pretty girl in her little red cloak and the wolf dressed as a kind, old grandmother. "Oh! Grandmother, what big eyes you have got!" Would you buy that fable, too?'

'Sure! And I'm make a fight for it! I'd choke that damned wolf!'

Very New World. Eden before the Serpent. If only Adam had been an American Jew! I got up. I explained that I was planning to go to the opera: an old fable called *Manon Lescaut*. Smiling we glanced sharply at each other, the one challengingly, the other dismissively, neither of us inimically, and a tiny flag of memory fluttered: once before this I had obliquely considered another woman I loved with a man who also loved her, walking with him, the father-to-be of his Chris, among the hills of Wicklow, each of us aware that my Nana walked invisibly beside us.

'Let's have breakfast together, here in the coffee-room,' I proposed and he nodded. 'If there is no news from Texas we might even go for a stroll around Manhattan. I'm sure you could tell me a lot about your native city.'

And, perhaps, I thought, about more important things? What image, what symbol, I wondered as I sat into my taxi for the Opera, does he find in Chris? Into what symbol of her had I, before him, translated her? For, of course, everybody must perforce brush aside all human appearances in the effort to know what life throbs behind the public mask. What his Leonardo had seen behind his most famous model's mask nobody knows, and perhaps even Leonardo himself did not live long enough to know. Certainly only the longest experience can tell us whether or not there has been a fair consistency between our imaginations of men and women and their experiential reality. Mostly, alas, we dream brittle dreams. We do not dream cold enough, hard enough. Later, listening almost in tears in the darkened auditorium to the Chevalier des Grieux's exquisite aria to Manon about a little cottage beside a purling stream where they would live alone in blissful quiet – not at all that lovely little Christabel's sluttish idea of happiness! – I thought, 'Another man who has not dreamed hard enough' about his woman, nor had I. Nor Bill Meister, with his two wives, nor Manon herself whose soft fancies about happiness were so often turned into smoke blown about the sky by her passion for pleasure; nor had her creator, the irreverent Abbé Prévost, before he wrote his immortal novel that has become the libretto for an immortal opera. Three times at least Prévost skipped from under the yoke of his priestly vocation only to find himself deceived by love's middle-aged dreams, his last skipping being from that towered monastery on Boulevard Saint-Germain opposite which we nowadays sip our aperitifs with our own modern Manons – which is to say that he lived and wrote. As I do?

Unable to sleep, I rang Dublin. She was sleepy. She said, 'Oh! It's you? Where are you?' I told her. I begged for news. When for

God's sake could I return? She told me that in virtually two years and a half Ana Two would take her degree. She told me that the child was both very intelligent and very lovely. Hair like daffodils shaken by the wind, slim, reedy, fearless, laughing, the toast of the whole college. She reminded me that in less than two and a half more years I would be fifteen and that she would be forty-eight. She told me she loved me as much as ever. No! No! No! What nonsense! How could she love anybody else? Never would! She told me that it was raining in Rosmeen Park, and ra-a-aw – the word became a yawn. She asked me where I would ring from next, to which I said I was returning to Boston because it was nearer to her, at which she chuckled so unbelievingly that I saw her generous Titian form snuggling deeper down under the warm bedclothes and I reverently said good night, and she said a sleepy good morning, darling, and there was a heart-rending click and I was back in Manhattan.

The next day while waiting for that promised confirmation from Texas I wandered about the city with Bill Meister, checking back with the hotel every hour on the hour. We went on foot, by bus and underground, all the time arguing and confessing, which naturally means inventing, resting in corner drugstores, saloons, public parks, hotel lounges until, quite worn out, we found ourselves, lying like the sunset from across the Hudson on a flat tombstone in Trinity Cemetery away uptown on the west side at, I think, 157th Street. It was characteristic of him that he should end our day's wanderings there. To every born New Yorker, the authentic counterpart of any Paris *gamin* or Neapolitan *scugnizz'*, his native city is certainly not just a place to reside in, hardly a place even to live in, but excellent as a private pad once he has learnt how to exploit its last square inch, a sovereign city to hate and love, to fight for and against, to dream in, die in, return to as dust to dust.

He observed that the two great merits of every cemetery are that it is quiet and for free – to visit – which quality, I found, appealed to him in a great many things, not because he was frugal or miserly but because he hated to be exploited. So, he might say, 'Where do you want to go now?' and I might say, 'I've never seen Chinatown, or Harlem, or the Village or the Bowery' at which, still talking, he would raise a forefinger of assent, glance around to take his bearings, and still talking stroll on to the correct underground station and come up for air at or near the exact, 'good-value' saloon, store or restaurant that he had had in mind from the start. He knew the city's best swimming pools (for free, or almost); places where we might hear good music (f.f. or almost); the commercial galleries worth having a look at (f.f.); spread his open-air proffers from The Cloisters down to the Bronx Zoo, on through The Botanical Garden, down to the Central Park Zoo (for free), away down to Coney Island with its crowds and sideshows, (f.f), its aquarium and baby whale.

There was, I noted, only one section of his city where he did not feel cock-of-the-walk – although he granted that for art and to impress girls it was unbeatable – the hard core of expensive hotels, cinemas, theatres, the symphony, the opera, all those swank restaurants, fashionable stores and prestigious offices crammed between 42nd Street and the Park, though he did admit that without its showy centre New York would be almost as dull as say Philadelphia, just as without the fantasy of its downtown skyline it would look like another fusty old, musty old, empty old, cosy old Boston Bay. What unsettled him in this midtown core was the implication that taste and skill must always go along with pretentious show-off and flossy piracy. So, it was just one more declaration of his self-assertive egregiousness that he should suddenly say that he wanted to go up to the Amer-Indian Foundation's museum at 157th Street West (free of course) and that feeling tired after it he should bethink himself of the nearest patch of enfranchised real estate, and that I should presently find myself stretched on my back beside him in Trinity's graveyard's oasis of mortal quiet at the hour when the rest of Manhattan's citizens were fighting their way both under the ground and on the ground back to, like us, shoeless ease in their cramped crofts of peace. Anyway I had long ceased to be surprised by anything Citizen Meister did, so deeply had he by this time impressed on me how much it can mean to possess the only fully endowed city in the only English-speaking republic in the world – always provided you knew how to use it instead of letting it use you.

By this time we had discussed at length the nature of trust between man and man, and of distrust between man and woman, the honesty of the male, the ambivalence of the female, the element of durability in love-affairs and of solubility in marriages, the independence of a mistress as compared with the dependence of a wife, the unreliability of all written history, the even greater unreliability of all spoken memories, the solid single-mindedness of the Jews and the as ancient severalty and dissensions of the Irish, the decline and fall of empires (we had by that time visited not a few pubs), from which we smoothly passed on to the crucial question – the shattering of all our certainties in the modern West, especially those comfortably entertained around the time of the marriage of the Age of Reason to the Youth of America by such explosive powers, people and events as the French Revolution, the Romantic Revival, Darwin and Marx, Freud and Einstein, two world wars and the greatest of all the twentieth-century's many calamities, the abrupt Decline and Fall of the world's last empire, The British.

'Emancipating,' said he, 'oppressed people like the Irish.'

'Elevating,' said I, 'oppressed people like the Jews.'

We stopped chuckling. A light, as they say, had burst on me. Only a few days ago I had been re-reading one of my master William James's lectures, the one called *A Pluralistic Universe*. I only got the full force of it when we stopped making those flippant remarks about the decline and fall of empires, pre-Roman, Roman, Roman-Catholic, French, Dutch, British, followed by their far more tyrannical replacements rising like the sun (as usual) in the East. Two sentences that James uttered in the course of that lecture came back to me like a light switched on in a dim room: *'Pluralism lets things really exist in the each-form. Monism thinks that the all-form is the only form that is rational.'*

I suddenly saw, like a lofty vision floating above our tombstones, that great powers do try to glue every individual unit of life into one vast single collective all-form, down to our dearest, smallest, littlest, most precious private, secret lives, until every man unconsciously begins to live through, for, in, and by one all-embracing, powerful ethic. Anybody who prefers to this all-form of institutional life some alternative form, or no form at all, is a heretic, a dissident, a rebel, Sinn Feiner, freak, outsider, misfit, odd ball, cad, bounder, Commie, traitor to be sent hot foot to Coventry or to Siberia. With my hands behind my head and my face to the sky I explained all this tolerantly to Bill Meister.

To my observation that the result is that civilisation is now in bits he replied, 'Maybe it is but I am still I!'

I declared my faith.

'Bill! There is no such person as I. The word is just a convenient manner of speech. Your Jewish monism, your notion that you and yours are one solid, singular, seamless weave is a delusion. Every one of you, of us, is a plurality, shimmering with variety, endlessly changing, as honeycombed and tangled as the back of a telephone switchboard, as mobile as a ballet, or a circus. All life is. If it were otherwise we would all go mad. Our multiplicity of mind saves us from the madness of the idea of a homogeneous reality. In variety and changeability is freedom. Consider. . . .'

Warily I watched a pigeon passing overhead. Higher up, no larger, a plane passed irreverently over the cemetery.

'. . . Consider the multiplicity of Mr Einstein. He had jiggered up Time. He had rightly insisted that the import of every temporal phenomenon depends on its observer's position in space. He discovered relativity. Still, when his housekeeper asked him when he would like to have his lunch, he said "Now!" She said, "Where?" He said, "Right here." When she asked him what he would like to eat he said, "A turkey sandwich", ignoring the number of viewpoints involved in those three words: those of the baker, butcher, dairyman, cook, messenger, Sicilian salt-miner, housekeeper, the laundryman's, the poulterer's and the turkey's.'

'All you mean,' Bill snorted, 'is that certainty is a relative thing.'

I sat up on our tombstone.

'Relative to what?'

'Time?'

'Which is itself relative to?'

All he could do was to grunt. I resumed my explanation: 'Time and change are inseparable. Watch any farmer watching the weather around harvest time.'

He lightly kicked his heel on the stone beneath us.

'Ask her about Time. Or is it a him?'

I turned round to look.

'Here lies . . . He or she lies under your bottom. Time is man's greatest enemy.'

'Why should it be? You are young, your life is all before you.'

I wish it were. I wished I could, with the dying Hotspur, shout that that Time which surveys the history of the world should itself have a stop. Bill, as if seeing, though not understanding my discomfort, went on in a kindly voice, 'Time is nothing but a personal notion, an egoistical mode of measurement. It seems to be boundless but each ego, divided or not, has his own special portion of it and his own units of measurement for it, all different. We kill time, pass it, have lots of it, have none of it, employ it, are its slave, beat it, waste it, do it, are behind it, up to it, lose it and find it. Youngsters want to hurry it up. Old men and lovers want to halt it.

If you like change you have to accept the mother and father of change. Which do you want most?'

'Since I believe that man becomes a honeycomb as he grows, I want lots and lots of it. I want to be able to plug into Jane if June deceives me, into Jenny if Jacky betrays me. But I also in-between would like to be a cop halting the traffic of time.'

He sat up beside me and laughed and laughed.

'You Irish! You always want every goddam thing both ways. The old ways and the new at the same time.'

'Because we are multiple!'

'And don't know it. You all want the same thing, eternal change and eternal immobility. Well, you cannot have it. That is not the way the world is made. Descendants of kings!'

I jumped to my feet and glared down at him.

'You should talk! Descendants of David!'

He surveyed the toes of his shoes, opened them to a V, closed them to an I, made a V again, looked up at me silently.

'One could have the *illusion* that time stops. I have had that illusion of eternal change and eternal immobility in only two places, both of them cities that have been lived in continuously for over two thousand years. You can guess the first. Our Jerusalem. I have had the very same sensation in your Rome. Only so ancient and unbroken a history can give the impression of frozen time.'

He stood up, dusting his pants.

'As for your being multiple,' he smiled at me, 'when I was at college I read about Ockham's razor, his idea, so true, that one can have too much plurality, too many entities. Sooner or later,' he laughed, 'the guillotine has to fall, the private is trimmed to the general. Civilisation depends on accountability. It took the Roman Empire to teach us Jews that much. You Irish never learned it in spite of the British Empire's and the Roman Catholic Empire's most forcible persuasions. It is what makes you simultaneously attractive to the rest of the world and a screaming pain in the ass.' He threw his arm affectionately about my shoulder and laughed at me. 'Who *is* your accountant, Bob?'

Amiably though abashed, I held his wrist. We would have made an attractive photograph at that moment, he laughing at me, I looking down at the tombstone. *Here lies Jane Abbott Perkins, Beloved wife of.* I remembered a grave in Richmond, England.

'One's accountant? Aristophanes called her "the longed for, shining, with wings of gold".'

He released me.

'Let's go back to the Biltmore and see what she has to say to us there.'

We changed at Forty-Second Street. We were silent the whole way. At the Bilt he hastened to the desk where there was at last a telegram for each of us. Frowning, we read and compared. *Everything now absolutely okay but a sad goodbye eternal thanks fondest memories Chris.* He waved an intense hand to me as he rushed to the travel desk to book a seat on the next plane for Dallas. I was not sorry for him, a third man who had not dreamed hard enough about his Manon. Like me he had thought her strong, vigorous, independent, her only accountant herself. We had underestimated her father. Other loves. Younger and Younger, Inc.

Six months later I got a card from Texas, twice forwarded, grey with silvered edges, announcing the marriage of Christabel Mary Younger, daughter of etc., to one Patrick Pearse O'Brien of San Antonio, Texas.

It was only after Bill Meister's taxi drew away from the Biltmore that I realised how alone I was. True, I had acquaintances here and there in the eastern states and in the south, but one does not fly 1,000 miles to have a cup of coffee with a pleasant acquaintance in say Houston or New Orleans. I went upstairs, sat before a martini in the lounge and wondered how many places in the world there are where a fellow can feel more alone than in a trafficked hotel lounge at martini time. I think I could still paint the pattern in that sea of carpet. At which point a trauma that had been inactive for two years and a half rumbled and began to spit fire. I was back drinking in a pub near the State House in Boston with two teachers from the economics department of Boston College and a revisiting Bostonian named Sullavan or Sullivan who was planning to abandon a fine career with, I think, Heinz of Pittsburgh in order to marry a girl who insisted on living near her people (the old familiar Irish phrase that invoked a sick mother or an ageing father and squads of cousins) in Boston's featherbed; which bed, I had been given to understand by my disgruntled economics teachers, is the nearest to the long sleep that snores all the way across Ireland from Dublin to the Aran Islands. By this time, I felt sure, Sulli(a)van had gone back to the capacious, oozing teats of Mother Boston. The traumatic effect of that able young man's dilemma turned to lava, slow, smoking, oozing down the sides of my Etna or Vesuvius in an image of shame, defeat and despair. I now was, I must remind myself, only four months short of 17. I had rather be Ahasuerus the Wandering Jew than return to Boston.

I hung on in New York into January – through a chance meeting with a man I met in some shamelessly neon shamrock saloon on Third Avenue I got a counter jumper's job in Tiffany's over Thanksgiving, Christmas and the New Year. Then my real wanderings began. Afterwards, in nightmares, I am still wandering around the States after five dreadful years. In fact they were only two years and not dreadful. I met a number of people I liked who, had I stayed anywhere for a longer period, might have developed into real friends. I even still get greeting cards signed by such names, now meaningless to me, as 'Bob and Cherry', or scribbled initials that evoke neither occasion, face nor feeling from California, Maine, New Mexico, Florida, the state of Washington, from towns so small that I have to search for them in a gazetteer to find out in what segment of the vast American compass they lie, such as that village in Omaha where the train, one a day, will halt only if it is flagged down, townlets where no plane not even a hedgehopper descends. What did those two years do for me? I once decided that they persuaded me to sign an armed truce with life. Would that strike the gods as one of the worth while teachings of that commodity they call experience? Those two years also persuaded me that Nana was right when she insisted that night on Lake Maggiore that the often asserted antithesis between Realism and Idealism is false. Body and Spirit really are one, or can be one. From that village where they flag down the train-a-day I remember nothing except a man who helped me up the steps of the train the morning I left his lousy village: he glowed like a little diamond in mud – I do not remember anything about him except that he glowed, and he was as factually real as his completely forgotten village from which he has twice sent me across the world his greeting signed 'B'.

In the end I even accepted Boston. I wanted the featherbed, the however distantly half-familiar, maternal bosom. My year there I cannot describe: it would take a Beckett, Behan, Joyce, Baudelaire, Genet to give some idea of what that last year of exile did to me. When I could bear it no longer I wrote to her and felt ashamed that what impelled me was nothing less inexplicably sentimental than St Patrick's Day, my sixteenth birthday. I had gone down into the streets to look at their vulgar, silly parade, far, very far indeed from being interested in it, let alone impressed by it until there came around a bend in the street a female contingent, a fife and drum band which enchanted my scornful misanthropy by being preceded by two shapely girls in short-short pants bearing a street-wide banner that read THE BLESSED VIRGIN'S ROCKETTES, followed by a handsome majorette with splendid thighs twirling her baton of green and gold, flanked by two young priests, hats slanted, eyes challenging, 'Right, down, out there,' I could hear them boasting it, 'near our own people'. And I was ready to scoff at the whole, damned, show-biz cheapness of it all when I saw coming like a ship under full sail around the curve of the street a great, big tricolour, my country's flag, billowing and flapping in the March wind, and I had to back into the doorway of the store behind me to hide my sobbing gulps of tears at the whelming memory that these were the same Irish whose kin had come back here in the Black 'Forties, famine-starved, lice-ridden, sidewalk beggars, sleeping ten to the cellar, white slaves – now proud and free.

I went back to my pad and I wrote to her. 'Dearest love, I can bear it no longer. I want home. I need you. I am sixteen years old today. At my next birthday I shall be fifteen. I want you. I have kept my half of our bargain. Can we not at least meet now, at last, in Europe? Say in eternal Rome?'

I have her written reply. She wrote that in June Ana Two would both take her degree and be married to an apparently promising young gynaecologist from Johns Hopkins who had been having a look at a few of the better known maternity hospitals in these islands including 'our' Rotunda. They proposed to spend their honeymoon in the Bahamas and then go on to Baltimore. She would love to meet me in Rome; but first she must attend a Philosophical conference in Helsinki. We would make lovely plans. Her sentences seemed nervous and tentative. She wrote she was very well. She mentioned that she was almost three times my age. It would be exciting to be with me again after so long. Had I changed? Her sentences were as clear as well-water but they did not connect – it was as if she wrote one and then put down her pen for several minutes before writing the next. I naturally thought at once, 'She has a lover.' Then I thought, 'No.' What she means is not have I changed but has she? She is vain – at her season four or five years older could mean a lot. But, at my season to be four or five years younger could mean even more. At what age would I recross the threshold of puberty, become sexless again? Thirteen? When she would be in her supernal fifties, the glorious, the vintage, the maturing years of every woman's life. Must I lose her for ever?

Even already, when at last I saw her there looking for me in that crowded Rome airport, she was a golden goddess. Lavish was the word that came to my mind. Lavish without being maternal. Or was it lavish and maternal? I had not anticipated such astonished delight. I could not guess what she thought of me, a youth, that is to say a young old man, but I thought I saw bewilderment in her eyes. And did I see desire?

I am writing this one year later in Rosmeen Park. It is my fourteenth birthday as the world wags, in my hundredth and sixteenth year thanks to the fancy of the gods, fifty-one years ago since I was reborn. I have fourteen more years to live. To live? Consciously to decline into infancy. This March wind in from Dublin Bay is a white hare flying fur-blown under the north-east wind across Rosmeen. How soon should I start sleeping alone? Last night as she undressed she said, 'You remind me of a warm tom-cat, a very young tom-cat stretching himself on my sofa, lazily unsheathing and sheathing his claws on my brocade.' Was that 'young' a reproach? Or a taunt? I made love to her like a Young Turk. But for how long more?

I am entering my thirteenth year.

PART FIVE

Farewell

2030

He was a darling boy, slim, eyebright, innocent, unworldly, in many ways what I on occasion crossly used to call stoopid, i.e. adult-male-silly, but with an immense fund of love to spill over anybody who would take it and give it back to him. That time in Rome the instant I saw him at the airport coming through the barriers into the baggage-claim area I remembered that long ago in Paris as we started out on our informal honeymoon he surprised me by suddenly saying 'Don't betray me.' I did not know, and still do not know what spurred him to say those three words but I did know by them that he would always be faithful to me, that it was not just a confidence trick, that he had always been faithful to me even though later on the memory of those three words often did make me feel guilty, anyway feel uncomfortable, anyway develop a conscience at my least lapse from his idealising image of me. I remembered it very easily with that redheaded Foucault-ite philosopher in Helsinki who took such a shine to me, and I to him, that when he made the expected pass at me I was at once able to say (trembling in every relevant part of me) 'It isn't, God knows, that I don't want to, but there is this young fellow in Rome waiting for me!' He hooted, 'And what do you think he's doing tonight in Rome?' I only needed to say, 'The devil of it is he is not!', and as I said it I once more felt rather ashamed of my own few unfaithfulnesses – two and a half, at most three – since I had edged him out of his own house, home and bed five years before. I could have defended myself: I had a daughter to consider, and his return from the States, I could have argued, must ruin my life, turn me (as transpired) from a mature, level-headed university woman into a maudlin old fool in love with a teenaged youth, sexually virile I agree – oh all that! – sufficiently handsome, well heeled, telling me hourly that I was the rising sun and the golden moon, and, I swear it, meaning every word.

Gratefully I gave him my Indian summer. Gratefully he gave me his boy's body, his springtime, bird song and nesting time, daffodils, bursting buds, even though I knew at the back of my bewildered head that all these were the hints and fore-signs not of his opening summer but of the shut-time of his life. And where would I be then? A professor of philosophy with fog in her hair, wrinkles under her ear lobes, sad little pouches at her elbows and a big-eyed, babbling, blethering, boring adorable baby in my lap begging me to explain again Descartes' doctrine of innate ideas. I nevertheless loved my lover as a vanishing infant more than I ever loved him as an oncoming man, though, of course, in an entirely other way.

Already in the Leonardo da Vinci airport, I had foreseen trouble in the swell of maternal joy that rose in my belly at the sight of this smiling boy approaching me out of his lustrum of exile with his bundle of canvassed tennis rackets in the crook of one arm like an acolyte bearing flowers to an altar. (I had never known him to play games before. Had America and youth done this for him?) I admit that my second thought was a cool and comical 'What will everybody say?' The third, sanely frightened, was, 'Is what I am feeling unnatural? Am I a pervert?' For from that hesitant moment on there came foaming past the crags and rocks of the sane and the impossible, cascades of the possible and the insane, the one-could-do-this-es-and-thats, so youth-bestowing was his grin, so rich his whole person to create nostalgia for times I had for ever lost. Young again? Two? More! Three, three and a half years of youth all over again? A stronger minded woman than I am may have resisted the faustine temptation. I could not.

For weeks he bored the pants off me with his 'philosophical' ideas. (Why the hell do people who have never studied philosophy, stockbrokers, insurance men, Revenue Commissioners, always want to tell me about their private 'philosophy'?) He talked of Pluralism, Time, Change, Pause. Inexplicably I sometimes liked him all the more for it, so juvenile he was, and I was insanely in love with the boy in him. Besides, who was I to blame him for wanting Time to pause who, myself, wished only to turn it backward. I laughed to see him happily drinking in Rome's timelessness at the oddest moments and in the oddest places; as when, one day, in UPIM (Italy's Woolworth's) while I was trying to buy a zip-fastener and he a tea-infuser, so dim were the tea-bags of our hotel, he looked out from an upstairs floor towards the Piazza Colonna and the winding spool of the column to Marcus Aurelius Antoninus and said:

'Look! The noblest Roman of them all! That great Stoic. The first man to say that Time is a river whose current is so strong that no sooner is one event floated into sight than another event takes its place, and this in turn is replaced until we begin to believe that everything that happens has happened before as surely as the browning of the harvest and the scent of the summer rose?'

I can still see him thinking it as he looked later at the Tiber's fleeting wrack, doubtless thinking as that greatest of the Antonines has also written that the universe is Change and that short life on it is whatever we choose to imagine it to be.

'Nana! This is the oldest city in the world to have lived an unbroken life. All the others are either in ruin or seen their power destroyed. Thebes, Athens, Babylon. Even Jerusalem. Here alone is layered time.' He touched the window-sill. Looked at the dust on his fingertip. 'Caesar?' he whispered.

I ran my forefinger around the edge of his beloved jaw.

'Indeed! But, my darling, I do want to buy myself a zip-fastener.'

He sighed.

'And I a tea infuser.'

He was right. One does tend to feel pluralist in Rome. Numbers of people must in every generation have fled from it to Siena or Florence where the challenge and the answer is simpler and more singular. Rome is inextricably multiple. She withholds her full self from any mind not multiple enough to respond to her timeless sameness and endless variety.

Now that he is slipping away from me and I am distanced from him far enough to see him more clearly I think that this obsession of his about multiplicity arose from the fact that having lived so long he became impressed and distressed by the equation Time = Change = Repetition = Confusion of Vision. It could well be that if each of us lived much longer than normal with, like him, all our original faculties unabated we would become more diverse, and from frequent movement through our diversities not more wise about our Selves but more uncertain of them. He and I often talked about Yeats's vain search for what he called a 'Unity of Being' and when we came down to actual cases had to agree that in history all that those men and women who seem to have been completely unified had was a concentration on one aspect of their selves to the exclusion of all the others.

I remember suddenly this misty morning how when he was about eleven he told me, on waking of a like misty morning, that he had been dreaming that he was back in his lost boyhood in search of a tailor named Holmes from whom he knew he could buy a 'heather-speckled' Irish homespun tweed suit for the sum of £3.00 in some back street room lost to his memory in the old Liberties of Dublin – the area so called because it had been once surrounded by a wall protecting its residents from the wild Irish squatting like dispossessed Red Indians up in the hills to the west. It was the sort of street that a lazy writer might describe as Dickensian; not at all picturesque, crumby rather, even crumbling, quite run down in his boyhood, not quite a slum but not far from it, a place of old and not too clean shops, small dealers, mean and tough, dim electric light bulbs shining blankly through bare windows. He had in his dream kept on wailing, 'Where has my tweedy old Holmes gone to?' as he wandered by night-light through those streets on the dusty borders of Dublin's Danes and Normans, Irish and Anglo-Irish; Sytric Silk-beard in the crypt of Christ Church, Strongbow prone in the nave, Sir Henry Sidney in the Castle, Dean Swift, Robert Emmet hanged hard by the old weavers quarter, Lord Edward Fitzgerald shot by Major Sirr. All I understood about this dream was that it had an unusual effect on him. On questioning him about it, to find out why, I realised that his homespun heather-speckled suit, adhering like a burr to his deficient memory for over a hundred years, was a symbol of some desirable mode of life that he had once had or touched or guessed at as boy or youth, an image of some other simpler world of pause or peace in the endless tension, crudity, rapacity, commercialism of everyday life, perhaps even in the young animal drive of sex that he could neither live with nor do without; a symbol of something as 'desirable' (as I have used the word) and as unattainable as an exile's image of a return to a homeland that when he sees it is not at all what he had expected.

Every exile, it was he who put it to me, is an exile from something desirable that does not exist otherwise than as an idea or a dream, like an inexperienced boy's idea of ambition, heroism or of love. This I could follow. Every symbol is by definition anti-realistic. It pierces through things. Why else does a man marry this girl rather than that except that this one represents some personal image of life that he needs. We all seize day after day on people who represent – or so at the time one is convinced – some absolute personal necessity, some one aspect of life that for the moment excludes every other aspect. That he had done so I could guess from the manner in which his thought suddenly slid away from that speckled, homespun, Irish tweed suit, loose fitting, easy, baggy, still smelling of the oil of the wool and of peat smoke, to my mother Anador Longfield's trim, formal, tight-fitting, almost armorial, almost military and certainly androgynous *tenue*. 'So suitable', he said, 'for a horsewoman', though to my knowledge she never rode a horse. After which he was talking of this young woman he met in Texas, Chris Younger, whom he had obviously admired, speaking of her as a young heroine on horseback. What those three had in common – Anador's imagined woman-on-horseback vigour, this girl's actual dash and style, his wild homespun boyish suit – was, however, more than I could understand. He apparently did.

I have often thought since that all symbols are divisive. The symbolist is like a surgeon who falls in love with the patient's liver, or heart, or eye, a specialist who develops an exclusive interest in one organ or one limb. Predator or cannibal? What in him devoured what in me? In me what in him? And each of us playing up to our image in a mirror held up by the other? Had he been as interested in other sides of me and of himself he might also have formed much clearer images of all the other people in our circle – of the attractive Des Moran for example, about whom he never knew, and I thought it unfair to tell him, that his Reverence was not indignant for my sake or for Anador's sake at those love letters B.B. lifted from Hugo. He was indignant for his own sake. And Anador at the end told me he was much more than 'fond' of her. And I could have told her that the old boy twice made a very heavy pass at me. From which more follows since he would have done neither if he really had been Anador's father.

But who was then? My mother always took it for granted that she was the daughter of her mother's husband, Reggie ffrench. When I read Bobby's manuscript years ago, or as much of it as he had written of it up to then, I realised that my grandmother, Ana ffrench, had composed four possible fabular librettos about her child: that Bobby had made her pregnant that night in Nice; that Des Moran had done so later; that she had earlier or later a never-to-be-revealed lover; and – which I believe to be the truth, but which was much too unromantic and undramatic for her to accept – that her drunken husband had done the job. She was a woman, or so I gathered from my mother, for whom life was tolerable only when her imagination had chewed it up, like a spy with a secret code, and rewritten it in her own fabulous code. Like the gods creating good and evil she was a great hand at thickening every plot.

I wrote the foregoing when he was thirteen. Having reread it I observe that I did not there decide what I see – saw in him and I still think it wiser not to try. Everything he has written in his manuscript is a warning against the futility of trying to write a wholly truthful autobiography. Somebody has said that one would need to live twice to find out whether such-and-such an alternative decision would have worked better. His ms. suggests forcibly that if he were to live not twice but six times he would still be composing rather than recording, still groping in dissatisfaction for those missing pieces of his jigsaw which, if found – or indeed if only imagined; I do not like to say invented – would reveal some sort of personal pattern of character or feeling in the otherwise apparently formless (or so he thinks) chaos of his life.

Unfortunately it is doubtful if there is any consistent pattern in any man's life. Man is not a roll of wallpaper. So far he is right in maintaining that man is not homogeneous, that he is instead a multitude of particles, full of those contradictions, inconsistencies and incompatabilities that are our efforts to adapt to change, to chance, to fate, to unforeseen experiences, to new discoveries and to our own manifold mistakes. Some of the most famous autobiographies in literature prove it. Rousseau's *Confessions* are riddled with proven fiction. *The Confessions of St Augustine* are highly imaginative. Yeats, Benvenuto Cellini, George Moore, Goethe, Tolstoy, Paustovsky, Charlie Chaplin are as fascinating for what they leave out as for what they put in, and that not always reliable. One of the most honest of writers was Stendhal and he has been called a rhapsodic liar. His so-called Roman *Journal* is a web of invention. On the margin of one of his published reminiscences of Naples he cheerfully wrote, 'I was in Naples at the same time as M. de Stendhal and he is a great liar.' How few writers of travel books have been so frank! Fewer have been as charming and persuasive. I do not know what my boy-lover set out to write in his now obese ms., but to my world-weary eyes what he has written is less about what he saw or was than about what he would have liked to have seen or been, in this at least though in nothing else like the Stendhal who spent so much of his otherwise unexciting life walking in and out of mirrors presented to him by a conspiracy of flattered woman. My grandmama Ana ffrench, a sybilline fabulist, was evidently made for him. My mother, Anador, elevated to the unenviable role of venturesome Vikingness was ill made for him. Too literal, too frank, too honest. That American chit acting out the role of heroine on horseback not for his benefit but for her own was probably using him as her mirror-bearer. Narcissa?

What particular need or bias in his multiple nature had I the enormous honour to represent? I know at least what in him appealed to me: his duality, a man split down the chine, wouldbe rationalist, wouldbe romantic, that fatal self-deceiving Irish type that has addled more sane men's heads and broken more sane women's hearts . . . Otherwise I have used the essential word above. Conspiracy. He made me a fellow conspirator, and after all one of the great attractions of love is that it is a secret world inside a public world. For some forty years after he shared his ultimate secret with me in a Paris café I must have been the only woman, perhaps the only human dotty enough to believe his truthful story. Do I now regret my belief? Not wholly. Though I do dearly wish that since his fable is true he could more quickly become the baby at my breast as he once was the man crushing what he sweetly called its surging swell.

Five younging to four. I observe that he has given up mowing our lawn. The machine is too heavy for him. I mow it. Those effing Irish husbands!

March 17th. Anno 2027. St Patrick's Day. His 127th birthday. Entering the first of his final three years.

I have wondered how I would behave if some Olympian doctor were to have told me at some earlier point in my life, 'You have exactly three more years to live from today.' I believe that after the first shock I would have delightedly planned. If I had saved or were certain of a certain amount of money to spend during those last years how lavishly I would have spent every penny of it! How wonderful each new sunrise would become, every sound, every smell, every touch, every meal, every kiss. Total appreciation of every second of life! In his case it has not been quite like that because – there had been no cheating, he had been warned beforehand – with his necessarily abridged memory and adult consciousness he had to accept and endure the continual torment of his ignorance about the nature of the man thus accepting, enduring, enjoying or putting up with this or that unprecedented experience. It is the old Sartrean taunt: there is no recognisable Self, we can know ourselves only by observing the effect we make on others, who in turn only know themselves by the effect . . .

I weighed him this morning after his bath. Three pounds. He was naughty, splashing me with bathwater. I put him across my knees and with pleasure whacked his bottom soundly. He leered back at me disgustingly. Does it *never* die in them? After all the brat is 128 years old!

During the next two years I must become like a woman concealing a wanted man from the Law. I have already discovered that it is a relatively easy task provided one happens to live in that most impersonal of all modern hiding places, a middle-class surburban enclave in a large city: e.g. some such thimble of Dublin's modest million and a half people as Rosmeen Park's thirty-six little private houses. In a vast modern metropolis it is less easy: there private houses have mostly given way to lofty apartments and blocks where privacy is far from easy to maintain. Certainly none of my neighbours in the park appears to show the least personal interest in me, as I know nothing about them. My sociological colleagues in Trinity assure me that life was not at all like this in a younger and more intimate Dublin. If I ask them why the answers have always been alike: that Dublin's life-way has changed with its increased prosperity, evident in the expansion of its middle class, the total disappearance both of its leisurely wealthy class and of its equally leisurely O'Caseyian indigent class, all evident in the spread of suburbia, the rape of our old eighteenth-century central homes by office builders, high salaries and wages, and keen competition to get them. The happy result that concerns me vitally is that Dubliners no longer have time to be inquisitive.

After all it is now nearly a century and a half since this city first attracted the amused if also Swiftian attentian of a young student named Jim Joyce, much as Christiania alerted without at all amusing young Henrik Ibsen. Whenever I now happen to open *Ulysses* I find myself reading about a wholly unfamiliar city, small, intimate, comfortless, scruffy, impoverished, dirty, easy-going and as gossipy as a provincial town anywhere in the world. Joyce could no more write his book about this modern Dublin, so impersonal and private has it become, than Ibsen could peer through the lace curtains of modern Oslo at its one-time puritanical, lecherous, secretive and splendidly inquisitive old Christianians.

If I were to peer out this morning through the nylon curtains of my own front window in Rosmeen Park what would I see? I could by craning right and left see across the road six front doors, something of their six front gardens, the greater part of my own small garden and to its right and left two isosceles triangles of green, the gardens of my proximate neighbours. How little I know about the lives of the occupants of those houses! Thirty years ago I did at least know their surnames. Now only two of those old neighbours remain, bedridden, invisible. The rest? A doctor's car. A hearse. A furniture remover's van. There are over a score more similar houses in the park. I do occasionally in passing one particularly ancient resident lift a paw in amiable salute. I do not know the old lady's name. I cannot remember how we became so unusually intimate.

To be sure I take precautions in defence of my secret husband. For instance I once enjoyed the daily help of a young woman whom I treasured. No more. I once employed a regular gardener. No more. The milkman does not come beyond my doorstep. I attend no church. Formerly my social life revolved satisfactorily about Trinity College. No more. Since I retired I have no social life. I am, I have gathered, known to the local grocer who obligingly delivers goods to my door as 'the ould professor'.

A macabre thought that illustrates the secrecy of our lives. The houses to my right and left have been unoccupied for over a year. I do not know why. This leaves me insulated on two sides by silence and inscience. My rear garden is enclosed by three seven-foot walls, a number of trees, macrocarpas, a prunus, two scarlet crabs, two apple trees. In this enclave within an enclave I could safely smother my child-love, bury him in the rear garden, take a single ticket to New York and live there for the rest of my life without anybody on earth being a scrap the wiser. Or I could do so if the gods had not ordained otherwise. I should of course need to make careful arrangements beforehand about the transfer of the cash – he has left me everything in his will.

So, I do not find it unbearably difficult to conceal my diminishing secret. What a public splash it would make if I suddenly died and it were to be discovered! Nobody could believe that I was his wife. More likely I shall all too soon become a widow, or so I hope and pray. For if I should die sooner than Bobby what will they do with my babykins?

One. Fully grown is the phrase. At two he was ready to move to a small perambulator from his go-cart. Now he could almost sleep in a boot box like a wounded bird. Presently a cigar-box will do. Last of all a match-box Well, I have seen old, senile men crumble dirtily.

How awful for them. This way he will not so much die as, like a moth, perform a vanishing trick, his last meal a tiny hole in one of my woollies or my scarves, his last words: 'Her scent? Balanciaga 10?'

Dearest Nana,

You have just gone out again giving me another of my longed-for chances to have the last word. 'I shall be back in an hour. Don't stir.' I have been for months looking and looking up at my Memoirs skied to a top shelf until a month back when you were searching up there for some book, toppled a few other books, and my ms. fell down unnoticed behind my old desk. I am able to crawl that far.

By the time you find these pages tucked into the front of my ms, the whole game will be up, and a game with loaded dice it has been both for the gods and for me since they knew from the start what I only suspected – that it is not possible to live a whole life again. That morning so long ago, gurgling into my pink wash-basin, wondering whether or not to accept their offer, I did splutter feebly-furiously at them that without a memory I'd have to spend half this second life of mine reconstructing a new artificial ambience in which an artificial reconstructed 'I' might slowly take shape. Ten minutes later I faced the blue truck that killed the child at the end of the park and was ready to kill me. I decided that I did not want to die. I chanced life-at-any-price.

Not that at the end of it all I am ungrateful to the gods for doubling my span. How could I be? I would otherwise not only have missed so many of these primal joys of life – new friends, new places, new wrestlings with new problems created by others and by myself, more of what we call passing people in whom to seek with curiosity for further clues as to the nature of our common existence, and among the throng those few rare dear lasting ones, three whom I have loved passionately and unforgettably, including above all you.

Further, and quickly now, the referee is looking at his watch, can I, you may well wonder, say this *above all you* without dishonouring those others whom I have also unforgettably loved? I not merely can but, in honour to them I must because the dice were loaded against them too. By being cut off from my past, from pasts behind that past, from shadowy pasts of countless pasts that are not even shadows, it was not until the year I first saw you and began to inch into love with you that I had amassed enough new-born memories to be able to offer to anybody more than a questionable past, a scanty present and the embryo of a self. I might call it the garret or the basement of a self, or what landladies and estate agents call 'a fully furnished apartment' which may mean two chairs, a table, a sagging bed and a three-ply wardrobe lined with a six months' old *Financial Times*. It is no wonder then that I now put you 'above all', you with whom I have lived, loved and learned for nearly forty years, thanks to whose generosity I grew rich enough to live in a present equipped with years of recall which, as neither of us can ever have forgotten for long, bind us together at least as far back as the maternal plain of the Shannon, ffrench Chase half empty, dark nights, old loves and new beginnings that are now about to end.

You have done still more for me: you have given me at least the key to my beginnings even though I shall now never turn that locked door, never pass into bodily contact with them. (How deeply I now sympathise with poor old Bob Two boozily fondling his faked memorials of a faked ancestry!) You gave me the key less than a year ago when, without knowing it or wishing it, you yielded me the tiniest, simplest, silliest but clearest glimpse of light, a keyhole perspective extending to the landscape of generations. You know what happens if you take a card and stick a pin through it and then hold that pinhole close to the eye. It can see not alone a landscape, wide as far lakes, tall as far mountains, real but also more than real: an ideal framed by desire, memory, imagination. Remember? You were bathing me one morning and smacked my backside. I looked back at you and saw by your expression that you had quite misunderstood. I was not looking at *you*. I was looking lovingly at my mother in your guise, the end of my life translated into its beginnings.

Every item about me changed in a second to a lost Then – house, walls, carpet, pictures, weather, windows, smells, sizes, forms, colours, the morning light, the texture of the bath, the spongy scent of the soap, a loving woman's palms wandering over my infant body. I have no hope – I have tried once or twice – of making you realise what an agony of emptiness it is never to be able to kick aside all abstract ideas, all general drifts or concepts and clamber back into one's primal, animal human self that, having branded one for ever, fell asleep at the unremembered centre of this confusing convoluted maze we call Now. I cannot, likewise, hope to make you conceive, let alone imagine what a corresponding joy it was for me that morning to recapture after my lifelong thirst this vast gulp of infancy, a joy as exquisitely unbearable as one's first life-giving orgasm with one's life's love, a joy as vast and piercing as what? – the sky to a caged lark, a flooding sunrise, an overflowing spring tide, a complete daffodil moon balanced on the horizon, a spoon of cold water to a man parched to the verge of death. I was once again a hungry baby receiving at last the pneumatic pressure of its mother's breast and moist nipple.

I felt the same sated infant's wonder when a yellow-billed bird flew fast across the window of suburban Rosmeen; wondered wide eyed again after almost one hundred and thirty years at a nutbrown leaf slowly twirl down from the blueness, saw on the carpet a hurrying spider. I heard outside on the country street the cries of children who were not there, the cric-crock of a slowly passing donkey-cart, by this a whole century gone to rot, my first smell of burning peat, the far mooing of a cow wanting to be milked, the smell of new mown hay, all the fated modalities, symbols, dispositions of my nature shaped in my unknown mother's womb after the first wild second of my conception. Last night she came again and sat by my bed, i.e., my bootbox, my maker, shaped like you, your colouring, your very presence and essence. Into whose belly shall I in four months' time re-enter? Ovum eagerly awaiting sperm? Since how many centuries? Who was she? You? Too late – I only know for certain you who are my beginning and my end. *Dulcium mater saeva cupidinum.*

You and I have argued so often, meaning that I have babbled and you have patiently, boredly listened – Oh! I know, I know! – about your *I think therefore I am* Descartes. He was such a brainy, such a methodical, original, if manifestly peculiar philosopher, before whom there had been nobody as clear in style, as illuminating, as original, and he was so fatally wrong! He thought the body divisible (it is) and the soul, he called it the mind, indivisible (it is not) because he had to according to his method of thinking and doubting his way to certitude, to perfection, and thereby to God. Yet if I say 'I have changed my mind', is not merely that little much the end of his mind's indivisibility? The fatal breach in his dyke? And what about all the people who have complex personalities? Poor Descartes! His idea of Self was an empty abstraction. He was unlucky: he lived before men discovered that thoroughly divisive element, the unconscious. (Was it in New Orleans or in Paris that I met the woman who said to me, 'We French are all cool, rational Cartesians until we fall in love and then we become as big fools as everybody else.') Darling Nana, I have held and I hold that we are not only divided in our minds but honeycombed, and you have however rightly insisted that each of us is nevertheless accountable to some immutable indivisibility. I know now for certain to what and to whom that points. To some inner principle in me since my mothering childhood, and to my life's love, which means to you.

Thank you for all you have given me, above all for not being an abstract philosopher with me, for feeling with me, for opening my past to me, for being a fool with me, for being one with me in love.

Is that your car turning? Ciaou! I must fly.

B.B.

Fly was his last word, appropriately. He dwindled and dwindled until he became as tiny as a clothes moth, though still talking like a man. I had long before that stopped feeding him with a spoon as small as a snuff spoon or with milk from a rubber teat. At the last I was cultivating him like a silkworm in its pupal stage, except that he was not moving onwards from larva to imago but, as all his life he had been, backwards towards his final condition of becoming his own spectre. The last night I saw him, a ghost in a padded match-box, he was as beautiful as a scarab. That is how ever since I see every clothes moth, its delicate antennae outstretched above its four wings, the brown and the pale, the patterned and the plain. When I came back the next morning, his birthday, to look at his beauty again the box was empty.

The norwester brings me the sound of bands playing. Another St Patrick's Day. His birthday. Soft rain floats by in curtains – I see why I feel so chilly. It makes me glad he went before me. My body begins to show the first signs of age; not that he would have noticed, or rather, for he was an observant man, not that he would have heeded – he saw everything in the form of some ideal that he nourished and that nourished him. On my lap lies his manuscript. I have gone through all his personal effects and destroyed, sold or given away to charity every other sad reminder of him. I do not know what to do with this one. Leave it to my executors? Show it to Miss Poinsett? But I know what she would say. She would call it a farrago, point out that on the mere ground of ages it was sheer hocus pocus. No philosopher whom I respect could live inside her tight rational cage. She did not know her man. I had lived with and loved him. I am sure that if she were listening to a *cavatina* of Handel's on The Queen of Love she would observe that there is no known record of the historical existence of such a woman. And yet I do not wholly condemn her. Edges of puzzlement remain. The paradigm of B.B.'s life is patently incomplete, the purpose of its repetition inconclusive enough to make one wonder whether we are not all 'as flies to wanton boys' etc., not to be killed but forced to live for their godships' sport. After all most of the purpose of the experiment of making Younger grow younger and younger was to demonstrate mockingly that no gods' amount of experience teaches us mortals a damned thing. But for us mortals to decide this question we should be able to make a comparison between the Bobby Younger we all knew in his second life and the Bobby of his first, and since among the active characters of his manuscript he was then known intimately only by my grandmother Ana ffrench and the gods, and they have not spoken again and she was a fabulist who never could divulge anything as it really was, we still do not know the answer to that mocking question. My own feeling is that the gods have long since forgotten the whole thing as they so often seem to have forgotten this world they idly made one supernal morning when playing with a handful of Olympian cloud, out of which, boredly kicked into limitless space, man has through millions of years created every speck of the splendours and miseries of civilised life.

As I lie here in bed scribbling on what will have to be the last page of his journal, barely hearing the faint, far away St Patrick's day bands, or looking out at the rain's silent procession, I amuse and torture myself with a rather different question. I pretend that I hear a mouse scratching outside my bedroom door, and that if I were to glance down at the foot of it I would see a yellow page being pushed under it inviting me to grow younger and younger, with Bobby beside me no bigger than a clothes' moth growing older and older. For his first couple of years he would be a baby sleeping in my bed, hot in the curve of my arm. At five he would be my small messenger. At thirteen he would begin to fall in love with me again! and why not? – I would then, bordering fifty, be in my woman's prime. That tune on the wind? Is there some French band visiting? *Aux armes, citoyens! Formez vos bataillons!* I am losing touch with everyday life. I see a tiny fawny moth flitting about my face. I have glanced half-hopefully down at the bottom of my door. But would I? I mean supposing the yellow page really were there would I accept its return ticket? *Would* I? Not half! Every single moment of him, boy and man. Again and again and again and

Stamps
Margarine
The London Library
Elastic for knickers